PRAISE F̶O̶R̶ ̶K̶H̶A̶N̶ ̶W̶O̶N̶G̶

"Khan Wong gives us an ̶ ̶ ̶ ̶ ̶ ̶ ̶t hard-hitting space fantasy notes w̶ ̶ ̶lusivity and respect. Featuring an ace protagonist, the consent dynamics of the book are particularly adept. The Circus Infinite *explores the nuances of gender and sexuality while punching you in the gut with soaring feats of gravity and interrogations that will make you gasp out loud."*
TJ Berry, author of *Space Unicorn Blues*

"Wong luxuriates in sweet scenes between Jes and his first love, Bo, and develops heartwarming found family dynamics in Jes's other relationships. The worldbuilding is just alien enough while still inviting readers in, and it's a pleasure to witness the world through the lens of its progressive social dynamics. It's a thoroughly enchanting adventure."
Publisher's Weekly, starred review.

*"*The Circus Infinite *is an action-packed tale of found family set against a finely wrought canvas of different genders, cultures, and sexuality. Jes's journey of personal discovery is as fascinating as it is heart-warming. This one is sure to both entertain and enlighten the reader."*
Ginger Smith, author of *The Rush's Edge*

"Khan Wong has made the book for which so many of us have been yearning! The Circus Infinite *is not only a gripping science-fiction tale set in a lushly imagined universe teeming with fabulous aliens, extraordinary powers, and political drama, but also a story that celebrates our real, lived spectrum of gender and sexuality. To top it all off, it revolves around a circus, the perfect manifestation of outsider community, artistic expression, and a sense of wonder.* The Circus Infinite *renews faith in the power of science fiction to represent our world even as it lifts our imagination beyond it."*
Justin Hall, editor of *No Straight Lines*

Khan Wong

THE CIRCUS INFINITE

ANGRY
ROBOT

ANGRY ROBOT
An imprint of Watkins Media Ltd

Unit 11, Shepperton House
89 Shepperton Road
London N1 3DF
UK

angryrobotbooks.com
twitter.com/angryrobotbooks
Come one, come all!

An Angry Robot paperback original, 2022

Cover by Kieryn Tyler
Edited by Gemma Creffield and Paul Simpson
Set in Meridien

ISBN 978 0 85766 968 1
Ebook ISBN 978 0 85766 969 8

Printed and bound in the United Kingdom by TJ Books Ltd.

9 8 7 6 5 4 3 2 1

MIX
Paper from
responsible sources
FSC® C013056

For Marty – my greatest joy will always be sitting under the oak tree with you

CHAPTER ONE

After an hour scoping out the waves of tourists flowing in and out of the terminal, Jes spots what he's been waiting for: a clueless human clearly on his first trip away from Indra. One of those who are completely unaware of their surroundings, of the possibility of ruffians in their midst. The man fumbles with a bag as the holographic stripe of the pass pokes out of his slacks, winking at every passerby. A quick bump of shoulders and a swipe so delicate it barely happens, and Jes has a ticket off this miserable hell world also known as his home planet.

Overhead, glass panels set within the vaulted arches stream with rainbow-stained light. Holographic displays glow in amber, green and blue, destinations and launch times scrolling over their sleek surfaces. Travelers of multiple species, but mostly human and Rijala, move through the atrium as if performing some kind of obscure choreography. Jes casts his eyes about looking for orderlies but there's no sign of them. The spaceport is clear.

A Bezan girl behind the ticketing counter returns his smile, both of them performing the expected expressions of friendliness. "Slip and return to Opale Lunar Station, please." He looks into the camera set in the counter – he wants to make sure he's recorded making this transaction.

"Opale! Are you going for the Mudraessa Festival?" the

1

ticketing agent asks. Her eyes are wide and gem-toned, a brilliant cerulean blue, deepened by the violet-to-purple tones of her skin. Her hair is pulled back, but maintains the characteristic phosphorescence of Bezan hair.

"Yes..." He scans her uniform for her name-tag, "Alys. I love opera in all its forms. Ever since I was little. I've never heard Mudraessa, of course, since the Asuna don't allow it off-world. It's supposed to be the most perfect. That's what everyone says. I can't wait to listen with my own ears." Jes can't stand opera, but in the moment he's quite certain that whoever he's pretending to be loves it deeply. Jes's mother and father wouldn't stop going on about the festival after they attended that one time, but he's glad he retained some tidbit to deploy now. He decides he doesn't want to think about them though, and fidgets with the strap of the satchel on his shoulder.

"Well, you must be thrilled to have gotten lucky in the lottery. The Asuna are so restrictive about off-worlders on Opale."

"Yes, I'm very lucky."

She arches an eyebrow as she proceeds with the transaction. With his empathic sense, he susses mainly indifference – he's one of many such transactions today and she doesn't really care, however well she fakes it.

"Node?"

He hands over the sleek palm-curved pebble of glass; she takes it and slips it into a groove on the surface of her workstation. Jes's buddy in town helped him get the alias – a favor banked for all the locks picked and safes cracked over the months they ran together before the Institute got him.

"You're all set," Alys says.

"Thanks." He takes the node back and slips it into his pocket.

On his way to the gate, the blazing white of orderly uniforms sets panic alarms pinging in his head. *Shit...* Jes looks around wildly for the nearest exit, heart pounding, sweat prickling at his skin.

No wait, he breathes. *Not them. Just a couple wearing matching white outfits.*

Jes exhales relief. Flashes of his past come to him without warning – the orderlies at the Institute, stunning him, shocking him, injecting him. All to make him weak and compliant. The pain. So much pain...

Jes shakes his head to clear his mind. How long will people wearing all white set him off?

At the departure gate he scans his node. With a beep and a flash of green light, he's registered boarded. He heads toward the boarding ramp, then spins on his heels, bringing a hand to his forehead in fake befuddlement. His pulse quickens as it always does when he's about to lie.

"I left my briefcase at the cafe!" he exclaims to the no nonsense Rijala gate attendant. It's the first thing that comes to mind, despite the fact that he doesn't look like the briefcase-carrying type. "Can I just run and get it? It won't take long."

"We depart in ten minutes," she says flatly without looking at him. She tucks a stray lock of hair behind her ear and smiles at the next passenger, simultaneously welcoming them and abruptly dismissing him.

Her disdain for Jes pokes like bony fingers. He can't tell if she's annoyed by him being a forgetful passenger, or if it's because his typically Rijalen blue-white hair and silver eyes combined with his human-toned, deep-tan skin makes his mixed heritage obvious. Rijala don't like hybrids much, but are always just short of being outright discriminatory.

"I'll be quick," he promises, despite the fact that she is no longer listening. His heart pounds like it did when he busted his way out of the Institute, but nobody is chasing him this time. He wipes his sweaty palms on his trouser legs as he walks away, then tosses the node into the first waste bin he walks by. The decoy alias has served its purpose. He's on his way to Opale, as far as anybody tracking him is concerned.

From the satchel on his shoulder, he pulls out the cape he

acquired from one of the vendors in the bazaar outside the spaceport. It's made of green satin rimmed with gold – gaudy trying to look classy. It's a much more ridiculous thing than he'd normally wear, which is entirely the point.

The cape slips lightly over his shoulders, and he delights in the fake luxury of it, the aspiring glamor. He puts up the hood as he scans a destination board. He takes out the purloined all-travel pass; the rounded edges are smooth against his fingertips as he worries it. He can disappear on any world within the 9-Star Congress now. So… where?

He is tempted by a trip to Indra, but the Institute staff already know about his fondness for that world. It would definitely be the first place they'd think to look once they figure out he's not on Opale. Maybe a place that's the farthest away then? What star system would that be?

Vashtar. The principal world there is Lora, the other human world. Jes has met people from there before, and he didn't like them. They were polite, friendly even, but a strange aggression simmered under their surface. It rubbed roughly against his empathic sense, like sandpaper. It could have been down to the specific individuals he met, but his grandmother had warned him that they were like that; humans born there, who grew up without connection to Indra, come off that way. Though there are multiple species there, it's dominated by humans with this vibe. So – not there.

Also in the system is the notorious so-called pleasure moon, Persephone-9. That far-flung hunk of rock bears the most decadent reputation in the galaxy. The moon is truly a multispecies panoply as no single species dominates the mostly transient population there. The mix of his empathic sense and sexual aversion, however, would likely make being there uncomfortable at times. But, he reasons, that would be preferable to the harshness of Lora and maybe it would be easier to blend into the background in a place like that. Jes nods with his decision.

When he arrives at the departure gate for Port Ruby Station, he smiles to himself – with his cape, he fits right in. Of course the passengers traveling to a place famous for hedonism would be a colorful crowd! He can suss the general, collective feeling of the group: happy, buzzing anticipation. A lovey-dovey kind of vibe. He flips a panel of his cape over one shoulder in imitation of a Bezan dandy ahead of him in line – is this how these things are worn? In the crowd, he spots people of all the species that make up the 9-Star Congress, except the Mantodeans, who slipstream travel in their own vessels and by their own network of tubes.

There are even Asuna here – he has only seen them in person a couple of times, when his father received delegations as part of his duties as a commerce leader. He admires their pale green skin, the hints of yellow and white. Most of all, he admires their halos. The crystals sprout around the crown of their skulls and, like their eyes, appear in a multitude of colors.

An inner knowingness tells Jes he made the right call. He remembers childhood conversations with his grandmother when she explained the importance of that sensation. "Our intuition is the force of our life moving towards what will fulfill it, like a plant moves towards the sun. Follow its pull and you'll find what you need."

He hadn't been aware of it before but now, as he looks down at his all-travel pass, he gets it. He's grateful that even what he endured and witnessed at the Institute didn't overwrite this essential lesson his grandmother had imparted. He heeded it without thinking. It is a part of him still.

"*Last call for Port Ruby Station, Persephone-9,*" the smooth robotic voice of the attendant intones. He flashes his pass for the scanner and is waved on board.

He grabs an empty seat among some humans and straps in. Behind his eyes, his grandmother's face smiles – she is still teaching him about intuition. In his pocket, he carries his only memento from the life he is fleeing, a crystal shard on a delicate yet strong chain of tiny titanium links, threaded with colored spheres of other coded minerals. His grandmother had given it to him on his tenth birthday. It is the only tether he has to his past.

"I can't wait to hit the clubs," a young human behind him says to her Rijala companion. "We'll have a couple of nights before the forest gathering."

"I've heard the forest is beautiful," her friend responds. "This is my third trip to Persephone-9 and I still haven't been to that side of the moon."

"That's because you're a party whore," the original speaker teases.

"You flatter me!"

The two friends laugh as the shuttle vibrates, preparing to depart. With the vibration comes relief – he is *really* escaping now. He can see Matheson's face in his mind – the pale skin that obviously did not get enough sun, the pale, watery blue eyes, the limp ashy blond hair and the fake smile that didn't hide the man's impatience nearly as much as he thought it did. The man who thinks of Jes as his prize lab animal. He hopes to never see that face again. But a deep buzzing in his intuitive sense tells him that he will, someday. But right now he has to focus on getting away. He can only hope that "someday" is far, far away.

The chatter about party plans, and which casinos are best, and which clubs have the best vibes, all settles down as the engines increase their pitch. Jes leans back as the shuttle glides gently to the guiding strip. It hovers a moment before the press of speed pushes him into his seat and they launch out of the bay, away from the city, the ground, the planet of Rijal, the Institute and all its horrors.

In seconds they've pierced the atmosphere and zoom out into open space. From where he's sitting there's no porthole, but a viewscreen option is available. Once they're in space he shuts it off, knowing there will be a viewing deck when the lounge opens. Instead, he looks around at the rabble surrounding him. The range of species comforts him. Definitely the right call.

There are Rijala and Bezans. There are humans of various shades of brown and a bewildering array of hair textures and colors. A couple of Hydraxians occupy a wide bench on the side of the shuttle. They're orange-skinned and four-armed, and against his empathic sense are much softer than one would guess from the sour expressions they wear. As a hybrid himself, Jes feels more comfortable in this multi-species array than he ever did among homogenous Rijala society.

The ones who fully captures Jes's attention, however, are the Asuna sitting a row ahead on the other side of the craft. With their hoods down, the characteristic iridescence of their skin is visible from this distance. He can also see that the crystals that sprout from their heads are a deep emerald green. If he remembers his Asuna sociology correctly, emerald green is the Council Class of civic and cultural leaders. One of them looks younger than the others, and she doesn't have the shimmer yet – a characteristic only the fully mature members of the species manifest. He remembers being told that they often looked younger than they were and that their lifespans were much longer than that of the other known humanoid species. He guesses they are a family unit, as their halos are all the same color. But he is confused. If they are as upper caste as he thinks, why would they be taking a common transport?

The two females wear their long hair in ornate braids; the younger one's hair is the color of rose gold and her braids sit loosely around her face, while the older one's braids are knotted atop her head and are a deep auburn in color. The brilliant green of their crystal halos reminds Jes disconcertingly of the serum they shot him up with in the lab, the one that kept him sedated and unable to use his ability while they performed the more invasive procedures. He remembers the heavy, sleepy feeling falling on him. How everything moved real slow, how the places in his body where his ability usually buzzed went numb and dark and cold. But he is not numb now.

Jes wakes from a dreamless sleep to find the shuttle well into its time in the slipstream. The lounge is open, so he gets up to stretch his legs. Standing at the viewport that takes up almost a whole bulkhead, he stares out at the lightshow before him. The slipstream, gift of Zo, the sentient star who called to order the 9-Star Congress of Conscious Worlds, displays colors of violet and indigo and white as they writhe and intertwine and shift between shades. The stream cuts the length of interstellar travel to a fraction of the time that such trips take in regular space at sub-light speed. Jes doesn't fully understand how it all works. He suspects most folks don't.

"It's so beautiful," a voice says from beside him. "I've never seen it in person before. Have you?" It's the Asuna girl, and she's speaking Ninespeak without first asking if he knows it. But, he supposes, it's probably a safe assumption that anyone going to Persephone-9 would know the common language used in the unaffiliated sectors.

"Yes," Jes answers in Ninespeak also. "A few times. But it's been a while."

"Esmée." She bows slightly as she says this, then looks at him expectantly.

He struggles to remember what he learned in his Interspecies Etiquette class and dredges up a vague lesson on greetings. The Asuna simply state their names and bow, by way of introducing themselves.

He's about to give the name of his discarded alias, but then remembers that Asuna are empathic, in their own way. He reasons that in this moment, the truth makes the most sense to give. His intuition pings back to him that this is the right call.

"Jes," he says, bowing back.

She says something that sounds like "orkut". The r sound rolls like a purr.

"I'm sorry – I don't speak Mudra-nul."

She laughs. "It means 'well met.' I think humans would say 'nice to meet you.' Though it could also mean 'nice to see you.' You are human and Rijala? I hope it's not rude of me to ask." She seems about to say something more but holds back.

"Yes, I am. Human mother, Rijala father."

"I'm sorry if I'm prying. Hybrids aren't common where I'm from."

Jes is aware of the Asuna's reputation for xenophobia – their restrictions on other species visiting their homeworld is well known. "It's fine," he says.

"Is your human side Loran or Indran?"

He wonders if all Asuna are this direct or if it's just this Esmée person. "My mother's from Indra. But I was born and grew up on Rijal."

"So do you possess the Indran talents?"

"I can see auric fields when I concentrate. And I have the intuitive and empathic senses, but I'm not emerged so no telepathy or telekinesis or any of that stuff. But even if I were emerged, psi-abilities don't work away from the world of origin anyway. That's true of Emerged Ones from all species."

"Of course. I wasn't thinking." She pauses. "I haven't met many other species. This is my first trip off Opale."

This doesn't really surprise him, but he holds his tongue and looks back out at the lightshow. "Some people have questioned whether all Consciousness Holders could access their abilities if they were in orbit of Zo, since it connects all our worlds."

"That's an interesting question."

A few others join them on the observation deck. The Rijala keep their distance from the other passengers and look askance at everyone, especially the humans and Bezans from whom they turn away if one gets too close. It's as if they fear picking up some kind of parasite from them. Odd how the Asuna have the xenophobic reputation while it's Rijala who behave like this in public. A pair of Bezans, whose bright clothes give off the insistent smell of reef and incense, giggle together in a corner and point at the slipstream lights. He wonders if they experience the streaming colors differently than he does.

"Are they your parents?" he asks. "The two you're traveling with?"

She nods. The slipstream reflects in the golden glint of her eyes.

"I'm surprised to see Asuna of your status traveling by shuttle."

She smiles wryly. "Persephone-9 is a place of depravity. Any Asuna who wishes to sully themselves by going there may only do so by common means, regardless of status." She meets his eyes and adds, "Those are the rules. My mother isn't happy about it."

"So why are you going? Needing some depravity?"

She laughs. "You're funny. No. My mother must deliver some news to a relative who lives there."

"Do you not have comms where you're from?" Jes susses her curiosity, openness and a friendliness he hasn't encountered all that much in his life. He finds himself relaxing in her presence and is relieved he can still have a conversation with someone without having his guard up.

"This news must be delivered in person," she answers. "It is our custom. Most Asuna don't have to go off-world to do it though."

"I'm going to guess it's not happy news?"

"My aunt died. My mother's sister. We're on our way to inform my cousin."

"I'm sorry for your loss."

"Thank you." He senses sadness from her, but gets the feeling it isn't really connected to her aunt. She stands with her arms crossed, looking out the viewport; her halo's deep green crystals glitter in the reflection it holds. She has smaller crystals too, along her collarbone and at her wrists – these aren't as dark and shine a bit brighter.

"Are you training in an approved field for your caste?" It's an awkward change of subject, but he figures she probably won't mind not lingering on the death in her family.

"In my own way," she replies. "Emeralds are civic and cultural leaders, mostly in the realm of policy and administration. But I hope to be an artist. Artists are technically a type of cultural leader but it's rare for Emeralds to pursue the arts. It's not unheard of, of course, though Rubies are more typically artists. In my opinion, artists are the ultimate cultural leaders – I mean, they're the ones that actually give creative expression to a society, a culture. Somehow, bureaucrats took over that leadership."

He picks up a resentment that is familiar in its emotion, if not in circumstance. "What kind of artist are you?"

She brightens at the question. "I'm training in Mudraessa – do you know what that is?"

He susses from her that she expects his ignorance. He is happy to surprise her. "Asuna opera," he responds. "I've never had the honor of witnessing it first-hand. But I understand it is the most harmonically perfect music produced by any species in the 9-Star Congress. Are you sad to be missing the festival?"

Incongruently, she smiles at this. "You're familiar with the festival?"

He shrugs. "I know of it. I know it's a big deal for off-worlders to be selected in the lottery to attend." He can tell she's impressed. "So, you're a singer then?"

Now she is less impressed. "If you must boil my identity down to such simplistic terms." After a pause, "So why are *you* going to Persephone-9?"

Jes hopes his face doesn't betray the fact that he hasn't thought about this part of his story. He had been so focused just on getting away from Matheson and the Institute that he hadn't yet invented a cover story for himself. He panics a little, knowing that she is empathic too, but then remembers that the Asuna mode of empathy focuses almost exclusively on desire. Sexual desire. So his panic starts to ebb. But he wants to make a connection, so he makes what he hopes is a neutral-yet-cheerful expression. "Seeking my fortune, I guess."

"Surely finding your fortune relies on more than guessing?"

He smiles against the nervousness rising inside him as lies formulate on his tongue. "I have an uncle who runs one of the... casinos. I came to see him about a job. I didn't want to stay on Rijal anymore." At least that last statement is true. He brushes the knuckles of his left hand against the hem of his cape, taking comfort in the smooth coolness of the satin.

He stiffens reflexively as a green-haloed figure steps onto the deck, coming up behind Esmée. Her startling green eyes intimidate and judge, though she visibly relaxes as she gets closer to them, as if something she'd been worried about proved to be of no concern. Though he feels no desire, Jes's breath catches at the ripple of light and soft color across this older one's skin. The shimmer is truly hypnotic up close. Flashes of gemlike glamor glint across her face, up her temples, right up to the glittering crystal formation of her halo. She places a hand on Esmée's shoulder and the latter flinches at the touch.

"*Attention passengers,*" the smooth AI voice says over the intercom. "*We are about to re-enter simple space. Please return to your seats and strap down.*"

"Esmée," the tall Asuna woman says. "Come."

"I'm sorry for your loss," Jes says to Esmée's mother. She looks taken aback, and shoots her daughter a glance loaded with what can only be interpreted as annoyance.

She collects herself and sniffs. "Yes. Thank you, stranger. Esmée, come along. You know your father doesn't like to be alone in public."

"Nice talking to you, Jes."

"Yeah. You too."

Her mother says something to Esmée in Mudra-nul as they

walk away. She doesn't sound happy. She doesn't seem happy in general, but then again, her sister just died.

Jes has to go the same way they are, but he waits until they're out of the lounge before he does so, to avoid that awkward going-the-same-way-as-someone-you-just-said-goodbye -to thing.

As he takes his seat and straps down, the reality of his situation dawns on him. He may have eluded the Institute's – and Matheson's – grasp, but he'll need more money sooner than later, and a place to crash. He wonders how much rooms on Persephone-9 cost, then shudders at the thought of what a room on a pleasure moon would be used for. Especially one on his budget. He suddenly wishes he had paid more attention to the cleansing rituals his grandmother tried to teach him when he was a child.

The shuttle rumbles and shakes and the vertiginous rushing sensation of transitioning back to simple space overtakes his thoughts.

"We have entered the Vashtar System," the AI informs them. *"Arrival at Port Ruby Station, Persephone-9, in twelve minutes."*

He looks over at where Esmée sits with her parents. The older two have their hoods up, covering their halos and shimmers. He bets there are all kinds of hungry pervs on the pleasure moon who would pay handsomely for a romp with an Asuna. Esmée's mother doesn't seem the type who would tolerate a solicitation for a second. Her mother nudges Esmée and she puts her hood up also.

Jes wonders how the unbridled lustfulness of Persephone-9 must feel like for a species attuned to the desires of others. He decides it must be awful. He worries that it might be difficult enough for him – even though his empathy isn't fine-tuned to sexual desire to the same degree as the Asuna, he is able to sense general horniness. While he is not totally sex averse, Jes's asexuality means that even horniness is an uncomfortable thing for him to suss. He realizes then that Esmée must have felt comfortable being near him because she could sense no desire in that way. Her mother's relief must have also been due to the same thing. He smiles, realizing that it's the first time his asexuality has felt like a huge positive.

Jes considers following them, thinking that they surely would have accommodation arrangements and would be heading for a much less sketchy area. Asuna of their status would likely be staying someplace nice. But nice meant more expensive.

From his pocket he pulls the dowsing crystal. Small colored beads punctuate the silver links: red, orange, yellow, green, blue, indigo, violet. He recalls memories of his grandmother: her kind, brown eyes lined with the traces of a lifetime of laughter; her white hair flowing and wild. *Help me find my way.* He releases this silent prayer as the shuttle jostles to its landing. The passengers immediately unstrap themselves, stand, smooth out their clothes and check their possessions. He stands too, slipping the crystal back in his pocket.

The hatch hisses open and, once it touches down on the dock, the passengers pour out. As space opens up around him, Jes relaxes, realizing how tense he'd been holding himself. He steps into the flow of people heading for the exit, for the transit stations and roto stands, and tosses the travel pass he used into a trash chute as he goes. He wants no traces of his escape from his former world left on his person.

This spaceport is not as grand as the one he departed from, but it feels much more comfortable. It takes several minutes for him to make his way through the terminal, then finally he steps outside onto a plaza bustling with vendors selling trinkets and refreshments. The air is redolent with incense and grilled food, and pulses with the syncopated rhythms pounded out by a group of Bezan buskers. A bowed instrument threads a sinuous melody over it all, adding dramatic accompaniment to the large pink petals that bloom and fall in the glowing arcs projected by the holographic lenses that curve around the edge of the plaza. The city beyond is a kaleidoscope of neon, dizzying.

He holds the crystal in his fingertips as he makes his entreaty. "OK grandma, help me out here. Help me–" He's about to say "Help me find a place to rest," but decides that's too temporary – too much about surviving immediate circumstances. If he's really going to do this, he figures he should really go for it. "Help me find a place to belong. Help me find a home."

He lets the crystal hang, pinching the other end of the chain with thumb and forefinger. He breathes deep, exhaling for longer than his inhale. It's a technique Matheson taught him as a way to keep his ability under control during stress or panic. He hates that he learned anything from that man, but there were useful lessons mixed in with the torture.

Whether randomly or genuinely controlled by something ineffable, the crystal begins swinging at a distinct angle from Jes's chest, and points to the right. He walks in the direction the crystal indicates, looking up occasionally to make sure he's not about to walk into something or someone, but mostly keeping his attention on the crystal, watching for any change.

The surrounding area is awash in colors between the advertisements, the aesthetic displays and the signs. The neon catches in the crystal, an upside down refraction of the city. Then the crystal changes direction suddenly, back and forth in a horizontal line. He pivots left and walks straight ahead until something is in his way. It is a hologram advertisement for one of the many shows available in town, this one for something called *Cirque Kozmiqa*, a performance event of some kind happening at the Luna Lux Resort Casino.

He looks from the advertisement down to the crystal, still hanging from his fingers. "Really?" he asks. It hangs perfectly still.

He wishes he had a node and for a second regrets tossing his alias. But no. That subterfuge was necessary. No regrets. He looks around at the passersby, and spots a human woman in a long, pink and glittery coat, lined at the edges with pink and white feathers, her hair a cloud of white above her oval face. "Excuse me!" he calls, catching her attention.

She eyes him warily, cautiously responds, "Yes?"

"Do you know how to get to–" he points at the holoboard "–the Luna Lux?"

Her face relaxes, and Jes susses her relief that here is a young man with a genuine, non-creepy question. She points down the avenue to a river of lights. "Do you see the big white beam shooting straight up into the sky? That's it."

He nods, understanding. "Thank you."

"Good luck," the stranger says as she sashays away, her long coat swinging behind her.

The upward beam doesn't look that far away, so Jes chooses to walk the distance. He doesn't want to spend what little coin he has on transit just yet. He steps off the plaza and onto the promenade, joining the hustle and bustle of Port Ruby.

Is he really going to go by what his grandmother's crystal told him to do? He doesn't really have another plan, and this at least provides him a destination. The column of light he walks towards is a beacon, the apparent next step. But, of course, he has no idea what he'll do once he gets there.

CHAPTER TWO

The front gate of the Luna Lux Resort Casino curves around the entrance to its grounds like parentheses, two silver-white crescents holding a secret. They open onto a curved walkway that winds around a large pool, throughout which jets of water shoot up in multicolored arcs, creating showers of gems raining through the air. Jes flips both panels of his cape over his shoulders so that the green satin shines bright. He thinks it's a bit classier and will make him fit in better – he has witnessed far more flamboyant fashions than he's accustomed to in his small walk to get here.

He wishes he'd thought to find a washroom and freshen up a bit before making his way, and wonders if he can do that once he's inside. The garden he walks through is fragrant with flowers, and the path is lined with pale white lights that leave rainbow tracers in his eyes when he looks away. Benches are set along the path intermittently, and a couple of gazebos host small groups – clouds of reef smoke make stoned weather around them. Swings hang from some of the larger tree branches, and their solo occupants sit gazing out at the water, swaying lightly in the dark. The whole area is much less gaudy than the strip outside, peaceful even. The rushing sound of the crowded strip is muffled, distant. Constellations of white and golden lights twinkle from the places they've been set into the wall that contains the property.

The purple globe of the planet Persephone dominates the sky, and three of its other moons are visible. The towers of the Luna Lux reach for the heavenly bodies, gleaming silver and white surfaces and dark grey glass – clearly of Rijalen design. The light that marks the sky above it, the beam that guided him here, shines from the top of a central dome, and the main entrance presides over a grand courtyard that hugs a fountain at its center. He approaches the front door and spots a sign pointing towards the back of the casino: *Cirque Kozmiqa*. The lettering is gold holographic type on a matte, dark red surface. The sign hangs over a path of stars stenciled with the same gold holographic substance. It leads him along a route edged with gold velvet ropes that winds around the inside perimeter of the casino. The clicking of giant wheels of fortune, the clacking of roulette tables, the pinging of slot machines, and chatter in a multitude of languages fill the air, punctuated by the occasional cheer as someone reveals a winning hand. Servers walk by, carrying trays of drinks. He sees members of most species of the 9-Star Congress present, the love of games of chance common across cultures it would seem. There's a part of him that wants to wander around, out of curiosity and to get his bearings, but he feels an urgency to get to the destination the crystal indicated, to figure out how to settle himself in this place. He stays on the path.

Eventually he reaches a set of red curtains held open with golden sashes. He steps through the curtains and finds himself outside, on a lawn. Several meters away, a trio of large, lotus-shaped tents rise. They're made of swatches of red and gold fabric, and look heavy and sturdy. From the top of the center dome a star system spins, a radiant sun of amber glass ringed by planets, each a smaller sphere, glinting against the night.

Ticket takers are stationed at each of the entrances. Shit, he didn't think about that. There aren't any people going in or milling about outside on the lawn, and from inside the tent comes faint music – the show must already be going on. He doesn't think he can bluff his way past the ticket takers and so continues walking.

Without getting any closer to the tents, he strolls casually around the edge of the lawn and looks for other ways in. He comes across a side tent that contains a kitchen. Through the clear panels that serve as windows, lines of cooks prepare what look like little desserts. This is a dinner-and-show kind of deal.

There are a couple of kitchen workers smoking outside and he hears one of them say to her friend, "You owe me, Lucian. Next time you're buying."

"Yeah, yeah I know I know," Lucian – presumably – replies.

Jes keeps walking, hoping for a side entrance – surely the front doors aren't the only way in or out. His hunch proves correct, and he spies a back door unattended. He rushes to it and pushes the panel open slowly. Just a couple of meters from the door stand two attendants with their backs to him. He slips in quietly and begins heading away when one of them calls out, "Hey!"

He turns to face them, all smiling and innocent.

"The show's already started," the attendant says.

"I know. I was having a smoke," he replies. "With my friend Lucian. In the kitchen? We got distracted. You know how he is."

The attendant chuckles. "I'm surprised that reefhead hasn't gotten fired yet. Come in through the front next time."

"I will. Thanks." He continues down the corridor lined with dark curtains, hearing light, delicate music. The crowd makes deep *mmmm* sounds, clearly appreciating whatever they're seeing. Finally, he reaches a door to the main arena, and steps through. He joins the standing room only section at the back of what must be the central tent. He sees that the audience is arranged in sections: standing room where he is, then a circle of arena style seating, then an area where a dinner service had clearly taken place at the tables set along the curve of the stage.

Onstage stands a tall Hydraxian. He wears a sparkling black

vest that exposes all four of his lean and muscular arms, and tight pants that are black but reflect rainbows. His orange skin appears to be dusted with glitter, his face painted up as some kind of mythological creature. He juggles eight balls with his four arms, forming complex and dizzying patterns with the arcs of their flight. He uses two of his arms to catch a series of balls, balancing them at different points along their length. They fly into the air, then land solidly, right where he wants them, and they stay there, perfectly still. He begins rolling these balls around his body, waving a couple of them fluidly with two hands while tossing with his other two, then catching and balancing one on his face.

He moves his body like a dancer and the balls are his partners, but two of his arms are doing one kind of dance while the other two are doing another. He juggles shifting patterns of diminishing numbers as he divests himself of one ball at a time, tossing them to the waiting assistants, until there is just one rolling on his palm. It looks like it's floating as he passes it from hand to hand to hand to hand. A series of short rolls, then an elongated one across a bridge formed by two arms one way, then back the other way along the other two arms. He changes his positions fluidly and Jes can't help but wonder if there's some kind of complex code being transmitted by the hypnotic movements. Finally he draws to a close – all four hands waver around the ball and again it looks like it's floating. As the spotlight dims and the crowd cheers its approval, Jes can't help but join in.

The stage goes dark as the crowd shuffles and coughs in anticipation of the next act. Then the center spot opens slowly on an amber gold mound of fabric and spangles as the music fades in. A face appears, flipping up from the mound. A beautiful human face, framed by legs – the performer's legs, he realizes, that are not in places they should be. Her chin is on the floor, framed by her feet, and her body is bent in half. The contortionist unfolds herself to the murmur of the crowd.

She tumbles across the floor, the embodiment of grace, lands in a split before sliding her front leg behind her, then bending them both forward over her head so that the tips of her toes are in front of her forehead. She presses down with her hands and lifts herself off the floor before slowly rising up into a handstand. She spins and walks on her hands to the center of the stage, kicking her legs gracefully.

A large silver hoop descends from the fly space above the stage; she grabs it and they rise up in the air together as she hangs, moving her legs as if treading water. Jes realizes that what he'd taken to be a tight bodysuit is, in fact, her skin. She wears a spangled bikini which keeps her from total nudity, but the iridescence is her, not a costume. Though she has human features and human toned skin, she has a shimmer. And what he'd thought to be a headpiece with crystals of rich amber has a familiar glitter – she has a halo, though hers is smaller than expected. Could she be interspecies? Asuna and human? The Asuna notoriously do not approve of interspecies mating so this performer is a rare creature indeed.

She hangs from the hoop, bends her body through a series of shapes that draw applause each time she stops and holds one. Now she hangs from one arm while her legs bend over her head; now she adds her other arm and flips over into a split; now she pulls herself up into the circle and presses her body into the curve, making herself a crescent moon. She contorts herself within the hoop, glides through a sequence of poses, her body seemingly boneless. The hoop lowers down to the stage and she flips to the floor. Then, gripping the bottom of the hoop, she begins to twirl and the hoop rises again, and she spins and spins and spins – a living jewel taking flight. Faster and faster she spins as she draws her legs up, then the spin slows as she brings her legs back down, held in right angles, bent at the knees. She continues spinning as the hoop lowers, then her feet make contact with the stage again and she finally stops as the crowd erupts with cheers. She beams, takes her bow. Jes wonders what it must feel like to belong as perfectly as she does on the stage.

Could *he* belong here? At least for a little while? Was it too much to hope that this bawdy, gaudy moon could be his refuge? Somewhere the Institute would never come looking? Because why else would he have been guided here? He knows perfectly well that he could be standing here, now, in this alien crowd, by random happenstance. And yet something feels familiar about what he's watching.

A succession of acts take the stage: a trio of acrobats, a group doing flying trapeze, some annoying clowns. He barely takes them in as he strengthens his resolve. He wishes he could will his body to such feats as he's witnessing, but he can't. There *is* something he can do that would dazzle and delight the crowd into ooohs and aaahs. But he can't. Not as a public performance.

The crowd thins out after the show, but Jes doesn't move from his spot. He leans casually on the barrier that separates the standing section from the seats, watches as everyone makes their exit, chattering excitedly about the show. A few workers enter the space discreetly, invisible to all but the one looking out for them. They are humans and Bezans, and they quietly set about their duties: clearing glasses and empty bottles, cleaning the tables from the dinner service, sweeping the floors.

The house lights come on, and the air of mystery vanishes in sudden brightness. The space becomes not quite garish, but is certainly no longer the magical otherworld it had just been. "Excuse me," he says, politely as he can, to the young human woman tossing empty bottles into the receptacle floating behind her. "Who would I talk to about getting a job here?"

She sticks out her lower lip and blows a lock of pink hair out of her face as she continues working. "Aleia handles house staff, but if you're interested in crew, talk to Quint. Aleia's probably gone for the night, but Quint'll be backstage somewhere. Big Hydraxian guy."

"Oh, the juggler?"

She laughs. "No not him. Quint's a *big* guy." She pauses and looks at him closely, taking in his hair, his eyes. She's trying to piece his heritage together but says nothing about it. He likes her for that.

"Big Hydraxian," Jes says. "Got it."

He begins heading down the steps towards the stage.

"Oh, don't go that way," the busgirl says. "You won't get through. Go to the crew door – out into the corridor there," she points to the door he entered by. "Go right, it curves around. There's a little alcove with a black door. It's unmarked, but you'll hear people and probably smell the clouds of reef."

"Thanks," he says and follows her instructions.

An attendant walking the other way steps in his path. "The exit is behind you."

"I'm here to talk to Quint. About some possible work."

The usher sniffs in response and steps aside. Jes continues down the dim pathway, towards the sounds of chatter and laughter. As the girl predicted, the pungent smell of reef fills the air. He follows the sound and the smell, and sees a space where the curtains lining the walls are parted. He heads for it, then freezes when a multi-legged form emerges from the shadow. An insectoid being as tall as him steps into the corridor. It walks out on four back legs bearing a long abdomen, and its two front arms (or legs) are bent forward in front of it. Its head is triangular with rounded corners and two long, feather-like antennae sprout from the top of its face, wavering slightly. Its large, bulbous, oblong eyes are violet and black, like the rest of its body, and they seem to refract the dim light. A Mantodean. Jes has never seen one in person before.

The being emits a soft hissing sound, some clicks, then says in Ninespeak, "They will accept you when you make them float."

As creeped out as he is by the large compound eyes gazing at him, Jes can't look away. He feels the alien's attention unpeel him to his very essence and he finds, disconcertingly, that he wants to be seen. Is he being judged? Jes can't suss this individual yet feels certain that he is being assessed somehow. He hopes he passes muster.

"Thank you," he stammers out. He's embarrassed to be so flustered by the – for lack of a better word – *alienness* of a member species of the 9-Star Congress. But the Mantodeans are the most alien of all of them and he's never met one before. Not that he accepts that as an excuse. "Thank you for the... advice?"

"My pleasure. It's what I do. My name is Kush O-Nhar and my pronouns are he/him. After you," the Mantodean says and gives a little bow, gesturing toward the door while emitting soft clicking sounds.

Jes pushes the door open, tamps down a feeling of revulsion at all the legs of the creature – person – behind him. He imagines the fine filaments of the front pincers whispering the air on the back of his neck. He wonders if that's speciesist of him.

The room is warmly lit as he enters, and he steps into a haze of reef, chordash leaf, and incense. To his surprise, nobody really pays him any mind, but he feels the keen attention of the Mantodean behind him. There's not much of the crew left, just a few lingering clowns gathering their things and dashing past him out the door. The trio of Bezan acrobats, triplets it looks like, stands together in a loose cluster, dressed in street clothes, satchels slung over their tiny shoulders, looking ready to go but in no hurry. They laugh together at some private humor.

"I thought you left," one of them says to the Mantodean with a look at Jes. Her sisters join her in looking at him and he susses from them mild curiosity tempered by indifference.

"I wanted to see how this plays out," the insect-person replies.

Curious.

The space is a mirror of the theater space, minus the stage

and seating. It is filled mostly by mats, and trampolines, and aerial rigs and other equipment. On one of the towers of trusses rising towards the circus top, a Bezan male in a safety harness climbs among the lighting instruments. At the base of the tower stands the biggest man Jes has ever seen – he must be the "big Hydraxian guy". The Hydraxian he saw on stage was tall, but thin and long limbed, lithe even. But this guy is even taller and all brawn – thick and hefty, corpuscular in his musculature. He gazes attentively up at the Bezan in the rafters. Jes finds his concern all the more touching given his bulk.

"Excuse me," Jes says, modulating his voice to be quiet and respectful, but not timid. "Are you Quint?"

The Hydraxian keeps his eyes on the Bezan, who's still in costume – he must be one of the acrobats – then glances down to Jes for a click of a second, then back up to the guy climbing around high above them. "Who are you?"

"I'm wanting to ask you about a job. On your crew maybe?"

"How's it looking up there?" Quint calls to the upper reaches of the tent.

"Almost got it!" comes the distant call back.

The hulking four-armed man turns his attention back to Jes. His brows are thick, his jaw square, and nose broad. Despite his intimidating build, his eyes are kind. "What's your name?"

"Jes."

"Ever crewed before?"

"Can't say that I have."

"Built stuff?"

"No."

"Fixed stuff?"

"No."

"Well, what can you do then?" His tone isn't snide or sarcastic, he's genuinely curious.

Jes wonders how he should spin his particular set of skills and wishes he had thought a bit more thoroughly before coming back here.

Before he can formulate a response, the contortionist-aerialist lady walks up. She's draped in a dark red cloak, her lustrous brown hair tied back in a loose ponytail. Her halo, though small, catches and refracts the light just as much as the Asuna on the shuttle. It's a golden amber color with some pale yellow that complements her deep copper-toned skin. The effect of the shimmer on human skin captivates his gaze. He tries not to stare but she catches him at it. If she minds, she doesn't say so.

"Hi Kush O-Nhar," she says to the Mantodean, who bows in return, bringing its front arms up in a sort of prayer pose. Its movements are graceful, delicate almost. She turns to Jes. "I'm Essa. You are…?"

"Jes."

"Jes. If I were to take a guess at your heritage I would say human and Rijala?" Her voice is silky and resonant.

"You would be correct."

"That's very unusual."

"Not any more unusual than human and Asuna."

She smiles faintly at this, nods her head toward him. Then she wraps her arms around Quint in an embrace, and her torso looks as thick as one of his legs. He rests one of his hands on her back and smiles down at her fondly.

"Jes here is asking about a job with the crew," Quint informs her.

"Oh really?" Essa arches an eyebrow and looks to Jes with fresh interest. "What can you do?"

"We were just getting to that when you made your enchanting appearance." Quint rubs his hand on her back gently as he speaks.

Essa giggles. "Flatterer. Someone's looking to get lucky tonight." A flush flows between them, one that Jes recognizes instantly. He looks away from the couple and shakes off the echoes their attraction leaves in him. Quint's suavity impresses and makes for an easier focus than his attraction to his apparent lover.

"So," Quint begins again. "What is it that you—"

A yelp of alarm from overhead interrupts the conversation.

"You OK, Bo?" Quint calls up.

A loud crack sounds through the air, struts high above them snapping. A wedge of a support beam plummets towards them, cracked off the main structure along with a couple of big lights. Bo, tethered to a strut by his harness, yowls as he falls.

Reflexively, Jes reaches up and emits one of his fields. A pale blue bubble of light envelops the falling man and gear, suspending them in the air. Then the crewman, the broken scaffolding and the lighting instruments all float gently down at Jes's direction.

When everything is safely on the floor, Jes closes his fingers into a fist and the blue light vanishes, winking out.

Bo, Essa, and Quint all stare at him. He can feel the intense looks of the Bezan triplets and the Mantodean burning into the back of his head. No use hiding it now...

"That," Jes says nonchalantly. "I can do that."

THE INSTITUTE

They remove the collar on days of gravity tests. Jes has to use his power, after all. But they make sure he knows who's in charge with stunners mounted in the corners, and handheld versions in the holsters they all wear. They're ready to fire the moment he breaks protocol, disobeys instructions, or tries to use his talent against them. During the long, boring days in his cell, he fantasizes about the leaden feet he'd inflict on them, imagines gravity so strong they can't stand upright. He's not stupid though – even in his most surly and rebellious moments, he's never directed his ability towards them. Any thought of doing more grievous harm makes him queasy, just as it did growing up, with bullies and violent vids and stories alike.

On this day, he's in a room with a five hundred kilogram cube of unknown material and a lab assistant with a metallic rod. Jes wears a heavy crown: an array of sensors in a ring around his head, connected by a stalk of lit-up cables that lead to the main diagnostic console. The lights are color-coded: red for vitals, blue for autonomous nervous response, purple for psionic abilities, and white for the paratalents he's about to demonstrate. Patches of the same kinds of sensors are stuck all over his torso, only these transmit wirelessly. He stands in his underpants; the sensors require bare skin and the lenses that the telemetry beams through must be unobstructed. The room is cold and his skin raises goosepimples.

"OK," Matheson instructs over the intercom. "We want you to reduce the gravity until the cube lifts off the floor."

It doesn't feel possible to him, but Matheson had said that based on the findings from other experiments where Jes floated smaller objects of lesser weight, he should be able to do this. He attempts to fulfill the command, and creates a field around the cube. He susses the gravity inside the field in a similar but altogether different way than from sussing people's feelings. Gravity is an invisible force in the room – not just this room, everywhere of course. But for now, he only needs to focus on this room. He connects to a sense he has, a sense it seems that nobody else has, and feels the gravity's hold on everything he sees, the waves that keep the world from flying apart. It's like heat, like electricity, and at the same time nothing close to them at all.

The sense of emotions or graviton particles or gravity waves, or whatever it is, isn't in his head, but in his body, in the very core of him. He focuses on the waves within the field he's created, and hones in to that limited area. *Lighter, lighter, lighter, softer, lighter, softer.* He repeats this mantra and something inside him opens. He becomes the mind of the waves, and wills gravity's hold on the cube to loosen, to relax, like letting a taut line go slack. He wonders what Matheson sees in the control booth, what, exactly, his wicked instruments measure.

The cube floats.

A lab assistant walks up to it, puts one end of the rod under one of the cube's bottom edges and, using his foot as a pivot, makes the rod a lever and raises the cube even higher off the floor with ease.

A flare of surprise and wonder fills him. He knows the feelings aren't his. There's no collar restraining him, and no collar means he can suss. His empathic sense blazes now that it's unbound. Throughout the procedure, the personnel in this room keep their emotions tamped down, in check, stoic. But the lifting of the cube causes a surge among them all and feelings flood him in a rush.

He susses the intense focus of the researchers and technicians, their awe at the shift in the mass of the heavy cube. He also feels their fear, fear of him that he can effect such changes to the power of physics, to the material world. If he were to focus, he could identify which feeling flows from which person, but in this moment, being so unused to functioning, and while he's floating the biggest object he's ever attempted, it's all just a jumble of confusion.

But above all of that, like a harsh yell over a cloud of hushed tones, he susses a drive to understand, a drive to control, a twisted pleasure.

And in there somewhere, small and ignored, his own loneliness and defeat.

CHAPTER THREE

"So no one knows you're here?" Quint asks, leaning forward as he interrogates Jes, his face looming like a rising moon.

"Nobody." Jes repeats his answer for who knows how many times. He can't blame the big guy for being cautious. He hadn't planned on telling them about his ability or the Institute so soon, if at all, but the equipment failure happened, and people were going to get hurt and he had to show them some reason, some value he could add to their operation. Disclosing his ability just opened the door.

"And they just *sold* you?" One of the triplets asks the question, but he can't tell which one. "Your parents?" one of the other ones asks, but they mouth their words so quickly it's hard to tell which spoke. He nods and they all look at him with an expression of deep compassion.

"Because of my ability." People having powers is a known phenomenon in the Congress, but encountering such abilities is still met with astonishment and curiosity by those that witness them.

"Explain again what you do?" Quint says.

"The Institute called it 'Localized Gravity Manipulation'. I make these sort of bubbles, and inside them I can increase or decrease gravity. I can make things float or crush them with their own mass. Before, with Bo and everything falling, I made the gravity incredibly light so that they floated. Then, I increased it bit by bit, bringing them slowly down to the floor. I don't hold them up in the air the way a telekinetic would, but it has the same results, I guess. A telekinetic would have a much bigger range of motion than I can achieve."

Jes looks around at the group facing him; Quint, Essa, Bo, Kush O-Nhar, the Bezan triplet acrobats, Zazie, Lula, and Jujubee – he wonders if he'll ever be able to tell those three apart – and he feels glad that he shared his ability and situation with this bunch of weirdoes. Having people respond with curiosity rather than fear is a welcome change. Besides, he needs them on his side. He needs someone on his side.

"Crazy," Essa whispers, gazing at Jes, her eyes wide.

"Please don't tell anybody else," Jes says.

"Your secret is safe with me," Kush O-Nhar says in his soft, susurrating voice, followed by a set of soft clicks. Again, Jes feels the Mantodean's attention on him, and gets the sense that Kush O-Nhar is looking beyond him somehow but what he sees, Jes can't guess.

"And us," the triplets say in unison. "We won't tell."

"Who'd believe me anyway?" Bo quips and they all laugh nervously.

"I won't break your confidence," Essa says.

"And I look out for everyone who works for me," Quint says with a smile.

"So I got a job?" Hopeful excitement rises in Jes's chest.

"I'll have to clear it with Aleia, but she usually goes with my recommendation. Besides, a little while ago we had a couple guys go off and join the Jasmine Jonah interstellar tour. It just so happens we're prepping some new set pieces. So there's openings."

Jes thanks Quint profusely as the group murmurs its approval. "I won't let you down." As they shake hands, Jes is dwarfed by Quint's bulk but feels comforted rather than intimidated. His overall gentle nature came through very quickly after the initial grumpiness. Jes decides he wants to please this guy and make sure that he's kept around.

"You'll be an apprentice at first. We'll shift you around to different tasks and see what suits you."

Jes agrees to this, then it's time to broach another topic. "Can you tell me where there's some cheap rooms? I kind of need a place to crash."

Essa's laugh bubbles delightedly. "Of course you do! Poor little fugitive. I have a guest room. It's yours until you find a place."

"Really? I appreciate that. Thank you."

With that, the motley crew gathers their things and make their exit.

"I owe you my life," Bo says as they leave. "I feel like I should at least get you drunk. If that would be a treat for you. Or high. Whatever you like."

Jes chuckles – playful energy pulses from Bo, along with gratitude. "Why not both? I'm always up for a buzz."

Bo smiles. "Well alright then. I can't tonight though, but soon."

They enter the lobby and its opulence is dazzling. Red velvet drapes tied with gold silk sashes cover the walls. Three high-backed circular sofas are spread out across the space, above which hangs a chandelier dripping with beads of red glass. A cocktail bar consisting of baroque curves occupies the wall by the theater entrance. And above the bar is another light fixture – a long branch of a tree whose leaves are slices of amber glass and whose trunk is covered in fractal patterns. A Bezan motif.

Posters hang in the front lobby featuring various acts of the Cirque Kozmiqa: Jes spots the triplets in pyramid formation – *The Pirouetting Pixies of Port Ruby*; Essa is pictured suspended in two flowing bolts of silk – *The Aerial Queen of Pleasure Moon Nine*, and prominently, in his own frame of bright bulbs, the "Special Feature": *Kush O-Nhar, Mystic of the Future*. Something about his pose in the picture is so self-serious that Jes has to suppress a laugh. He suddenly realizes the Mantodean is watching him.

"Nice shot," Jes says, pointing to the photo on the wall. "Really captures your essence."

Kush O-Nhar tilts his head, and his antennae vibrate. Is he amused?

A soft hiss, some clicks, and then: "You're strange."

They all walk outside together and without another word, Kush O-Nhar unfurls his wings and lifts off, hovering for a moment before dashing away with a buzzing sound.

"Whoa. Where's he off to?" Jes asks of no one in particular.

"He lives in a treehouse in a restricted area of the gardens. Come on," Essa says, holding a gate open for him.

They are let out onto a side street off the main drag, which saves having to go through the casino to leave the premises, which Jes is grateful for.

"Thank you for saving me," Bo says again, turning to Jes. "Would've been quite a mess if I went splat."

"Anytime," Jes replies.

"Are you staying over tonight?" Essa asks Quint, who nods as he calls a roto.

Bo and the triplets go their own way. In seconds one of the silver and orange spheres rolls up; its side swirls open revealing the welcoming cool leather seats. Jes climbs in after Quint and Essa, then the side of the sphere swirls shut and they roll off down the street. The inside of the sphere is softly lit with pink light; the inner sphere that sits still, cradles them within the rolling outer sphere they can see spinning around them. A catchy Jasmine Jonah song plays softly from all around.

"What made you decide to hire me?" Jes asks. "Just some rando off the street?" His fingers stroke the soft upholstery of the seat and he finds the sensation grounding.

Though the question was directed at Quint, it's Essa who speaks. "Are you aware that Asuna are empathic?" She stares at him intently.

"Yes. Of course. So you – even though you're..."

"Even as a hybrid I have the Asuna sense, yes. Plus, my human side is Indran. Which is how I can tell you're not malicious. Back at the tent I could tell you were desperate for safety even as you spoke calmly to us."

Jes considers this. Both Indran humans and Asuna have their own ways of sussing, so that makes sense.

"Also Kush O-Nhar told us we could trust you and that we should help you," Quint adds. "Before you got there. He told us to expect you."

"He did? What did he say?" Jes leans forward in his seat, looking eagerly at his companions.

Essa and Quint turn towards each other and confer in whispers. Finally, Essa turns back to Jes. "He said the hybrid boy would need help. He said helping him would help us too."

"Huh." Jes considers this. "How might I help *you*?"

"That remains to be seen," Essa replies.

"I've got a few ideas," Quint adds while she shakes her head. "What did he tell you?"

"To make stuff float. That I would be accepted if I made them float."

Quint lets out an "ohhhh" of recognition and Essa says "Of course."

"So Mantodeans really *can* see the future?" Jes is all attention, intrigued that he might finally get an answer to a question he's had since he was a child.

"It's more complicated than that," Essa says. "Kush O-Nhar can explain it. You should ask him sometime."

"Ask Kush about seeing the future," Jes confirms. "Got it."

"Not 'Kush'!" Essa and Quint exclaim in unison. Essa continues, "His name is Kush O-Nhar. He'd be offended if you called him simply Kush. It's a cultural thing."

Jes takes in this information. "Understood."

The roto rolls to a stop and the side opposite the one they entered swirls open. They climb out and find themselves standing in front of an apartment complex, whose curved shapes look organic. Persephone and two moons loom overhead. The roto rolls away as Essa and Quint walk into the complex, Jes following. Quint holds Essa's hand with his lower right one as his other three arms hang, relaxed, at his sides. One of those arms probably has more muscle than Jes has in his whole body.

They take a path that goes by a pool where laughter and smoke drift from the shadow of a gazebo. The glowing ember of a spliff goes bright with someone's draw and Jes savors the perfumed scent as they enter one of the globular structures and take a spiral staircase up to the second floor. There, Essa pulls out a keycard, swiping it over the glass panel beside the door. She steps into the doorway, turns and extends her arm. "Welcome."

Quint hangs behind in the corridor as Jes enters ahead of him, then shuffles through with a slight turn sideways, since the door is too narrow for the broadness of his shoulders. The door slides shut behind him.

Soft lights come on in a neatly appointed home where a large purple sofa with green and orange cushions dominates the room. There are plants all over the place, and a couple of large pieces of art including one of the holographic fractal mandalas popular on Indra. His grandparents had one in their home.

"Are you hungry? Thirsty?" Essa asks as she removes her cloak and drops it on the sofa.

"I wouldn't mind a bite," he answers. The last thing he'd eaten was a stale nutrition bar at the spaceport bazaar back on Rijal.

"I'll whip up something for us," Quint says. "I'm hungry too." He heads for the kitchen, stoops slightly and turns sideways again to get through the doorway.

"He's an amazing cook," Essa says with a loving look at the four-armed hulk in her kitchen.

Through the doorway to the kitchen, Jes sees Quint pulling

out a pan, a knife, and a cutting board all at once, each with a different hand. He sets the items down simultaneously before turning to the fridge.

"A little brandy?" Jes's hostess offers.

"Sure." He takes a seat on the sofa and looks up at the holographic art on the wall.

"Are you a fan of Indran art?" Essa asks, handing him a snifter of dark green liquid and taking a seat beside him.

"Yeah. My grandparents had a lot of it in their home." He juts his chin toward the geometry on the wall. "That one reminds me of them."

"So which of your parents is…?"

"My mother's Indran, my father is Rijala. I grew up on Rijal."

"Is your mother a psion?" She sips her brandy and looks intently at him.

Jes nods. "Not a Consciousness Holder, but her parents were. And my Rijala grandfather was a mager."

She raises her eyebrows. "That's some heritage. Could that be how you're able to do what you do?"

"The Institute sure thought so."

"It must have been hard for your mother on Rijal, being cut off from those abilities." She curls her legs under her as she speaks.

"I suppose. We never really talked about it. We never talked much in my family, except about what a disappointment I am."

Essa lets out a sound like a laugh. "Oh believe me I know about that."

"So what's your deal then?" Jes asks, sipping at the brandy. It has a grassy kind of flavor. "Human and Asuna must be even rarer than human and Rijala."

"It is. My grandparents thought my mother was crazy for falling in love with a human. I grew up on Indra of course. They don't let half-breeds set foot on Opale."

"I never knew that," Jes says, startled. The ease with which she tosses off "half-breeds" saddens him.

"They don't want anyone getting the idea that interspecies coupling is acceptable. The Asuna are quite possibly the most xenophobic species in the Congress. It's a miracle I exist at all really. My Asuna family still maintain that my father used his telepathy to ensnare my mother. They met at a Moonsbreath Festival, so that just made them even more suspicious."

Moonsbreath is a famous festival on Indra, when the eponymous flowers bloom and release a perfume that causes a psychotropic reaction. Apparently orgies happen there, amongst other revelries. Jes had been curious about the festival at one point in time, but after hearing about the orgies he decided to avoid it forever. Essa's parents meeting at such an event could certainly induce skepticism in her family. He says nothing about this though, not wanting to be judgmental.

"What brought you to us? Tonight?" Essa cups her drink to her chest with both hands and gazes at him earnestly with deep brown eyes.

Jes reaches into his pocket and pulls out his grandmother's crystal. He lets the weight of it drop while holding the end of the chain in his fingertips.

Essa's eyes widen with recognition. "A dowsing crystal!"

It's Jes's turn to be surprised. "You know what this is?"

"Raised on Indra, remember?"

The crystal swings gently between them before settling to stillness. No question posed to it, no path to discern.

"Well, I asked for guidance," Jes explains. "After stepping out of the spaceport. And it led me to a holoboard promoting your show. And here I am."

Quint walks in, carrying three plates on one arm like skilled servers do, a pitcher of water in another hand, glasses in another, and silverware and napkins in the last. He hands a plate to each of them, as well as a fork and napkin, and places the water and glasses down on the coffee table.

"Bezan hominy crêpes! Yummy." Essa eagerly sets the plate in her lap while Quint settles down beside her.

"I hope you aren't vegan or anything," he says to Jes. "I should've asked first. There's cheese in it."

"Don't worry, I'm an omnivore," Jes replies. The delicate skin of the crêpe gives way to its filling, a gritty mush of the signature Bezan grain mixed with what he recognizes as Rijalen sheepsmilk threefold cheese. The combination is soft enough to reward the pleasure-yearning parts of the brain while substantial enough to settle hunger. The flavors – the sweet of the grain, the salt of the cheese, the dance of unknown herbs on his tongue – burst spectacularly and course through his body with nourishment and pleasure.

After their meal, Quint cleans up and Essa shows Jes to his room. It's modest, just large enough to contain a simple bed and a small Starlink-enabled desk with matching chair. Jes is touched – it's the most luxurious space he's had to himself in a long time. He is also given a private bathroom and decides to shower before bed. His last time bathing was in the Institute. When he woke to this day, it was in a squat near the spaceport in Nooafar Prefecture, just a day after he broke out. What a difference a day makes.

As Jes stands under the hot water, he imagines his old life washing away. He can still hear the alarms blaring and the yells of confusion that broke out as he ran through the complex, making his way to the gate. In his mind he can see the fearful looks of the orderlies that he brought down with his gravity fields – they must have thought he would crush their flesh and bones to pulp. While he was tempted, he just couldn't bring himself to harm any of them, even in the heat of escape. He thinks of Matheson, the lead researcher, and wonders if he would have felt the same way about him. Could he hurt that awful man if he had the chance? Would he?

Matheson must have informed his parents of his escape by now – would they care? They got paid and it seems to him that's all they ever cared about.

He gets out of the shower, towels off, climbs into bed naked and delights in the feel of the clean sheets. Sheets! He barely knows these people, yet this is the most welcome, the most safe he has felt... well, ever. No, not ever...

In his first home, his parents always treated him like a nuisance they could barely tolerate until he became a commodity, and then they couldn't wait to sell him off. At the Institute, he was nothing but a source of "Important Findings", a curiosity to be deciphered. At the squats, among his fellow street urchins and petty criminals, he felt like one of them, but he was also a potential snitch and backstabber, like they all were. Only in his grandparents' house, his human grandparents, had he ever felt safe. His last visit there was ten years ago, and not since then had he felt like a person who had every right to exist in the world. Not once, until stumbling into the circus tonight.

Jes wants to lean into this feeling, of just being a person. He wants to make it last. But the Institute darkens his hopes with a long shadow. He figures it can only be a matter of time before they find him, but he hopes it's a long time. A long, long time.

GRANDMOTHER

The crystal glints in the sun as Jes sits with his grandparents in the meadow near their house in Indra City, the great domed capital of the human world, Indra.

"It's called a dowsing crystal," she explains. "It helps to focus your intuition. Use it when you are needing guidance, like when you need to make a choice and you don't know what to do." She shows him how to use it, how the mind must focus on the question being asked. Binary choices worked best: this or that, yes or no.

She shows him how to hold the end of the chain, how to let the crystal hang still while the question is posed, how to gently let it start swinging. There's a tingle when his fingertips make contact with the sphere at the end of the chain, a satisfying weight as the pendulum part hangs.

"Don't you think such a gift is wasted on a child?" his mother asks his grandmother. She's barely paying attention to what's happening, her eyes on whatever she's reading.

Since Jes learned to suss, he's learned some new words that describe people's feelings and he's learned a couple that he sadly realizes apply to his mother – disdainful, detached. How could she be the daughter of the warm-hearted and generous person giving him this magical thing?

"The child will grow into a man who will call upon this gift and understand it," his grandmother explains with a patient voice, but he susses the impatience underneath her words. "You've let your Rijala mate's pragmatism seep into your mind. Hard to imagine he's descended from a mager. Though, on second thought, they do tend towards the cold and logical side of things." There's *disdain* here too, directed at his mother. It's deserved.

His mother rolls her eyes. His grandparents don't like his father and though he doesn't fully understand why, he doesn't think it's speciesism. He doesn't like his father either. He doesn't really like his mother for that matter. They are cold and mean and he's just in the way, a nuisance whose existence they're annoyed to remember. What did he do to deserve that? He's always tried to be good. He's starting to think maybe he shouldn't bother trying to please them, they either can't be pleased or they don't care.

His grandparents though, his grandmother especially, are different.

His grandfather snoozes in the sun in what he calls his nap-chair. It hovers a meter or so off the grass. He snores lightly, and his tunic is splayed open, revealing a forest of white hair that stirs in the breeze. He always naps when they come to this meadow. Jes can't say why, but he loves knowing that about the old man, knowing that tidbit of his habits.

"Never mind your mother," his grandmother says. Jes looks up at her lined face, her warm brown eyes and ruddy skin that still has a youthful glow despite the wrinkles. Her curly white hair blows about like wild wisps of clouds. He remembers when it was mostly dark with streaks of white; it seemed to change so quickly. "Now that you can suss, you are ready for such a tool. Remember this always: it is one tool of many that you can use to guide your choices. May it grant you clarity when you need to find your way."

She kisses his forehead. The kiss is soft, and warm, like the love he susses from her. He wishes he could stay in this moment, and never go back with his parents to stupid Rijal at all. He wishes this moment didn't have to be tainted by knowing it will end.

CHAPTER FOUR

Jes stands before Aleia Siqui, General Manager and principal owner of Cirque Kozmiqa. As the new hire, he must present himself to her scrutiny. She sits at attention, her arms resting on the desk in front of her, hands clasped, her gaze intense. She is full-blood Rijala, and her features are characteristically thin and angular, her skin pale blue. She wears her blue-white hair swept back with a silken band, and her silver eyes examine him coolly. Her suit is pale violet in color and makes her eyes appear almost blue when they flick towards him. "You're staying at Essa's," she says.

"Yes, ma'am," he responds in best-behavior mode.

"If she and Quint trust you, I trust you." He relaxes a bit at this comment, but not all the way. "What are your specialties?"

"I'm a quick study, and I'm good with my hands. I'll be working on carpentry, but I'm interested in lighting and sound."

"So, no performing aspirations?"

He shakes his head. "No interest. But Quint's not in charge of casting, is he? I figured that'd be you."

"Perceptive." She smiles and nods slowly. "And it's a good thing you're not a performer. I don't think I can take any more delicate flowers. Don't get me wrong – they bring in the crowds and for that I'm grateful. But show folk are a special lot."

"Oh, I know that." He doesn't really know that, but he'd taken a course in theater when he was still in school, and could extrapolate from the behavior of the aspiring thespians.

The continued eye contact makes him uncomfortable, and he glances up at the painting of a forest landscape on the wall behind her.

"I sense there's something you're not telling me." Her eyes narrow and she leans back in her chair, crosses her arms.

That's weird. Did somebody in the room last night already spill the beans about his ability – one of the triplets, perhaps, or Bo? He knows to his core that Essa and Quint would have divulged nothing, but he can't say about the others. They were all earnest in the moment, and he'll just have to trust that.

"I'm not sure what you mean." He's thankful that Rijala don't have empathic or telepathic abilities. Had he behaved suspiciously to prompt the question?

"You're part human, yes? Do you possess any Indran talents?"

"The psi abilities don't work off-world," he says. He makes the effort to sound like he couldn't be happier to be discussing such matters for the zillionth time. "And I was raised on Rijal anyway. I have the intuitive and empathic senses, and I can see auric fields, sometimes, if I try really hard. I'm not a psion."

She's clearly making a mental note of this, indexing the potential usefulness. "Why did you leave Rijal? Why come here to this little moon?"

Time to reveal his other backstory. "I couldn't take it anymore on Rijal," he begins. "Being a hybrid there... limits opportunities. People make assumptions. People pre-judge."

She nods. Being Rijala herself, she knows the truth of this. She waits for more.

"And I got into some trouble when I was there."

"What kind of trouble?"

"I fell in with the wrong crowd. It turns out I'm good at picking pockets. And also locks and sneaking into places. I never *needed* to steal – my parents were well off – it was just something to do when I got bored."

Her eyes open wide at this, though she doesn't seem taken aback. "Do Essa and Quint know about this?"

He shakes his head.

"Do you have a code?"

He looks at her quizzically.

"A code of conduct? A moral code."

With her clarification, he does not hesitate, "Never would I steal from anyone in my circle." He speaks with as reassuring a tone as he can muster. "Only strangers. Only strangers who are..." He struggles to say what he means without being crude about it.

"Who are easy marks?" she finishes for him, with a sly smile.

He matches her smile. "Yes. Some people really do just ask for it. I was trying to find a more polite way of saying that."

"That you even cared to do so is a check in your favor. I might have some use for you. Beyond whatever tasks Quint sets you to. Would you be open to other assignments apart from crew?"

"Of course. Whatever you need. I aim to be indispensable."

"That's the spirit."

After passing Aleia's adjudication, he joins Quint and some others in the crew area where a group is at work on a new set piece. He notices a box labelled "Free Box" that is full of clothes and some random items: balls, rings, board games, a cone shaped thing he can't fathom the use of.

"Help yourself to anything in there," Bo says as he passes by. "There's lots of good stuff. Other people's trash, you know."

Jes doesn't, in fact, know. "What do you mean?"

"Other people's trash can be your treasure," Bo says. "It's a Bezan thing." He pulls his hair up and ties it into a top knot – it's pale orange with pale lavender highlights. Bezans have the coolest hair, famously bioluminescent and almost holographic-like. Bo's amber eyes contrast sharply with the dusky violet of his skin.

"Makes sense, I guess." The Rijala upper class tossed so many things aside so carelessly he understands the Bezan saying right away. Jes rifles through the items – he does need clothes as he only has what he grabbed from the squat. And that cape.

"I was thinking tomorrow night after the show." Bo speaks quickly and seems to assume Jes knows what he's talking about.

He meets Bo's gaze, "You mean hanging out? Yeah, OK. You're on."

"OK. Later."

Jes watches Bo walk away with a bouncy sort of gait and can't help smiling after him. Turning his attention back to the clothes, he picks out an orange and green striped shirt, a gray shirt, and a pair of pants that look like they will probably fit. He takes the items, folds them and sets them aside in the lounge area.

Quint's talking to a group of crew members and waves him over.

Through a transparent wall in the loft area, the costumers are busy making repairs on various pieces of wardrobe. Directly below the loft are the dressing rooms. The curtain separating the performance-facing and performance-making parts of the venue is drawn back and the two are one. Earlier today, one of the clowns explained that the front of house is called "outer space" and the backstage area where they are now is "inner space".

Out on the stage, Essa and the triplets work out a collaborative routine that involves each of them balancing on their hands around an array of canes – poles of varying lengths capped with a square knob of polished wood. They pull off one of the positions, one leg bent and the other stretched out, then they all drop out of it, coming to rest on the floor.

Quint assigns Jes to cutting long pieces of wood in half. It is the raw material for the frame of the new set – the one for the act Essa and the triplets are rehearsing. It is a simple enough task and he's glad to be put to use. He places each piece of wood on the table, where a preset frame indicates where to cut. He activates the cutter in his hand, sends a band of red photons through the wood. The cutter slices the material effortlessly, leaving each cleaved edge smoking slightly. After the pieces are cut, the assembly will begin. It's an ornate design, a miniature of the Port Ruby cityscape.

There's a sudden flurry of activity at the crew door as one of the ushers, out of uniform, rushes in, runs up to Quint and speaks to him in muffled tones. Jes notices but keeps going with his task. Quint turns from the usher and heads over to where Essa is rehearsing. She's giving the triplets choreography notes. It's a conversation that piques his interest and that he's been listening in on – he's curious how a performance is made.

"...hold that pose an extra eight while I move into the second combo..." Essa explains to her performance partners when Aleia walks in. Everyone continues their work, but all are definitely paying attention. Jes senses that she rarely comes into the inner space.

"You have some visitors," Aleia says to Essa. "They say they're your family?"

Essa looks puzzled by this. "Did they give you names?"

"Enovo and Eronda."

Essa pales at this information, her knees weaken, and she catches herself on one of the canes. One of the triplets reaches out, and helps steady her. Aleia says something else to her that Jes doesn't catch, but Essa nods. One of the triplets helps Essa over to the lounge area while Aleia steps outside again. She returns with three Asuna in tow. Jes immediately recognizes them from the shuttle. The two older ones – presumably Enovo and Eronda – walk side by side, while Esmée walks behind them. They're all dressed in the Asuna long robes.

Esmée carries a smooth black box that looks like it's made out of some kind of stone.

"Greetings, niece," Enovo says. His voice is smooth and cold.

Essa bows. "Uncle."

"My niece," Eronda says and steps forward, giving Essa a kiss on each cheek. There doesn't seem to be much genuine affection there. "Might we go somewhere more private?"

Essa shakes her head. "These people are my family. You can speak in front of them. And if you're here it can only mean one thing."

Eronda stiffens visibly, looks around at the crew. Nobody is making any pretense of working or rehearsing, but the costume shop keeps buzzing in their enclosed loft. Jes wonders what Eronda makes of the motley group gathered here. Quint looms large beside her wearing carpenter pants and a form-fitting tank. The triplets are in leotards and tights, their bright hair tied up in buns. Some of the clowns, a mix of human and Bezan, are paused in the middle of a juggling routine, holding clubs in their hands, some of them shirtless.

Jes can tell Enovo and Eronda are used to being around much fancier folk than this – their manner, their robes, say so. Not to mention, he susses how uncomfortable they are, but maybe that has something to do with the purpose of their visit.

"My sister and your mother, Eminy, has passed through the crystalline portal and into the celestial vault. She waits to take her place in the firmament."

The triplet with Essa gasps and brings a hand to her mouth while a couple of the clowns wearing hats remove them and hold them over their hearts, bowing their heads. Essa bursts into tears at these words, but it is clear she knew what the news was before it was spoken aloud. Jes remembers what Esmée had told him on the shuttle – that they had to deliver some bad news, and it had to be done in person, that was their custom. Esmée steps forward now, still holding the black box. "Cousin," she says.

"Esmée," Essa replies and embraces her awkwardly, the box being in the way.

"I present your mother's zaiharza." She holds the box out for her cousin.

Essa takes it and opens it gingerly. Quint, beside her, looks down at the contents and rubs Essa's back.

"It would have been preferable to bring this to your home," Eronda says. "But we don't know where you live. We only knew that you... perform. Here."

"This is fine," Essa says.

"As you are barred from coming to Opale, the zaiharza will be with you to sit zaijira. If you wish it. I hope that you do."

Essa takes a long look at whatever is in the box, then closes it. "Thank you," she says. "You should come to my home for supper. Later. All of you. Aleia can give you the address. I need... I need to keep working right now."

A look of annoyance swipes across Eronda's face, but she settles it back into her prim and proper mask quickly. "Of course."

Enovo's expression hasn't changed at all. Jes doesn't think he's moved since greeting Essa. Esmée has stepped back behind her parents and mostly stares at the floor, though she sneaks a look up at her cousin. Jes wants to catch her attention but has the wherewithal to know this situation is not one where he can just rush up to her and say hi.

"If you come with me..." Aleia says, indicating they should follow her.

"I'll see you later," Essa says.

The family all bows to her, and as they turn to follow Aleia out, Esmée catches Jes's gaze. She smiles faintly, quickly, then follows her parents out of the room.

When they're gone, the other two triplets rush over to Essa and all of them surround her as her shoulders shake with crying. Quint steps away from them and calls out "OK, everybody! Back to work! We still gotta put on a show!"

The clowns go back to their group juggling routine while the triplets return to the canes. Essa and Quint speak, and she hands him the box, which he leaves to take somewhere.

"You gonna get back to cutting or what?" one of the human crew says as he grabs the pieces Jes has already prepped.

"Yeah," Jes replies. "Yeah, I'm on it."

Later, once they're back at Essa's place, it's a flurry of rearranging and putting things away while bringing other things out from where they were stashed in the closet. Quint fluffs the pillows on the sofa, arranges them so that they alternate colors. Several art pieces are taken off shelves and put into cabinets: a carving of a human deity that possesses many arms and appears to be dancing, the Bezan sculptures that look like genitalia. In place of these, Essa lays out a purple cloth. On top of the cloth she sets candleholders made of panels of colored glass – these are placed but not lit. Finally, she opens the black box her cousin had handed her.

She pulls out a stand made of some kind of shiny silver metal, and on the stand she places a deep green gemstone, almost-teardrop shaped. Essa places it onto the stand with the narrow end down. It pokes through an opening at the base, a stem framed by the struts. The bulbous end is faceted and sits on top. The pinlight that had illuminated the dancing deity sculpture now glints off the stone. She lights the candles and whispers something in Mudra-nul. Jes is fascinated by the gem. He doesn't want to interrupt, though he is bursting to ask about it.

"I'll get dinner started," Quint says. "Jalaya stew?"

"That would be perfect," Essa says quietly. She flashes a sad smile at Quint who leans in and plants a quick kiss on her cheek before heading to the kitchen. She turns back to the stone.

"What is that?" Jes asks as he steps beside Essa.

"It's my mother."

"What?" Jes isn't sure if she means it's a representation or symbol or something else entirely.

"It's my mother's remains. I guess that's a more accurate way to say it. The Mudra-nul word is *zaiharza*. It means 'soulstone', roughly. When Asuna die, our bodies are placed inside a crystal case for last rites at a temple. Every temple has a giant lens on the southern wall, which is kept covered by gold foil most of the time. When a funeral is held, the lens is uncovered and when the sun is focused through it, it hits the crystal case and the body within. The body burns and the zaiharza is all that's left. It's cut and polished until it looks like this." She gestures at the stone. "It's kept in the family home for nine days, then at their temple for nine days. This period is called the *zaijira*. The soul's journey. It's a time for family to sit and grieve their departed. Normally this would be placed in my mother's home, or my aunt's, then at their temple. But because hybrids aren't allowed on Opale, my aunt and her family brought my mother's zaiharza here, so that I can sit zaijira. After zaijira, the stone is brought to the family vault, where all the zaiharza of our family are kept. The vaults are called the *zaimira*, or soul's home. I imagine they're quite beautiful."

"The Asuna are really serious about their ways, huh?"

"I wouldn't have been a performer if I was raised on Opale..." She runs her fingers lightly across her halo. "Topaz isn't the color for that. But my parents raised me *Asunasol*. That means, roughly, 'person who abandons tradition'. It's what they call any Asuna that chooses not to abide by their caste. Such individuals are banned off-world just like hybrids, of course. But they're not only banned from Opale – they're exiled from the entirety of the Crystal Imperium."

Her parents must have really loved each other, to live with all that. "So, does that make your father Asunasol? Will he sit zaijira too?"

"My father passed a few years ago," Essa explains and his

heart sinks with all the loss. Her loss, his loss – it's hard to differentiate whose feelings he feels. It happens sometimes when feelings are deep and intense and of a similar emotional tenor. His empathic sense picked up on a sort of haunted vibe from her when they first met, but sadness and grief is right at the surface of her being now.

"He lived and died on Indra. Not long after that I came here to pursue performing and my mother decided to go back to Opale, to her family. Indra is welcoming, but she still would have been an alien there, with no family."

"I'm so sorry," Jes says and winces at the inadequacy of his response. He wants to reach out and put a hand on her shoulder in comfort, in support, but he isn't sure they're at that point in their relationship yet. As if sensing this, she reaches for his hand, grabs it, gives it a squeeze. In the kitchen, Quint whistles as he chops something.

"You should join us for supper," Essa says.

"Are you sure? I don't want to impose."

"It's no imposition if you're invited. Besides, a buffer would be useful. My aunt can be a bit much."

And so, after a quick shower and putting on the new-to-him clothes he grabbed from the "Free Box" earlier, Jes sets the table for six, laying out mismatched silverware and dishes. Quint fusses that the place-settings aren't fancy enough for their guests, to which Essa responds, "It's who we are. Fuck 'em if they don't like it."

When the door chimes, Jes answers it. "Hello," he says to the surprise of Essa's aunt and uncle. "Welcome. Please come in." Growing up, he picked up on the way his father greeted guests of import and does his best to mimic that formal-yet-friendly tone.

Eronda and Enovo walk in stiffly, followed by Esmée who flashes a smile. "It's nice to see you again."

"Orrrrkut." Jes tries out the Mudra-nul word she taught him.

Sharp spikes of surprise come from her parents, but Esmée is amused. "Nice try," she says with a laugh. "You have to roll your tongue more." She demonstrates.

Eronda and Enovo are so taken aback by this exchange they don't acknowledge Essa and Quint at first, and awkward greetings follow when they do.

"Thank you for having us in your home," Enovo says.

Jes detects an undercurrent of guilt and figures it's because they would never reciprocate the gesture. Partially due to the prohibition on hybrids and interspecies coupling, but he wonders if Essa would be welcome in their home even if the law permitted it. He can't help but notice the difference in the colors of their halos. He doesn't know the ins-and-outs of what every color means, but he knows enough to understand that Essa is not the same caste as her relatives.

"I see you have set up the altar," Eronda comments, eyeing the zaiharza in its display.

"Yes," Essa replies. "I was hoping we could sit zaijira for a bit before we eat."

"That would be acceptable," Eronda says.

"Can you help move some chairs?" Essa asks Jes, and gestures to the area in front of the altar. He catches her meaning and grabs chairs from the dining table, and sets four of them up. The Asuna family each take a seat, facing the stone at the center. Essa lights the candles, a stick of incense, then sits down herself. They hold their hands up, palms facing out toward the stone, and begin chanting in Mudra-nul.

Feeling like an interloper by watching them, Jes steps into the kitchen.

"Are they praying?" Quint holds the lid of the stewpot as he inhales the fragrant steam rising from it. He gives the whole thing a stir.

"Yes. Is it a prayer for the dead or something?"

"Something like that. Essa explained it earlier. The chant guides the spirit of the deceased home or something. It's all mysterious to me. Hydraxians don't go much for ceremony and..." he gestures at what's happening in the next room, "stuff like that."

"How do you honor your dead?"

"We burn 'em. Want a beer?"

Jes is amused, charmed even, by Quint's brusqueness and can't help but smile as he sits down. "How did you and Essa become a thing?" he asks as he accepts the bottle from Quint, who joins him at the table.

"We met at work. I remember when she came in for her audition. I'm not involved with casting, that's Aleia's deal, but I see a lot of the auditions just because they happen where we work, you know? So, she was just another acro-contortion-whatever. It's all exotic and ooh and ahh for our audiences, but when you work it and see this stuff all the time, it just becomes part of your world, you know?"

It's another thing Jes doesn't know and he can't imagine getting to the point where the amazingness he's witnessed so far at the circus could become ordinary. Still, he nods in reply.

Quint continues, "Anyway she was there, waiting her turn with the others, one of the hopefuls. But when she got up on the lyra–"

"The what?"

"The lyra. It's the hanging hoop thing. Mental note to me – we're going to have to give you a crash course in circus equipment. Anyway, when she got on that thing, it was magic. Everybody stopped to watch her, and that never happens at auditions. It wasn't just the shimmer – which, wow – but the way she moved. Like she was doing a dance with it and not just a bunch of tricks. There's something really special in the way she moves. And when she's on – it's so weird how she can turn it on and off like that – but when she's on in her showgirl thing, you can't take your eyes off her. She just radiates specialness. I was awestruck. After her first show with us, I asked her out and she said yes. Best decision I ever made. I'm thinking of asking her to get a place together soon."

"Oh, that's awesome." Jes raises his beer in a cheers gesture and they clink bottles.

Quint nods in reflection. "It's time. I'm always here anyway because we have privacy. I live with a bunch of clowns. Literally."

Jes laughs at this.

"It doesn't sound like you've had time for love in your life, from what you've told us?"

Jes fidgets with the label on the beer bottle, picking at a corner. "No. I'm not sure that I ever will. It's so far from my mind right now."

"How old are you?"

"Twenty. In Rijal years."

"You're young. You've got so much time ahead." Quint says this with the certainty of someone who takes romance as a matter of course. "You are kind of weird looking though." He smirks, then swigs his beer.

"I prefer 'exotic', thank you," Jes jokes back. "But seriously, I'm ace. That kind of puts a damper on things a lot of the time."

Quint raises his eyebrows mid-sip. "Oh. I'm sorry. Shit I didn't mean–" He sets his beer down, fumbles for words. "I mean, I didn't mean 'sorry you're ace'. I meant sorry I didn't realize. I wouldn't have pushed all this romance stuff on you otherwise."

Jes is touched by the big guy's sensitivity. "I understand. It's OK. And I'm not closed to the idea of a romantic relationship. With any gender really. I'm just not wired for sex. So, you could say, I'm asexual panromantic." Jes smiles at the term. "I thought for a long time I was a late bloomer or whatever, that it would just switch on one day like it seems to for everyone. But it didn't. It hasn't. When I suss people's feelings, it's usually familiar things. Emotions that I've felt myself at some point; angry, happy, sad, alienated, lonely. But with sexual attraction – when I suss that, it's really the only time I sense something I haven't organically felt myself. The first few times it happened, I didn't know what it was besides super uncomfortable. But I figured it out eventually. It's weird."

Quint is about to say something when Essa pokes her head in. "We're done," she says.

"Well supper's on!" Quint exclaims.

After moving the chairs back to the table, the gathered group takes their seats as Quint brings out bowls of fragrant stew. He's also prepared a salad of peppery greens and slices of some kind of pulpy fruit in a light green dressing.

Jes finds himself sitting next to Esmée who is much more at ease than her parents. They seem uncomfortable in such a "rustic" setting. It's apparent they're used to finer dining and fancier environs.

"Thank you for having us," Eronda says after the wine is poured. "I would have thought you'd have a show. Isn't nighttime the time for you... folk?"

"They're subbing my act for the next couple of nights," Essa replies. "Given the circumstances."

"Well, that's nice."

Though her tone is polite, Jes susses a rebuke beneath Eronda's words. Jes doesn't even need his empathic sense to know Eronda doesn't really care.

"We look out for each other," Essa adds. There's a barb beneath this simple statement as well.

"It's nice to see you again," Esmée says as she turns to him. "So, your uncle owns the Luna Lux?"

"What? No... I..." Jes fumbles, forgetting for a moment the story he told her on board the shuttle.

She smiles, enjoying watching him squirm.

"OK, you got me," he says. "Would you believe that I had no plan for after I got here, and that I was led to the circus by my grandmother's dowsing crystal, and that I asked for a job and they gave me one because a Mantodean told them to?"

She considers this with a bite of salad. "Yes," she says after she swallows. "Yes, I would. That story's too outlandish to be a lie. So why did you leave Rijal?"

"Oh, you know... youthful folly. The call of adventure. I told you on the shuttle I was coming to seek my fortune. That part's true."

"Not the whole truth though."

Jes has a fruit slice on his fork, looks down at the bits of pulp all shiny like tiny jewels of scarlet red and purple. He turns to her, meets her eyes. "That's a story for another time."

"OK," Esmée replies. "I'll hold you to that."

The older adults chat among themselves, scarcely paying attention to the conversation between the younger ones. "What are your plans for the rest of your stay here?" Essa asks her aunt and uncle. "I don't imagine Port Ruby is really your kind of place."

"No," Enovo sniffs. "Gambling, debauched parties, sexual depravity and pedestrian entertainments are not for us." Then, realizing who he's talking to, he quickly adds, "Not that your performance is pedestrian..."

Essa takes a prolonged sip of her wine. "No offense taken. You haven't seen the show so you wouldn't know." Jes susses that she was indeed offended.

"You should come to a show!" Quint interjects. "When Essa's back on stage, of course. It's something to behold." He winks at her at the other end of the table; she returns a smile.

"Oh, that would be wonderful!" Esmée exclaims. "I would love to see you in your element, cousin."

Essa reaches out her hand and grabs Esmée's with a little squeeze. "We can arrange tickets for you easily. Jes, will you speak with Aleia about it tomorrow?"

Jes nods his assent in mid-chew.

"So you're my niece's secretary, then?" Eronda asks.

Jes meets her gaze and finds himself intimidated. "Well," he swallows, "we're still figuring things out–"

"He earns his keep." Essa and her aunt meet eyes over the table.

"You know, if Port Ruby isn't to your liking," Quint says casually as he takes a bite of stew, "you could visit the Mytiri Forest on the other side of the moon. Essa and I love it there."

Essa takes up the suggestion right away. "Yes, that's a marvelous idea. There's a spa resort that will probably be better suited for your tastes. The falls are beautiful, and the waters have healing properties. Allegedly."

"That does sound like a pleasant way to wile away some time during your zaijira with your mother," Enovo says. "I could use a massage."

"Speaking of zaijira, do you have a temple here?" Eronda looks pointedly at Essa as she asks this. "Where will you conduct the community portion?"

"I've given that some thought." Essa takes a deep breath, gearing herself up. "I think the zaiharza should be on stage with me nightly."

Eronda blanches at this and sets down her fork. "Excuse me?"

"The circus is my temple. It is my community. My performance is my way of… praying."

"I don't think such a debased environment–"

"You haven't seen the show." Jes speaks up with a sharper edge than he intends. "It's not 'debased'. It's magical. It's inspiring. Truly." He meets Essa's gaze, and her eyes are grateful, but she gestures with her hand: *settle down.*

"It feels profane."

"Eronda," Enovo's tone is matter-of-fact, not quite stern. "It isn't our decision. The right path is within the heart of the ones who sit zaijira. We will have our own back on Opale. The journey here is for Essa."

Eronda looks down at her plate, then takes a slow sip of wine.

"Come to the show," Essa reiterates. "You'll see."

Her aunt nods in agreement, but remains unconvinced.

THE INSTITUTE

Today they have him strapped face down. His arms are cinched to his sides and his face is in a cradle so that he stares at the floor. He gets an occasional glimpse of the tops of shoes. They've kept the collar on so he can't access his abilities, but they're keeping him awake for this procedure. Whatever it is. He'll know soon enough. Matheson always likes to spell it out right before he starts, like Jes is a colleague he needs signoff from. As if consent were on the table, not his naked body.

"We'll be giving you a local anesthetic right back here," Matheson says as he taps the base of Jes's skull, where it meets the spine. Even though Jes can't see the scientist's face from his current vantage point, he can picture him. The pale flaxen hair and the round lenses of the scope he wears, reflecting his face with colored dots of tiny data points scrolling across it.

"We need a tissue sample, you see, from the mager's gland." He'd wondered if this was what they were going to do today. He'd heard about this procedure from a boy in the therapy group. Before that boy went away and never came back.

Jes is positive that if he could suss Matheson right now, he'd be delighting in the feel of the scalpel in his hand.

"You mean *my* mager's gland."

Matheson tsks. "I wish you could learn to be a bit more generous, more cooperative. We are all a team here, after the

60

same thing. You are sacrificing for a greater understanding of paratalents and biology and, not to sound too grandiose, the fabric of the universe."

Jes feels the slice through his skin. The anesthetic works and there's no pain, but the pressure of the cut still registers. Then the buzz of the laser comes and a sickening smell of burning bone as they cut into his head. Needles prick in his brain as he squirms uselessly against his bonds. It doesn't hurt, exactly, but he can tell something's happening there in the back of his head, and the sounds and smells aren't exactly comforting. He whites out – he isn't sure if he loses consciousness or not – and listens to the muffled voices of the researchers, the sounds of the monitors, the tools they use.

Matheson patches him up afterwards with a suture-wand and some Bezan gel that helps close up wounds. It smells herbal, like many Bezan medicines do. It's a soothing smell that he might have enjoyed in other circumstances, but he wonders if he will forever associate it with his head being entered against his will, with parts of his brain being cut out.

His legs are a little floppy after the procedure, so they pour him into a convalescent chair, one of those that hovers. "You'll experience some dizziness for the next several hours," Matheson says in his "soothing" tone. "We'll give you a sedative to help you sleep; the dizziness should pass by morning." He thinks he's being kind. Jes is collared – not able to suss – but he can still tell. He has to wonder if the man is delusional or just has a fucked-up idea of what kindness is.

Jes glides down the hall in his chair. He likes the floaty feeling of being in the chair, knows he could glide by himself if they'd let him. He's pushed along by an orderly and accompanied by a wellness aide. They're both Rijala, as most of the staff are, and they are perfunctory in their dealings with him, which he prefers. The humans trying to be nice just make things worse.

When they pass the room next to his, he sees that it's open. There's a new kid being installed – a human and Bezan hybrid by the looks of him. He's collared and his face is puffy from crying. Poor kid. He'll get used to it all soon.

Jes waves as they go by. The hopeful way the kid's face lights brings on a torrent of guilt. He didn't want to give a false hope of friendship. That's not a thing here.

Back in his room, the orderly dumps him onto his cot. He gets under the covers and lays still as the wellness aide administers the sedative. They leave, locking him in with a beep. He thinks he hears knocking from the other side of the wall, but he can't be sure. He doesn't tap back, he can't with drowsiness overtaking him. His hands are heavy and everything, including the wall, seems so far away. He can tell he'll be out for a while. He hopes they let him wake up on his own.

CHAPTER FIVE

"So my plan is: Jes, you do your thing," Quint wiggles his fingers in the air, "and me and Bo will secure the filters. We'll use the scissor lift so nobody has to climb up there." It's early morning, before anyone else has arrived at the circus. Bo wouldn't normally take part in the task before them, but they need someone who already knows what Jes can do.

"I'm so excited for these air filters," Quint says. "Especially with all the reef smoking that goes on back here. The smoke won't linger any more. You'll see. Clear air makes for clear bodies and minds!" Jes finds it cute, how hyped Quint is by such pedestrian equipment.

The operation is straightforward: Jes will generate his gravity fields and float the new gear up one at a time. Quint and Bo, on the platform of a scissor lift, will then bolt them to their places on the trusses – including the replacement for the one that broke on Jes's first night here. Quint had explained to Jes on their way over that this task would normally take more gear and personnel to accomplish, as one person would be required to hold the filters in place while the other secured it. But with Jes floating more than one unit up at once, the task will take a fraction of the time.

True to Quint's prediction, it goes by in a flash.

"Well, that was easy," Bo says. "Thanks." He claps Jes on the back.

"Any time." Jes is surprised at how satisfying it is to use his ability this way, for such a simple and unglamorous task.

"So now that that's done, can I take a nap?" Bo asks Quint. "This is an unnatural hour to be up."

Quint laughs. "Fine."

With that Bo makes his way to the lounge and curls up on the couch. He immediately begins lightly snoring, just as Aleia walks in.

"I thought I heard people here," she says. "Bit of an early start?"

"Just had something to get out of the way before everyone's here," Quint explains.

"Well, I hope you're finished with that. I need to borrow him for a bit today." She indicates Jes with a glance.

Quint shrugs. "Fine by me."

"Follow me," Aleia instructs brusquely. Jes complies.

They exit inner space and walk the short length of corridor to her office. Jes susses her agitation, her nervousness and... is it fear? She closes the door behind them once they're inside.

Without preamble she says, "I need you to accompany me to a business meeting this afternoon."

Jes is taken aback by this – it seems beyond the scope of his duties. "I'm happy to do that–"

"I need your empathic sense," she says, anticipating his question. "You won't need to talk. Just stand to the side and listen. I'll introduce you as my secretary. Do you have any better clothes? More professional?" She paces her office, wringing her hands.

"Not really."

"We'll need to get you something a little dressier. I'll have Moxo help you." She notices his confusion. "Our juggler," she explains. "He's the best dressed person here. He'll be able to get you sorted."

"I don't know if I can afford anything nice," Jes says,

thinking about what little coin he has left. He hasn't received his first wages yet.

Aleia brushes this off. "Don't worry about that."

"Who are we meeting?" Jes can tell it's somebody important, or at least *about* something important, given the waves of anxiety coming off of her.

"Niko Dax," she replies. "He owns the Luna Lux and half the major properties in Port Ruby. Nothing happens in this town without his say so."

"I see."

"I just need you to… read him. Or whatever you call your Indran talents."

"Ah, it's 'suss'. And, OK. I can do that. But I'm not telepathic, remember."

"I understand. You can't read his thoughts. But whatever insight you can provide will help. I just need an edge."

"You're afraid of him."

Aleia stops pacing at these words, and stares at Jes, clearly startled. She seems to have forgotten he can sense her feelings too. "Can you ever turn it off?"

He shakes his head. "I wish I could sometimes."

She looks at him some more, and her gaze softens. "He's the boss of this town," she says after a moment. "Of course I'm afraid of him."

Jes arrives at Moxo Thron's home in the forested hills at the edge of the city, a curved white bean with a deck jutting off the cliff behind it. He is perfectly on time thanks to the roto Aleia arranged. It deposits him at the door, then rests itself on a park-pad. The door opens before he even has a chance to knock, and in the curved doorway stands his host. It's strange seeing him in casual clothes, but even in silk lounge pants, slippers and a loose tunic, he has an elegant air about him. Rather than the top-knot he sports in performance, his long hair is arranged in a loose bun.

"So you're the ragamuffin I'm making presentable?"

"Hi – I'm Jes – thanks for having me." Jes wipes his feet on the doormat before coming in, something he gets the impression Moxo will appreciate.

Inside, it's cool and the air is sweet and floral. There's a side-table on top of which sits a large crystal formation of vibrant lime-green points. A flowering vine is trained up one wall and Jes guesses that's the source of the fragrance.

"It's a hybridized Moonsbreath," Moxo explains when he notices what Jes is looking at. "You know what it is?"

Jes nods. "It's a tree native to Indra. There's a whole festival revolved around it. The flowers have a psychotropic effect."

"OK, you're not completely clueless then." Mild surprise. "This vine was engineered to produce flowers that bear the scent without the psychotropic effects. It's still just intoxicating, though, isn't it? Come this way."

Moxo leads him through the house, to a room that's empty but for a trunk full of juggling equipment and a small table and chair. One wall is a mirror, and a large oval window overlooks the valley; Port Ruby sprawls in the distance. Jes can just make out the silhouette of the Luna Lux.

"Sit," Moxo commands, gesturing at the chair in the middle of the room with his two right hands while his left ones unfold a towel. He drapes this across Jes's front and over his shoulders when he takes his seat. On the table rests scissors, a set of combs and a spray bottle. Moxo picks up the bottle and begins spritzing Jes's hair. "First step is to tame... this. Luckily your hair is more like Rijalen hair."

"Why is that lucky?"

"It's more manageable, easier to keep clean. The keratins form a different sort of bond. Biology." He sets the spray bottle down and runs the fingers of all four hands through Jes's hair and across his scalp. "What's this? A scar?"

Moxo's fingertips slide over the rough tissue. At his touch, the lab flashes in Jes's mind like a needle. "I fell and hit my head this one time. Did you used to be a stylist or something?"

"In a manner of speaking. When I was in circus academy I became the go-to person for haircuts in the dorm after doing a half-way decent job on another Hydraxian. It was a base for an acro-duo. Anyway, after that everyone asked me to do their hair, since I was decent at it and didn't charge. That time of my life was an education not only in circus arts, but all different species of hair. All the members of the 9-Star species train at Branch of the Tree Circus Academy. Well, everyone but the Mantodeans." Moxo picks up a comb and scissors. "I know what to do here. Trust?"

He's never been one to care much about fashion or style, and he figures with Moxo's clearly well-developed aesthetics, he'll end up with something decent. "Go."

Moxo proceeds combing parts in his hair with two hands, while snipping the scissors with a third, and his fourth tucked into his back pocket. "What brings you to our fair land?" Just a hint of a smirk.

Flurries of white hair fall before his eyes. "Not much of a story to tell really. Mongrels like me aren't that well regarded on Rijal."

"I am aware."

Waves of hair get snipped and tossed over. The air around his head starts to feel different. "Well, opportunities would have been limited for me there. What better place for a mutt with a questionable skillset to try his fortune than the anything-goes pleasure moon?" He susses that Moxo knows there's more to be said, and he also susses that he understands the value of discretion.

"I know how colonialist mindsets can be. Tilt your head forward, please."

Jes does as he's told and feels the hair getting shorter at the back of his head in diagonals. His time at the Institute falls away with every snip.

"As much as Hydraxian society has evolved to the point where we can be earnest participants in the 9-Star Congress, lingering prejudices remain. Nothing to the point of persecution of course, but there's a certain pity towards those judged to be less-than: queer folks such as myself. That's why I also came to seek my fortune on the anything-goes pleasure moon. Chin up."

It takes a moment to understand he means mentally and physically. Jes raises his head and immediately a flurry of comb maneuvers and the nearly martial rhythm of the scissors fly all around his head.

"And besides, performance opportunities are rare on Seraph. Nevermind for a runt who dances with balls." A laugh. Genuine humor, but sad. "That's starting to change, though. From what I've heard."

"Your juggling is the most elegant and artful I've ever seen." He looks through his asymmetrical bangs that stretch across his gaze like a canopy.

Moxo's hands pause and he meets Jes's gaze. Then more spritzes go in his hair, and the longer edges of his bangs flip. Combs. "You either have impeccable taste or really know how to kiss ass. Go look at yourself."

Jes susses an appreciation under these words, accompanied by suspicion. He rises from his seat and walks over to the mirror wall. In the reflection, Moxo follows and Jes notes that despite being taller and broader than him, the juggler is still quite lanky in proportion. They reach the mirror and stand side by side as Jes inspects his new hair.

"This is a more professional look. I suggest you wear it this way for the meeting you're attending with Aleia. You can also muss it up and bring your bangs down like so." He reaches over and ruffles the hair, knocking down the swept-up locks so they form bangs. What had all been overgrown shag is tapered now.

Jes sees part overgrown lab-rat, part urban sophisticate reflected in the wall. He looks at his new hair from different angles. Yeah, OK. He can be this person. "I like it."

"I'm so glad. Now for the next part of the mission. Come along." Moxo turns and heads out. Jes follows him through to a great room consisting of a comfortable looking living area with a few large pouf chairs and one high-backed rigid chair that looks like a throne. Jes imagines Moxo sitting in that one, holding forth for his guests. There's a sideboard behind the sofa, on top of which is a photo of Moxo, his arms around a smiling, mostly naked human man. They're both mostly naked.

They continue on: the kitchen is spare and clean, with fixtures of reddish wood and silver. The countertop is of pink stone, on top of which rests a vase full of flowers. On the other side of the great room, Moxo opens a door, flicks on a light, and Jes steps through into a space stuffed with gear: bolts of silks, hoops, juggling equipment and racks of costumes. "This was supposed to be temporary storage," Moxo explains. He beelines for a rack towards the back of the room. "We've updated the looks in the show a few times and the costumes that are still in decent condition I keep here since we don't really have storage at the venue."

"I'm supposed to attend this meeting in costume?" Jes imagines himself in a clown outfit, pretending to be Aleia's secretary. Amusing, and fitting in a way, but he suspects it's not what she had in mind.

"Everything we wear is a costume, isn't it?" The scratchy sound of hangers sliding across the rack fills the space. "We used Rijalen business dress this one time–"

"Why is all this stuff at your house?" Jes stands at the room's center, the only clear space, looking around at bits of past shows, forlorn at the edges of this room, hopeful they may get a chance to shine again.

Moxo shrugs. "I had the space. And I'm fond of the circus. It has been my artistic home and community for some time now. I had the means to help out, so I did. Though I must say Aleia could show a bit more gratitude." He sniffs. "But I'm happy to be a team player and all. Ah, here we are." He pulls out a suit that's very familiar to Jes – a conventional Rijalen style that his parents used to make him wear when he accompanied them to official functions. But this one is made out of a different fabric, soft with a subtle sheen. "Rijalen cut, Asuna silk. A combination that works very well, I think. Try it on. There's a mirror in the corner. I'll give you some privacy."

Jes slips out of his clothes and into the suit. It's a silver-gray color, shot through with purple threads. The tunic has a square, violet collar that gives a subtle hint of color to his silver eyes. The pants are a bit long, so he cuffs them and it looks OK. The silk feels luxurious against his skin; the weight and drape of it is comfortable, almost like pajamas. Much more comfortable than the stiff, scratchy things he used to have to wear for his parents. Jes pushes his bangs back with a swoop of his hand. He doesn't look like a vagabond anymore, that's for sure.

A knock on the door. "Come in."

Moxo pokes his head through the cracked door and appraises his make-over project. "I think that'll do," he says. Jes's mismatched socks catch his eye. "I'm not sure what to do about shoes though. Do you have shoes?"

"Those are my only shoes," he says, pointing to his kicked-off black ankle boots.

"Hmm. You'll look scruffy making an effort. That will just have to do. I think my work is done." He ducks his head out but leaves the door open.

Jes decides to keep the suit on and slips back into his shoes. It's not perfect but it's not like he can afford dress shoes. He leaves the room, turning off the light and shutting the door behind him.

"It's my training time so I'm afraid I'll have to send you along now," Moxo says as he holds out a large satchel. "For your clothes."

Jes slips his clothes into the bag and slings it over his shoulder. "Thank you."

"Aleia owes me another one," he says. He walks Jes to the door. "It's been a pleasure. See you around the circus."

With that, Jes is out the door. He walks over to where the roto has parked, gravel crunching under his feet. As soon as he slides into the spherical interior of his transport, it whirs away, having been programmed for a round trip. Looking out at the woods he rolls through, Jes marvels how other-worldly this feels, just a few minutes' drive outside of Port Ruby.

When the roto reaches the center of town and has stopped at an intersection by the central square, Jes decides to get out and walk the rest of the way. He finds the roto's control panel, sets it back to on-call, and climbs out. It's a bit warm so he unbuttons the tunic of the suit. He brims with excitement at just this short walk – he hasn't seen much of Port Ruby since arriving.

The plaza is dominated by a large screen that bears the face of the human-Bezan-Rijala popstar Jasmine Jonah, her hair blowing artfully across her face, purple eyes gazing across the square, taking possession of all they see. Her Intergalactic tour will be here on Persephone-9 in a few weeks; he's overheard several among the cast express their excitement to see her live.

As he strolls, he can't help but gape at the garish signs advertising reef and opium lounges, whorehouses, casinos and nightclubs. He wants to take it all in, but he doesn't really have a lot of time to dawdle. He tries not to gawk too hard so that he doesn't come across as a hick from the sticks, though Rijal is hardly the sticks. Still, the flagrant promotion of a multitude of vices is new to him, and he wonders about the folks that work in these establishments. Where do they come from? Is hedonism the guiding light of their lives or do they want something different? The barely dressed bodies of pretty girls and pretty boys light up the holoboards, even in the morning light. They are mostly human and Bezan, though a Hydraxian female is prominently presented. All these escorts look very happy. But these pictures are advertisements. Of course they would look happy.

"Mongrel!" somebody calls out.

He knows this person is yelling at him, but he tries to ignore them. He walks by several street performers setting up their pitches, musicians turning on speakers and tuning their instruments, circus acts laying out their props.

He keeps walking but the drunk has stumbled beside him. "You are a little mongrel boy," he says, eyeing Jes salaciously. The drunk is Bezan, and his purple skin looks pale and wan. His eyes are a cloudy yellow and his hair sticks up in thinning red tufts above his round face. He has a bit of a belly and his shirt strains tight against it.

Lust oozes from the Bezan, and Jes struggles to hold back his revulsion, closing off his aura the way his grandmother taught him. "I like mongrel ass. How much for your mongrel ass?"

Taking a breath to steel himself, Jes steps up to him, placing his hands on the drunk's chest. "More than you can afford," he says, patting. He slips his hand quickly to the inside pocket of the man's loose jacket and in a second he has the man's coin-purse between his fingers. He withdraws, palming it, then places it in his own pocket.

"You're a snooty one!" the drunk exclaims before he wanders off, muttering to himself.

Once he's gone, Jes takes three deep breaths, exhaling the grimy echo of the drunk's lust, and releasing the ghost sensation of touching him. So gross. Then he pulls out the coin-purse and inspects its contents. He chuckles. This has been a productive morning.

NOOAFAR PREFECTURE

Jes stands watch at the base of the Nara bridge on the first warm day of spring. Ramis and some of the other boys his mother refers to as his "so-called friends" are throwing up a new mural and he's tagged along just to get out of the house. He's not skilled with this stuff but likes to watch the images arise from blankness, the seemingly random colors and shapes that somehow coalesce into something: a nude woman wearing a crown, a Mantodean face, sometimes their street-names in the stylized script they wrote in that he can't read at all.

Today they're doing a portrait of a new singer who's just released her first single, a Bezan-Rijala-human hybrid named Jasmine Jonah. He likes the song OK, but the others make fun of it and predict she won't have much of a career. "Hybrid trash," one of them says, then throws Jes a dirty look. Not all of them like him so much.

"Cut it with that talk," Ramis barks. Ramis is the de facto leader of the crew, and thankfully he's taken a liking to Jes – mostly because of his thieving and pickpocket skills, but he takes it as a win. Ramis is friendly and amiable towards Jes, not just with words and behavior, but in his underlying feelings too.

Ramis clearly has a thing for this Jasmine Jonah girl because the mural of her is detailed, beautiful, loving even. And she's not wearing much. Jes susses Ramis's infatuation for her and wonders if he maybe has a thing for hybrids.

"This girl is gonna be big," Ramis says, stepping back to appraise his work.

Jes likes sussing him in these moments – the focus, the loving attention to detail, the honest self-assessment and confidence in his talents. He admires these qualities and wishes he possessed them himself. He wonders how they would all react if they knew he could suss.

"Patrol!" comes a sudden yell from Pipa, the other look-out, who has an unrequited crush on Ramis that everyone is fully aware of, including Ramis, but she doesn't think any of them know. "Run!" she cries out and the group scatters.

Jes and Pipa run off together, under the overpass. He wishes it were Ramis he was with instead, but she's better than one of the other boys who've made clear they don't care for hybrids. She pulls him up against a wall suddenly and says, "Just go with it." She kisses him, shoving her tongue in his mouth. He fights back a wave of disgust, but he goes with it because he understands what she's doing. Kissing is better than getting picked up by Patrol again for graffiti.

The patrol unit glides by slowly, stops.

"You kids should do that somewhere more private," an officer chastises, getting out of the unit.

Pipa turns to him. "We figured down here would be out of the way enough," she explains, all fake sweetness. "Our parents don't approve of us being together, you see."

The officer eyes them both. His gaze lingers on Jes, obviously noting his skin tone and the human face disguised by Rijalen hair and eyes. The officer shakes his head and Jes is prepared to defend any insult on his hybrid nature, even if it means getting into trouble. But the officer only says, "I remember young love. Anybody run by here smelling of paint? There's some renegade muralists at large."

"No," Pipa replies, shaking her head. "Nothing." She turns to Jes.

"We haven't seen anybody, officer," he says, as innocent as he can muster.

"Alright. Stay out of trouble, kids."

The officer climbs back into his patrol unit and continues his glide, searching for the unsanctioned artists. When he's gone, Jes pushes Pipa away.

"Don't ever kiss me again," he says.

"Sorry," she replies sullenly. "You queer?"

He doesn't answer. He knows what he is, but he doesn't want to say it out loud. Not to her. She'll tell them all and he doesn't want them to have another thing to hold against him.

"I don't care if you are."

"I just don't want to be kissed like that." He can tell she's insulted, but he doesn't care. She doesn't know he can suss; he'll just pretend to be another oblivious boy. He's fine with that. He wishes he could actually be more oblivious.

CHAPTER SIX

"Yes, this will do," Aleia says as she examines Jes's new style. He's in the new clothes and has swept his hair back the way Moxo showed him. "Shame about the shoes, but at least you look more presentable. Let's go."

She leaves her office at a brisk pace and he follows closely. They pass a couple of guys on the crew, and the triplets, all of whom open their eyes wide at his new look. He smiles and waves. He likes the way he looks all dressed up, but he's also a little embarrassed. It doesn't really feel like him. But, he reasons, who is that anyway? For so many years he's been controlled by everyone else. Shouldn't he take the chance to be someone new?

They take the path that leads from the front of the tent across the lawn and into the hotel. They walk past the long counter where guests check in, past a cocktail lounge and the High Stakes Room. He wonders just how high the stakes get in this place.

Aleia leads them past the banks of silver elevators to one with a shiny black door that's in an alcove by itself. She places her hand, open palmed, on the security panel set in the wall beside it, and the door slides open, revealing a back wall that gleams like a portal in whose mirrored surface they're greeted by alternate versions of themselves. The doors close and their ascent begins without Aleia pressing any buttons or speaking a command. This elevator must only make one stop.

"Now remember," she says, a slight quiver in her voice. "You are my secretary, and you say nothing. Stand where you're told to stand. Just pay attention to... how the feelings flow. I guess."

"I understand," Jes replies. He wants to give her hand a squeeze, or pat her on the shoulder, to offer some encouragement or reassurance. But it's not his place so he says nothing.

The ride up goes on for longer than it seems it should. Aleia appears as comfortable in silence as he is. When they finally stop, the doors open to a foyer where a young human woman sits behind a simple glass-topped desk. Her skintone is of a deep, ruddy hue that is more common to Indran humans, but he can tell she doesn't have the Indran gifts – she's not sussing him back.

"Mz Siqui." She rises from her seat, smooths her skirt as she walks them to the office door. She wears a sleek dress of soft blue material and a matching jacket – standard Rijalen business attire. "Please," she continues, opening the door and entering, then stepping aside to let them through. "Mz Siqui and associate," she announces.

"Thank you," a silky voice says from deeper into the office.

The receptionist steps out and closes the door behind her with a soft click. The room smells faintly like fresh carpet and chordash leaf. His father used to complain about the increasing frequency of chordash smoking in business settings. He wouldn't have approved of this environment.

"Come in, Aleia. No need to be shy."

They walk deeper into the office, toward a desk that sits in front of an arched window overlooking Port Ruby. This curved pane of glass is framed by other windows that are long and rectangular, both of which are open; curtains flutter in the soft breeze coming through them. The slate grey walls are lined with paintings;

pedestals are dotted about, upon which sit pottery pieces that must be very expensive. Closer to the desk, the walls are lined with sparsely populated shelves. Behind the desk is a Rijala, a bank of holographic displays glowing in the air in front of him.

The fact that he is Rijala is no surprise – it makes sense that the big boss would be, or maybe a Loran Human. Both groups have reputations for unscrupulous business practices, after all. To put it mildly. Jes is slightly ashamed at the way he's profiling; he's glad he said nothing aloud.

"Hello, Niko," Aleia says brightly, feigning cheerfulness. "This is my secretary, Jes."

Niko Dax takes Jes in with a glance. "Human and Rijala."

Jes nods. "Yes, sir."

Dax quietly chuckles as he pulls out a sleek silver case from a drawer. He takes out a rolling paper and pinches of shredded purple leaves from within. "Humans must be the most prolific cross-species breeders in the universe." Jes is put off by this comment, but also acknowledges the truth of it. He himself had just, moments ago, been profiling in much the same way. This similarity between him and the man behind the desk is discomforting and he shuffles his weight anxiously. He says nothing, and just watches as Dax methodically rolls himself a smoke. "Have a seat, Aleia."

She takes the one chair available. Jes stands behind her, slightly to the side. Dax puts the smoke to his lips and lights it, filling the air with sweetness. Jes susses him, and the overall impression is not so different from the Rijala that surrounded him back home. No, not home. Just back where he came from. There's a formality, an almost clinical detachment. Aleia, on the other hand, comes off so much like a human. If he were to suss her with his eyes closed, he might take her for human. It's no wonder she left the Rijalen Expanse. But why did Dax? Jes senses someone firmly in control of his emotions, highly intelligent, and somewhat cold.

"How can I be of service?" Aleia asks.

"Please, Aleia. We've known each other for a long time. No need for obsequiousness."

"Well, 'what do you want?' seemed a little too forthright."

Good. She's relaxing.

Niko takes another remarkably graceful drag of his cigarette. He is fine featured with high cheekbones and a sharp nose and a thin mouth. His eyes are deep blue, a vivid, dark shade that is unique to Rijala, though the silver hue of Jes's own eyes, or Aleia's, is more common. Dax's eyes look like sapphires set into his pale blue skin.

"The Cirque Kozmiqa has done quite well over the years," he says. "It's been a good investment. Mostly."

"Yes. We're all very proud of what we've created."

"It's really given the Luna Lux that extra little spark. Something more elevated than the strippers and cheesy bands out there." He waves a hand dismissively at the window behind him. "And all thanks to your vision. I commend you for that, Aleia."

Aleia smiles, gives a small nod. Jes senses her nervousness rise again – she's waiting for the other shoe to drop. He turns his sense toward Niko, but finds it hard to get a read on him.

"But you and your merry little band of misfits have been at it for a while, and revenues are starting to slip."

"We are playing to full houses–"

"But not sold out. Not anymore. No more waiting lists. And six shows a week instead of eight."

"We couldn't keep up that pace," Aleia protests, her nervous energy dissipating and giving way to indignation. "The performers need rest. It's very strenuous on them, what they do–"

"Then recruit some more. Bez is crawling with circus folk. Indra is full of musicians and performers. Besides, the show needs freshening up, Aleia. It's getting stale. Adding that Mantodean was a nice touch, I give you that. An intriguing side attraction. But I want more."

His voice is smooth, lulling even, but Jes senses the impatience beneath, the building threat.

"I have another associate who has quite a successful production on Bez. Some similar acts to what you present, but they're also doing *different* things. Sexy girls in big bowls of water. A whole group bungeeing from the top of the theater. That show tells a story. Where's your story, Aleia?"

"Well, it's–"

"That show has fire too. Literally people dancing with fire. I want fire, Aleia. Where's your fire?"

Aleia is bewildered. "I… We can do that. Had I but known you were unsatisfied–"

"Consider this your notice. My associate has made a proposal to bring his show to Port Ruby. I don't think this town needs two circuses. Especially since the one that's here isn't even selling out anymore."

Jes tenses. The man had already come to a decision before he called her here.

"I'll give you the next quarter, Aleia. Zhuzh it up. I want sold out houses again. I want demand so great you must turn people away at the door. That's what I need to see." He stubs his smoke out in a glass dish on his desk. "Got it?"

"Yes," Aleia says, forcing stillness to her voice. "I understand."

"And I'll need another ten percent of the proceeds. To make up for the lost revenue." It's obvious Niko doesn't need more money, and he smiles as he tightens the screws.

"That will make it hard on the staff," Aleia pleads. "And to make the changes you're asking for, we'll need some new acts–"

"Cut some of the old ones then. Do you really need all those clowns?"

"They're acrobats too."

"I don't care how you make it happen." He holds his hands up, casting an unquestionable apathetic air. "Just do it." For the first time, there's a discernible edge in his voice that makes Jes's stomach clench.

"Don't cut the Asuna half-breed though," Niko adds. "Keep that one around."

"I... I understand."

"Very good." He spins around in his chair, turning his back to them, a blatant dismissal. Then, as an afterthought, he adds, "Do give my regards to your sister." He doesn't turn around when he says this, just looks out the window, surveying his realm.

Aleia stands, meets Jes's eyes and begins heading for the door. They make a hasty exit and the receptionist smiles without saying anything. Once the doors close, Jes asks about Aleia's sister.

"They were lovers once, she and Dax. My sister had the audacity to break it off, a risky move, considering." She brushes it away, not wanting to discuss details. "What else did you pick up?"

"He's having fun with this challenge and he likes power tripping. That's not a surprise, I guess. He's pretty much made up his mind about the other circus, but there's a part of him that wants to be surprised. He wants to be impressed. But there was something else – he's not being as rational as he pretends. I sussed a kind of... vindictiveness. This quarter he's giving us is really just a courtesy."

She huffs at this. "We'll have to really razzle dazzle him then. With acts and with profit. So much so he can't deny us. I don't know how we'll manage the extra ten percent though. The margin is so tight as it is."

"That was just petty. He's toying with you for amusement."

Aleia laughs a humorless laugh. "You're right. It is petty. He didn't need to make this even harder. I noticed something though, just now."

"What's that."

"You said 'this quarter he's giving *us*'."

Jes senses Aleia is touched and he's not sure he can take it; his face flushes hot. "I guess I did."

She smiles again and says nothing more.

Aleia wastes no time sharing the news and calls a meeting of cast and crew. Everyone is there: the set builders, the riggers, the lighting guys, the costumers, all the performers, the house band, even the ushers, food runners and kitchen staff. They're all gathered in the performance space and occupy the seats where the audience usually sits; several performers sit on the stage. Jes spots Lucian, the cook whose friend he pretended to be to sneak into the show. He spots the pink-haired human girl who told him to talk to Quint that first night. Everyone is being jovial, but he can tell they're all nervous too. Evidently Aleia never calls everyone together like this. He's taken a seat next to Bo, who prods him. "You know what this is about, don't you? I like your haircut by the way."

"It's not my place to tell. And thank you." He's changed out of his suit and sits in his regular clothes and has ruffled up his hair again.

"We've been given an ultimatum," Aleia begins. "Our benefactor wants to see an uptick in earnings and audience and he's threatened to bring in another circus to replace us." At this, the gathered group erupts into protestations and grumblings. Aleia holds her hands up, calling for silence and attention. "He's suggested that I make staffing cuts–"

More grumbles and protestations, louder, angrier. A little fear.

"I fully intend *not* to do that," Aleia goes on. "If we can revamp the show enough to accomplish what Mr Dax wants, we can avoid that. Maybe. But we need to work together on this. I need a new concept, new routines, new music, new menu. He's given us a quarter, which is not a lot of time, but we can do it if we hustle. My door is open to anyone who's got suggestions. I want a plan of action within a week's time. We're all in this together. Let's save our show."

With that the group is dismissed, and the performers and kitchen staff dash off with more urgency than the others, eager to prepare for the evening's performance.

"Wow, this is intense," Bo says. "Did you know all that already?"

Jes nods. "Yeah. I was there."

"What's Niko Dax like?"

"Like a cat who enjoys playing with mice."

The curtain separating the inner space from the outer space is parted, and the dressing rooms are abuzz with the performers who go on during the first act. They're all discussing the news as they get into their costumes and do their make-up. The triplets are on the mats in the tumbling area going through their stretches, and Quint supervises the final safety check of the aerialists' rigging. Sound check is happening in the main house and the amplified "Check One Two Check," can be heard distantly. Some of the clowns are already in makeup and costume and practice juggling passes. It's a controlled kind of madness and Jes loves it. There's a comfort he hasn't felt since his visits to his Indran grandparents. He vows to himself to do what he can to save all of this from the petty machinations of Niko Dax.

"Hey, I grabbed this for you out of the free-box," Bo says and hands Jes a bundle of fabric.

Jes takes and unfurls it. It's a pale orange and lavender shawl of a soft wooly fabric, printed over with white stars. He drapes it across his shoulders, flings a flap across himself.

"I thought those colors would be good against your skin. And your hair. You look like a proper Bezan hobo now."

"Uh... thanks?" Jes doesn't know how he feels about looking that way, as the drunkard from earlier fills his mind. But he's touched by Bo's gesture.

"I have to get ready," Bo says, placing a hand on Jes's shoulder. "You're staying for the show and we're hanging out later, yeah?"

"Wouldn't miss it."

With that, Bo scampers off to the dressing room.

Jes takes one of the house seats and settles in, excited to view the show in its entirety. He also decides to take the opportunity to look for flaws, places where the pacing sags, or areas that feel redundant. He's not a show-person of course – what does he know about making shows? But maybe only an outsider, a layperson, can see the show for what it is. He senses anticipation as the crowd begins filling in. As the appetizers are brought out for the people who have dinner seating, an idea occurs to him.

He removes the shawl from his shoulders and drapes it across his seat. "I'll be back," he says to the Rijala couple sitting beside him. He walks a circuit around the theater, reaching out with his empathic sense, making mental notes of the swirl of feelings he picks up. What do the feelings tell him about people's attitudes towards the show? He susses pockets of mild excitement and curiosity. There's a group of humans – they don't look like Indran humans – who seem bored. He wonders if they'll stay bored once it gets going. He senses skepticism from some Hydraxians standing in the back. He'll have to check in with them and the humans again later, maybe during intermission.

The house lights blink on and off and he returns to his seat, draping the shawl over his shoulders again. Free Box or no, it was nice of Bo to think of him.

The lights dim and the house band plays a rollicking, upbeat theme. The clowns come out to warm up the crowd and he spots Bo among them, cavorting about, doing back flips. There's a lot of tumbling and pratfalls and general foolishness. The crowd laughs, not uproariously but it's not dead either. The couple beside him are amused but they're still waiting to be impressed.

The clowns all run through the crowd and disappear out the exits at the back and sides of the tent. The triplets come on, folding and contorting themselves, one center stage and the other two coming in from the sides. The people around Jes are all intrigued as they watch, and when the three come together into a pyramid formation, everyone is properly impressed.

The show continues, the spaces between acts punctuated

by clowning or a song from the band. The songs are met with polite applause. The clowns seem to garner more attention because of the hint of a storyline: one of the clowns has a box and is keeping it secret from the others. It's interesting but the audience as a whole is only half paying attention. The people down at the front feel more engaged though. He makes another mental note.

The acts continue apace: a static trapeze act, a dance routine with a little bit of gymnastics thrown in, two acrobats rolling about together in a big wheel contraption, a tightrope walker. This last act elicits some genuine anxiety in those seated around Jes and he is pleased to feel their intrigue piqued.

At intermission he walks through the crowd, feeling, feeling, feeling. Sussing everyone. People are generally impressed, but not equally so. The clowns, for example, are tolerated but don't wow. Do clowns ever wow? The audience vibe is happy and entertained, but there is a general feeling of anticipation... of wanting *more*. Maybe that's the intention of the show? He detects something else among some of the crowd too: mild disappointment. He wonders what kind of show those folks were expecting, what other circuses they might have seen. He thinks about what Niko Dax had said about the other circus he knew of, with people dancing with fire. Maybe Dax has a point? But he also wonders if they'd burn down the tent accidentally.

The acts in the second half impress more: Moxo Thron's transcendent juggling act, the triplets' second routine. A human aerialist is suspended in long, flowing sheets of silk while two other aerialists – a human and a Bezan – slither around each other, hanging from and crawling over a silver cube that hangs high over the stage. Three of the Bezan clowns, including Bo, do an act on long poles, climbing and dropping, sliding and holding different poses as they spin around. Jes is amazed at the control of their bodies. All of these acts elicit awe and even joy from the audience. He wonders if the show should start with these... but then where would it go?

The flying trapeze predictably thrills, before the final act – a large set piece featuring multiple trampolines – brings the crowd to the edge of elation. The acrobats – the clowns and the triplets – bounce and flip and spin around each other, sometimes grasping hands briefly or high-fiving in mid-air. Jes finds himself following Bo's movements and feels utterly delighted watching his new friend in his element. Essa's absence is notable, he is sure all of these people would be dazzled by her, but she is sitting zaijira tonight and nobody here knows what they're missing.

After the show, Jes joins the group heading over to the house Bo shares with the triplets and one of the other acrobat clowns named Beni. They call it the "circus mansion" and Jes sees why: it's an enormous, shambling house that looks like a Bezan and human home smashed together. The lower levels are all curved edges, with a couple of levels that are more square, and there's a peaked roof that rises next to a dome. It's the strangest structure Jes has ever seen. The house sits atop a hill far from the strip, on a lot surrounded by a short wall covered in murals. They remind him of the unsanctioned art his crew in Nooafar Prefecture used to throw up, but much better, more intricate. The lights of Port Ruby flash and strobe and swirl in the distance, calling, enticing. Persephone, as always, fills a chunk of the sky and it's like the lights of Port Ruby are signaling it, sending some sort of message. *See us. Love us.*

Beni puts on some music, breaks out a bottle and begins doing shots with the triplets in the kitchen. One of them packs a long pipe while singing along to the music: the latest Jasmine Jonah release. Jes remembers her old songs from his time on Rijal; they sounded like what a naive child would interpret as club music (having never been to a club). His old friends dismissed her as cheesy pop but Jes secretly always liked her music. The newer stuff playing now he hasn't heard before –

he supposes it's material released while he was in the Institute. It has an edge to it while still being catchy and Jes is surprised to be impressed by Jasmine Jonah's artistic evolution.

"I can't believe Tasso and Silas ran off to work on her tour," Beni says.

"They'll come crawling back when it's over, I bet," Bo responds.

Jes remembers Quint mentioning a couple of crew members who had left to join that tour. He makes a mental note to thank Tasso and Silas if he ever meets them.

Bo puts some supplies into a satchel and signals Jes to follow. "I'm taking you to my favorite spot," he says. They climb up a flight of stairs, arrive at a landing, from which several rooms are set. "Those are the triplets' rooms," he says, indicating three doors on one side of the corridor. "Beni's in there," he points to another door across the hall.

They climb another flight of stairs. At the next landing, Jes sees a lounge area, and they walk by a room with a very wide door. "That's Quint's room," Bo explains, "but he's always at Essa's." Across the hall is another door, left ajar. "That one's mine." They continue down the hall, at the end of which is another door, which opens to yet another flight of stairs.

At the top of these stairs is an attic, which is decked out like a den of vice. The faint scents of reef, chordash, and incense color the air. A couch and pouf chairs are arranged in a circle in the center of the room, and to the side is a shelf full of board games. The walls are covered with tapestries of Indran and Bezan origin. On the ceiling above the circle, an Indran fractal geometry holographic print is mounted.

"This way," Bo prompts as he crosses the room. He goes to a window, pushes it open, and steps out onto the roof outside.

The night is brisk and Jes pulls the shawl tighter around him. Persephone is behind them from this vantage point. The view that meets them is a wash of stars punctuated by the silver crescents of three of the other moons. "Oh wow," Jes says.

"Sit," Bo instructs and settles down. From his satchel he pulls out a small pyramid-shaped lamp. He switches it on and it begins cycling through a rainbow of colors. He also pulls out a squat cork-topped bottle which Jes recognizes as the traditional bottle shape for barat, the Bezan liquor made from the fermented leaves and berries of some kind of shrub. He also pulls out a spliff: Jes can pick up the piquant combined scent of reef and chordash. He lights the spliff, hands it to Jes, then pulls out two cups and pours them each some barat.

Jes takes a puff of the spliff, then another before passing it back. Bo raises a cup and Jes does the same.

"To my hero," Bo says. Jes blushes at this and is grateful they're sitting in the dark. They clink cups.

"Do you have to swear eternal allegiance to me now?" Jes jokes.

"I don't know. Do I?" Even in the dark, there's a mischievous glint in his eyes. Is he flirting?

The barat is sweet with a delicate nutty flavor, but it also burns. "I like this stuff," Jes says.

"Bez's number one export. Besides circus folk and associated bohemian weirdoes." His hair glows faintly in the dark, the lavender highlights particularly bright. "I'm glad you like it though. I can't really trust people who don't like barat."

"What about those who don't drink?"

"Boring. I mean, I can respect that choice. But still." He exaggerates a yawn.

The two pass the spliff back and forth, taking sips of their drinks in between.

"I can see why this is your favorite spot. This sky is amazing," Jes says. "I've never been on a moon before. I see three others now. Do you ever see more?"

"At other parts of the year. Never all eight of them though. Not all at once. In the summer we can see the slipstream gate when it opens. There's a special viewing shuttle you can take that gets up close. We should go sometime. It's a fun party." Bo uncorks the bottle again and refills Jes's cup. He leans back on the slant of roof, looking up at the moons. Jes follows suit, so that they're sitting beside each other. Under the influence of the spliff, the starlight is a blurry smear across the sky.

"Is everything a party around here?" Jes turns to look at Bo, who is gazing up.

"Pretty much. This is the infamous pleasure moon, after all. What happens here stays here, you know. I mean, I guess there's Chiffon too, over in the Rijalen Expanse. But it's all resorty spa treatments and fitness and junk. It's for stuffy rich people who don't know how to have fun."

Jes grunts. "My parents loved it. 'Stuffy rich people who don't know how to have fun' just about sums them up."

"I'm sorry they sold you." Bo turns to face Jes as he speaks. "I can't imagine having parents that cold."

Jes shrugs. He doesn't know any different. "My grandparents saved my life. My human ones I mean. I used to visit them a lot, sometimes with my mom but sometimes by myself. I wish I could have lived with them. Indra's a cool place."

"I've never been there, but I like the humans I've met from there. That festival sounds amazing, the one where everybody trips balls?"

Jes chuckles. "The Moonsbreath Festival. Yeah."

"Would you ever go back there?"

"I don't know. My grandparents are gone." First, his grandpa died of a stroke, and then his grandma followed. 'A broken heart,' according to his mother. His father always admonished her for being too romantic when she talked that way. "I think I just want to kick it here for a little while." He doesn't want to run the risk of Matheson looking for him there.

"What do you mean by 'they saved your life'?"

Jes takes a breath, exhales. "They were the only adults that ever showed me any kindness. They taught me that adults could be cool, and interesting, and loving. And that not everyone was like my parents. They gave me hope, something to look forward to when I could get away. It was hard on Rijal, even before the Institute got me."

"What was it like there, on Rijal? What did you do? School?"

"You don't wanna hear about that."

"I do."

Though Jes looks up at the sky, at the spray of stars and the moons hanging like diadems, the focus of his awareness is mostly on Bo's gaze. He senses the magnetic pulse of his attraction and it's not just gratitude for saving his life – there's an undercurrent of sexual attraction and something else, a feeling familiar and warm, like a favorite hoodie. This something else is why he doesn't pull back.

"I was a shitty student," he explains, "much to my parents' dismay. I kind of was intentionally bad at school because it bugged them so much. I hung with a bad crowd. It was fun, don't get me wrong. Some really talented graffiti writers and street artists among them. But we also stole stuff. I got good at picking pockets and locks."

Bo giggles at this. "Really? You're a petty criminal?" He punches Jes playfully on the arm.

"I did get in some trouble, yeah. I wasn't the best kid, I guess. I liked getting under my parents' skin because they were such assholes, but part of it was that full-blooded Rijala aren't so kind to hybrids. Not as bad as the Asuna are, but not much better. I really acted out. I mean, I can almost understand why–"

"Don't," Bo interjects, turns to Jes, takes his hands. "No good parents would ever sell their kid for money to be experimented on. I mean, fuck. What even is that? You deserve better. You deserve people who care about you."

Bo's hands are hot on his. There's a definite wave of attraction and he's not sure how to handle it. How do people without an empathic sense do this? He does like Bo too, but…

"Listen," Jes says, pulling his hands away. He picks up his cup and takes another sip, clutching it tightly. "I like you, but you should know I'm ace." He susses a wisp of confusion. "Asexual," he adds.

Bo's eyebrows lift with surprise. "Oh. OK." The colors of the pyramid light shift across his face: pink, red, orange, yellow.

"So… you know what that means, right?" Jes continues. "I don't mean to assume but I'm sensing your vibe. Empathically. I can feel your attraction." It's uncomfortable being so direct about it, but there's no other way to handle it really. He's not the type to ignore the issue. Well, sometimes.

"Yeah," Bo confesses. "You're cute. You're intriguing. But if you want the truth about me, I'm not all that into partnered sex myself. It's why I've never had a steady boyfriend or anything."

"Wait – so are you ace too? I'm confused."

"I'll just be frank," Bo says. He downs what's left in his cup in one swallow and pours himself another. "I'm not ace, but I'm not super into sex like other men my age. To be honest, if I'm horny I'd rather just masturbate than have partnered sex. But I'm attracted to fellas. So, you being ace isn't that big a thing. Not to me. But you're right, I do like you. I'd like to get to know you better and hang out more. I guess there's no hiding that from an empath."

"I'm open to that." Jes surprises himself with this response, he realizes it's the truth. "I feel attraction to you too. Not sexual, but…"

"Are you OK with snuggling?"

"I mean, when I get to know somebody better, I guess I could be open to it."

"Holding hands?"

Jes pauses for a moment, then smiles. "OK."

Bo slips a hand into Jes's and interlaces their fingers. The contact is electric, and Jes surprises himself again by not wanting to pull away.

Music and laughter drift up to them from the first floor, their circus comrades getting into the full swing of an after-party.

Bo rests his head on Jes's shoulder as they continue drinking together. Jes inclines his head so that his cheek brushes against Bo's soft and iridescent hair. He smells of earth and spice.

Jes thinks back on this day: the morning with Moxo, the meeting with Aleia, the company convening, the show, this. Can he dare hope this could be home?

After a little while, they decide to go back inside and head downstairs. The triplets are doing their bendy-thing in the great room, which is the space where a normal household would have a holo entertainment station set up. This room, though, has one long sofa against a wall, a couple of pouf chairs, but is otherwise an open floor. There's a storage console that holds a variety of clubs, rings and hoops on organized racks, and at least one drawer full of balls. One wall is covered by an enormous tapestry that bears the image of the Bezan Tree of the World; the treetop and roots are mirror images of each other, the top crowned by nine stars. Despite the high ceiling – two stories of open space – the room is hazy and redolent with reef.

"Oh good, the next shift," Beni says. He's stripped to the waist, his baggy trouser legs rolled up to mid-calf, and he's barefoot, red-eyed and bleary. "I can't keep up with these girls. Nighty." He hangs up the clubs he'd been playing with and heads upstairs.

"Good night Beni," Bo says as he and Jes sit next to each other on the sofa.

The triplets move as one fluid unit. One of them backbends while the other two move through the arch she forms. Then they're all up in handstands, circling around each other as they walk on their palms. They bring their legs together and apart in a variety of angles and shapes, slowly melting from one to the next. Jes susses the unity of their feeling as they move and wonders if it's born from their time performing or from being triplets. He imagines it's both; their familial and performing relationship so intertwined as to be inseparable.

"It's so cool seeing them do their thing up close." Jes checks the water-pipe sitting on the floor and seeing that it's not cashed, takes a long draw of the reef through the tasseled hose. A thought occurs to him as he exhales. "Do you guys do an after-party experience?"

The triplets stop their improvisation and drop to the floor in squats. They and Bo all look at him with curiosity.

"For the patrons."

"No. What do you mean?" one of the girls asks.

"Well, what if, for an additional fee, guests get a Cirque Kozmiqa after-party? There could be drinks, and reef, and up close and personal performances with select acts. Maybe it could be a VIP thing?"

"Holy shit," Bo says.

The triplets exchange looks. "You have to tell Aleia," they say in unison.

"Cute *and* smart too." Bo nudges Jes with his shoulder and a playful smile.

"Are you two…" one of the triplets asks. Is her name Zazic?

Jes and Bo look at each other then turn back to the expectant looks of the acrobats. "We're just friends," Jes says while Bo simultaneously says, "We're figuring it out." They laugh.

"We're just friends who are figuring it out," Jes says finally.

The triplets nod approvingly.

"Hey, can we try something?" another one of them asks. Is it Jujubee?

"Can you float us?" the third one asks. Lula, he's pretty sure.

Jes takes a breath. Everyone here already knows about his ability, and the one that doesn't is upstairs in bed. Why not? "OK," he says.

The triplets clap their hands and twitter excitedly. They arrange themselves in a triangular position and join hands. The one in front gives Jes a nod.

Jes reaches out with his left hand, and a faint aura of blue light appears around them. The three sisters gently lift off the ground as one of them lets out a squeal of delight. Jes floats them a couple of feet off the floor. They squeeze themselves together, bend their knees, then pushing out against each other's feet, fly apart. They swim in the air.

"Whoa!" Bo exclaims, sitting up excitedly. "Cool."

They each try to propel themselves upward, but without anything to press against they can't get momentum. All three look down at Jes with the same expectant expression. Understanding, he increases the gravity within the field ever so slightly to bring them down a measure. They bring their feet together again, and when he decreases gravity again, they once again push apart against each other's feet, only with more force this time, and fly upward, arching their backs and flipping over once, twice, three times. They flip towards each other, finding a center point between them. Their movements are graceful, balletic, and the weightless environment Jes projects around them makes it magical. The two at the sides turn and toss the third upwards. She flips high into the air, somersaulting all the way, then slowly drifts back down and settles with one foot on the shoulder of each of her sisters. They float in a pyramid formation, gently bobbing up and down in the air.

"Bringing you down," Jes says as he gradually increases the gravity until they're on the floor again, then he releases the field.

The triplets land and Lula – if he's tracked them properly – drops to the floor from her sisters' shoulders.

"Oh, we *have* to develop that!" she exclaims, bouncing up and down. "Please, Jes, please! Can we?"

Jes sits back in the sofa. The request fills him with trepidation – he doesn't want to risk discovery. And yet, he enjoyed doing it. It was fun. It's a novel use of his ability and it feels good participating creatively with his new friends – he feels a locked up part of him opening.

"Don't be pressured," Bo says. "Don't do anything you're not comfortable with."

Jes doesn't say anything, but they all know what his answer will be.

BOYHOOD GAMES

"Kill it! Kill it!" the boys from the neighborhood chant in unison. Jes looks up at the blue faces surrounding him, eyes open and wide with excitement at the promise of violence. He's only recently come into his empathic sense and he's not at all sure he knows the right names for all the feelings he's sussing. But at a guess, he'd name what he feels from these boys as *lust*. But it isn't sexual – nothing of that nature is happening here. They just want to see violence done to this creature they've captured. They want to see him do it because they think he's soft.

What is wrong with them?

Or is something wrong with him?

Should he want to do this thing this group demands? Should he have no problem with it? No. The intuition blazing inside him tells him no – he is not the problem here. But he still has to deal with this situation.

One of the boys found a nest of green and silver hedgerats wreaking havoc in Sontu Park. They were eating the roots of the new plantings and destroying the lettuces and edible flowers being raised by the botany students in the food gardens. Most of the pups dashed away in their underground tunnels once the roof of their nest was ripped off, but one didn't get away. Jes wonders if it was the runt.

Two boys hold down the mewling creature while Jes's hand hovers over its head, rock at the ready. He thanks the maker of all that he can't suss animals. This pup's terror would be too much; it's already too much.

"Kill! Kill! Kill!" the other boys chant as they hold down the pathetic, squirming thing.

Jes grips the rock so tightly its edges cut into his fingers. They want him to bring it down hard on the head of the squealing thing, crush its skull, squirt its brains across the patch of dirt they crowd around.

He looks up at their blue faces, the same faces he's craved acceptance from, the same ones that have crowded around him taunting *half-breed, mongrel, shit-child of a human whore–*

"No!" he shouts, anger and frustration and yes, fear, boiling over. He hurls the rock away from him and turns to run away.

One of the boys grabs him, eyes full of derision. "Weakling!" he spits in his face, "Cowardly trash! Whore-spawn!"

It isn't only the words that hurt this time. Jes susses the depth of the boy's hatred, feels what a lowly creature he believes Jes to be, though barely more than an animal himself.

Jes throws his hands over the boy's face, squeezes so tight he digs his nails in and draws blood. He susses the boy's surprise and alarm and is glad. He doesn't hit him, or knee him in the groin, or use any of the standard fight moves. He doesn't know exactly what he's trying to do really, but he keeps squeezing. He focuses all his fear and misery into his hands as if trying to make the boy's eyes pop out, or make his brains ooze from his ears. With a hard push, Jes releases him and knocks the boy to the ground.

In their astonishment, the other boys don't even try to stop him as he runs away. He runs and runs, tears burning. He doesn't know what will become of the pup he left behind and wishes he'd thought to grab it. Is he a weak waste of space because he didn't save the poor thing, or because he couldn't smash in its head?

When he gets home, out of breath and tear-streaked, his father catches him in his distress.

"Not getting along with the neighborhood boys?" His voice is ice. Like always. "I really don't know what's wrong with you."

"They hate me," Jes says bitterly. "They called me a half-breed."

"Maybe if you made more of an effort, they'd accept you." He susses his father, and finds that he holds the same disdain for him that the boys do. Like so many Rijala do.

"Why did you even have me if you hate hybrids so much?" Jes spits.

His father tenses, holds back. There's something he's not saying, but Jes doesn't care anymore. He runs up to his room and locks the door behind him. He doesn't know what's wrong with him either. From his nightstand drawer, he pulls out the crystal his grandmother gave him. As his fingers make contact, a thought occurs to him: maybe it's the world that's wrong.

CHAPTER SEVEN

"You've given me a lot to think about," Aleia says as she leans back in her chair, her hands up behind her head. Jes stands in front of her desk excited and hopeful, as he shares what he learned from the audience the night before. He's happy she's taking him seriously.

She continues talking through his ideas, "So, we'll freshen up the show with some new acts. Tell me again which ones lose audience interest?"

"The static trapeze and the dancers." Jes feels bad for sharing this information. He doesn't want to cost anybody their gig, but with Niko Dax's demand, there's dead weight to cut. "And the band was fine when they played music for the acts, but when they did songs in between, people got a little restless."

"And the clowns?"

"Oh, people enjoyed the clowns." This isn't totally true, so he stresses the caveat: "When they did the bit with the box. There seemed to be interest in a narrative, even that little one. If there's not going to be a host, telling a story through the show might be a good way to go."

"I'll think about that. I love the afterparty idea though. Something exclusive. Something with mystique. It's very on brand for Luna Lux. Something we can do instead of adding full shows. Good thinking."

The satisfaction at being able to contribute flushes him with warmth, reassuring him that he's on the right path.

"I'm not convinced about the story part."

"It will hook people in," Jes presses, making his case. "I felt it happen during the performance. People love the spectacular stuff, the acrobats and contortion. Moxo leaves them in awe. That wheel thing, people really like the wheel thing. But having one after the other with only music breaks in between, it all starts to blur together, no matter how great each individual act is. But I could feel the surge in... curiosity when there was a hint of a story." He's overstating the situation, but his intuition is telling him this narrative strategy will bring about the optimal result. He just needs to convince Aleia.

She rolls her chair back away from her desk, crosses her legs and arms. "Let's say a narrative hook is what we need. How would we accomplish it?" OK, good, she's not dismissing the concept.

"There needs to be a main character," Jes enthuses. "An audience stand-in. One of the clowns probably would be best. As they go about, they encounter each of the different acts, who are other characters in the story. The acts wouldn't even have to change that much, if at all. Just put them into a context with the narrative framing. Maybe the clown is looking for something. Like on a quest. Maybe he's a runaway lost in a mysterious world looking for someplace to belong..."

"Alright," Aleia says with a finality that indicates she's done with the conversation for now. "I'll think about that. A consult with Kush O-Nhar would be helpful. Could you rouse him for me? He doesn't have a node in his quarters because the network's frequencies interfere with his sleep. He's in the restricted gardens on the south side of the grounds."

Jes leaves her office and passes by a quieter than usual inner space; Quint's called a halt on the creation of the new set pieces until the changes to the show are finalized – no need to build stuff that might not work with the new concept. But he does hear wisps of music, some laughter – a few of the performers rehearsing, or coming up with ways to revise their acts.

He steps out into the bright day and makes his way across the grounds. Gardeners trim trees and refresh the sharp lines of the topiary – the edges of the bird shapes that had been slightly overgrown are in focus once more. A group of humans and Bezans have sprawled out on the patch of lawn he approaches. They're all playing with different props: hoops and spheres, staves and balls on the end of leashes that are spun around to make different patterns. None of them are part of Cirque Kozmiqa and he wonders if any of them are professional performers. He susses their lightheartedness as he passes, and wonders what it's like to live life so unburdened.

The gate to the restricted gardens is locked when he arrives. He peers through the slats, thin rods of black metal with a matte finish, twelve feet high. He could easily float himself up over it but it's too open, too public here. Besides, there are security cameras aimed right at the spot where he stands. He'd expected a guard or something.

He looks around and finally spots a call button beneath a small round speaker, both made of the same black metal as the rest of the gate. They're so small, they're easily missed. He presses the button and waits.

A voice crackles through, *"Yes?"*

"I'm here on behalf of Aleia Siqui. I need to see Kush O-Nhar."

"Wait."

The monosyllabic abruptness is a bit jarring – the staff elsewhere in the complex are so polite and helpful. After a minute the gate slides open silently without another word from the speaker and he walks through. The trees are denser here, and after just a few steps it feels like he's travelled into the woods. There's only one path to follow and when a fork appears, he prepares to intuit which way to go before a patio area comes into view. There's a table there, and at the table drinking tea is Niko Dax.

"Well, if it isn't Aleia's secretary boy," he says. Sunglasses cover his eyes and the combination of his unreadable expression and silky voice gives Jes a shiver. "You're here for our bug friend?"

"Um – isn't that a slur?" Jes struggles to maintain a neutral tone.

"Are you going to challenge my casual speciesism by asking why I don't refer to humanoid species as monkeys because we're descended from primates? And then, if I don't, why do I refer to Mantodeans as common 'bugs'?"

"Well, I just meant–"

"Don't be so reductive. They know what they are. How are things going at the circus?"

"Everyone's excited to rework the show." Jes doesn't sound excited at all. Oh well.

"Is that so?" Dax remains cool, clearly unconvinced. He slowly takes a sip of tea. "Did you arrive here from Rijal?"

The sudden change in subject throws Jes for a second. "Does it not seem like I'm from here?"

"Don't be absurd. Nobody's from here."

Jes realizes he has to play nicer. "Yes. I'm from Rijal. Grew up there."

"Was working for a circus your long-cherished dream?" Dax holds a smoke in two long fingers; it sends white curlicues around his grinning face.

"I kind of just fell into it. I like it though. I'm glad I'm there. It feels special."

"How lovely," he replies with no warmth. "So… you mentioned excitement about the show. There must be some bold ideas put forth?"

Jes susses genuine curiosity, which surprises him. But behind it is something else, something greedy. "I'm not authorized to speak on that."

A toothy smile from Dax. Jes never knew a smile could be cold and threatening. "Of course. You'll find Kush O-Nhar further up the left path. There's a clearing. The treehouse."

"Thank you," he replies, calm, polite. Even as he turns to leave, the greedy feeling he susses from Dax persists with a needling sensation that's almost physical. He can't get away fast enough.

The treehouse is two meters or so off the ground, and made out of a waxy, paper-like substance. It's a bulbous shape, drab green in hue, with veins the color of copper and gold running through it. It is nestled in a cradle where three limbs join together at the trunk. It induces wariness of what it might contain.

Jes calls Kush O-Nhar's name but receives no answer. He examines the abode more closely and notices a platform on one side. It's a thick panel of glass held in a frame of silver metal. Overhead, through a slot that a lift slips into, he sees a doorway into the bulb. He steps onto the glass and it lights up. He begins ascending.

Once on the deck above, he gingerly approaches the arch that opens into the bulb's inner chamber. "Kush O-Nhar?" he calls into the doorway.

There's still no reply. The arch leads into a short corridor that is open at the other end. Standing right at the doorway, Jes peers into the bulb – something casts pink light on the inner walls. He walks in slowly, taking in the silence and sussing a sharp and focused intelligence. No emotion, only presence. As he enters the bulb, he sees the source of the light: a fibrous pod hanging from the ceiling at its center, the cords that comprise its shape are interwoven in an intricate pattern of curlicues punctuated by spirals. There are two star shapes on it, bound by an infinity loop. Jes wonders if they're meant to represent Ixia and Ixiz, the binary stars of the Mantodean homeworld. The structure itself reminds him of an egg. Standing at its base is Kush O-Nhar, his antennae pulsing with the same pink light. The rhythm of the pulse feels like breath.

Jes looks around and realizes he is standing in a foyer – to his right he sees a sofa, lounge chair, and coffee table that present a welcoming human environment. Jes looks across the space to where the Mantodean stands connected to the glowing pink pod. Dappled spots of sun light up the places where the shell thins. For the most part though, the interior is shady, its sides rough, with occasional shelves and basins flowing right out of the material that forms it.

The space chitters with a series of clicks, then resonates with a humming tone like a large string instrument being bowed. Jes realizes it's from Kush O-Nhar rubbing his wings together rapidly.

Jes watches as the Mantodean retracts his antennae from the cocoon and the appendages stop glowing pink and revert to their normal color. That insectoid face turns toward him.

"Hello, Jes," Kush O-Nhar says. He scuttles over, steps onto the floor and settles in front of Jes, antennae quivering.

"Aleia would like a consult," Jes says, "And so would I."

A series of clicks and the insect face tilts quizzically. He says nothing. The globular eyes peer at him, eternally patient.

"I'm here because of you, apparently," Jes continues. A mix of gratitude and wariness swirls inside him as he stands in this strange space, eye to eye with this being who gives off an air of knowingness. He wonders how much those big eyes see. He's thankful that Kush O-Nhar's words resulted in his finding a place in this community, but he also can't help but wonder if there's more to it. One thing he's learned from his parents and the Institute – there's always an agenda.

"I cause nothing," Kush O-Nhar explains. "I just describe the paths that are likely, given specific choices."

"But you said stuff that inclined Quint and Essa to taking me in. And you encouraged me to use my powers."

A series of clicks without the hiss. "What led you to the circus that night?"

"A dowsing crystal. My grandmother's. And intuition."

"So, it was nothing to do with what I said. If you had made

a different decision, if you hadn't shown up at the circus, my words to Quint and Essa would have been meaningless. And I would never have said anything to you, for we wouldn't have encountered each other in the corridor. So, you see, you're here by your own choices."

Jes has no counter to that. But there is something he's been wondering. "How does your seeing ability work?" he asks.

A set of clicking sounds before the words come out. "I'm a weaveseer, a Consciousness Holder of my species. We can use our abilities away from our worlds of origin because we see spacetime, and spacetime is everywhere. Everything in creation vibrates. There are patterns in the weave…" He gestures to his eyes. As he does so, Jes sees the weave Kush O-Nhar is talking about. At least he thinks he does – filaments of energy buzzing through the air. Everything wavers, like an illusion about to give way. He shakes his head as the Mantodean continues speaking.

"There are paths these eyes perceive even down to the quantum level. Sometimes we weaveseers observe a result and by examining the weft of the spacetime around it, we can see what choices led to it. Sometimes we see what might result if specific actions are taken. I saw one path where the circus was ended and another where it continued on. The path where it continued included you. The path that included you was the result of other choices…"

"The choice I made to come to the circus and ask for a job and the choice Quint made to give me one. And Aleia's choice to affirm that decision when she could have overruled it."

"All that you say. And also, the choice you made to save Mister Bo and all that equipment."

"That was a reflex. I didn't even think about it."

"Because long ago you chose what kind of person you would be."

Jes isn't keen on talking about his character. He's not ashamed exactly, but grows uncomfortable with the attention. "Why are you here in Port Ruby?" he asks in an attempt to deflect that attention. "The Mytiri Forest seems like it would be more suitable for you, if you're going to be on this moon."

"I need to be where the action is." The Mantodean emits a series of rapid clicks and twitches his antennae rhythmically; the fine feather-like edges quivering gently. Though Jes can't sense emotions from this being like he can from others, he gets the impression of amusement. Kush O-Nhar is laughing. "You are an interesting development, Mister Jes."

"How so?"

"Your way of manipulating gravity. It is not emergent from a connection to a planetary sentience like other special abilities. It is something else."

"I'm real special I guess."

"Special enough that I'd like to extend to you an invitation. You are welcome to attend a gathering my people host for the worlds on which we settle. The locals call them Orbitals. It's part ceremony, part celebration. Bring Bo."

"Ceremony and celebration of what?"

"Connection."

Jes wants to prompt him to elaborate but gets the distinct feeling that no further explanation is forthcoming.

"When is it?"

"You'll receive directions when it's time." A set of clicks.

"So when the directions come I'm supposed to just – what – stop whatever I'm doing and go?"

"That's how it works. It won't be at an inconvenient time."

"Is that your way of saying I won't have anything else going on?"

"You could put it that way, though I didn't."

Jes looks away from the Mantodean, looks around at this odd domicile. The cocoon-thing catches his eye. "What is that?" he asks, pointing.

"It's for communications," Kush O-Nhar replies crisply. "I will go to Miss Aleia now. I'd prefer to fly there. Would you mind walking back by yourself?"

Jes shrugs.

"Until next time then." Kush O-Nhar stands still and gazes at Jes with those large globular eyes.

Jes takes his leave and exits back the way he came, taking the glass platform down to the ground.

"Goodbye, Mister Jes," Kush O-Nhar calls from the deck, then he takes off with a buzz of his wings, flying over the tops of the trees.

"Are you serious?" Bo asks disbelievingly when Jes tells him about the invitation from Kush O-Nhar. "Orbitals are the most exclusive happenings on this moon. You have to be personally invited by a Mantodean to go. You sure I'm invited too?"

"He said to bring you," Jes replies. "By name."

"He's never invited someone from the circus before. Well, some of us think maybe he's taken Moxo, but he won't talk about it. Wow."

Jes had simply taken the invitation in stride, but after Bo's reaction he's more intrigued. What exactly happens at these events? He'll see for himself soon enough.

Later on in the day, Essa arrives with Esmée in tow. She's giving her cousin a tour of the circus and is currently showing off her apparatus: the canes, the silks, the lyra. Esmée is engrossed, and impressed.

"Do you use all three in one show?"

"Right now, silks in the first half and lyra in the second," Essa explains happily. "The canes are for an act I'm creating with the triplets. But who knows if it will have a place in the new show."

"It will," Jes says confidently.

Essa smiles and casts him a curious look, as if wondering if he knows something she doesn't. "You were out late last night," she says. "I don't think I even heard you come in."

"I was hanging out with Bo and some others. At the mansion." He gives Esmée a nod and says, *"Orrrkut."*

She laughs and appreciates the effort. "You're improving."

"I'll say it in Ninespeak then – nice to see you. Kind of surprised actually."

"My parents finally let me out of their sight. I think they're terrified I'll be corrupted by this 'debauched' moon. Essa even had to come get me at the hotel this morning. They wouldn't let me come over by myself. They were afraid some pervert might kidnap me."

Jes remembers the drunk Bezan who wanted to pay for his ass. "There are a lot of creeps around. Even I've had to fend them off and I'm not an exotic Asuna female."

"Good thing I had my chaperone then," she quips.

"I can't believe the last time I saw you your halo hadn't even come in yet," Essa says as she continues showing her cousin the space.

Quint sidles up to them and looks at Jes. "You're on lighting duty tonight."

And so, an hour later, Jes finds himself in the lighting booth with Noor, an amiable human. His attention is half on the console he's being introduced to and half on surfing the vibe of the audience.

"These are the house lights," Noor says, sliding down one of the many knobs in the array in front of them. "Then we bring up the base stage setting. What we use before the first act comes on." They tap the control panel. "The settings for each act are preprogrammed; we mostly need to pay attention to transitions, and if any acts run out of order."

The show is mostly the same as before, except Essa's back and he sees her silks act for the first time. The brilliant purple fabric ignites against the copper tone of her skin and seems to refract in her shimmer. Her modest golden-yellow halo adds another glint of interest. She wraps the fabric around parts of her body – an ankle, the crook of an arm, behind her knee – then scales the wide ribbons and hoists herself up as she bends her body in one crazy pose after another. It's a dance, the way she hangs, then rolls, unfurling the richly hued fabric. Noor points out that the light on her is in the amber range with a little hint of pink. "It catches her shimmer the best," they explain in a whisper. "I'd never use this palette on the triplets."

Essa ends her act on the stage, holding the two bolts of fabric together. She runs around in a circle then the silks rise up off the stage and she's flying. Jes feels his heart, his spirit, lift as she soars. She bends her body into a myriad of different positions as she hangs from one arm, spins around and around, silk flowing behind her like a comet's tail.

Jes reaches out with his empathic sense, searching for Essa's visiting family who are in the audience tonight. Judgmental as they are, surely even they must be moved.

After the show, there are more cast and crew hanging out than usual. They've begun the countdown to the final bow of this iteration of the production, and want to catch more time together. Though Aleia pledged to keep as many as she could, some cuts are inevitable, especially as new acts have to be brought on. Jes watches Bo showing one of his fellow acrobats a new tumbling run. The room is full of reef and juggling when Essa and Esmée come in with their family.

Quint and Jes head over right away.

Jes picks up on a feeling coming from Eronda and Enovo: wonderment. OK. So they're not totally dead inside. "How did you like the show?" he asks.

"It was most impressive," Enovo says. "As was our niece."

Essa beams with pride at this remark.

"I understand now how Essa can consider that sacred," Eronda says. "Though there is no explicit call to Spirit, there is beauty here. And awe and exaltation. So, a call of spirit in its own way. I felt more stirred than I normally do at temple."

"Mother!" Esmée exclaims with faux-shock.

"So do I have your consent to conduct zaijira here?" Essa asks hopefully.

"It was never my place to consent," Eronda answers, "And you could have conducted zaijira here without my approval. But I see why you want to do it here. You have my blessing, niece."

"Thank you so much, Eronda," Essa says. "That means a great deal to me."

There's a rush of warmth from the overspill of her elation. It's infectious.

Eronda sighs. "With that we will take our leave. Thank you for an enlightening evening. Esmée, come."

"I want to stay here a bit." She squeezes Essa's hand as she says this. "When will I ever get a chance to experience all this?" She gestures around with her free hand.

Eronda is about to say something – issue her denial, no doubt – but Enovo speaks first. "Essa, you will stay with her?"

"Yes," Essa says firmly with a nod. "I'll be her chaperone."

"Let's leave the youth to their fun then, Eronda." He takes his wife by the arm and starts leading her away. She seems about to protest but holds her tongue.

Esmée turns to Jes. "I finally get to see what the nightlife is like on the seedy pleasure moon!"

"So the mission tonight is to corrupt your soul," Jes says with a chuckle. "Challenge accepted."

They drink and smoke and laugh and the group dwindles until it is just Jes and Bo, Quint, Essa and Esmée and the triplets still lounging in inner space. None of them had intended to just hang out here all night, but they fell into a groove and didn't want to leave it. The triplets practice the formations they explored the night before, pretending they're floating as they mime swimming through the air. They each make eyes at Jes: imploring, daring, demanding. Jes actually considers floating them but isn't sure about revealing his secret to Esmée despite deciding he was going to, the other night at dinner. Now, he's not sure if he's ready.

Bo has picked up a Bezan lute that one of the clowns left behind and picks out a sweet, lilting melody. It makes Jes think of twilight and flowers. Bo catches him watching, winks and flashes a smile, sending a flush of warmth to Jes's cheeks.

"That's nice," Esmée comments. "It reminds me of 'The Nightbird's Heart'."

"What's that?" Bo asks as he continues plucking.

"It's an aria from an Asuna opera of the same name. I've been studying it."

"You're studying Mudraessa?" Essa asks, surprised. "How lovely," she adds in response to her cousin's modest nod.

"Sing it!" Quint exclaims.

"I'm not really supposed to," Esmée replies.

"Of course," Essa says. "The Prohibitions. Stupid xenophobic Asuna."

"You're talking about the cultural laws of Opale?" Bo says.

"Yes," Esmée confirms. "I am Asuna and proud, but my people are stupid with our cultural edicts." She glances briefly at Essa, and Jes senses a twinge of guilt for Essa not being allowed access to her family's zaimira.

"We respect your tradition," one of the triplets says.

"But you can't sing? Even if it's just us?" another inquires.

"Nobody's recording anything," the third adds. "This is totally private."

The triplets have this way of unabashedly tempting people to voluntarily stray from their own boundaries. Jes can't tell if he's annoyed by that behavior or admires the skill. Maybe both. He continues to wonder if he'll ever be able to tell them apart with any degree of certainty. As for Esmée, he can tell she is truly tempted, and that she actually wants to share her singing, but years of indoctrination holds her back.

Esmée looks around at all the eager faces and seems to have a "why the hell not" moment with herself and stands. "The Prohibitions are stupid," she says in response to Essa's wordless surprise.

She nods at Bo, who resumes playing the tune he'd been playing before. She sings. Bo continues playing through his astonishment which unfurls all around him. The others stare, stunned by the clarity of her voice, the rich, alluring tone of her alto. Though she sings in Mudra-nul, the ache and longing in the song comes through. It comes from Esmée herself, as she fully inhabits the music and sends it out of her body. She's practically glowing with song. In fact – she *is* glowing. Or is she? Essa whispers something and the song ends.

"Oh wow," Bo says and begins clapping. The others all join in.

Esmée is clearly flustered, and touched, by the attention. "Thank you. It's nice to share what I do with all of you."

"Asuna opera should be all over the universe," Bo says.

"Maybe one day the Prohibitions will be lifted," she replies. "The younger generation of Asuna certainly think they should be. My father is a cultural minister, and while he's not a shake-up-the-system kind of man, he's made little comments here and there that make me think he's sympathetic to the idea. In the meantime, the universe has Jasmine Jonah."

Everyone chuckles at this.

"I bet there could be a place in the show for you," one of the triplets comments.

Esmée laughs it off, but Jes senses she's tempted.

"Let's not pressure the poor girl," Essa says.

"It's so nice you showed us what you can do," another triplet says. "It's so great when people share their talents." Jes knows this last comment is pointed at him. He meets her eyes. *Lula.* She continues, "Hey we have an idea for a new act maybe." The sheer force of her will shoots stun rays as she holds Jes's gaze before smiling at Essa.

"Yeah," one of her sisters says. "A new act, since we all have to do our part to save the circus." She, too, looks pointedly at Jes. *Zazie.*

"It'll really wow 'em," *Jujubee* says as she gets into position. "Jes? You do your thing too."

"Oh Jes, you perform something too?" Esmée exclaims, clasping her hands. "Is this the whole truth you promised to show me?"

Quint and Essa look both intrigued and cautious as they glance over at Jes, who meets their gaze and their caution. He sighs heavily. What the hell.

"Let's go," he says.

The triplets clap their hands excitedly and get into formation. He reaches out a hand and a field envelops the sisters as they slowly, slowly float into the air. Esmée gasps, but then looks on, leaning forward in her seat, eyes wide.

The trio goes through the same pattern they'd discovered the previous night, but smoother, adding little flares to their movement, like twirls of their hands. Already they've come to understand how to move their bodies in the strange no-gravity space of Jes's fields. Jes senses their kinesthetic understanding, the fine-tuned control they've developed over their own musculature. It's like an additional consciousness in the mix, shaping the field. The combination of the weightlessness that Jes provides with their acrobatic and contortion ability mesmerizes.

"Whoa," Quint says, stunned.

"Yes," Essa says softly, mostly to herself it seems. "Using each other as leverage, to break inertia in the weightlessness…"

The triplets move through a few strokes and patterns, doing a variation of things they do on the floor which look even more thrilling in the air. After a few combinations, he brings them slowly back to the ground where the three of them exude relief even though they were so fearless and confident flying. Jes turns to Esmée and is about to explain his situation to her, about the Institute and everything, when a voice interrupts them.

"Now *that* is going in the show."

Jes looks over just as Quint and Essa whip their heads around at the sound of Aleia's voice. She stands behind them, having walked in when all eyes were on the girls. Her face is calm but Jes susses her curiosity bloom like a nighttime flower.

"Someone want to tell me what the hell I just saw?"

CHAPTER EIGHT

Aleia finally accepts that she must cut some acts to make space for new ones, and so she reluctantly releases some of the longtime performers, calling the unlucky ones into her office for private meetings. Dread at being called to her office takes hold of the cast. The static trapeze artist takes the news in stride and decides to go back to Bez; the human dancers are rather more distraught when their turn comes around. "I guess I'll need to dance and take my clothes off now," one of them says spitefully as she collects her things from the rehearsal area. Her resentment and bitterness fouls the room. "Probably make more money than at this shithole anyways. Unless you're some stuck-up half-breed bitch." Quint starts charging her, but Essa holds him back.

"That wasn't very nice," Bo calls as she walks past him, then the rest of the cast makes a rumbling "Boo!" as she slinks out. In the moment, Jes is swamped by a wave of affection for Bo and the others. She should've stopped after shithole.

In addition to those acts, two clowns are released, as well as a number of front of house staff. Their departure makes way for the new acts, who've been practicing in the space for the past couple of weeks. One of them is human and performs a discipline that's never been in the show before: he dances within and manipulates a large ring of Rijalen platinum, known for its lightness and rigidity.

He spins while standing inside the ring, his body cycling through a multitude of positions as he hangs from an edge. He rolls edge over edge, positioning his hands just right so his fingers don't get crushed between the metal tubing and the floor. There's a move Jes loves when he hangs from the ring, his arms up and over the top edge as if he were embracing buddies or assuming the final pose of the martyred prophet of an old, forgotten religion.

He tells Jes that he's the only person practicing this discipline in the known systems. He trained at a circus school on Bez and while contemplating a dismantled double-ring wheel, he imagined a universe of movements within a single one. The apparatus has since come to be called single ring wheel, since it's part of a double-ring wheel, but he calls it, simply, the wheel.

Another new act is a Hydraxian duo who practice multiple disciplines. One of their acts involves one lying on his back while flipping the other on his feet. The flyer flips and twists high in the air, landing on his partner's feet with his feet, hands, or back. Another of their acts involves leveraging their respective body-weights to balance in intricate poses. Their movements are deliberate, smooth, graceful, and display great flexibility and strength.

They also perform on the poles. Their way of moving on this apparatus is more aggressive than the Bezan and human ways, but no less impressive. These styles are contrasted to great effect in the sequence they're currently rehearsing: a set of poles are scattered across the stage and the two Hydraxians with four Bezan acrobats – one of them being Bo – chase each other through them, climbing up and down, swinging and leaping between them.

After consulting with Kush O-Nhar, Aleia accepts Jes's suggestion of adding a narrative to the show. The story is developed with input from the whole cast: Bo's character falls through a portal and finds himself in a strange world. With the assistance of that world's denizens, he makes his way home but then, in the end, decides to stay in the new place. Each of the acts are people of the strange world who help him on his journey, or attempt to thwart him. It is only a whisper of a story, but it is enough.

Jes works on the set-piece Quint's devised for the levitation-contortion act – something they'll pass off as an invented piece of antigrav tech. Jes will be the operator of the device so he can be onstage with a view of the triplets in order to float them. He'll wear a mask as part of his costume – hiding his face was his only demand for participating in this. The set looks real enough: there is an authentic-looking control panel he put together from scavenged computer parts and a round platform acting as the faux field-generator that the triplets will float over. The floor of the platform even lights up and emits a suitable whirring engine sound. More importantly, the sides of the aerial rig are covered with a sheer fabric, upon which various lighting effects will be projected. The triplets will be floating, but the lighting is designed to portray it as an illusion based on holographic effects and show-trickery.

"You're gonna be behind that thing a lot," Quint says as he walks by. "Better get used to it."

"It's not crazy, is it?"

Quint takes a breath and steps closer. "It's gonna be great," he says. "And the Institute of Para whatsit–"

"Paragenetic Institute."

Quint places his hands on Jes's shoulders, a sensation Jes has come to appreciate, and speaks calmly. "Those egghead assholes at the 'Paragenetic Institute'," he puts on snooty airs to say the name, "are not gonna look for you in a circus on Persephone-9. And anyway, what's so crazy about floating contortionists? It's just circus magic." He gives Jes a wink and a nudge. "OK?"

"OK. Thank you." He steps out from behind the contraption and gets back to work. He pauses to marvel at the men swinging around the poles. A part of him wishes he could do that, move with that kind of freedom and grace and abandon. The Hydraxians don't look like they'd be able to do what they're doing, which is part of the great surprise of their inclusion in this act. Bo maneuvers through the poles like he's a monkey in its natural habitat, spinning around in iron flag position. Craziness.

"Hi," Esmée says as she steps up to him. "How's the antigrav coming along?"

"It's getting there."

Jes knows she has a lot on her mind – she's been offered a place as singer for the band. At Essa's urging she sang for Aleia who invited her to join the show on the spot – an Asuna opera singer would certainly be a draw. Ever since, she's been sitting in with the musicians as they rehearse, doing Jasmine Jonah covers, Bezan folk songs, and classics of Indran Thrum. The bandleader, who's been coming up with original songs for the show, has been conscientiously writing melodies to show off the unique tones of her voice. No Mudraessa though – everyone involved wants to be absolutely certain there's no violation of the Asuna's cultural edicts.

But even with all this work with the band, she hasn't given a final answer yet. Now that Essa has completed the zaijira, her family's sojourn to the moon is nearing its end, and she has to decide. Her parents, surprisingly, fell in love with the Mytiri Forest and stayed out there longer than they'd planned, but by now they've had their fill of the pleasure moon.

For the past couple of days, whenever Esmée's close by, Jes susses she's on the verge of something.

"We're coming over tonight, for one last supper together," she informs him. "My parents wanted to take us all out to a nice restaurant but Quint insists on cooking."

"Of course he does. He's not going to pass up the chance to make a going-away dinner for his loved one's parents. No way."

"And… I've decided to stay."

"Whoa. That's big! Congratulations." He gives her a hug. "Does this make you *Asunasol*?"

Esmée's eyes widen, and she laughs. "How do you know that word?"

"Essa explained it to me once. You're being autonomous, right? Making your own decisions?"

"In a way. Asunasol is used specifically in the context of someone rejecting the caste system and leaving Asuna society permanently. What I'm doing isn't really about caste."

"Well, whatever social thing it's about, your parents are going to freak out. On so many levels."

"I know. That's why I'm telling them tonight at dinner. So there's witnesses." She laughs ruefully at this. "Essa and Quint already know. I wanted you to know too."

"I'm with you. We have your back."

Like the night when she first shared her song, she glows.

Jes runs into Moxo Thron in the corridor as he heads out for the day.

"You must be so very proud," the juggler says, peering down his nose. "The genius who saved the circus."

Jes susses prickliness from him, barbs of – is it envy? "It might be too soon to call," he replies. "We won't know until the show goes up."

"Oh, don't pretend to be modest. You've seen the development of the acts just like I have. The new additions are brilliant. This show will be tremendous. How did you do it? How did you convince Aleia to go with having a story?"

There's a simmering bitterness beneath Moxo's words, and the hostility surprises and unbalances him. Hadn't they gotten along? "I don't know if it was me really," Jes explains. "She was really skeptical about it when I talked to her. It wasn't until after she consulted Kush O-Nhar that she agreed."

"I suggested adding a story element ages ago. She wouldn't

hear of it. She insisted on keeping the showcase format." Moxo has his upper arms crossed over his chest, but his lower arms hang at his sides. His fists clench and unclench. "You have some kind of magic way about you. Apparently."

"I don't know what to say..." Jes shuffles his feet, and looks at the floor nervously. Moxo's shoes are incredibly shiny. His temples begin to throb. "She asked for ideas and I gave her one–"

"*More* than one. The afterparty concept came from you too, as I understand it."

"Yes, that's true... I'm sorry, Moxo. Have I offended you?"

The juggler quivers with resentment.

"I'm just wondering how you show up here and convince our boss to run with concepts I could never get her to consider, despite being here for years."

The understanding dawns on Jes that in his eagerness to contribute, he's stepped on some toes. "I'm sorry, I didn't know about any of that. Aleia asked for suggestions and I gave her some that came to mind. I just wanted to contribute–"

Moxo leans down, ever so slightly, just enough to compel Jes to back away. "Just watch your step." With that, he stalks off down the corridor. Jes watches his departure until he rounds the curve and disappears from view.

His head pounds. What the hell was that?

Eronda launches into a fourth-glass-of-wine inspired rhapsody on the wonders of the Mytiri Forest. Jes marvels at how loose and relaxed she is – a far cry from the formal, uptight woman he'd met before. "The smell was delicious," she says. "And the leaves! All the purples and reds. Though I must say the waterfalls were my favorite part. I've never seen water that blue."

"I had several wonderful spa treatments. A Hydraxian four-hand massage! Can you imagine?" Enovo, too, is more relaxed than usual.

Jes hopes it maintains through Esmée's news. He helps Quint clear the table after dinner and overhears the conversation in the living room.

"Yes, I know how four hands feel," Essa says demurely, gazing lustfully at Quint.

"Essa!" Eronda exclaims, shocked at the impropriety. Then she laughs. "Of course you would, dear. But seriously, truly, that side of the moon needs more promotion. All anyone thinks of when they hear 'Persephone-9' is Port Ruby. And I see why. But the forest is something special, and it's half the moon!"

"I'll be sure to bring it up with the tourism council," Essa says jokingly.

Jes and Quint join the group, each with a glass of Hydraxian whisky, a beverage that Bo and the other clowns refer to as "donkey balls". Jes understands why, but he likes it. He's not sure what that says about him, though.

They take seats on the sofa. Eronda is uncharacteristically wistful, and Jes realizes just how tightly controlled she usually is of her emotions. She's much less intimidating this way. Her eyes settle on the zaiharza, sitting on the altar for the last time.

Esmée follows her mother's gaze and says, "You should have seen Essa's performances. It was like a prayer to her mother every night."

Jes agrees with this assessment. The zaiharza was onstage each night, set on a pedestal stage right, spotlit and glittering. Every act was a benediction for Essa's mother, Eminy of the House of Emerald Flame.

"She would have been so proud of you," Eronda says. "You have a wonderful life here. It's nothing I would choose for myself, and yet..." She trails off and her eyes drift to the middle distance.

"What?" Essa prompts.

"I can't help but wonder at other choices I might have made. In my youth."

"Come now, Eronda," Enovo chides. "Don't get maudlin."

"I hope you make a life with no regrets," Eronda says to her daughter.

"Well, I'm glad to hear you say that," Esmée says as she downs the last of her wine. Jes catches his breath in anticipation, and senses that Quint and Essa feel the same.

"I've decided to stay here in Port Ruby. I've accepted a role as singer with Essa's circus."

Enovo stiffens visibly and stares into his cup as if it will reveal the mysteries of his daughter's thinking. Eronda's face has gone pale, and the fuzzy warmth she displayed so far this night dissipates instantly.

"You cannot be serious. You can't possibly intend to perform Mudraessa off-world—"

Esmée holds up her hands. "I have no intention of doing such. The prohibitions of Opale are ridiculous, but I will not defy them. However, nothing prohibits performing the songs of other species. Or original music."

"This is your doing," Eronda says to Essa, her voice venomous. But Jes susses no true anger or maliciousness beneath the words, rather just sadness and fear. "You've corrupted her!" she exclaims, leaping to her feet. "You've set her against us!" She begins pacing the room and hugs her arms close, clutching her elbows.

"I've done no such thing," Essa counters, bristling. Jes susses how hard she's trying to keep her temper from rising.

"You will tell the Rijala boss-lady at the circus that you are backing out of this," Eronda orders her daughter.

"I will not," Esmée counters, defiance glinting in her eyes. "And besides, I've signed a contract."

Eronda's face is stricken. "How can you possibly have done this? You are not yet *edermapor*."

Jes doesn't know this word and looks around.

"The age of being able to enter into contracts," Essa explains. Then she turns to her aunt and uncle. "I co-signed it," Essa says. "As a family-member who is of age. An allowed practice here in the Vashtar System."

"Oh, oh, oh! You... mongrel cow!"

"Hey!" Quint exclaims, getting to his feet. "No need for that kind of language!"

"You just said you hope I make a life with no regrets," Esmée says, keeping her voice calm though Jes can suss she is anything but. "If I pass up this opportunity, I will always wonder. I'd rather regret a choice I make than a choice I don't. I can still come see you at home. You can still come here. You said you love the forest."

"A beautiful landscape and soothing waters do not make up for a lost daughter–"

"Don't you think that's overstating it?"

"Enovo!" Eronda turns to her husband, practically willing him to step in and take her side.

"This is a big decision, and it won't be settled now." He gives Esmée a sharp look, then continues, "Why don't you give us some time to get used to your announcement?"

"I've already decided," Esmée states matter-of-factly. "But fine. Take all the time you need to get used to it–" Her words stop abruptly and she wavers on her feet. She sits down quickly on the sofa, glowing with a soft, ruddy light. Across her skin, a wave of iridescence ripples, full of copper and violet and pink hues. In a few seconds it's over, and the glow has subsided, but her skin reflects and refracts, flashing with color.

"Oh, your shimmer has come in!" Essa exclaims. "It's beautiful. Some water..." She taps Quint's arm and he dashes to the kitchen.

Esmée looks down at her hands and forearms, smiling.

"So, it happens just like that?" Jes asks. He's dazzled by her changed appearance; it's not radically different, but is enhanced.

"For me it happened overnight," Essa says. "I went to bed with no shimmer and woke up with one. I wasn't even sure

I'd get a shimmer. Not being full-blooded Asuna and all." She casts a glance at her aunt.

"Mine came during an argument with my father," Enovo says quietly. Jes gets a wistfulness from him, a soft melancholy. "It happens when we are ready to assert our independence. Not necessarily at the same age for everyone."

"There are limits to independence," Eronda says. She has steeled herself, and Jes can tell she won't let her daughter go without a fight. She turns to her husband. "We certainly can't leave now."

"I didn't think we would, dear," Enovo replies wearily. "I'll extend our suite. And besides, we have to be here for opening night, don't we?" He casts a quick smile to Esmée before slipping back into serious mode for his wife's benefit.

"Don't encourage this," Eronda says before turning back to her daughter. "You'll want what we want before we leave this moon."

"I wouldn't count on that, Mother," Esmée replies. "You'll only be disappointed."

MOTHER

She isn't happy when she fetches him from the holding center –
disappointment radiates from the core of her, deeply shaded by
a sense of bother. He wishes he could turn the sussing off, use it
only when he wants to. He wishes he didn't have to feel every
damn thing everyone around him feels, but it doesn't work
like that. She's come alone. Whether his father is truly engaged
with important business matters or just couldn't be bothered,
he doesn't know. But it doesn't matter; same result either way.

After the death of her parents, they stopped making trips to
Indra, and the difference in his mother shocks him. She was
never a warm person, but had been capable of moments of levity,
of kindness, in between the long stretches of indifference. But
with her ties to her human roots fully severed, she's adopted
Rijalen ways and Rijalen manners. Those human moments are
gone, and he wonders if she's even capable of them anymore.

"This is your third detention," she says when they're alone
in the autopod taking them home. "Your father's patience
is running thin, along with the authorities'. They're not
going to dismiss charges so easily forever, no matter your
father's position. Why must you do these things? Breaking
into an ambassador's office? Shoplifting? What was it today,
pickpocketing tourists at the bazaar?"

He wants to say, *"You wouldn't care about me at all if I behave."*

But he'd feel like such a tool if he did. He doesn't want to be a little boy desperate for Mommy's love. He summons as much surliness as he can muster and says, "Life is boring and I hate this planet."

"I know you miss your grandparents and Indra," she says. "But they will never accept a hybrid there."

"Indra's not like that and you know it," he says. "They don't accept hybrids *here*. Do you really think I'll believe any shitty lie you say?"

"Watch your tongue. I'm your mother and I deserve some respect."

He can only laugh at this, and he susses she's insulted but also not surprised. He susses she doesn't really know how to handle him. He susses she's annoyed that she even has to try. "Why did you have me? You know how Rijala are about hybrids – even Father has the same attitudes. That came through loud and clear the last time I bothered to engage him about it. Why even reproduce with him? Why have a child you knew you didn't even want... Don't bother telling me that's not true, I can suss, remember?"

Her mouth opens and closes and all he can think of is a fish gasping for air. "Life doesn't always go the way you plan."

"That's all you have to say? What the fuck is that?"

"Language!"

"What the fuck are you gonna do about it?"

She closes herself off, and looks out the window at the city zooming by. They're on the Nara Bridge, and he wishes he could make the autopod crash over the side and plunge into the bay below, drowning them both. He doesn't care if he goes, he doesn't care if he takes her with him.

"Jes..." She's clearly struggling with what she wants to say, stops, closes her mouth again and goes back to looking out the window.

For a moment he was curious to hear what she would say. He hates that he even cared.

CHAPTER NINE

Jes is attaching a metallic trim to the edges of the platform on the triplets' new set when a visitor arrives. He sees her enter and recognizes her immediately – Niko Dax's receptionist. She walks in as if she belongs here and though many on the crew wonder who she is, nobody questions her. Quint is seeing to preparations in the new after-party tent or he surely would have stopped her. She scans the area briskly, and meets Jes's gaze from across the room. Curiosity and apprehension mix and tingle along his spine as she approaches. What could she, or her boss, want with him now?

"Jes," she says. "Mr Dax would like a word with you."

"Alright. I'm almost done here–"

"Now. It won't take long." She smiles. A polite for-show-in-front-of-all-these-people kind of smile.

Oh. So it's like that.

He sets down the tool he's working with and gets to his feet. "Should I change? My suit–"

She chuckles, out of genuine amusement. "You're cute. No, you're fine."

She leads him out and he follows a couple of steps behind. They walk by a few clowns practicing juggling passes. Moxo is there and pauses the runthrough of his routine to watch them. Jes meets his gaze briefly, then looks away, still feeling awkward about their last interaction.

They take the same route he took with Aleia only instead of taking the private elevator to the office, they head for the VIP Lounge where Dax sits ensconced in a booth, eating a salad of what looks to be mostly flowers.

"Jes! How lovely of you to join me, please have a seat." He's dressed in a dark blue suit, punctuated with an apricot cravat.

Jes slips into the booth as invited and the receptionist disappears as soon as Jes sits down. "You wanted to see me?"

"Yes. I was wondering, Jes, how you are enjoying your time on our fair moon? Your work with the circus, is it rewarding?"

Jes gets the same greedy feeling as before, a sort of joyful possessiveness. It sets his teeth on edge. "I like it a lot. Everyone's really great."

"Oh, that's wonderful to hear. I imagine you'd like to keep your place there a good long while, yes?"

"For as long as they'll have me, yes." He gets the sense he needs to humor this man and offers a faint smile.

"I'm sure they'd keep one such as you around if they could. If I recall our previous conversation correctly, you are from Rijal?"

"That's right." Jes shifts in his seat, takes his hands from his lap and places them on the table.

"As a business leader of Port Ruby, I have taken on the responsibility of supporting the work of our local magistrates. This includes keeping abreast of the goings-on in other star systems. Including Rijal's home system. Did you know this?"

Jes shakes his head. He doesn't like where this is going.

"I'm in possession of an interesting bulletin from Rijal, about a young human-Rijala man who escaped from the Paragenetic Institute of the 9-Stars with excessive violence. He disappeared around the time of your arrival here. And you, too, are a young human-Rijala man. Isn't that funny? What a small universe."

"It is quite a coincidence." Jes fights to keep his face

impassive, his voice calm and steady. "But there are a lot of hybrids these days."

"I suppose. This particular young hybrid has also had some run-ins with the law – petty theft, entry without consent, burglary. It seems family connections prevented him from facing severe criminal consequences at the time though."

"He sounds like a real winner," Jes says, hoping the sweat arising to his skin doesn't burst in a flood down his face.

"Oh, I'm sure there are reasons for that. I don't really care about those. What's done is done. Wouldn't you say… Mr Tiqualo?" He touches a small gem on his lapel and a bulletin bearing the Institute's logo and Jes's face is drawn out in light between them. Jeszoson Tiqualo. It's been a while since he's used that name. Seeing it now, drawn out in photons in front of him, makes his chest ache with panic, and all he wants to do is run.

"What do you want?" He manages to fake calmness well enough.

"The Paragenetic Institute of the 9-Stars has issued a bounty for you, are you aware of that? There must be quite a bit more to you for them to do that."

Jes shrugs.

"Given the nature of the Institute's work, with which I'm familiar, I surmise you must have a paratalent of some kind? What can you do?"

A deep sigh. He doesn't really want to share this information with this man.

Dax senses Jes's hesitation, however, and adds, "I could always request your file, but then they might wonder why I'm asking for it."

Fine. Jes can see no way around this. "It's what they called 'localized gravity manipulation'. I create these fields, and can control the strength of gravity inside them."

"Show me."

Jes pushes away the spoon and napkin from the place setting in front of him. Holding his hands out, he generates a pale blue field around each of them. "You see the fields? I can decrease the gravity inside it–" the items float off the table " or increase it." The napkin slams down heavily to the table as if it were made of rock.

"Fascinating." Dax drums the fingers of one hand on the table as he speaks. "Given your heritage, do you have any of the mager or psion talents?"

"No mager talents and I'm not a fully emerged psion. I have the Indran intuitive and empathic abilities."

Dax raises his eyebrows at this information, peaking so high they look like they're trying to escape his face. "Empathic? So... you can sense my emotions? That's why Aleia brought you to that meeting." Chuckles. "I'm beginning to see just how much to you there is, little ruffian."

Jes wants to shudder at the thought of being Dax's little anything. "There's really nothing else."

"We'll see. You'll be interested to know that I've reported to my contacts in the Oaloro System that there have been *no* sightings of the individual they seek on Persephone-9. I haven't passed the bulletins on to local magistrates so the authorities here know nothing of this. My continued participation in your little scheme of evasion is worth something to you, is it not?"

Jes stifles an urge to throttle this asshole, to crush him down into the very fabric of existence. He wonders if he could really do that to someone. He doesn't know and isn't sure he wants to know. He manages a nod.

"I need you to accompany me to a meeting tonight. You will do for me at this meeting as you did for Aleia at ours: read the other party and confer with me about it. Fairly straightforward really. Planetset, this evening. Find my roto at the front entrance. Got it?"

Jes doesn't want to go, but sees there's not much choice if he wants to keep the Institute from finding him. He nods.

"I'll need your verbal assent."

"Got it."

Dax goes on, "Very good. And one more thing–" He slides a node across the table.

Jes just stares at the shine of the device's glossy surface, its soft curves sending panic through him. "What's this?"

"It's my private line to you. Take it. If I ever need to get a hold of you, I'll ping you. I can't be sending my assistant after you every time."

"Every–"

"I'm sure I'll have further need of your talents." Dax smiles, relishing Jes's discomfort. "In the meanwhile, I wish you well on the show preparations. What is that odd phrase you showfolk use – break a leg? Do that."

Jes steps out of the lounge, his heart racing, palms sweaty, the node heavy in his grasp. He leans against the wall beside the lounge door and takes a deep breath, willing his panic to leave his body with his exhalation. The node is the weight he's chained to as dark waters rise over his head.

"Taking meetings with Niko Dax now, eh?"

Jes opens his eyes to see Moxo standing in front of him, glaring down. "Did you follow me?"

"Our circus isn't enough for you, apparently," Moxo ignores the question, bitterness edging his words. "You're really intent on working your way up the ladder, aren't you? And you play at being this innocent, confused young man searching for his place in the world. I see your ambition, Jes. I see it. And soon everyone else will too."

Jes wants to protest, to tell Moxo that he's got it all wrong, but he susses that he'd be wasting his breath. Besides, his head is beginning to hurt. "Whatever you say, Moxo." He manages to get the words out without his voice quivering. He walks away, bringing his fingertips to his now throbbing forehead. This is going to be a hell of a headache.

The roto waits at the curb in front of the Luna Lux when Jes arrives. He hasn't told anyone about this outing with Dax, and now, as he approaches his ride, he wonders how wise a choice that is. This roto is more luxurious than the standard model, a matte black interior sphere with an outer sphere that has a silvery sheen. Its side whirs open, to reveal Dax waiting inside. He's in the same suit he wore earlier today, which surprises Jes somehow, though the apricot cravat has been replaced by a black one.

"I see you had the good sense to make yourself presentable." His intuition pinged that he should wear the suit he got from Moxo and he's glad he listened. Dax is all smiles and predation as Jes slides into the dim, sumptuously upholstered confines of the vehicle.

"I gathered this is a business meeting. A suit seemed appropriate. Who's the meeting with?" He shifts in his seat, placing his hands on the upholstery – it's incredibly soft.

"Business associates. It's none of your concern who they are. I want you to read them–"

"Suss."

"Pardon?"

"The word is 'suss'."

Dax tilts his head toward Jes in acknowledgment. "I'd like you to *suss* them and tell me if they're lying and what they're hiding."

"I'm not a telepath. I won't be able to suss their thoughts, just emotional responses."

"Understood. I'll ask you when I need to know."

Jes nods and looks out the window. Eye contact with his companion is just too uncomfortable right now. They're passing the edge of town, out from the center by a road heading through one of the solar farms that powers the city. The blossom-like arrays are all closed up, giant buds tight against the dark sky, that will open again at first light.

They're heading out onto the grass plain at the northwestern boundary of Port Ruby; the jagged silhouette of mountains scribbles the horizon in front of sister moon Persephone-8, who's sinking down to join the planet they orbit for deep night. The road is a ribbon of light stretching in front of them. The treeline wavers beneath the vault of stars.

"Where are we going, exactly?" Jes asks, his palms beginning to sweat. He doesn't much relish the idea of being out in the middle of nowhere with this man. He has a node –

But it's the one Dax gave him. What if something happens? No, nothing's going to happen. He'll be fine.

"A private shuttle dock," Dax answers. "My associates and I prefer to do our business away from the major spaceport."

Not shady at all.

He can feel Dax watching him and steadfastly avoids meeting his gaze. The darkness outside is broken only by the illumination of the roadway. Finally, the roto slows and veers, rolling off the main road and down a driveway. At the end sits a round structure; past it, the blinking lights of a shuttle pad form a constellation on the ground. There's a shuttle already parked.

"Looks like our friends are here already," Dax says as they roll up onto the pad. Jes slides out after Dax and looks around. The air is crisp and there's a unique scent in the air – something green, some kind of plant. It reminds him of a plant his grandmother showed him once, something called sage. Four guards in gray uniforms stand at attention at the doorway to the structure. Tinted shades cover their eyes, though it's dark outside. Two of them leave their post and walk over to the shuttle, staying a few paces behind.

The shuttle door opens as they approach and a ramp extends. "Niko!" a human man calls out jovially as he exits the craft. "It's been a while."

"Hello, Kreshus." Dax's tone is light and friendly, but the shadow of threat lies beneath. "How are Noria and the girls?"

"They're doing fine, fine." Kreshus answers as he approaches Dax, and is followed by a younger man with the same wiry build, the same dark hair. A son? The younger man pushes a cart ahead of him, on which rests a stack of slim black cases. Dax walks ahead, but signals with his hand for Jes to hang back.

"My eldest just birthed my first grandchild, with her Bezan mate."

A wave of curiosity from Dax. "You don't care that the offspring is hybrid, do you?"

A shrug. "I don't mind it. Humans once were organized by distinct ethnicities, but during and after the Migration, we all blended. Mostly. Mixing with others is not something the majority of us are hung up on anymore."

"A distinctly different view from our galactic cohort."

"Certainly different from your people, I'd say. Jor?" He gestures to the younger man, who pushes the cart toward Dax and opens the top one with a flourish.

"Look at that sparkle!" Dax exclaims. He reaches out and pulls something from the case. Dax dips a finger inside and brings it to his mouth – Jes can guess what it is.

"Best twitch in the galaxy," Kreshus says. "Our guy is a genius chemist. Engineered the crash right out, but the craving hits harder after it wears off."

"Have you tried it?"

Kreshus opens his eyes wide. "Oh no! I don't sample my wares. That way lies ruin. Plenty of market research though."

"You'll have to put me in touch with this genius drugmaster."

Wry laughter. "And let you poach my talent? I know you're a little crazy, Niko, but not like that."

Now it's Dax's turn to chuckle. "No. Not like that." He snaps his fingers and waves at the stack of cases, and one of the guards walks over and takes the handle of the cart.

Dax and Kreshus maintain an air of joviality, but despite the friendly tenor of their conversation, there's a current of wariness that they're both adept at hiding.

"There's something I've been meaning to ask you," Dax

says, and Jes is taken aback by the sudden sharpness of his focus, which is not betrayed by the lightness of his tone.

"Oh?" Kreshus has his guard up. He's been expecting this.

"There's been an influx of swirl in town, and it didn't flow through me. Since you're the only supplier of swirl out here in this sector, I can only assume it must have been sourced from you. I'm wondering if you supplied any of my competitors, or if maybe you have competition I don't know about?"

"I don't know anything about that," Kreshus says. "I haven't had a run of swirl since two quarters ago, when I last delivered to you." Deception – wavering, fragile and uncertain.

"You're sure nothing is slipping your mind? I know how busy you are, and it must be hard keeping track."

He shakes his head. "No, Niko. I only make runs for you in this sector, you know that."

"Jes."

His name is fired like a clip; it hangs in the air. He walks over to Dax, who leans in close for a whisper.

"Well?"

"He's lying," Jes affirms. "And he's really nervous about something."

Dax begins pacing around Kreshus, his hands behind his back. "I want you to think hard. I can forgive a lapse of memory, even a lapse in judgment if amends are made. You're sure you've not met with anyone else?"

"No, Niko. Only you. I swear."

Dax sighs deeply. "Something you should know, Kreshus, about my associate here." He points at Jes. "He possesses the Indran talents. He's an empath and can suss all our innermost feelings and emotions. *He* says you're lying." With a quick swipe of his foot, Dax brings Kreshus down to his knees, then pulls the human's head back by a handful of hair. From inside his jacket, he's pulled a dagger whose jeweled hilt glimmers in the low light. The curved blade gleams against Kreshus's throat. "Between you and him, I'm inclined to believe him in this moment."

Jes feels himself go clammy at the sight of the knife on the man's throat. Dax really wants to use it but is holding back. Fear rises in him, cold and prickly. He wipes his palms on his pants.

Jor has his weapon out, aims it at Dax and he looks as scared as Jes feels. "Let him go," he says shakily. No one is convinced by his tough guy front. A plasma round bursts from behind them and strikes Jor's hand, sending his blaster flying from it and skidding across the ground. He moves to retrieve it, but the guard fires another round between him and the weapon. This gives him pause, and he's reduced to looking at his dropped firearm forlornly. Jes doesn't think he's ever actually used it much.

"Tell me who else you've been supplying." Dax's words are cold-edged, sharp as the blade in his hand. Jes can't read him – he's blank. But he's not blocking Jes's empathic sense, more like there's nothing there *to* suss.

"It was Danae," Kreshus sputters. "Danae Siqui!"

Dax's face betrays surprise at this as he looks to Jes for confirmation. With a nod, Jes confirms that the man is telling the truth, and Dax's smirk is back. He releases Kreshus, who crawls away on his hands and knees a couple of yards before rising to his feet.

"Danae," Dax says under his breath. "That conniving vixen."

Gunfire pierces the night, and the bright bursts of energy bolts strike the ground near their feet. A couple of crewmembers have appeared in the doorway of Kreshus's shuttle, a human and a Bezan it looks like. They fire at Dax's party, rounds sending clouds of dirt puffing up from impact. Jes slips into full panic, and looks around, watching Kreshus's men and Dax's guards shooting at each other, not knowing what to do. "Get behind the roto!" Dax calls and Jes wastes no time. He scrambles behind the roto with Dax, who's sputtering, "They're firing at me? At *me*?"

The two guards that had been stationed at the structure

have joined in the fight, and now four of Dax's men fire as Kreshus and Jor scramble back on board the shuttle. As soon as they're safely inside, it begins lift-off.

Dax's hand on his shoulder sends a shudder through him. He hopes Dax chalks it up to nerves rather than revulsion. "Can you bring the shuttle down? With your ability?"

"I've never–"

"Do it! Do it *now*!"

With adrenaline coursing through him, Jes doesn't stop to ask why or wonder if he can. He stands up from behind the roto now that the shuttle is no longer firing, and raises his hands. The ship is thirty, forty feet in the air and rising fast, but Jes wraps a field around it easily. He increases the gravity enough to stall the shuttle's continued launch, but the counterforce of its thrusters is stronger than he expected. He brings his conscious awareness to the graviton waves tugging at the craft, and he understands what he needs to do. He pulls sharply. The shuttle drops, its back end lurching down towards the ground. It maintains this lower altitude, then plummets the rest of the way with a crash, and parts of the bulkhead buckle in. Sparks and smoke pour out of the cracks.

After a moment, the hatch opens and the crew climbs out, coughing and waving the smoke from their faces. One of them singed – it looks like Jor. Kreshus helps him to the ground some distance away from the vessel. A crewmember raises her blaster, then the bright orange bursts of pulse weapons fire converges at her chest. Jes whips round to see all four guards with their weapons raised. They unleash another round, the orange comets trailing away from them as they take out the other crewmember.

"Please, Niko," Kreshus whimpers as the boss strides towards him. Beside him, Jor moans softly, the left side of his body badly burned. "It's business," Kreshus says. "It's nothing personal. I'll cut ties with Danae immediately. I promise. I swear it."

Dax kneels down in front of Kreshus, strokes the man's tear-stained face. "This isn't personal either." With a quick swipe of his glinting blade, he cuts the human's throat, sending a spray of blood arcing into the cool night air before the drops splatter on the ground. Before he even has time to react, Dax does the same to Jor. "See if anybody else is aboard," Dax orders one of his men. "Kill them all."

Dax turns to Jes. "Can you suss any others?"

"N–Not from out here." The echoes of fear left by Kreshus and his crew still flow through his sussing sense, and merge into his own so that he can't tell if he's feeling his own fear or theirs. The bodies of Kreshus and his crew are strewn on the tarmac. They had been alive just moments ago and that thought brings a fresh surge of terror. To distract from his own feelings, he brings his attention to that of others. From Dax he susses a strange mix of sadness and pleasure, from the guards a calm placidity that is the most frightening of all.

"Go with him, then."

Dazed by what he's just witnessed, Jes does as he's asked without really thinking about it. The assigned guard watches him coolly as he steps onto the ramp – he can feel the stare even though the man's eyes are shielded by the visor. They enter the shuttle together.

"Are you picking up anything?" the guard asks.

Jes stops in the middle of the corridor they're in, and closes his eyes. It's been a while since he's done this but the feeling of how to comes back to him easily. He visualizes ever-widening concentric circles as he extends his awareness outward. He would sense any emotional energy present as bumps in the empty air. There's no emotional pingback at all. If anybody were hiding on board, they'd be radiating anxiety, fear, maybe even the same placidity in the face of a potential skirmish as the guards are projecting. He opens his eyes, looks at the guard's visor-covered face, and shakes his head.

In short order, they check the rest of the small craft: a cabin, a weapons room, the cockpit. On their way back to the cargo hold where the exit ramp is, the guard removes a fake panel in the corridor and checks for contents. "A drug runner's shuttle always has at least one secret compartment," he says when he notices Jes's curious glance.

He pulls a case out from the compartment, like the ones previously unloaded. He thrusts it into Jes, who raises his arms to accept. The guard opens it, revealing rows of sparkling red gems.

But Jes knows they're not gems.

He reaches back into the compartment, pulls out another case, then another. Then he indicates with a jut of his head that they should exit the craft. Jes closes the case in his arms and follows the guard back outside.

"There's nothing," the guard reports. "Except these." He indicates the cases he and Jes carry. "Swirl. Crystals."

Dax chuckles. "Send word to Kreshus's family, and that of his crew, that there's been a terrible accident. A malfunction in the shuttle's thruster array or whatever, no survivors. Send our condolences. And take care of this." He gestures around at the wreckage, the bodies.

Without a word, the guard he'd accompanied on the shuttle places the cases in Jes's arms and attends to his new task of clearing the shuttle pad.

Jes walks in silence back to the roto. After he sets the cases down alongside the others in the storage compartment, he climbs in and joins Dax. He's witnessed murder, helped load drugs, and has an assigned node. Is he part of this whole operation now? He really hopes not. They set off immediately and Dax turns to him, "I've got another assignment for you."

He supposes that answers his question. A bright flash breaks through the darkness and Jes looks back to see a fire flare, then settle to quiet burning. The shuttle. Destroyed in a tragic crash. He swallows rising bile at the thought of what he will be asked to do next.

From a raised panel in the seat, Dax pulls out a sleek silver case. He opens it and pulls out yet another case inside, much smaller, and hands it to Jes.

When he opens the container, Jes sees contact lenses and a small pin.

"This task might require a little more finesse than what I needed you for tonight. I imagine you'll be able to draw on your... *unique* skillset to accomplish this. You heard the conversation tonight. Danae Siqui has been edging into my market, it seems, and running a narcotics operation without my approval. I need you to find evidence of this. You're aware of the party drug swirl?"

He nods. "I've heard of it, yes." He remembers some of the folks he ran with back in Nooafar Prefecture used it sometimes. Their eyes and their minds would go all sorts of far away.

"Well, it's more typically sold in powder form, but this batch I'm concerned about is pressed into red, crystalline capsules. Did you see what was in the cases you helped retrieve from the shuttle? Yes? Well, that's what you're looking for. Little fake gemstones. I want you to run a simple reconnaissance of Danae's place of business and see if you can find a stash. Don't take or sabotage anything, just see if what's rightfully mine is in her possession. Can you do that?"

An office break-in? A relief in comparison to the murder he's just witnessed. He can probably handle this, besides he doesn't see he has much choice. If he doesn't want to end up cut open and sliced up in Matheson's lab, he has to go along.

"I can do that."

"I will require you to wear those lenses during the operation." He gestures at the case Jes holds. "Not that I wouldn't take your word for it, but I'd like to see what you see. I'll be notified as soon as you start broadcasting. I may even send you instructions, which you will see as captions in the display. I hope you're OK with contacts. The club bans cameras and recording devices so we have to be discreet. Do this before opening night of the new show. Do you understand?"

Jes nods.

"I'm sorry, I'll really need you to verbally affirm your understanding." He seems to pick up on Jes' unspoken *why?* "I like to make sure there's no misunderstanding of my requests, or room to claim such. And, I'm a believer in respecting the free will of others. I need to hear explicit acquiescence to my demands. So, again, do you understand what I'm asking you to do?"

"I understand. What is this business that I'll be scoping out?"

"Ah yes. Pertinent question. It's the Apogee Pleasure Club."

Oh great – a sex place. His stomach sinks as if contained in one of his gravity fields.

"The target is the sister of Aleia, your circus boss." Jes wants to add, *and your ex,* but keeps his mouth shut. "She must know nothing of this operation. Understand?"

"I understand."

"Excellent. And just so we're clear, in case you're tempted to go to the authorities about any of this, know that I have Magistrates loyal to me throughout the precincts. Know that I will not hesitate to inform them of the fugitive from the Rijalen Institute in our midst, and of the bounty on his head. Got that?"

Jes swallows. "I got it."

That feeling of possession pulses from Dax again, and it reminds Jes of how Matheson considered him: property. Not a person at all. He looks out at the dark road through this flat plain they roll down. The lights and towers of Port Ruby rise ahead of them in the night.

GRANDFATHER

"It's time for you to taste the waters of Indra," his grandfather says. They're finishing breakfast in the garden, and his grandfather sits bare-chested in the sun, sipping his tea. His white hair contrasts sharply against his brown skin, and his light grey eyes twinkle. There's a playfulness to him, that he always seems to have, and so Jes isn't that nervous about "tasting the waters of Indra" even though he has no idea what that means. "It's a good time while your mother's away."

Jes's mother and grandmother are spending the day together on another island in the archipelago. Jes wonders if that outing had been planned just so his grandfather could take him on this mysterious tasting. "Why is it good to do this while Mother's gone?"

"Has your mother told you about the Indran talents?"

Jes shakes his head.

"I didn't think so. Well, I'll explain on the way. Go get your shoes on."

It's a bright morning and Jes loves the light that's filtered through the dome enclosing the city, dappled by the trees. His grandparents live in an area called Featherwood, so named for the soft and fuzzy-barked trees that grow throughout the district. Grandfather, who has put on a loose tunic while Jes was busy with his shoes, takes him by the hand, and together they make their way through Featherwood, towards the canals.

"Do you know what the Emerged Ones are?"

Jes nods vigorously. He is proud to know this. "We learned about them in school. Every species in the 9-Star Congress has those who Emerge, and they have special abilities which are different for each species. Rijala call theirs magers, and Humans are psions... and I don't remember the others."

"That's enough to know for now," Grandfather says cheerily. "Well, for people here on Indra, when they get to be about your age, they take their first sip from the Waters of Indra. Indra is this planet, as you know, and these special waters flow in a special place which is where we're going."

They've reached the canal station, where the brightly painted boats, color-coded by destination, wait at their slips. The one they head for is aqua: the Waters District. Grandfather and the boatman greet each other with nods as they get on board.

"The waters awaken our connection to the planetary consciousness," Grandfather continues. "For those of us called to be psions, this is what activates our intuitive capacities, and our sussing. This is the first step we all take. Understand?"

Jes nods. "Will I be a psion? Will I stay here?"

"Oh, my boy," Grandfather smiles, puts a hand on Jes's head, the side of his face. "You have to live on Rijal for a while. I know you like it here on Indra. Maybe you can come live here when you're older. But if these talents wake in you, you might find them helpful back home."

A detail from the school lessons on Emerged Ones comes to him. "I thought the abilities don't work off the planet of origin."

"The major psionic talents – telepathy, telekinesis, clairvoyance – aren't accessible off-world. But the base talents of intuition and sussing work anywhere."

"It's time for him to taste the waters, eh?" The boatman addresses Grandfather while continuing to guide the boat through the canal. They're in Flowers District, and the surrounding air is redolent with the perfumes of who knows how many varieties of bloom. The railings at the top of the canal walls are laden with vines bearing yellow and white flowers. "Will it work, considering...?"

Though the boatman doesn't finish his question, Jes knows he's wondering about the fact that he's mixed species.

"Don't know," his grandfather replies. "Worth a try though. His mom's side of the family, we're psions. There's a mager on his Rijalen side. Chances are good."

The boatman lets out a low whistle. "That's some kind of mix." He eyes Jes appraisingly, but not in a judgmental kind of way like he gets a lot of back home, more like he's wondering what Jes will turn out to be.

They arrive at their destination slip, clamber out of the boat, and walk some more. The light has a bluish tint because of the dome, and the waters in the giant pool and the waterfall are crystal clear. They walk to a cave near the far edge of the city – Jes can tell they're at the edge because they're very close to the inner wall of the dome; he can see it from where they are. The arch that frames the mouth of the cave is made of a burnished bluish metal – a special alloy made only on Indra that he understands from his father's dealings is a highly prized commodity, though he doesn't understand why. There's only one marking on the arch, at its top: an etching of an eye.

They enter a cave and head down a long tunnel. Water burbles and colored lights dance across the walls. He gapes in wonder at the cavern: the walls are like a gemstone his grandmother once showed him called an opal. Brilliant colors flicker within their smooth surfaces, waving and moving and glowing – they are the source of the light. In the center of the cavern is a rock, and out of the rock gushes water in a steady stream that flows into a pool.

Grandfather leads him, still holding his hand, to the edge of the pool where there is an array of geodes and gourds. "Pick one for your cup," his grandfather instructs.

Jes runs his hands over them and settles on a geode that's gray on the outside and full of purple crystals in its curved interior.

"Amethyst," his grandfather says. "Good choice. Hand it to me."

Jes does as he's instructed and watches as his grandfather cups the geode in his hands and whispers over it. Something about "Mother Indra" but he doesn't catch it all. After the chant, he dips the geode into the water and brings it up to Jes's lips. "Drink."

Jes sips the water as his grandfather pours it into his mouth. It's the sweetest water he's ever tasted. And he feels something, a tingling that starts in his belly and spreads out through his body until the top of his head and the bottoms of his feet are also tingling.

He's overwhelmed by love for his grandfather, who watches him expectantly, a smile slowly appearing on his face. He doesn't just feel love for his grandfather, but he can feel his grandfather's love for *him*. Like he's loving himself, like he's both inside and outside the love.

"You're sussing," his grandfather says. "That's my boy."

CHAPTER TEN

The directions take them out to a Spaceport dock, though this one is so far afield Jes wonders if it's really part of the main port at all. He gawks at the ship: a black sphere fused with a pyramid. The main sphere has a matte finish, a black so deep the ship looks to be made of shadow. In contrast, the points that jut out from the curves of the sphere are highly reflective and Jes can't tell if they're made of metal or stone or something else. The vessel hovers several meters off the ground, and he can feel the antigrav tug on his awareness. He's never seen one like it.

"It's a Mantodean intraspatial sphere," Bo explains. "The shape is called a sphere tetrahedron. I've only ever seen pictures. Spaceports usually have a special dock for them that's far away from the others. Something about the energy they give off interfering with the nav systems of regular ships. I had a friend back home who was all into starship engineering and he used to go on and on about these."

A jade green Mantodean greets the guests, gazing at each one with large eyes of a slightly different shade of green. Their red-tinged antennae wave gently as Jes and Bo step up. Jes feels looked through rather than at, a sensation he's experienced under Kush O-Nhar's gaze, so it isn't entirely new, though still unsettling.

"Jeszoson Tiqualo and Bolo Valen, guests of Kush O-Nhar, welcome."

"Your name is Bolo?" Jes asks, his voice edging up with surprise.

"That's just the name on my official records. I'm Bo." He turns to the Mantodean, "How did you know who we are?" His curiosity glows as bright as a signal flare.

"The Weave around you tells me all I need to know." The Mantodean continues watching them, antennae quivering, front legs rubbing together. "Please proceed to the boarding port. Under the blue light." They gesture their head behind them to the floating orb, where a column of blue light extends from the bottom of the sphere to the ground.

There's a disc at the bottom of the light beam, similar to the one at the entrance to Kush O-Nhar's house, and Jes and Bo step onto it. It rises gently and in a moment they're inside. They find themselves in a welcome area, a dome-shaped space lit with pink light.

"Please step off the disc," another Mantodean instructs. This one is also green, and looks identical to the one that greeted them.

They do as requested, and a Bezan attendant beckons them to follow.

"You're an acolyte," Bo says. "Of the Ones Who See."

The attendant smiles. "Did my lack of hair give me away?" His head looks dusted by an iridescent fuzz of stubble.

"And your robes. I have family members who serve. I didn't know acolytes went off world."

"Some of us serve the Mantodeans in this capacity as part of our training," the attendant explains. "Prospective Consciousness Holders of all species do. Here we are."

They've reached a large chamber with a high domed ceiling lit in tones of soft peach and violet. Below it is a sunken floor, across which are strewn rugs, pillows, blankets, and small tables bearing jars of water, cups and mortar and pestles. There are only six other guests: one other pair, and the others appear to be here solo. Each party is accompanied by an attendant in the traditional acolyte robes of the Consciousness Holders of their species. Their auras all glow gold in Jes's sight.

Their attendant guides them to an empty table. "My name is Toma, and I will travel with you this evening."

"What exactly is going to happen?" Jes asks, peeking into the mortar and pestle, curious about its contents. He sees dried tendrils of some kind of plant matter, and what look like small, jet black rocks.

"You will be administered the tonic, then we travel to the planet's portal spots. Well, moon in this case. We'll be making a circuit around the moon. That's why these gatherings are called orbitals, even though we won't technically be orbiting."

Nervous laughter as a human male and Hydraxian female are guided to a neighboring table by their Asuna attendant. Jes can't help but notice the color of her halo – pink, like rose quartz. The human, tall and broad-shouldered compared to Jes and Bo, seems small next to his companion, who makes no effort to play it cool in this environment – her awe is plainly apparent.

"All the guests are here," Toma informs them. "We'll be departing shortly."

Jes looks around, counts the guests. "There are only eight of us?"

"The Mantodeans keep these gatherings intimate. Sometimes there are up to twelve guests, but I suppose they found fewer that fit the Weave tonight."

"Is Kush O-Nhar here?" Jes asks. Since he was the one that invited them, it would feel strange for him to not be present.

"He's not on board tonight."

Jes susses Toma's energy: a placidity he struggles to maintain, broken by anticipation, and a wild sort of joy he's making concerted effort to rein in. What are they in for?

"I bet Esmée would get a kick out of this," Jes comments. "I get the impression she likes new experiences."

"Well I'm glad it's just us," Bo replies, giving Jes's hand a squeeze.

A chime rings throughout the space, clear and piercing. A door slides open at the far end of the chamber, and a Mantodean of extravagant coloration enters. If coloring and features are indicative of status in Mantodean society, this one must be far higher in rank than Kush O-Nhar or the attendants they've encountered tonight. Their carapace is silvery-white, and a multitude of hues glint off its surface. Their eyes are elongated and are mostly violet, but for a gradient of red-yellow-green where they taper to points above its face. The face and antennae are a color somewhere between pale orange and pink. From the space between the antennae stalks on its face, an aquamarine jewel glints. The being's candy-colors are radiant, and Jes can't take his eyes off them.

"I guess Kush O-Nhar is a bit plain for his people, huh?" Bo whispers.

"Apparently."

They make their way to each table, where the respective attendant grinds the contents in their mortar and pestle. Each party speaks with the brightly-hued Mantodean in voices too low to overhear. It looks like some kind of ritual is performed, but Jes can't quite see what's happening. Finally, it's their turn.

"Jes and Bo," the Mantodean says with a voice like silk, soothing, lulling. "Summoned here by Kush O-Nhar. I am Hela A-Nor, my pronouns are she/her, and I am your Gateway for tonight's journey."

Toma has picked up the mortar and pestle, and methodically grinds its contents, making crunching and scraping sounds that are rough in contrast to Hela A-Nor's voice.

The Mantodean continues, "I see in the Weave that your summoner explained nothing to you."

"Should he have?" Jes asks nervously.

She emits soft clicks and her antennae quiver – a gesture that Jes now recognizes as how these beings laugh. "That he didn't only indicates his confidence in your readiness. Bo, look at me."

Bo does as he's requested. Jes susses a shift in him as the anticipation, curiosity, and excitement he'd held for tonight's experience smooths out into a placid calm. After a moment, she turns to Jes. "Your turn."

Jes meets her eyes, and is captivated by their surfaces. They look like mesh, but for raised spots of tiny crystalline structures that glimmer like sequins. They're so different from Kush O-Nhar's smooth eyes. Her antennae bend towards him as she examines him, their tips wavering. Her eyes seem to grow, become huge in his vision, and he sees his face reflected in each one. Then his face vanishes, replaced by a shuttle-pad at night, a crashed shuttle, a knife, sprays of blood, the smirking glee of a killer.

"Darkness and violence," she whispers. Her gaze draws further from his past – flashes of Matheson's face, the memory of bindings and shocks, electrodes and cold, clinical faces. "You mustn't let these past experiences taint this one. Can you be present with the here and now?"

His grandparents' faces arise in his mind's eye, smiling, beaming tenderness, care and affection. Without breaking his gaze with Hela A-Nor, he reaches his hand out for Bo, grasps empty air until Bo's hand returns his grip.

"I can," he replies. "I can be present."

She seems to accept his word, or maybe she sees something in the Weave that affirms what he's said, because she steps back and breaks her gaze with him.

Toma raises the bowl in which he's crushed the ingredients for the tonic, and the Mantodean lowers her head, opens her mandibles, and releases a clear, viscous substance from her mouth. Upon contact with the contents of the bowl, the whole mixture turns a vivid purple color as Toma mixes it. He pours a portion into the cups on the table, and hands one each to Jes and Bo. Jes tries not to think about the fact that it's part Mantodean spit.

Hela A-Nor, meanwhile, has taken a place in the center of the space, and a pedestal has raised up from the floor, bringing her up close to the zenith of the dome.

"Drink," Toma instructs, "then lie down."

Jes looks at the concoction in his hands with some trepidation. He's aware the substance the Mantodean exuded may not technically be "spit" but it still came out of her mouth. "What was that stuff?"

Toma chuckles. "I understand if you found the sight unsettling. It's a substance called *hona*, which is produced by a gland only Gateways possess. It's not that dissimilar to honey from bees. Now drink, before it loses potency."

Jes looks over at Bo and sees that he's already downed most of his portion. He shrugs and follows suit. It's bitter – not like honey at all – with a mineral kind of taste that reminds him of his "vitamins" at the Institute. He pushes the memory aside. Be present.

He lies down beside Bo, and they hold hands once more. Jes doesn't feel different, and waits for whatever effect the stuff they just drank to kick in – surely something will happen?

The pillow under his head is plush and soft, maybe the softest thing he's ever felt. They look up at the dome, still aglow with the same colors as when they arrived. But when Hela A-Nor touches her antennae to its surface, the room is plunged into darkness and the dome goes black. Slowly, spots of color appear in the dark overhead, and these quickly proliferate until the visual field above them swirls with fractals, dizzying patterns that repeat in interlocking echoes of each other. They shrink and grow, undulate with the breath of the colors and complex geometries unfolding and folding up again. Are these shapes outside of his head or inside his head? He can't tell and for a moment he's not separate from the colors, or Bo or Toma or Hela A-Nor or any of the others on board this vessel or the vessel itself. He turns inside out and the geometry is all there is. His breath catches, and then everything is normal again – everyone and everything separate once more.

"We're at our first stop," Toma informs them. "The Ontari Canyon."

"What?" Bo asks, incredulous – the surprise Jes susses is sharp and loud. "The Ontari Canyon is on the other side of the moon. It takes half a day to get there by standard shuttle."

"This is no standard shuttle," Toma explains. "Intraspatial spheres move through space and time by folding dimensions. The tonic helps your bodies and minds make it through the journey. Think of it as psychic lubricant."

"You didn't have any tonic," Jes observes.

"I'm an acolyte," comes the response with a clear surge of pride. "Practicing these trips is part of our training. Now sit up, you have the opportunity to disembark at each stop."

Jes had forgotten he was still lying down and sits up slowly. He's prepared for a headrush, or some other symptom of being psychotropically altered, but there's nothing, other than an awareness of his body, and his breath. Toma helps him and Bo get to their feet, then indicates with a tilt of his head that they should follow him.

They file out of the chamber with the others and gather in the pink domed room. This time, instead of a small disc bearing two guests at a time, the entire floor lowers to the ground below. As they exit the ship, they see they're on a high plateau, and before them is the largest canyon Jes has ever seen, extending all the way to the horizon ahead. The river at its bottom glints with the reflected light of the moons and planet that dominate the sky. It's half-day where they are, meaning they're on the shadow-side of the moon facing the sunlit side of the planet. Persephone's vibrant purple makes a royal backdrop for the brilliant sister moons.

The attendants didn't descend from the ship with them, and one of the green Mantodeans is their only guide. "Welcome to the largest canyon in this star system," they say. "Feel free to explore, though we advise you not to descend into the canyon. Listen for the chime, it will let you know when departure is imminent."

"Come on," Bo says, grabbing Jes's hand. They head off the platform, away from the ship and towards the edge of the plateau. "How do you feel?"

Jes feels his fingers intertwined with Bo's, and the warm breeze bearing the scent of sagebrush. The heavenly bodies sing to him, and he susses the music of their contemplation, intelligences locked in a dance of space, time, and gravity. The dance that holds whole worlds together. And people. And relationships.

Maybe he's higher than he thinks.

"Awake," he says after a long pause.

"I know what you mean!" Bo exclaims. "Like everything is super sharp, right? We sure are having a time, aren't we?"

Jes can't disagree. He looks around: in front of them, canyon and river overlooked by planet and moons, behind them flat desert plain. The flatness is broken by craggy mountains in the distance and the constellation of the Chalice rising behind them. There's no city and the associated noise and light, no sign of civilization at all except for the ship they arrived in, which glows like a lantern in the distance, dwarfed by the landscape.

"We're really on the edge of the galaxy."

Bo chuckles. "Quite a spectacular place to bring me on a date."

Jes flushes, hopes the strange twilight that bathes them isn't bright enough for it to show. "This is a date, isn't it? I didn't really realize, it was just this thing Kush O-Nhar invited us to…" He's embarrassed but susses only amusement from Bo, no judgment.

"You're cute."

"This is better than the party, right?"

There's a party at the circus mansion tonight, in honor of two former crew members being in town. But then the summons to the Orbital came, and who turns down an invitation to one of these, direct from a Mantodean?

"Yes, this is way better than the party." Bo looks down at the ground, out at the vista in front of them, then back to Jes. "I want to put my arm around you. That OK?"

Jes nods, and a warm flush fills him as Bo's arm slips around his shoulders. He reciprocates, slides an arm across Bo's back, his hand coming to rest on the opposite hip. Bo tilts his head onto Jes's shoulder and sighs.

"Do you see what I see?"

"If you mean the fractals streaming over the landscape, then yes," Jes replies. The ground beneath them, the canyon, the river, all of it is made out of fractals. "I think it's the Weave the Mantodeans talk about. I think that stuff we drank helps us see it. Whoa."

It isn't just the landscape that's fractalated – Bo is too, and when Jes looks down at himself, his own body is formed of fractals blooming from some inner space, lit up from within.

"Everything is made out of the same stuff," Bo comments sagely. "Part of the same dance."

Jes suppresses a giggle at his friend's corny psychedelic musings.

"Your grandparents were Emerged Ones, right? Do you think they saw fractals?" Bo asks.

"I'm willing to bet they did. Fractals feature prominently in Indran art. I bet seeing these patterns is common to all Emerged Ones. I don't know why I think that though. It feels intuitive."

"Heightened intuition is one of the Indran talents, right?"

Jes nods. "Yeah. My grandparents taught me all about the talents, how to suss. My grandmother gave me this." He reaches into his pocket, pulls out his dowsing crystal. "This led me to the circus." The crystal point dangles from its chain, flashes in the bits of moonlight it catches.

"So I have that crystal to thank for bringing you into my life?" Nervous laughter as their eyes meet. "How does it work?"

"You ask it a question, and pay attention to how it swings. Usually, it tells you yes or no, but sometimes, like the night I found the circus, it tells you which way to go."

"Have you asked it about me?"

Well, that's a question. He takes his arm from around Bo, turns so that they stand face to face, and asks: *Should I pursue this relationship?* The crystal swings gently back and forth, from Jes's chest to Bo's. The crystal is a concentrated fractal bloom, and the patterns that make up the world around it stream into it, become focused.

"It says you're alright," Jes says with a smile. He hopes he's being cute, but isn't sure he pulls it off. When did he ever care about being cute?

"I feel validated."

A chime rings through the night, a clear, pure tone. It's time to get back on board the sphere.

"Wow, right?" a human female says as they gather back on the platform, her eyes full of wonder. She seems very, very stoned.

"Right," Jes agrees. "Wow."

The group shares a chuckle at this scintillating exchange as they rise back up into the sphere.

"So how exactly are we traveling tonight?" Bo asks Toma when they're back at their spot in the main chamber.

"As I explained earlier, these spheres travel using dimensional folds. There is a network of folds throughout the galaxy, some believe throughout the universe. There are certain hotspots where entering and exiting the folds is easier. If you think of the network like a tree branch, these locations are like the places on the branch where a flower would bloom. The network and these spots were revealed to the Mantodeans when they made contact with Zo a long time ago." He pours them each a glass of water, hands them over saying, "It's important you stay hydrated."

He continues as they drink their water, "The orbs can only

launch and land from these places. Each world has a set of such spots, and tonight we're hopping from one to the other. The only location where infrastructure has been built is the spaceport."

The jaunt around the moon continues with a stop at the Cosmia Falls deep in the heart of the Mytiri Forest, where they all stand in awe of its roaring cascade for what seems like hours. It's a location Bo says is a few days' hike from the town of Mytiri, and he expresses over and over again how he can't believe they're there.

They make a stop in a mountain glade in the Sigil Range, where Bo introduces Jes to a tree native to Bez that has thrived on this moon. Its wood is yellow and bears a spicy, peppery aroma and a wistfulness comes over Bo as he talks about this tree from his homeworld that Jes finds endearing.

Finally, they alight on the shore of Lake Tourmaline, the great freshwater lake of the eastern hemisphere. It's deep night on this side of the moon, where its night side faces away from both planet and sun. The sky over the water is a spray of stars, punctuated by the luminous fuzz of a nebula.

The lake spreads before them, all the way to the horizon – there's no other shore visible besides the one on which they stand. The water is calm and glassy, reflecting the stars above. The Mantodean attendant releases glowing orbs into the air – they float gently, casting soft yellow light. The different parties spread out along the shore, and a set of orbs follows each one. Though there is a sense of connection over the shared experience, none of the different parties mix, which is just fine with Jes. He wonders if this is how it always is, or if this dynamic is particular to this outing.

"Let's get close to the water," Bo suggests, and they walk hand in hand toward the edge of the lake, trailed by three of the glowing, floating orbs. Once there, he pulls off his shirt. "We have to get in," he says in response to the puzzled look Jes flashes.

Jes susses Bo's excitement, longing, even, for the water. But he isn't so sure. "Is it safe?"

"During full day, people come to boat and swim, it's totally fine. And it's shallow close to the shore." He's kicked off his shoes and pulls off his socks. He stops suddenly. "Do you know how to swim?"

"Yes, they taught us in school. And my grandparents used to take me to Indra Bay."

Bo pauses his disrobing, stands at the water's edge topless, in bare feet, his pants undone. "We can't come all this way and not have a dip."

Jes is overwhelmed by a bout of shyness and getting undressed in front of Bo, but he reminds himself that it's just swimming, and it's dark, mostly, and they'll be covered by water anyway. Flashes of fractal patterns ripple across the lake's surface. He slips out of his tunic.

"That's the spirit!" Bo exclaims. "But we won't get totally naked if you're uncomfortable." With that, he kicks off his pants, and wades into the water in his underwear. "Oh it's nice. Get in here."

Jes finishes disrobing and gets in the water – Bo's right, it is lovely.

"The water is crazy though, are you seeing this?"

The water ripples out away from them, illuminated, made of the same geometric patterns they've seen all night, only liquid. The ripples fan out, and their colors and patterns eventually fade where the water darkens once more.

"I'm seeing it. Just to be clear – the water's not like this normally, right?"

In the distance, laughter and splashing; it seems like everyone in the group had the same idea. The lake near the shore is shallow and deepens gradually, and they walk out until it's shoulder high. Bo takes a deep breath and dunks himself under the surface, rising up again, spraying water all around, the luminescence of his hair even brighter in the night.

Jes follows suit, takes a breath, goes under. The water feels like body temperature, and he can't tell where his body ends and the water begins. It's a delicious sensation. When he resurfaces, the night air kisses his face, neck and shoulders with coolness. He floats on his back, looks up at the sky. The lake is remarkably buoyant, and floating is easy. Bo does the same, and after a moment his fingers snake through the water to grab Jes's hand.

"Such a trip travelling this way," he says. "Do you think the Mantodeans hop around the galaxy the way we've been hopping around this moon tonight?"

"I think probably they do. I always wondered why they don't use the slipstream like everyone else does."

"Now we know they trip and bop around in their spheres."

"I wonder if they drink that stuff too. Or if it's just for non-Mantodeans. I got the impression from Kush O-Nhar they see geometric patterns all the time."

"Hey, I've been wondering, did that stuff we drank earlier affect your powers?"

"Not really," Jes says. "Though I haven't tried any gravity stuff and I don't really want to. I'm sussing like normal." He squints his eyes – vestiges of fractals whisper across his sight.

"What's it like, having powers?" Bo rubs his thumb against the side of his hand as they float side by side.

"I barely remember what it's like not having them at this point. At least the Indran ones. The gravity stuff feels like second nature now too, but I kind of feel like I'm only scratching the surface, you know? If I only had the Indran talents, I'd probably have gone to Indra to study with the psions there. I might have followed that path like my grandparents did. The gravity fields... well. Without them I wouldn't have been locked up and experimented on. I wouldn't be hiding from the Institute. I wouldn't be here, that's for sure. I don't know why else I would've come to Port Ruby, or this moon. I didn't know about all this."

"I'm glad you did. Come to this moon, I mean. I know the reason why sucks, but..." Bo's voice trails off.

Jes susses a rushing swell of nerves and affection – and something else he's too scared to name. Bo stands up in the water again and Jes does the same. They face each other, the light orbs floating over their heads.

"Can I kiss your hand?"

Jes nods. His pulse quickens as Bo takes their joined hands up to his face, touches his lips delicately to the back of Jes's hand once, twice, as their eyes remain locked on each other. Bo runs the fingers of his other hand through Jes's hair, strokes his face.

"Is this OK?"

Jes nods again, his heart beating fast. He hasn't experienced affectionate touch since his grandparents died – nothing from his parents and only intrusive handling and pain from the Institute staff. There'd been crude come-ons from other kids on Rijal, during which his aversion to sex revealed itself. But this is different. He susses Bo and what he gets is tenderness – not lust. The same tenderness rises in him – not just a sense of Bo's feeling but his own. It's strange being able to feel them both simultaneously, like two strings on that lute Bo likes to play, in harmony.

The chime rings clearly as if it were right beside them. When they get back to the platform, there are stacks of warmed towels waiting for them. "Everybody goes swimming," the Mantodean says by way of explaining their presence.

"Do you ever go in?" Jes asks as he towels off.

"Most Mantodeans don't like the water."

When they get back to their table, Toma is there with two shot-glasses of something milky and blue. "These will help ease your transition back to regularity."

The sweetness of the drink makes it feel as if he could woo anyone with the next words that come out of his mouth. After they down them, they lie back on their pillows, once more looking up at the dome above. It pulses with a soothing amber hue, then changes when Hela A-Nor touches her antennae to it. There's that folding inside out feeling, but then Jes feels suspended in space. He can sense Bo and Toma beside him, can sense the others all around though he doesn't see them with his eyes.

A field of stars takes over his awareness, he's in a bubble filled with them, and the bubble breathes. The stars begin streaking, wiggles of light dazzle his mind, then fractals emerge from the light, rising up and falling back, blooming out of his body and curling back in. He sees that everything is this fractal field, all the stars and worlds, the joined consciousness of all beings. He and Bo both arise from this field, and by this field they are connected. But not just Bo – Toma, Hela A-Nor, everyone in this room and out of it. Esmée too, and her parents, and, though he wishes it weren't so, his parents. Matheson. Dax. They are all emergent from this field of whirring patterns that underlies matter and thought. He wants to hold onto this feeling of connectedness, but doesn't think he will once he's off this craft and the potions wear off, once he's back in regular life.

This is the transition back to regularity. The inside out feeling comes once more, for the last time tonight, and they're back. Jes doesn't really know how long he lies there before he slowly realizes he's staring up at the dome. The dome in the chamber. The chamber on the Mantodean sphere.

"We're back," Toma informs them. "To the same time as we left."

"Wait – what?" Grogginess fuzzes Jes's brain, he's not sure he's understanding.

Toma smiles, happy that a secret he's held all night is revealed at last. "I told you that this sphere travels in folds of space and time. We have made a full circle, and have returned to the place and time of our departure. Everything you saw and experienced tonight was part of one extended moment."

Is that the lesson in this? How much experience and connection is contained in a moment? Is this what time is like for the Mantodeans, all of it an eternal "now"? Is this what time is like for Consciousness Holders in general?

Hela A-Nor exits without another word, and the attendants lead their guests out.

"Thank you for joining us," Toma says after he leads them to the exit. The parties exit one at a time, the way they entered.

They're deposited on the spaceport dock where they started.

"I can't believe it's the time we left," Jes says, mind reeling.

Bo lets out a laugh. "You know what this means, right?" When Jes shakes his head in response, he continues. "We still have the whole night ahead of us. We didn't miss the party after all."

CHAPTER ELEVEN

"Donkey Balls!" Beni yells from his perch atop the kitchen counter when Jes and Bo walk into the party. A wave of laughter and music washes over them as they make their way to him. The hedonistic energy of the gathering nearly bowls Jes over, especially after the quiet contemplation of the Orbital. The predominant emotional tenor he picks up is joy, and he quickly adjusts.

Beni has two shots waiting for them when they reach him – this whiskey is going to be a far different experience than the last shots they took. They down the drinks, say a round of hellos, then do another round of shots.

"OK, we're off," Bo comments as he slams his shot glass down.

"Hey, I like the new look," Jes says as Esmée walks by. She's ditched her traditional Asuna robes and wears much more revealing clothing than is typical for her: a noodle-strapped camisole, low cut with a shiny bronze satin finish, and the tight-pegged pants Rijala girls like. Her choice of top seems intended to flaunt her new shimmer to greatest effect. Her hair, normally down, is done up in two buns on either side of her head, above the line of her halo, in a style the triplets favor.

"Thank you," she says as she plants a peck on each cheek.

"Me and the triplets are talking about going to the Shadowlight later. You and Bo should come."

"Maybe," he says, doubting his own intention. "It's been a long night."

She laughs. "What are you on about? The party's just getting going. It's still early. Kind of."

She doesn't know about the Orbital. The message to meet the sphere came and they went immediately, telling no one, and now they're here, that whole experience having taken just a moment before this party even got started. "We went—"

He's cut off by Zazie exclaiming "Come dance with us!" as she wanders by, grabbing Esmée by the hand. *Talk later,* she mouths as she is pulled away by the tide of Zazie's enthusiasm. They head into the practice room, which currently serves as the dancefloor. The music blasts and Jes feels the beats and the bass rumble deep in his chest. The shots have warmed him up, and their buzz dissipates what floatiness remained of the Mantodean beverages and the dreamy space of the sphere.

Though the encounter with Hela A-Nor helped him set aside his situation with Niko Dax, it all comes rushing back. He still has a task to complete. He's supposed to do it before opening night, and the clock is ticking. The thought of being in such a lustful and explicitly sexual environment seizes his breath with anxiety, and the fact he has to do it even though he doesn't really want to sends him into a bout of alternating bitter frustration and self-pity.

Stop it. This is a party.

"Hey, let's go find the guests of honor," Bo says, taking his hand. Jes finds he's starting to really like holding hands.

As they weave through the crowd, Jes catches sight of Quint and waves at him from across the room – he gets a three-handed wave and a raised drink in return.

"Have you seen my cousin?" Essa asks when they pass her on the stairs.

"She's dancing with the triplets."

"I hope she can handle her shimmer! It's easy to get a little out of hand the first night out."

"Not going to warn her then?"

"She has to learn sometime!" Essa melts into the rest of the party at the bottom of the stairs.

They head to the second-floor lounge, where a multispecies group sits around a water pipe sat upon a short table. A long purple velvet tube snakes from it, a red tassel dangling off the end of the wooden mouthpiece. He knows the humans and Bezans from the circus, but the others are strangers. He guesses the human and the Bezan-human are the guests of honor.

"Hey this is Jes, you guys," Bo introduces him. "This is Silas and Tasso. They left us and hit the big time."

"Hey ya, Jes," Silas says. He's human but his whole aura is different than the humans he's known – he must be diasporic. From here in the Vashtar system – Lora, probably. He's very pale compared to the majority of humans who are typically some shade of brown. His skin is pinkish-white and he has light brown hair and piercing blue eyes. Jes knows from human history, people with this kind of coloring used to be more common.

"Heard you were alright," Tasso says. He has human features too but a pale lavender tint to his skin. The subtle glow of his hair and the brilliant green of his eyes display his Bezan heritage. It's also apparent from his eyes that he is very, very high. "Can I interest you in some of the galaxy's finest hash?" He offers the water-pipe.

Jes has never had hash before but heard it was basically just stronger reef. He feigns nonchalance. "OK." Owen, one of the human clowns, gets up and gestures for Bo and Jes to take the space he's vacating between Tasso and the Hydraxian. They settle in and Jes takes the mouthpiece, drawing gently until the floral notes whisper across his tongue followed by an intensely green finish. He exhales a plume of fragrant smoke and immediately words are gone from his mind.

"So, what's it like out on tour with the galaxy's biggest popstar?" Bo asks, taking the mouthpiece Jes hands him. Jes is happy Bo is beside him.

Tasso answers, "It's crazy – chancellors and royalty clamor to touch her hand."

"*We* don't get much of that treatment though," Silas adds.

"Silas is correct," Tasso says with a nod of his head towards his friend, "The help are invisible as always in the history of every world forever, right? But Jasmine treats us well. Her fans are… devoted. Devoted's a good word. I've never seen anything like it. But you should come see for yourself. We can get you in to the show, any night you want."

Bo bounces excitedly in his seat, gives Jes's hand a squeeze. "That'd be great!"

Silas goes on, "The media, as much as they overhype things, are actually right about Jasmine. No other musician's popularity has crossed cultures the way she has. The crowds are insane. Two hundred thousand even in the Hydraxian Range. Never seen a stadium like that. There were even Mantodeans at that show. It kind of seemed like they were observing everything."

"Isn't anyone who goes to a show an observer?" Bo asks.

"Not like that. You know what I mean. Jackass." Silas scrunches up his face as he gathers his thoughts. "Everyone was there to have a good time and see the show, right? But the Mantodeans seemed like they were there more for the crowd, you know? Almost like they were studying the whole thing."

"Not surprised the show there was huge," the Hydraxian says. "My people know the good stuff. I'm Theetee by the way." She offers Bo one hand to shake while waving the fingers of her other three hands.

Jes and Bo introduce themselves. "How do you know these clowns?" Bo asks.

"Life on the road," Theetee answers with a crooked smile.

"We hear you're ushering in a new era of the circus," Tasso

says. He takes the mouthpiece back from Bo, who's been holding it while they talked, hits it and hands it to Jes.

"I don't know about that." Jes takes the mouthpiece for another toke. He knows he doesn't really need it but he likes the taste and the aesthetics of the action; the water pipe burbles peacefully as he draws.

"Well, as we hear tell, you're the one who brought the narrative concept to Aleia, and used your empathic sense to evaluate the ups and downs of the show. From an audience perspective."

"Pretty smart to do that," Silas adds, then it seems as if he just catches on to Tasso's words. He looks at Jes with a suddenly more serious expression. "You can suss?"

Jes nods. "My human side is Indran." He exhales his toke. The hash has made his whole head feel bubble-like. He hears people speak but it takes a second for the meaning of the words to catch up to the sound. Everyone around the circle is comfortable, and sedated, so he feels at ease. While his mind moves a little slower than usual, colors leap out at him and the textures in the music get deeper and richer.

"Well we've been talking up the show to our boss," Silas says. "She might even come to the opening."

"No way!" Bo exclaims. "Aleia would flip."

Not to mention Niko Dax. The thought of Dax dampens Jes's mood – he suddenly remembers the special task ahead of him again. A wave of anxiety sweeps over him and his breath gets short. His head and body feel heavy and the layers in the music unpeel into the space of the room along with everyone's feelings.

He's grateful for Bo's contentment beside him, for that grounding presence. He also feels Theetee's burbling elation and her riding the edge of a laughing fit, and Tasso's satisfaction at where he is in life, being the cool kid back to see his friends with his cool new job. And Silas is... what is he? Nothing. He's closed himself off from being sussed. Curious. Most diaspora humans wouldn't know how to do that since they're not around psions or really train in that stuff. He remembers his grandmother once telling him that humans born off-world and who have never been to Indra were spiritually and emotionally more like the ancient humans who killed their planet. Was Silas's closure to sussing a sign of that? He felt him before. Weird.

In trying to suss Silas, he's expanded his empathic awareness and now the press of a party full of emotions starts to overwhelm. He pushes these thoughts aside and struggles to close off the swell of everyone's feelings. The auras of everyone in the circle and beyond swirl and pulse and blur together in a confusing haze of color. He usually has to push to see them but now he can't make the lightshow stop. So many bodies indistinguishable in his sight. Ghosts of fractals appear, only instead of leading to a feeling of connection like they did before, they dissipate in shards.

"Are you OK?" Bo asks.

"I… I think I need some water. Or air." He stands up, woozy and wobbling; he steadies himself.

"We're gonna mingle," Bo says to the others as he rises to his feet. "Thanks for the smoke."

"Yeah… thanks," Jes manages to say.

There's a round of nice-to-meet-yous as they step away from the circle. Outside of the lounge it's worse. People crowd the hall and the landing, and he's awash in waves and waves of euphoria, bits of despair – somebody here is very sad about something – and horniness. Overwhelming horniness as the young circus folk and their party people friends swirl around, wasted and flirting and wanting to fuck. Jes is drawn in by the happy sensations, and wants to comfort the sadness, and the lustful feelings are like magnets of the same charge pushing him away. The alcohol and the hash spin his mind, and the relentless thump of the bass vibrates in his bones. A storm of emotions assaults his empathic sense, and his vision blurs in a pulsing haze of color and light. There's a monster of want and need rumbling downstairs and hurling itself against the walls. He hopes he doesn't puke.

Bo reaches out for him and he recoils at the touch. "Roof," he blurts out and Bo understands.

"Can you walk?"

Jes shakes his head.

"Can I touch you? I want to help you get up there."

Jes shakes his head.

"How about you put your hands on my shoulders?" Bo turns his back towards Jes, taps his shoulder while looking over it.

Jes nods and gets his hands on both of Bo's shoulders and grips tightly.

"Lean on me if you need to," Bo says and walks down the hall slowly, cheerfully saying hello to people he knows.

"Is he alright?" somebody asks.

"Just needs some air," Bo replies casually. "Too much hash and donkey balls, you know how it goes."

"Been there myself." The guy who says this claps Jes on the back. The touch repulses him and the impact brings him that much closer to being sick. Thankfully the contact is brief.

They take the stairs slowly up to the attic room. It's quieter up here, the lights are low and the music soft and ethereal – someone is playing crystal singing bowls. The crystalline harmonics help – they slough away some of the emotional muck he's picked up. There's the smell of reef in the air and light incense; this makes him a little queasy, but they're almost outside. A small group sits in the sofas and circle of chairs, playing cards. Bo grabs a blanket slung on the back of a chair as they walk past. He steps out onto the roof first, then turns to help Jes out and over the window frame. "Careful," he says as Jes stumbles forward. "Sit," Bo orders and wraps the blanket around Jes once he's down. "How's this?" he asks.

Away from the crowd and the noise, out in the cooling night air, the turmoil inside him begins to settle. He takes a deep breath of fresh air, then another. "Holy shit," he says after a moment, covering his face with his hands.

"What happened?"

"All the... My empathic sense got overwhelmed. And my sight was too much."

"You mean seeing auras? I thought you had to force yourself to do that."

"Well I couldn't stop it just now. I still can't, not quite. At least it's just you and me."

"And me," a voice says from the window. Esmée steps onto the roof and joins them. "I heard you were having a rough time," she says. "Water?" She hands him a bottle.

"Maker of all, yes," he says, grabs it, chugs greedily. A sinking feeling grips him with each swallow – word of his rough time has apparently spread and Jes loathes the thought of being the newbie partier who can't maintain. But he remembers how it started, anxiety sparked by the job he has to do for Niko Dax, and trying to suss through Silas's block. "Thanks," he says, hands the water bottle back to Esmée, who sits down next to him. "I failed that one."

Bo and Esmée look at him with quizzical expressions, so he explains. "Back on Rijal, I used to grade my performance in social situations. In Rijalen school grades ranged from Outstanding to Fail. Most of the time I scored myself Needs Improvement, but just now was a Fail. So embarrassing."

"Don't be embarrassed," Bo says, sitting down himself. "We've all been there."

"I haven't," Esmée says with mock superiority.

"Oh look at you little miss 'gets her shimmer and now thinks she's better than everyone'," Bo teases.

"I've always thought I was better. I mean, I am."

Jes manages a chuckle at that and the friends share a laugh.

"Was it the hash?" Bo asks with concern. "I mean I've drunk with you, and we've smoked reef and you've never been overwhelmed before."

"Well the hash was a lot stronger than I thought it would be, and there's way more people downstairs than we normally hang out with. Everyone's emotional stuff was really intense."

"What's it like? Your empathic sense? I mean what's it feel like?" Bo's curiosity crackles between them. "I've heard about it my whole life, about how you can never put one over on an Indran human because they can suss you out, and how Asuna always know when you're horny and what you're horny for."

Esmée giggles at this. "That is true."

Jes ponders the question a moment. "It's kind of like smelling. Like, scents are just in the air, and you notice them, but you can't really *not* smell them. Like you can close your eyes and not see, or you can plug your ears, or you can not touch stuff or wear gloves or whatever so you don't feel. But you can't not smell scent. I mean, even if you hold your nose or breathe through your mouth you still pick up some of it, especially if it's really strong. And eventually, when you're in a place long enough, the smell of it just kind of fades into the background. And once in a while you encounter a really strong smell – good or bad – like moonsbreath, or Bezan irises, right? Happiness, satisfaction – those kinds of feelings are like good smells. And then anger or jealousy is like a pungent, sour smell. It's that same sort of sharpness, that same sort of punch. Only in your feelings instead of in your nose. Does that make sense?"

"That's a good way of explaining it," Esmée says, nodding.

Bo scrunches up his face as he makes sense of what Jes just said. "So, what happened to you inside was like... just too many smells stinking up the joint?"

"Something like that. The emotional currents, the auras – it all took over my consciousness for a spell. Some of it might be residual effects from earlier. And I think anxiety triggered it." He doesn't mention trying to suss Silas.

"Anxiety about what? Or just, like, general anxiety?" Bo's brow is furrowed with worry.

Jes sighs. It's time to confide in his friends. "So, I got called in to see Niko Dax…" he begins, and tells them about the meeting, registers their horror at the details of what happened to the crew of the shuttle. He tells them about what he's been asked to do at Danae Siqui's club, under threat of being sold out to the Institute.

There's a long silence when he's done, as they absorb what he's told them. Eventually, Esmée comments, "Asuna are taught that violence like this happens in the unaffiliated sectors. But I always thought it was just exaggeration to scare us from exploring."

"I've heard rumors about the kind of stuff the syndicates in Port Ruby pull," Bo adds, "but I've never known anybody that's witnessed any of it. Are you going to do what he wants?"

"I have to," Jes replies bitterly. "I don't want to go back to the Institute, and I saw last night what he does with people that cross him. I am a little nervous about going into the Apogee. All that sex going on, I'll feel everything. It skeeves me out thinking about it."

"I'll come with you," Bo says. "You might need backup. You'll need a lookout at least."

"I can't ask you–"

"You didn't ask. I offered."

Jes gazes at his friend – boyfriend? Whatever – and gratitude and affection swell in him. He did help him get up here when it got to be too much downstairs. What if that happens while he's trying to accomplish his mission?

"I'll join this little escapade too," Esmée says. "I can show you some Asuna techniques to help your focus. Besides, two wingpeople are better than one. And I don't want you going back to the Institute either. I want to help."

"You guys…" His friends are beautiful in the night, three moons hanging behind them, their auras soft, soothing even. He wipes tears from his eyes. "The people I hung with back on Rijal would not do this for me."

"Well they sound like shitty friends," Bo says.

"We're not them," Esmée adds.

"You're better," Jes says. "Way better."

Bo leans back against the roof. "What a night, huh?"

"You got that right," Jes says as he leans into Bo, rests his head against his shoulder, to Bo's delight. "I'm exhausted."

"It's just a party," Esmée says. "You two should get out more."

Jes and Bo exchange looks, then bust out laughing.

CHAPTER TWELVE

The entire moon's been anticipating her arrival for months and now that Jasmine Jonah's show has arrived, all of Persephone-9 is abuzz. There are detractors, of course: malcontents who think popularity automatically means the music is crap and only they are discerning enough to see it. And there are those who dismiss her as a talentless slut, with the misogynistic edge only frustrated male talents seeing a female artist succeed can manage. But Jes and his friends are stoked.

He and Bo have both been dusted with sparkly glitter, courtesy of Essa, who is positively radiant in a form-fitting scarlet dress. Jes, for the first time since his arrival here, wears the cape that he got at the spaceport bazaar back on Rijal. He wears it with the shiny green side out. He's tempted to wear it with no shirt underneath, but doesn't feel quite confident enough in his physique to pull that off, especially since Quint is wearing tight black velvet pants and a mesh top that reveals his chiseled definition.

The box Tasso arranged for them has a clear, unobstructed view of the stage and plenty of room for the group of Jes, Bo, Quint, Essa, and Esmée. There are a few others as well, dressed for a night at a club like everyone, presumably other friends of Tasso's or someone else involved with the tour. Esmée and Essa draw a lot of male attention but Quint's presence seems to keep them at bay, particularly the way he slings a protective arm around Essa's shoulders.

"This is so exciting!" Esmée says, clasping her hands together. "Aren't you so excited?"

Jes nods. He's looking forward to the show but isn't overflowing with exuberance the way Esmée is. He holds Bo's hand. "Can I kiss your cheek?" Bo asks.

Jes nods his consent and his heart races as Bo leans in and gives him a quick peck.

"Can I kiss your hand?"

Jes nods again and Bo lifts their joined hands up to his face and kisses the back of Jes's. His lips are soft. Though Jes doesn't have sexual feelings, he has come to appreciate such bits of physical affection from Bo. He and Esmée greet each other with kisses on the cheek in the Asuna tradition, and these are fine too. She understands that this show of affection, simple and even trivial to her, can be triggering to him, and she appreciates that he allows this intimacy between them. Quint sometimes pats him on the back or places one of his big hands on his shoulder when offering reassurance, and this too he's come to appreciate.

Although he's always understood it intellectually, he's slowly come to embody the understanding that physical affection isn't inherently sexual, and he wonders how it is that he's come to be OK with it, at least with people he's close to. Then he realizes – he's never really felt close to anyone before except his grandparents. That he can accept physical affection from his friends is a sign, to him, just how safe and close he feels with them.

The lights dim and the crowd erupts with cheers and everyone leaps to their feet. Jes jumps up too, grateful to be diverted from going down a rabbit-hole of rumination at the big show. The surge of emotion from the thousands in attendance is a rush and he closes his eyes for a moment to block himself off. He isn't able to close it off completely, but manages to dial it down so that the feeling doesn't blow his mental and emotional circuits. He's glad he chose to remain sober for this.

The first pulses of drum and bass fill the air and shake the stadium. Pink lasers shoot out into the crowd as colored lights fan across the backdrop of the stage. A tiny figure rises up from below the stage and everyone roars their welcome. The tiny figure waves, then a massive hologram flickers to life and the crowd goes wild some more. It's her: Jasmine Jonah magnified in a 40-foot high column of light. The hologram is live, and does whatever Jasmine does. She smiles brightly. "Port Ruby," she drawls and the crowd cheers. "The people of a pleasure moon surely must know how to have fun. So let's do it!"

More roaring. Jes, caught up in the moment, roars too, and his voice joins that of everyone else in the place. The rest of the band kicks in and Jasmine begins to sing, her voice sultry, the melodic hook of the song undeniable. Jes moves to the music, feeling it insinuate itself inside him. He dances; they all dance.

Song after song unfurls, mostly up tempo tunes that get the crowd moving and sweaty, with a couple of ballads in the mix. He marvels at the spectacle: not just the performance – though that is impressive. Jasmine's voice goes from low and sultry to high and breathy as the song calls for; her range is impressive and her tone unique and strong. She's a dynamic, magnetic presence and Jes finds himself focusing more on the small figure dressed in spangles on the stage rather than the hologram of her. But the spectacle that captivates him even more is this multi-species audience who knows every word, dancing together, singing together. He's part of a larger entity, this whole collection of bodies and minds connected by this shared love for and shared experience of the music.

Most of the songs are sung in Ninespeak, but occasionally she does a song in Bezti or Rijalic and these draw special appreciation from people in the audience of those specific backgrounds. In the moments when the stage lights go dark, he can spot the heads of Bezans, faint clouds of colored light scattered throughout the stadium, bobbing along. He doesn't have the Mantodean gift of seeing the Weave of spacetime, but what he does see heartens him. Different species of people with contentious histories among them, different ways of being in the universe, but here, in the container of this hybrid girl's adventurous music, for this moment, they're one.

After the show, Tasso greets them at the backstage entrance, dressed all in black, wearing a headset. "Incoming," he says into the mic. "Hey guys, welcome. Quint! Good to see you, big guy!" They greet each other with a hug, Tasso disappearing into Quint's arms like everyone does. "Essa. It's been a while." They greet each other with a peck on the cheek.

Their group enters through the door and Tasso holds up his hands to the crowd of people gathering at the entrance. "Friends only," he says. Two Hydraxian guards step in front of the door as it shuts behind them.

"Did you have a good time?"

"Oh it was amazing," Esmée gushes. "She's so inspiring."

"She'll be happy to hear that. Follow me."

The backstage area is oddly subdued. "I would've expected there to be crew running around," Jes comments.

"If we were breaking down tonight and heading onto the next tour stop then yes, there would be. But tonight's the first show of eight at this venue, so it's not as crazy. Here we are."

He holds open another door for them and they step into a surprisingly low-key scene of a fashionable, hip crowd. Jes had been expecting a dressing room, but the space is more like a large apartment. The colorfully dressed crowd stands around in small groups, sipping fancy-looking cocktails. Jes has no idea who any of these people are, but he imagines they must be the cream of the Port Ruby party and culture scene. There are only a couple of dozen people present, including them. He would've expected the backstage party for an intergalactic popstar to be a bigger deal. To his surprise, Jes spots Moxo Thron across the room talking with Theetee. The juggler meets his glance coolly, then returns his attention to his fellow Hydraxian.

"Jasmine," Tasso says as they approach a diminutive figure draped in a shawl. "I'd like you to meet the circus friends I told you about." He turns to them, "Everyone, this is Jasmine Jonah. I'd love to stay but gotta run. Official duties." With that, he takes off, leaving the room to attend to his tasks.

She turns to face them and in person her glamour is incandescent. She is surprisingly petite, barely five feet tall, and her mixed heritage is apparent and somehow adds to her mystique; Jes hopes it isn't exoticizing to think so. Her skin is pale violet in tone, and she has brilliant amethyst purple Bezan eyes. Her hair is lustrous bluish-white like Rijala, but it's tipped with iridescent highlights like Bezans – hers are pale green – and wavy like some humans.

"Hello, circus friends," she purrs. "I've heard all about you."

"You're amazing," Esmée blurts out. "I'm a singer too and if I could be half, a quarter, an eighth as captivating as you...!"

Jasmine laughs. "Oh you're too kind. You must perform Mudraessa?"

"Yes... well no... I mean..." She trips on her words. Jes finds it cute how tongue-tied she is in the presence of a star.

Essa steps in for the rescue, "She's trained in Mudraessa, but for our show she's doing hybridized songs. With our multispecies band. It's not pop, but it suits the world we're creating."

"Sounds intriguing."

Jes susses that she's genuine in her interest, not faking it to be polite.

"We open in a week," Essa adds, going in for the sell. "We'd love to have you as our guest of honor."

"I'd be delighted. Tasso's mentioned it, actually, and your opening happens right during our break, so the timing's perfect. I've heard so much about your circus from Tasso and Silas. It sounds like a marvelously fun life." She pauses, looks from Essa to Jes. "Human and Asuna. Human and Rijala. Am I right?"

Jes and Essa look at each other, then back to Jasmine, and nod.

"We hybrids are the future!" Jasmine exclaims. "No offense to the purebreeds in the room."

"None taken," Quint says, holding up all four hands.

"I agree," Bo says.

"We know what you mean," Esmée adds. "My father is a cultural minister and even he says so."

"Well if even an Asuna c.m. can see it..." She pauses, looks at Essa and seems to be debating whether or not to say what she wants to say, "...maybe you'll get to set foot on Opale one day."

Jes susses that Essa is both touched and confused. "Maybe," she manages in response. "I hope so."

"I'm sorry if that comment seemed random," Jasmine says. "I guess it was. I'm particularly interested in the treatment of hybrids throughout the Congress, for obvious reasons. I try to keep overt politics out of the content of my songs, but the way of being I try to model is inherently political. How could it not be, given my mixed heritage? My music has taken off beyond my wildest imaginings, and I'd be incredibly irresponsible to not leverage the platform I have to push our collective culture forward and make things better for everyone."

"It's appreciated," Essa responds.

"I admire you for it," Jes says.

"Well, I must say hello to some other people. Please enjoy yourselves. The mixologist has created some lovely concoctions, particularly the ones with the Bezan and Rijalen flavors. I hate to say that any species is superior to another, but Bez and Rijal do produce the best booze. As far as your show, give Tasso the details and I'll be there."

They all watch her walk off and Jes surprises himself by feeling a bit in awe. He can sense from her such a surety of self, and he could feel during her performance how much her music was a pure expression of that. He wonders how anybody gets to be that way. She must have grown up on Indra or Bez. The Rijal that he knows would not produce a hybrid artist of such confidence and positivity.

"She's so little," Quint says.

"Isn't everyone little to you?" Bo jokes.

Quint and Essa head for the bar, leaving Jes and the others to themselves for the moment. Before they can slip back into discussing the show, someone joins them; Jes can tell from the familiar unctuous vibration who it is before he sees him.

"Well if it isn't Aleia's little circus bunch!" Niko Dax exclaims joyfully. Jes winces at his presence and hopes he's not letting it show on his face. "Did you enjoy the show? Aren't we so lucky to have a star of Mz Jonah's magnitude among us? She's truly something special, wouldn't you agree?"

"Brilliant," Bo says.

"Wonderful," Esmée comments with a glance at Jes.

"It was great," Jes mutters.

"And you lot have your own show coming up! It opens in, what, a week? I'm sure you have much to do between now and then." He looks pointedly at Jes.

"Don't worry," Jes responds. "It'll all get done."

"So glad to hear it." He turns to Esmée. "I thought we were lucky to have a half-Asuna enchanting our audiences, and now a full-blooded Mudraessa singer! I am impressed by Aleia's casting coups I must say."

"I won't be performing Mudraessa," Esmée clarifies. "Per the statutes of the Collective Councils of Opale."

"Nobody will care if you do or don't. Your voice will enthrall. And your shimmer."

There's that hungry, greedy feeling again. It's a desire to own and consume that feels like lust minus sexuality and Jes finds it hypnotic yet repulsive. He fidgets with the hem of his cape.

"Actually, Mz Voulo, I'm pleased to run into you this evening. Your parents are persons of some importance in the Asuna cultural world, correct?"

Esmée is made visibly uncomfortable by this question, but is too polite – and scared – to tell him to fuck off, which Jes susses is how she would like to respond. "My father is a minister to the Collective Councils," she says. "And my mother serves as liaison for the Visual Arts Affairs division. Why do you ask?"

"Oh I make it my business to meet individuals of note from across the 9-Stars. You never know when the opportunity for collaboration might arise." He exudes that lusty vibe even more strongly now, and Jes does his best to withdraw his sussing.

"I'm not sure what kind of business you could have with my parents. I mean, nighttime entertainment venues aren't exactly their specialty."

"Dear child. My business interests extend beyond such establishments for discerning adults. One never knows what commonalities might be discovered, that's why conversation is so important." He smiles his predator smile. "In any case, I would be keen to host them for lunch or cocktails at some point during their stay here. Let them know, would you? They can send word through Jes."

With this, all eyes turn to Jes, who tamps down rising panic as best he can. "Sure," he says after what feels like a very long pause.

"I shall look forward to it. Well, enjoy the rest of your evening," Dax tosses the words over his shoulder as he turns and strides away so smoothly he almost slithers.

"What a creep," Esmée says once he's out of earshot and chatting up a group of Rijala. "But he thinks he's so charming."

"Are you going to tell your parents he wants to meet them?"

She's aghast at the notion. "Pardon my language, but fuck no. My mother already doesn't want me to stay here; if she knew a man like that was in any way connected to the circus…

she'd have a coronary. My career will be over before it starts."

"So you're thinking of a career now, are you?" Bo says, teasing.

"We've got to move soon," Jes says, struggling to keep his nerves calm. "On the assignment from Dax I already have. Like the show isn't enough to worry about."

"Tomorrow," Bo says. "Let's just get it over with."

"I haven't shown you the blocking techniques yet," Esmée frets.

"We'll have to do it on the fly. Learning stuff like that isn't totally alien to me. My grandparents showed me a few things." Jes thinks of the dowsing crystal tucked away in his room. It could help. Maybe.

"Was Niko Dax talking to you all?" Quint asks as he and Essa return with drinks for everyone.

"Just wishing us luck on the show," Bo says.

"I'm sure," Essa comments dryly as she glances around at the others in the room. A polite smile as Moxo Thron steps up next to Jes.

"Circus comrades," he says cheerily. "How lovely to see you. You enjoyed the show, I trust?"

"Oh it was marvelous!" Esmée gushes. "Did you like it?"

"Mz Jonah is an impressive performer, I give her that. Astounding set of pipes on that little thing. The music I don't care for."

"Ever the cultural elite, eh Moxo?" Essa chides.

"Some things will never change. No matter how much our show changes." He casts a sideways glance at Jes. "Speaking of, how's our leading man?" He directs this inquiry to Bo, who looks stricken at the question.

"Fine," he answers. A nervous spike right through the middle of him. He's a well-seasoned performer, but Jes susses that being referred to as the "leading man" upsets his balance.

Moxo Thron smiles inscrutably. "Yes. Well, it will be grand. Of that I have no doubt. I believe in our collective talents. Well, except for you, Jes. Other than convincing Aleia of a concept I suggested before, you're not really doing much, are you?"

Jes opens his mouth to respond but finds no words available. What the fuck, Moxo.

"Jes is a valuable part of the crew," Quint says. Jes susses that Quint is insulted on his behalf, and experiences a flash of gratitude.

"I wouldn't be here without his support," Esmée offers.

"I'm sure." A smirk curls the edges of Moxo's lips.

Jes sips his drink, a purple Bezan rum concoction, but really, he'd rather be on Bo's roof.

"Well I must be on my way," Moxo says after a moment that feels much longer than it actually is. "Big day tomorrow. Good night." With that, he makes his exit.

Essa turns to Jes. "What was that about?"

"He's mad at me because Aleia liked my ideas," Jes explains. "Apparently he had the same ideas a while ago and she shot him down."

Essa rolls her eyes. "He's always been a bit of a diva. Don't take it personally."

"It seems pretty personal." He rubs his temples. Moxo always gives him a headache.

"It'll blow over," Quint says. "We've seen him get himself all twisted up before. He settles down eventually."

"He is right about one thing though," Essa cautions. "We have a big day tomorrow. First full runthrough. We shouldn't stay too late."

Jes, Bo, and Esmée exchange glances in silent agreement. She's right more than she knows.

THE INSTITUTE

"Something different today," Matheson explains. He stands behind an array of holographic displays that receive the readings of the sensors attached to Jes. The researcher's curiosity is at the forefront of the emotional profile Jes susses today. He can almost respect this part of the man – the drive to understand. If only his means were kinder and less invasive. "Perceive the cube in front of you."

Jes stands, once more with the crown of sensors, once more with additional sensors attached to his skin, once more standing in the cold lab nearly naked. He looks down at the silver cube on the table in front of him. An array of sensors all point at it, reflecting it in their shiny surfaces.

"I'd like for you to crush it from within."

"What?" Jes is confused. He's crushed things before – many things – but something different seems to be asked of him now.

"I have a hypothesis," Matheson explains. It's strange that he speaks to Jes more like a partner in a joint venture than as a research subject like he usually does. It throws Jes off. "I want you to create a point of increased gravity inside the cube. Let's see what happens."

Jes understands. He creates a field around the cube, out of habit, then immediately disperses it. What Matheson is asking for now requires a different approach. He hates being so compliant, but rebellion has been shocked out of him. And besides, he's a little curious too.

He imagines the interior of the cube, visualizes where the center of it is, and he generates a field there, inside it. The field isn't visible as it normally would be, but he can feel the buzz of it, and he can suss the gravitons it contains. He increases the gravity, like pulling a line tight rather than loosening it, and the pull gets stronger and stronger. This point of concentrated gravity begins pulling at the cube that surrounds it and suddenly a dimple forms on the cube's surface as pings light up Matheson's display. More dimples, on other sides of the cube, then the whole thing crumbles inward on itself with a loud crunching sound. He releases the field and looks up at the scientist staring at the readings. Matheson smiles but there is no joy behind it, just a greedy sort of pleasure.

He seethes at being held in this place against his will, at jumping through whatever hoops Matheson lays out for him like a trained monkey. But this is a useful trick. He's going to remember this one.

Later, back in his room, there's knocking on the wall. The new kid. He knocks back.

I'm Minu. Jes isn't sure if he's really hearing this. *What's your name?*

"Jes." He never could hear through the walls before. Has something changed?

What did you do in the lab? With the cube?

Jes realizes he's not hearing the voice in his ears – it's in his head. Is Minu telepathic? And how…?

The collar only limits my range but my telepathy still works. He answers the unspoken-but-thought question. *Matheson doesn't know that. Don't tell him, OK?*

"OK." This is the most exciting not terrible thing since he's been in this place. "How did you know about the cube?"

I see it in your mind. I'm sorry. I don't mean to pry. Just being locked in here…

Jes knows what he means even without sussing it. He just knows. Without speaking, he answers Minu's question by replaying in his mind the process of crushing the cube.

Wow. That's cool. Oh, they're here for me.

Minu's voice goes quiet, and he hears, vaguely, his door opening. He wonders what they have in store for his telepathic neighbor. But then, he doesn't really want to know.

CHAPTER THIRTEEN

Jes replays the memory of watching Gregor, the wheel spinning guy, run through his act earlier that day. He's transfixed, everyone is. Gregor spins and rolls, stretches across the diameter of his large metal ring, shaping his body into various poses, sometimes just hanging from it as it spins and spins like a flicked coin on a table. He's manipulating the ring, but he also makes himself part of it, and is clearly very aware of how that merging effects gravity's pull on it. Them. It's a dance with gravity more delicate than Jes's own crude method. Gregor exudes a confidence, a mastery of self and skill that Jes wishes he can call upon now.

He stands at the entrance of the Apogee Pleasure Club with his two best friends and he's terrified.

"We can do this," Esmée says. "You aren't alone here."

She's right, he knows she's right, and yet. Nerves.

"Get your guard up now," she counsels. "Close yourself off."

He closes his eyes and visualizes his auric field withdrawing to the core of his body. He inhales, exhales a psychic sheath that repels the emotional cadences of others.

"Let's find the bar," Bo says, "get the lay of the land." He pulls the door open and a perfumed, velvety darkness embraces them. The curtained-off vestibule they step through spills into a warmly lit foyer that opens onto a lounge, through which a long bar stretches along the back wall. But before all that, there's the hostess stand.

The Rijala Hostess smiles broadly from behind her podium. "Good evening. How may we please you?"

"We were hoping for a drink to get a feel for the place before diving in," Esmée says nonchalantly. "Not many of my people come to Persephone-9, so I'm not sure of all the local protocols."

Esmée wears local party-girl style, a form-hugging dress in a blushing fuchsia shade that accents her skin and shimmer. She knows how rare it is for her species to make an appearance on this moon, and how desired they are, and she makes the most of it, just as she promised when they cobbled together this shambles of a plan. She flaunts her exoticness and speaks with the haughty air of a cultural minister's spoiled daughter, and people believe her.

"Of course," the Hostess says with a sympathetic tilt of her head. "You are a party of three?"

"Yes."

"And the nature of your relationship…?"

"I'm sorry but how is that relevant?" Bo asks, indignance edging his voice.

"Bo." Esmée's voice carries a stern yet patient tone, like a mistress to an impertinent pup. She bites the sound of his name right out of the air. Jes discerns in the circuit of feeling between his friend and the Hostess the way that Esmée anticipates the Hostess' reaction in order to gauge her own reaction to bring about the counter-reaction she wants. It's a fascinating dance he's never witnessed before. Learning on the fly indeed.

"We…" Esmée struggles to formulate the words and passes it off as discretion, "…are a polyamorous triad." She smiles. "I'm the apex."

"I… see," the Hostess responds, her blue lips remain flat and impassive, but her eyes betray curiosity. *You could do better than these two,* they seem to say. "There are a few options for you: we have the general entry which entitles each of you to the common areas – the bar, the lounge, the promenade, and private areas by invitation. There's the private suite with common access, and for an additional fee, hosted by attendants of your choice. We present a range of species, species-hybrids and genders across the spectrum."

"Can we start off with the general entry and upgrade if desired?"

"Yes of course." The Hostess taps symbols in the tablets of colored light before her. "I'll need a name to sort the tab."

"Voulo."

"And your honorific?"

"Mz Voulo is fine."

A press and swipe. "Enjoy your time with us."

Esmée smiles in response, says nothing, then steps past the velvet rope the Hydraxian usher lifts for them to pass.

"Here we go," Bo says as they step into the lounge and make their way through it to the bar.

Every bit of interest, curiosity, desire, dismissal ripples over Jes's empathic sense as they walk through the gauntlet of the focused attention of dozens of individuals from multiple species. There are a couple of large couches along the walls, and circles of armchairs set around circular, glass-topped tables. The clientele are mostly men, but not all, and they look middle-aged or older – Jes is aware that the three of them appear to be the youngest people in the room. Esmée draws most of the attention as they'd hoped she would, while Jes and Bo play her subordinate beta males nobody would really notice. Esmée walks ahead of the boys, who remain a couple of steps behind her.

Jes follows his friends to the bar where Bo orders him a Bezan bitters and soda – the herbs used in the bitters apparently help focus concentration.

"Alright. We're in." Jes breathes heavily and is keenly aware he's failing at nonchalance.

"Who are you talking to?" Esmée asks under her breath.

"Myself mostly."

She laughs as if he'd just made the most humorous remark. "Well stop it," she says through a smile.

Jes observes the surroundings: the lounge they just walked through and the bar where they now sit is all one great room. There's a doorway down by the other side of the bar, not visible from the lounge or lobby but he can see it from where they are. It opens into the deeper recesses of the rest of the club. From somewhere in the dark distance he hears dance music.

"First time here?" the Bezan bartender asks as he sets down their drinks.

"Is it that obvious?" Esmée asks demurely.

"I'd have remembered an Asuna visitor," the bartender replies. He's handsome, tall, with deep indigo skin the color of twilight and yellow highlights in his midnight blue hair. "Especially an Emerald female. Would you like an orientation, or would you rather just explore?"

"Oh an orientation would be marvelous." She shrugs her shoulders and smiles and it's as if her shimmer flickers just a little bit brighter; the pink highlights that swim across her skin flare.

The bartender pulls out a small data tab, taps its clear glass-like surface, and a map of the establishment is projected into the air in front of them. "Here we are now," he explains, and they see the layout of the level they're on. "The main lounge and bar. Through that door–" he points at the doorway at the far end of the bar, "–is the hash lounge and tea-room. There are private rooms off the lounge..." He's about to tap through to the next screen when Esmée touches his hand.

"What's this area here?" She points to a grayed-out area.

"Just storage." The bartender taps through to the upper floor. "We have Epitome, our dance club, and the Seduction, where we feature erotic performers of different species and genders. There are more single rooms and suites, and lastly, our group play den."

He swipes again. "The third floor is our male only playspace. It doesn't open until Blue Hour." Late night. The space is divided into one large room and an area that looks like a maze.

"No female only space?" Esmée asks.

"We used to have one, but we have many more gay male visitors than female. And besides there's a female only club in Sister Moons District."

"I see. Would you mind if we hang onto that?" She gestures at the data tab projecting the map of the facility.

"Sure. Just leave it with the Hostess on your way out." The bartender gives Esmée a wink and walks away to take care of a cranky-looking Hydraxian.

"Where to first?" Bo asks. "And how are you doing so far?" he asks Jes.

"Do I look as bad as I feel?" Jes replies. "It's OK actually. I just have to get settled." The place is full of lust, and even though he'd braced himself for it, the waves of sexual energies that ripple against his aura and his empathic sense make him a little queasy. They're not even in the main part of the club yet, where actual fucking will be taking place. He closes his eyes, inhales, exhales slowly. He can't bring his aura any tighter to him. He's as defended as he'll get. *Keep it together,* he chastises himself. *You're not actually having sex.*

"Let me try something," he says when he opens his eyes again. From his pocket, he pulls the dowsing crystal.

"Is that the one from your grandmother?" Esmée asks, leaning in for a closer look.

"Yup," Bo answers.

"Turn that thing back on." Jes juts his chin toward the data tab in Esmée's hand.

She switches it on, searches for a setting that projects the layouts of all the levels at once and there, above the bar-top, glow the floors of the club, each in its own bright rectangle.

"Show us where to find what we need," Jes whispers. He holds the end of the chain in his fingers, focuses his intuitive sense on the crystal point. It hangs perfectly still as he suspends it in front of the third-floor layout, it continues to hang still at the second floor, and begins a strong back and forth motion at the first. "It says to look down here."

"As good a place as any," Bo says with a shrug.

"I have a feeling."

"Between your intuition and your crystal, that's good enough for me," Esmée says as she slips off her stool. "Shall we?"

"You're the apex," Bo says, smirking.

"We should have planned a cover story ahead of time." Esmée flushes as she offers an explanation, "It was the first thing that came to mind."

"No, it's good," Bo says. "It actually makes more sense than a group of platonic friends going to a sex club together just for kicks."

"I should walk ahead," she says. "We should stay in role. Is that OK with you?" She directs this at Jes.

He nods – the formation will help keep his crystal dowsing a bit more discrete. He touches a button pinned to his shirt that activates the special contacts Niko Dax had instructed him to wear. A small green transmission icon illuminates in the upper right of his vision. They leave the bar and walk into a room redolent with the smells of hash and tea. The room is draped in dark red velvet and booths line the walls; only a few are occupied. Soft music plays, there's quiet conversation in the air, the burble of water pipes, the occasional spark of a lighter. A couple of the tables also have tea pots resting on them, and Jes sees a Bezan sipping from a steaming cup.

A hetero human couple walks by arm in arm and they both gaze lasciviously at Esmée, who is perhaps the most exotic creature they've ever seen. She maintains an aloof air, which Jes notes comes rather easily to her. The couple's desire sets off that queasy feeling again – he can't keep his sussing closed off and open his intuition at the same time. He takes a breath, does what he must and focuses on the swings of the crystal.

have an idea where it is? The words appear at the bottom of Jes's vision, like subtitles, in amber letters. Unfortunately, he can't answer back.

didn't tell you to bring your friends
but dirty looks after JJ make sense now

Damn. He should have thought to keep the other two out of sight. Oh well, too late now. They make their way through the lounge, past a row of doors and into a narrow corridor that opens into a sort of foyer area, around the perimeter of which are the doors to private rooms; some of them are open, inviting. The walls and floor are black but the doors are silver. A shirtless Bezan man stands in one of the open doorways watching the trio make their way through the space with more curiosity than desire. Jes is thankful for the welcome change in vibration, but it doesn't last.

pretty but not what you're there for

Jes wishes he could turn the words off.

The smell in this part of the club is very different from the other areas they've been in: the smell of sex is heavy and thick and the air is much more humid. A woman in one of these rooms is being loudly fucked, and other moans and groans can also be heard, in both male and female voices. The sexual energy here is intense and Jes does his best to shut it out and just focus on the crystal.

a crystal? ok…

They continue through this set of rooms and move through to another. As they walk past a curtained off doorway, the crystal begins swinging vehemently side to side.

"Here," Jes whispers hoarsely.

Esmée turns, pushes the curtain aside and the boys follow her behind it.

interesting

They find themselves in a short vestibule in front of a plain gray door.

"This is the storage area," Esmée informs them, without having to refer to the data tab map. "We'll keep watch while you scope it out."

"You're not coming in with me?"

"We'll be able to better pull off the lovers-who-can't-afford-a-room thing if there's two of us."

Jes nods his understanding. Such a scenario wouldn't have occurred to him so easily and he's impressed by how good Esmée is at this. He goes to the door. It's locked. The handle is sleek and smooth, with no visible locking mechanism, so he won't be able to pick it. Plan gravity it is. He generates a gravity field inside the door, feeling for the lock mechanism. Telekinesis would be much more graceful in this situation, but unfortunately that wasn't the ability he got. It's crude, but he can sense the general shape and mass of objects within his field, like the lock mechanism whose shape he discerns now.

what are you doing? Dax's question glows golden amber at the bottom of his vision and the words themselves are an imposition. He can practically feel Dax's presence through the signal.

He picks a point in the mechanism and increases the gravity just in that one spot and the rest of the lock collapses into it. A cylinder snaps and the lock is busted. He pulls the door open and steps inside.

fascinating

He looks around the storeroom: towards the front are shelves full of clean sheets and cleaning supplies. There are more clean sheets on the opposite wall, and a row of lockers. There's a separate room in the back, walled completely by glass. He heads for it, tries the door. Locked. To the right of the door is a retinal scanner. He prepares to do the gravity trick again when amber letters stop him: *wait.*

The vision in his right eye goes blue, but his left remains normal and the difference makes him dizzy. He covers his left eye with his hand. Better. Amber letters again, at the bottom of the blue screen his right eye has become.

put your eye up to the scanner

He does as instructed, and a strange pattern appears over his eye, webs of blue and silver and purple. The lock clicks. OK. His vision returns to normal.

i keep retinal scans of all my employees, the amber letters explain.

He opens the door and steps into this other chamber which seems to be climate controlled: it's noticeably cooler and less humid. He smells the warm scent of tea and the sweetness of hash. Varieties of tea and reef are arranged in jars lining a shelf, and a large multi-drawered cabinet is labeled with types of hash: Bezan Gold. Indran Double Moon Serpent. Spacetime Surprise. There's a tarp covering a stack of crates against the side wall.

what's that

Jes walks over to the stack, lifts the tarp and reveals wood-paneled crates, on top of which rests a gray metal case stamped with a sigil comprised of three crescent moons.

that bitch i knew it open it

Jes slides the latch and opens the case, revealing sparkling red gems arranged in neat rows – doses of swirl. Just what Dax suspected he would find.

that's all i needed to see
leave everything as you found it
don't want her onto us

Jes cringes at the "us" usage. He doesn't want to be complicit in Dax's plan, but he is, and Dax clearly sees it that way too. He doesn't know Danae at all, but he suspects he'd rather be on her side in this drama. He closes the case, puts the tarp back down the way he found it, and leaves the climate-controlled room, making sure the door clicks behind him. A red light on the retinal scanner console blinks rapidly. He's just about to open the outer door when he hears Esmée cry out, "Oh you caught us!"

OK, that's not good. He glances around the room and doesn't see many options for hiding places. He dashes for the lockers, tries each one frantically until he finds an open one. He squeezes himself into it and pulls the door shut just as whoever discovered Esmée and Bo comes in. He hopes they don't need this one. Through the slats of the locker door he sees a human man in a sleek slate-gray suit walk past. He's only within view for a second but Jes can tell what he's doing when he hears the beep of the door to the climate-controlled chamber. After a moment the man walks past again, carrying the case of the swirl crystals.

After the outer door shuts, he waits a moment, then steps out of the locker.

good thinking

bonus points for evasion

expect a call soon

He touches the button and ends the transmission, breathing a sigh of relief. But why would Dax call again? Jes did the task that was asked of him, shouldn't he be done? A sinking feeling grips his stomach – what if he'll never be done? With his stomach in free fall, he lets slip the filter he's raised against the sex energy filling this place and his next steps waver with the queasiness he can't keep at bay.

His friends are of course no longer in the corridor, and he cautiously pushes the curtain aside before stepping out from behind it. He doesn't see them anywhere. They wouldn't have gone deeper into the club, so he goes back the way they came. In that set of rooms, the second one they'd walked through, all the doors are closed, so of course they wouldn't have hung around in here. Passing through, he hears the slapping sounds of flesh on flesh, mattresses creaking under the pressures put upon them, the grunts of so many people fucking, the loud, breathless calls of "I'm coming! I'm gonna shoot!" in a loud male voice announcing his climax to all within earshot. The animalistic roar and grunts that follow seem to send all the other fuckers into a frenzy and Jes senses a sharp spike in the orgiastic energy: waves and waves of sex wash over him and revulsion shakes him, a wave of nausea. He makes it through that foyer, seeking relief, craving distance from the sex as desperately as sexual beings seek it.

Out in the foyer area of the first set of rooms, he spots his friends talking to the shirtless Bezan they'd walked by earlier. Esmée has an arm draped across Bo's shoulders, and Bo has an arm around her waist. A swell of jealousy rises in him, taking him by surprise. He knows they're just putting on a show, yet...

Bo spots him and his face lights up, "Here he comes!" he exclaims.

Jes walks cautiously over, practicing the breathing pattern Esmée taught him, a sharp inhale followed by a much longer exhale. He tries to pull his auric field in tight but can't seem to get it under control; he's too shaken.

"Here's our third," Esmée says as he joins them. "You alright, darling? Mission accomplished?"

Jes nods, struggles to smile at the Bezan like a normal person being friendly in such a situation.

"So nice to meet you," Esmée purrs. She reaches out her hands, one each to Jes and Bo.

Bo takes one and Jes understands he should take the other. He susses the Bezan's hunger for both of his friends... he doesn't seem to know what to make of Jes and there's no desire toward him, which is just fine. Jes needs to take the hand offered him or risk making a scene or sticking out too much. He takes Esmée's hand quickly and she gives it a light squeeze then leads her boys back out to the tea lounge.

"Are you OK?" Bo asks, concern crinkling his brow.

Jes shakes his head in response. Fucking hell. He wishes he didn't need Bo to help him out of a freakout. Again. Keep it together... keep it together...

A Rijala woman sits in one of the booths wearing a white robe, radiating satisfaction. Jes guesses she's the one whose fuck sounds they'd heard earlier. Her sated feeling is warm, lusty but easeful, and her aura is aglow in a way Jes hasn't witnessed before. He's felt the desire of others for sex, but hasn't really witnessed the afterglow. It's not as repulsive as the yearning to fuck part. There's something calming about it.

"Let's get out of here," he says. "I'm done."

They head through the bar where Esmée gives the bartender a friendly wave, then through the welcome lounge. A human male wearing only short shorts, one of this establishment's esteemed attendants, presumably, takes the hand of an older Rijala man and leads him away, into the promise of carnal pleasures that await upstairs.

"Leaving us already, Mz Voulo?" the Hostess asks.

"We'll be back," Esmée responds brightly.

"Until next time, then."

They step out of the club, past the Hydraxian doorman now on duty. Jes dashes away from his friends, away from the club and into the alley between it and the bar next door where a crowd of human and Bezan women are whooping it up at what looks like a hen party, as one of the humans wears a bridal veil. Jes pukes against the wall, letting all the unease and distastefulness purge itself from his guts.

Why? Why is he like this? Why can't he reciprocate the desire of the sweet Bezan boy tending to him, why can't he walk through a sex club with his friends and not get sick, like a normal person? Why?

"You're going to be OK," Bo whispers. Esmée stands a few paces away, looks on worriedly. "I've got you."

Bo gingerly places a hand on his back and he doesn't recoil, accepts the intended comfort. That's something.

THE INSTITUTE

"I hope you understand just how special you are," the Counsellor says. "All three of you." She's an Indran human – he can tell even with the collar on. Even with his empathic sense closed off, he can feel the press of hers.

They sit in a circle with his neighbor Minu, and a girl named Rosa. He knows there are more than just the three of them in this place – he can hear the cries and the wails and the pleading to be released. But he doesn't know how many there are. These two are the only others he's actually seen. Rosa looks human, but there must be more to her for her to end up in this place.

Matheson certainly thinks so. Minu responds telepathically to Jes's unspoken thought. From the flash of surprise on Rosa's face, he's in her head too. *Yes, I'm linking us,* he adds.

"The Institute wouldn't be keeping us here if we weren't special, so yeah that much is obvious," Jes says.

"Everybody here is using us for their agenda." Rosa doesn't bother hiding her anger. "Nobody has clued me in."

"I just get put through stupid tests." Minu tugs at his collar as he speaks. "And get poked and prodded. Is that how special people get treated? I'd rather be ordinary."

"I don't know why we're here. We're just your lab rats."

"Now, Jes. That's a disempowering position to take," the Counsellor counters.

"What power do we have here?" Jes yells, enraged by the tone of admonishment in her voice. Were they supposed to feel fucking empowered being locked up and collared and tormented?

Fuck this lady.

Rosa giggles, then puts her serious face back on when the Counsellor looks over at her.

"I don't want to be here," Jes continues. "I don't imagine these two do either. Speaking for myself, the ability I have–"

"Paratalent. We call them paratalents here." She holds her datapad loosely in her lap and smiles condescendingly.

"This *paratalent* that I didn't choose to have is just a toy for whoever runs this place. We're here against our will. Don't spin my presenting the actual fucking facts of the matter as 'disempowering'–"

That's some mindfucking crap right there.

"He's right," Rosa chimes in. "Spare us your psychobabble. Why are we here?"

The Counsellor clears her throat as a wounded look flashes across her face. She quickly smooths it over and turns her gaze to each of them in turn, her eyes wide with an attempt to communicate compassion. It feels like another form of torment; it makes a promise that he knows – that they all know – will never be kept.

This lady is so full of shit.

She sucks alright. Rosa's "voice".

"Each of you can manipulate a fundamental force of physics, in addition to your more conventional Emerged talents. That means you have a responsibility."

"What are your forces?" Rosa asks. "I'm electromagnetism. I'd show you but," she gestures to her collar. "You know. I can make lightning."

"Gravity," Jes offers.

"Strong nuclear force," Minu says. "I guess. I can make stuff come together and break apart."

"You each have abilities never manifested before. That makes you very important."

"So important that we have to be tortured?"

The Counsellor sighs. "The experiments yield very important data. Data we can use to understand how these abilities manifest and–"

"So you can make more like us?" Minu interrupts.

She doesn't answer this. "We all have our part to play in this great work. We all have our responsibilities."

Rosa spins around in her chair. "I didn't take on this responsibility willingly."

"I didn't either," Minu adds. He sits back, crossing his arms gruffly.

"I feel pretty dumped on," Jes says.

"There's more at stake here than any one individual's consent!" The Counsellor snaps, the veneer of her fake patience and kindness cracking apart. "You owe it–"

"Owe!?" Rosa exclaims, standing up from her chair. She reaches her hands out, scrunches her fingers up in frustration. "If this collar wasn't on, I'd fry your stupid face."

The Counsellor taps her datapad. "Your belligerence is noted. We'll take care of that."

That doesn't sound good.

"Why bring us together like this?" Jes asks. "Are we supposed to be having a group therapy session or something? None of this seems very therapeutic."

"It was our hope that if you three met each other, it could foster a sense of shared purpose. To know you're not alone in this. To help each other accept your place. It will be easier on you."

It is nice knowing I'm not alone.

Jes and Rosa meet each other's eyes, then glance over at Minu.

"Why can't we train with Emerged Ones?" Jes asks. "Why do we have to be here?"

"The Emerged Ones would be able to guide you with your standard abilities, but not the paratalents you each possess. Now, why don't we drop this acrimony and questions of why?"

Waves of calm wash over him, and he sees from their reactions that the others feel it too. They're coming from the Counsellor, who seems to be projecting this emotional state onto them. He never knew psions could do that. But they're not on Indra. Is the Counsellor a product of this place too? "Rosa, sit back down."

Rosa does as she's commanded.

"I was remiss in letting our conversation get out of control. Why don't we dial it back, get everyone comfortable." She smiles. "Why don't you each take a turn and share a happy memory?"

CHAPTER FOURTEEN

The triplets float inside the gleaming octahedron. It's like two pyramids stuck together base to base, mirror images of each other, one pointing up and one down. This geometry contains the morphing shapes of the triplets' poses, their bodies moving like a single unit, like some kind of sentient liquid in the air. Quint designed and built the thing because the triplets need surfaces to push off from for momentum when they get too far apart to use each other's bodies. They hover and twist inside the space contained by the apparatus of shiny rods, which spins slowly on the end of a cable descending from the fly space. They're in a formation they couldn't do on the floor: the tops of their heads meet together in the center of a triangular formation, each of them pointing away from one another at vertical angles. They hover and rotate in that orientation before using their hands to push themselves apart towards the rods that outline the shape they're in. They each catch a rung, swing themselves around, somersault through the air as they come back together.

Jes stands at the control panel set piece, twiddling the fake knobs while he maintains the gravity field within the boundaries of the apparatus. He loves watching the triplets go through their paces, but can't let himself lose focus on his field generation. It's a trickier balance than he realized it would be at first. He's getting the hang of it, though his mask slipping is a bit of a problem. Essa shared a tape-trick she uses with her costume to make sure no body parts pop out; maybe that will help with this mask situation.

The process of making this act has been very informative for him – he always just made fields to contain whatever it was he wanted to affect, amorphous blobs really. Giving actual shape to his fields is a level of control he's never tried before.

The hanging gem lowers and the triplets dismount, moving through their final dance and tumbling sequence on the stage floor, tempting Bo's character to enter their portal. Bo plays his part well, looking on as the mystical creatures from another dimension cast their thrall, entice him to join them, to escape his world of fear and pain. His character resists, raises high the artifact that Essa's character gave him earlier in the show – a sphere the size of Bo's head that shoots beams of light out of its luminous surface. The fog machine spews its mists as the trio of interdimensional interlopers is vanquished, their gem disappearing into the heavens as they exit upstage through the thick mists, to the soundtrack of Esmée vocalizing over the rumbling, carefully constructed chaos of the band.

The rest of the cast erupts in applause as the set slides back, and Moxo Thron takes his position center stage. He pauses.

"Excellent!" Aleia calls out. "We'll take lunch and pick up with Moxo."

The house lights come up and everyone splinters off into small groups and the tent fills with their chatter. The triplets beam and accept the compliments their castmates throw their way. Zazie makes eye contact with Jes and gives him a wink of acknowledgment.

"How'd you make the illusion?" somebody asks.

"It's a projection," one of them says.

"It's a trick of light," says another.

Jes is fine with receiving no credit, though he's proud of the beauty he's helping to create. The node in his pocket sounds with a single, clear chime and buzzes softly. His mood plummets like the shuttle he crashed, and his stomach knots up as he checks the display.

my office now

With a heavy sigh, he heads for the tent's exit to make his way to the main tower where Dax's office is. Bo approaches with sandwiches in hand, and his smile fades when he sees the look on Jes's face. "What's going on?"

Jes holds up the node. "I've been summoned."

Bo wants to say something, probably urge Jes to assert some autonomy here, but he understands the situation and that there's nothing really to say or do but obey. He gives a nod of resignation. "Be careful."

Quint's supervising the installation of the lighting outside and waves as he walks by. He manages a fake smile and waves back.

"My dear boy!" Niko Dax exclaims when Jes is ushered into his office by the receptionist. An array of holographic displays floats in the air in front of him like segments of a mandala he's piecing together. Dax swipes them away, then removes a data crystal from the socket in his desk and slips it into a case in a drawer. Once the receptionist has left the room and closed the door behind her, he adds, "Tell me exactly what you did to the storage room door."

"I used my ability."

"But not like with the shuttle."

Jes shakes his head. "I created a point of intense gravity inside the lock," he explains, "and made it collapse on itself."

Dax leans back in his chair, the look on his face shows he's impressed. "Clever. And I'm gathering this ability of yours isn't tied to being on your world of origin like others are. No wonder the Institute wants you so badly."

"But they're not getting me, right? That was our deal."

Dax raises his hands, palms out. "I said I wouldn't turn you in and I'll keep my word. But it's a big galaxy out there, Mr Tiqualo. Ruthless and mercenary individuals abound."

"Thanks for the tip."

Dax smiles that cold, unnerving smile. "You don't like me very much."

"I respect you."

A hearty laugh, disconcertingly jolly. Jes senses genuine amusement.

"Good answer. You're learning to play this game."

"I don't want to be a part of any game," Jes says.

"What do you want?"

Jes can tell the crime boss is prepared to dismiss, to laugh at his plebeian concerns. He can sense the derision bubbling up, ready to burst forth. He doesn't care.

"I want to make a life away from my parents and the Institute. I want to be part of something, find a place for myself. Find friends. Find community. Find a way to contribute."

Dax stares him down as if trying to measure his sincerity. "Your friends were certainly contributing, in some way, to the last task I set you to. I don't recall saying you could tell them about our deal, much less have them tag along on an operation."

Jes's heart starts racing. "I–I'm sorry. I didn't mean to… It just–"

Dax raises a hand and Jes falls silent immediately. "I trust you can guess my reaction if they prove to be less than discreet."

"They won't say a word to anybody. I won't say a word to anybody else. I promise."

A cold, unwavering stare. "I need you to do something else for me."

Jes sinks at this, like his own gravity powers have opened up a pit inside him and he's slowly being sucked into it. He should have known the break-in at the Apogee wouldn't be the only request from Niko Dax. "What is it?" he asks, trying not to sound sullen or put out or dismayed.

Dax waves his hand over his desk and a control panel appears on its surface. He touches a button and the shelves at the side of the room slide away and reveal a window, through which a room containing only a table, a chair, and a man can be seen. The man is tall, human, and he's pacing. Jes recognizes him as the man he spied while hiding in the locker at the Apogee.

"That is Hollan Zola, right hand to my deceitful employee, Danae Siqui. Now that I have seen evidence of dear Danae's duplicity with my own eyes, I need to send a message and discover what other plans they have. You're going to help me."

"What kind of message?"

"Let's say… a very *physical* one."

"What? I don't… I…" Jes fumbles for words, he's so taken aback. He hasn't used his ability to cause intentional injury, except for his escape. But that was different. He was running for his freedom, for his life. This man Zola has done nothing to him. Sure he might have injured that guy Jor when he took down that shuttle the other night, but what ultimately happened to him and the others wasn't his doing. "What is it that you want me to do, exactly?"

"Assist with the interrogation. Just follow my lead."

It's clear if he doesn't do as Dax asks, it'll be as if he never escaped at all. Or he'd have to run, again. And of course, Dax isn't asking. "Are we clear here?"

"I'll do what you want." A quaver in his voice he resents instantly.

Dax smiles, and a wave of that possessive feeling envelops Jes so hard that he's afraid he might choke on it. "Don't worry," Dax offers. "It won't be anything you can't handle." He touches an illuminated panel that's appeared in the glass, and a doorway opens up. Jes follows him into the room, feeling every bit like the unwitting henchman he's turned out to be.

"Mr Zola, how lovely it is to see you. Why don't you take a seat?" He gestures at the table and chair.

"I'd rather not," Zola replies. "Restless energy. You understand."

Dax radiates displeasure but says nothing about the refusal to sit. "Do you know why you're here?"

"Because you're a greedy control freak?" the human flunky retorts as he continues to pace the room. There's a bit of nervousness, but mostly Jes susses a feeling of annoyance, of bother. An intuitive ping that this conversation will not go how Hollan Zola thinks it will.

"Oooooh, sass from an underling's underling. That will get you far. Tell me about the swirl, Mr Zola."

"Swirl? I don't know what you mean. There's no swirl operation that I know of…" Increased nervousness. The man isn't totally clueless.

"I have seen the stash at the Apogee. I have been informed by Kreshus Shrop that he has been supplying Danae. Don't bother trying to lie. You're carrying on an unsanctioned operation. I don't like that sort of thing, Mr Zola. In fact, I consider it quite disloyal. Won't you take a seat?"

He doesn't take a seat. "Look, I don't know what arrangement you have with Danae, but I work for her–" He continues pacing as he talks.

"Everyone who works the Triple Moon Syndicate – and all affiliated networks, associations and concerns, including the Luna Lux and Extended Properties, of which the Apogee is one – works for me." He turns to Jes. "Stop him from pacing."

Jes focuses, creates fields around Zola's feet, makes them so heavy he can't lift them. The captive struggles against the floor.

"What the fuck?" Zola says. A little bit of fear creeps into his insouciant attitude.

Finally getting a clue, Jes thinks with satisfaction. Satisfaction? That's concerning. No wait – it's Dax's satisfaction Jes feels, not his own. He really doesn't want to be so attuned to Dax's feelings.

"You see, Mr Zola? You don't even walk unless I wish it. I'll release you if you agree to have a seat at the table."

Sweat beads on the human's forehead, and he sweeps a lock of damp hair off his face. He nods.

Dax snaps his fingers and Jes releases the gravity fields.

"How did you do that?" Zola asks warily as he sits down, placing his hands on the table in front of him.

"It's just gravity," Dax replies smugly. "Tell me who else is in on your operation."

"There's nobody big. It's all happening in-house. Danae got things set up with Kreshus, which you already know–" An understanding dawns on his face. "The crash – did you –?"

"Oh, come now, Mr Zola. You know if I told you about that I'd have to kill you." Dax laughs at the old mobster cliché. "But you were saying?"

"It's all in-house. Danae made the connection, and she's delegated distribution to me. A couple of Apogee staff sell at the club. That's all."

Dax casts a sharp glance at Jes, who susses he wants to know the truth of Zola's statements. He shakes his head.

"Swirl has been popping up all over town. It is definitely not being sold only at the Apogee. Who else is involved?"

"I'm telling you, it's just us." A note of defiance in his voice, but Jes can tell the man's not really feeling it. Just putting on a show.

"Pin his right arm down." The faux cordiality is gone from Dax's voice. He snaps and points at the arm in question with a glare.

Jes raises a hand and with a wave of fingers, has Zola's arm pinned to the table – it's as if a hundred-pound weight holds it down. Zola looks at his arm, then to Dax, then to Jes, then back at his arm. He shifts his weight in the chair and nervousness deepens to fear. The sweat from his brow drips down the sides of his face.

"I'll ask you again. Who else is involved in the swirl operation?" Dax pulls a knife from his pocket – the same one he used to slit Kreshus and Jor's throats. In the light of this room, Jes can see that the handle is made of a copper-colored metal and encrusted with green stones. He recognizes it as a ceremonial piece of Hydraxian origin. He makes a mental note to ask Quint about it. It's silly to turn his thoughts this way, he knows this, but he needs to keep the rising dread at bay. Whose dread is he feeling? The man being interrogated or his own?

"There's nobody." Zola looks straight ahead, makes his voice as steely as he can. "You can ask Danae herself if you don't believe me."

"Oh, she and I will have a conversation, you can rest assured of that." Dax stands opposite the table from Zola and places the blade against the man's palm. He sinks the edge of the blade in and begins tracing the perimeter of the hand while Jes holds it down with his gravity field. Zola winces. Stubborn pride won't let him cry out though he wants to. A ribbon of blood follows the blade's path, a ruby thread that begins dripping in sharp contrast against the skin. "The thing is, though, Mr Zola, I *don't* believe you."

"Please stop," Zola whimpers. "Please don't–"

"Tell me what I want to know." Dax drives the forward edge of the blade in towards the center of the hand, so that there's a loose flap of skin all around the palm. Blood drips onto the table.

"I can't–"

"You can and you will." Dax says these words calm as can be – Jes is struck by the absence of malice in his voice, the absence of anger. Then Dax takes up an edge of the cut skin of Zola's hand and rips off his palm.

The man screams and Jes is nearly bowled over by the sudden terror, the panic. He's grateful he doesn't also suss physical pain. Zola writhes in his seat, his whole body squirming but for the one arm that remains held down by Jes's gravity. He weeps and whimpers and moans.

Dax looks at the swatch of skin he holds in his hand, dripping blood over the sides of his own hand, onto the floor. He gestures with the knife, twisting it absent-mindedly in the air. "I understand your people believe you can read your futures in your palms? An ancient tradition, I'm told? I'm looking at yours now, and I don't see a very bright future for you, Mr Zola." He spreads the skin out on the table. "It doesn't look good at all. Who else is involved in the swirl operation?"

"Mag–Magistrate Romo. Chief Magistrate Romo."

"Romo!" Genuine surprise. "He's getting a bit greedy, it would seem."

"It's part of some other operation," Zola gasps out. "Something about a Loran syndicate... That's all I know... I swear."

Dax looks to Jes once again and Jes confirms the veracity of these words with a nod.

"Who do you work for, Mr Zola?"

"You. I work for you, Mr Dax."

"Jes. Please do your gravity trick on this hand. The one that you did to the door at the club."

Jes understands and is so repulsed he's afraid he may puke. Surely this man has experienced enough damage?

"No, please, no more, I beg you." Zola cries, his voice cracking. "I've told you everything. Oh, it hurts... it..."

Dax slaps Zola across the face. "No passing out. You don't get off that easy." He turns to Jes. "Do it now."

Jes knows just how to do what's asked of him, and he senses the shape of the bones within his field, and he susses Zola's sheer terror.

"Don't be squeamish," Dax presses. "Hollan Zola is not what anyone would call a good man. Do you think all the lovelies that shake their assets for the horny hobgoblins in the Apogee's Seduction lounge are there of their own volition? They're not trafficked, don't look so shocked. But he's got something on many of them much like I have something on you. You won't be hurting someone you'd consider a good person. And besides, with the quality of prosthetics in this day and age, he can get a replacement hand better than the original. If he can afford it. Do what you did to that lock in the door. Crush it.

Crush his hand." Dax exudes the hungry greedy feeling Jes has felt from him before, and also excitement at the prospect of witnessing more pain.

"Please don't hurt me anymore," Zola begs once again.

"Do it or you guarantee your precious circus goes away and the Institute comes knocking."

He's got to. Fuck.

Bringing his awareness to the field he's maintained around Zola's arm this whole time, he focuses his concentration on the center of the bloody palm, hones in on one of the tiny bones that make up a person's hand, and he turns it into a small but mighty gravity well and all the other bones and tendons and ligaments and tissues collapse into it and the hand isn't a hand anymore, but a lumpy ball of flesh, with shards jutting out of it that used to be fingers. Zola screams. He releases the field and Zola clutches the mess of a stump that used to be his hand to him, moaning terribly.

Dax watches him with a smooth and calm face, but Jes susses from him a primordial hunger surging and raging. This display has stoked, rather than soothed it. He turns to Jes, locks eyes with him. "I take it you sussed everything Mr Zola experienced just now?"

Jes nods, fear prickling up his spine, making him want to run. It's his fear for sure – no one else's.

"Never, ever cross me or you'll be using that gravity manipulation of yours on that Bezan lad you've been hanging around with. What's an acrobat with crushed legs? You'll bear witness to similar harm being done to that Asuna girl too. It would be a shame if something were to happen to her lovely voice, wouldn't it? But you do as I ask, and I remain hands off. Do you get me?"

"I do," Jes manages to sputter out. He feels faint, but he cannot pass out in front of Niko Dax.

"You may go. I'll be in touch when I need you again. Please ask my assistant to come in."

"Thank you," Jes says and hates himself for saying it. He doesn't want to bow and sway to Dax's authority and yet, here he is. He walks away as quickly as he can without breaking into a run. His hand shakes as he opens the door.

The receptionist looks up from her desk as he steps out of the office. Does she know what just happened? Her face is calm, friendly even, and he susses nothing from her. "Mr Dax wants to see you," he says, barely keeping the shake out of his voice.

She rises from her seat as he makes his way to the elevator. "Thanks." She eyes him with an expression he can't quite decipher through the haze that's descended upon him. Is it concern? Pity? "Take care."

"Yeah. OK." He keeps calm as the mirrored doors slide shut. Once he's alone and the elevator begins its descent, he breaks down and weeps.

The screams of the man he just tortured, that man's panicked terror, echoes in Jes as he makes his way back to the circus, dazed. He did it to save himself. He did it to help the circus. He had no choice, right? Right? Fuck, who is he even asking?

The sun casts long shadows across the lawn, and they're testing the outside lights on the tents. They look like mirages, mysterious entryways into hidden realms of magic and beauty. But there's pain too. And fear. And blackmail.

A figure in red catches his attention – a Rijala woman whose dress contrasts sharply with her skin and hair. He thinks at first it's Aleia, but she never wears red, and then he realizes it's someone who looks like Aleia, and then he notices the case she's carrying. He's seen that case in her place of business. She heads into the main tent and he knows right away who she is, where she's going, who she's going to see. He picks up his pace as he enters the tent and heads down the corridor to Aleia's office.

He hears Aleia say, "Hello, sister," then the click of her office door shutting. Why did Danae bring the case here? Is Aleia part of whatever she's doing? If she is, and if Dax knows, the circus is done for. And then whose hand would he have to crush? His own? Quint's? The thought of being forced to hurt anybody else makes him dizzy and sends his stomach flipping like the acrobats. He paces the hall near Aleia's office door. He can hear the sisters' voices but can't discern what they're saying.

Moxo Thron strides down the corridor. "Did you and your friends enjoy your excursion to that den of depravity?" He pauses in front of Jes, a single ball in all four hands. He butterflies the reflective silver orb back and forth, back and forth from hand to hand to hand to hand. Jes finds the repetition and the grace soothing and is momentarily distracted from Moxo's question.

"Well?"

"H–How did you know about that?" Goosebumps rise across his skin. A familiar ache begins pulsing at his temples.

Moxo just smiles. Like Dax, it is a smile that is profoundly unfriendly. And why does he always get a headache when they talk?

"Did you... Did you follow us? Are you stalking me?"

Moxo laughs with what Jes susses as genuine mirth. "Don't flatter yourself. You're not that interesting and I'm not a fawning fangirl. I was in the upstairs lounge of the café next door and saw you stumble out and expel the contents of your stomach on the alley wall."

Jes flushes with shame at this. The thought that Moxo witnessed such a low moment hurts.

"It's not what you think."

"As if you'd know what I think."

"Why are you being like this? I thought after that morning at your house, when you cut my hair, that we could be friends."

"Don't pull that 'I want to be your friend' tripe with me. I've encountered your type before. I don't know what your scheme is, but I'll suss you out. Ha! See what I did there?" With that he continues on his way to the main theater, leaving Jes to stand alone with his bewilderment.

A couple of minutes of nervous pacing later, and the office door opens. "Thank you for coming by," Aleia says. "I've got to get back to rehearsal."

"I have my own business," her sister replies. "Private event tonight for some Magist–"

She stops speaking and walking when she sees Jes in the corridor, her expression both haughty and surprised. They're not identical, but the family resemblance is distinct – the same small nose and eye shape, though the sister has pale aquamarine-colored eyes instead of Aleia's more common Rijalen silver.

"This is one of my staffers. Jes, this is my sister Danae." Jes susses that though they're making a show of being cordial, they each harbor deep resentments against the other. And as far as Aleia is concerned, a sharp, bitter annoyance at her sister.

"Pleasure," Danae says with a nod. Curt and frustrated.

"Hi. Nice to meet you." *Sorry about crushing your guy's hand,* he wants to add.

"Well, I'm off." The sisters exchange air-kisses on the cheek. Danae heads out, and Jes can't help but notice she's no longer carrying the case.

"It's time we get back to rehearsal–" Aleia says.

"I've gotta talk to you," Jes blurts out. "In private. It's urgent."

Aleia looks puzzled, but ushers him into her office nevertheless. As soon as the door is shut behind them, words tumble out in a rush, "Niko Dax knows Danae is running her own swirl operation and he's pissed, and he made me spy on her and he made me hurt Hollan Zola and she left that case with you didn't she and you're not involved are you?"

"Wait... What?" Her face is serious, but Jes can tell she hasn't fully grasped the situation. "How do you know about..."

He watches as her face reveals the calculations going on in her head as she pieces together a mosaic of the fragments he just shared.

"Tell me everything." She sits in one of the guest chairs and indicates Jes should take the other.

Jes fills her in on his interactions with Niko Dax, the threat to turn him over to the Institute, and the tasks he's performed. Aleia's face darkens with thunder as she hears him out.

"I appreciate you coming to me with this. Who else knows about your situation with Niko?"

"Bo and Esmée," Jes confesses. "They helped me at the Apogee Club. I don't think I could've done that by myself."

"Make sure nobody else hears about this. Not Essa, not Quint, nobody. Are we clear?"

Jes nods. "He doesn't seem to know you have anything to do with it."

"I *don't* have anything to do with it. At least I didn't until just now when Danae asked me to hold her stash. But that won't matter to him." Aleia says this with the resignation of someone who knows all too well the shitty ways of the world.

"What are you going to do?"

"What I must to save the show and protect what's mine."

"You can count on me."

She smiles a weak smile and her eyes well up. "You are a sweet young man. Thank you. But I don't want you involved any more than you are. If Niko summons you again, tell me, OK?"

Jes nods.

"Well," Aleia says as she stands and straightens her jacket. "I need to get a message to my sister. And we've got a show to get ready."

THE INSTITUTE

"Today's work is very important," Matheson says as they strap him down to a cold table. The table is metal with a sticky and gelatinous coating over its surface. "We're going to test how different sensations affect your ability."

Jes is in his underpants, and covered in sensors, including the cap of sensors on his head. This time they also put a rubbery tube in his mouth, which has a strap that goes around his head to hold it in place. Once he's all strapped in, the table raises so that he's upright, facing an array of cubes and spheres of different sizes.

"Last time you demonstrated that you can generate your localized gravity fields without using your hands to focus and control them. We'll need you to do the same today. Do you understand?"

Jes nods, apprehension causing him to break out in a cold sweat, despite the fact that the room is cold, despite the fact that he's mostly naked. His intuition screams that he must get himself out of this situation, but what can he do? There are stunners aimed at him and they'll only put him right back here and take away his meals and outside privileges if he acts poorly. He's got to do what they say. He's got to.

He's become so obedient. Father would be proud.

"Let's start small," Matheson instructs. Jes susses only

detachment, none of the hungry curiosity he's picked up from the scientist before. "When I give the signal, I want you to float a small cube. The one on the far left." With that, he leaves the room where Jes is, steps into a control booth behind a panel of glass. After a moment, he says through the intercom, *"Go."*

Jes looks at the cube, focuses and emits a field around it. He caresses every edge of it in his field, sussing the shape through his manifested energy. The process has come to be second nature. He brings his attention to the gravitons as usual, and then the cube lifts slowly up off the platform.

A jolt of electricity sears through him, causing his body to seize up. He bites down on the tube in his mouth, a trail of drool escaping. What the fuck is this?

"Keep the cube floating until the shock stops."

After a few seconds, the electricity stops and he drops the cube, hard. He's panting from the pain and effort.

"I want you to hold it longer next time," Matheson orders. He doesn't put on the fake niceness like he usually does, he's just matter-of-fact and oddly calm. *"Float it."*

Jes does as he's instructed, creates another field around the same cube and floats it again.

Another shock, harder this time, that makes him squirm against the table. He releases the field and the cube clatters to the floor.

"We're going to keep going until you can hold it floating for ten seconds. That's not a long time. You've held fields for much longer."

He has begun to cry. Was the man staying detached to better conduct this torment, is that why he susses so differently now? He wants to crush Matheson, crush them all, but then he'll never get out of here. He has to get through this, somehow.

"Float the cube."

Jes does as he's told, floats the cube, just a few inches.

The shock makes him yowl but he holds the field, he holds it, and he keeps the damn cube off the floor.

The shock stops and he drops it; it clatters when it falls.

He pants heavily, his body slick with sweat against the sticky surface of the table.

I'll never torture anyone, he swears to himself in that moment. *Never ever ever ever.*

They go at it until he passes out. He doesn't clearly remember the last few attempts, he doesn't remember them taking him down from the table and bringing him back to his room. He just wakes up in his cot, and the sheets and pillow feel downright luxurious. He hates that he thinks so, that he finds anything of comfort in this place at all.

They really fucked you up this time, huh?

He turns to the wall, places his hand on it, imagining his friend on the other side. "I don't get the point of what they do," he says softly, his voice hoarse, barely a whisper. He knows Minu is getting his response telepathically, but it helps him to say it aloud. He's not sure he knows how to "project" his thoughts the way Minu does.

They're breaking us down. I'll give them what they want.

That sounds ominous. "What do you mean by that?"

Minu says nothing further, and Jes gives in to the darkness behind his eyes once more.

CHAPTER FIFTEEN

My office

Now

The gang is about to go for post-rehearsal crêpes when the message pings. The words on his node leave wavering echoes in his eyes as Jes takes in his surroundings: the walkway outside the front entrance of the Luna Lux, his companions – Bo first among them. "I–I'll meet you there," Jes says, knowing it's a promise he'll break.

"Why? What's up?" Bo's face registers the answer to these questions before he's finished speaking them. "It's him." He spits the words out like he's referring to a rival lover. "You don't have to go whenever he beckons."

"I kind of do. That's the whole crux of our deal." Jes susses Bo's concern, Beni's distracted horniness, and the triplets' collective impatience all at once.

Bo sighs. "Find me later?"

He watches them head towards the glowing frame of the front gate. For a moment this group is someone else's friends, a group he wishes he were a part of. It's a perfectly framed shot in a vid for a cloying song about always being there for each other. And he's so jealous of the person whose friends these are – he wants to be the person that makes such friends. "You got it," he says aloud, even though they've moved out of earshot.

They're *his* friends. The notion sinks in: these people *are* his friends. It feels like the truth. He should tell Aleia about this summons as she'd asked, but he intuits that he shouldn't keep Dax waiting. He'll tell her later.

The office is quiet when Jes exits the private elevator to Dax's office. He doesn't see anyone when he first walks in, but hears voices coming from the side room. The interrogation room. He approaches the entrance framed by the slide-away shelves, and nobody really pays attention to his arrival.

In the room, he susses a scene of barely controlled panic under a surface of false calm. Dax supervises two of his security detail, who stand beside a body sprawled in the chair. His receptionist stands to the side, her face pale. Most of the panic emanates from her. The security personnel are even agitated which surprises him – he'd think they'd be used to such sights.

"Ah, you're here," Dax says when he sees Jes. "Come close, don't be shy."

Warily, Jes approaches the group. The body is that of a human in a Magistrate's uniform, his face astonished and pained. One eye stares out lifelessly, while a bloody absence screams from where the other eye should be. Jes's whole body goes leaden, his legs so heavy he's not sure he could run away if he tried. Though he wants to flee, he's glued to where he stands. He can't look away from the body, from the stiff and terrible face, even though he's repulsed.

"Meet Chief Magistrate Romo," Dax says cheerily. "He unfortunately succumbed to the pressures of questioning."

The name sounds familiar, and it takes Jes a second to place it – it's the name Hollan Zola gave up under duress.

"We need to dispose of the body. I was wondering if you could do that crushing thing you do? You know, what you did with Mr Zola's hand? Reduce the mass?"

Jes susses an intense curiosity from Dax, a fascination

that chills him. And anticipation, and a sense of entitlement.

"I–I think so."

"Do it then."

Revulsion fills Jes as he contemplates crushing the bones and tendons and flesh before him. He reminds himself the man is dead. He won't feel a thing. He looks around at the others present – the security, the receptionist.

"My staff will maintain the utmost discretion," Dax says. If Jes didn't know better, he'd think the boss was a mind reader.

He takes a breath, and upon exhaling generates a field around the body. He isolates a vertebra in the lower back, roughly the center of mass. The gravity he imbues it with does its work and the body begins drawing in towards the spot. Crunching, wet, squishing sounds fill the room and the receptionist blanches even more and runs out, her hands over her mouth as she heaves. Astonishment tinged by fear are what he mostly susses from the security guards, and from Dax he gets what he can only call glee.

Disgust fills him at first, but shifts to a strange detachment once the body no longer looks like a person. When the mass on the chair is about the size of a medium-sized, flesh-and-blood cake, he stops. "Is that enough?"

Dax nods, pleased. "Yes, that will do." He turns to the receptionist who has returned, wiping her mouth. She looks to be on the verge of tears. "Please fetch a container that can accommodate that." He points to the mound of stuff that used to be a person.

Jes thinks of his friends around a table at the Bezan restaurant with the amazing crêpes. He wishes he were there. He should be there. He's supposed to be there, with Bo and the others. How long will he be bound in this servitude?

"I have another task for you," Dax says.

Fuck, what now?

Dax pulls his node out of his pocket. "I need you to break into Chief Magistrate Romo's office and obtain something for me. It won't be a physical item, however. On the desk there's a port holding a data crystal set. You'll find this one," he taps his node and the image of a scarlet red sphere is projected in the air between them. "Navigate to a file called 'syntax'. You're going to find images related to a medallion. You're looking for a sigil, or logo – some kind of graphic mark related to 'syntax'. Snap it with your node and send it to me. You need to put the crystal back and leave everything as you found it. That last part is very important. Do you understand?"

"Desk, find an image of a medallion on the red sphere, leave no trace. I think that about covers it. But why go through all this? You must know somebody who can hack."

"Romo uses a scrying cage that's not networked. He was a bit zealous about protecting his information. With good reason, I suppose. In any case, his paranoia offers you another opportunity to use your gifts." Dax taps his node and Jes feels his own node ping. "I've just sent you a schematic of the Magistrates' Central Bureau, indicating the location of Romo's office."

"What happens if I don't find this thing? What happens if I get caught?"

Dax flattens his expression, unimpressed and impatient. "The terms of our agreement hold true. Do as I ask, and I keep your secret, you and yours remain safe and whole. Fail, and you'll be on a one-way trip back to the Institute. I imagine you wouldn't enjoy that very much. Nor would your friends enjoy the bodily harm that would befall them. If you are caught, my contacts among the Magistrates will see to it your throat is slit before you're interrogated and have a chance to tell tales. So find it, and don't get caught. OK?"

Dax nods at one of the guards, who steps forward holding an item in each hand, which he then hands to Jes. One of them is a lock kit. The other is a glass tube containing a severed eyeball, bloody tissue intact, optical nerve and all. Jes is afraid he might vomit.

"The scrying cage requires an optical scan," Dax explains.

Jes slides these items into his other pocket, trying not to think about the eye.

The receptionist returns with a waste bin. "This is the best I could do," she says, her voice shaking. Jes susses that she's summoning as much steely competence as she can, but she's barely holding it together. Poor thing.

One of the guards steps forward and takes the bin from her, then sets it at the base of the chair. He slides Romo's remains into it, where it lands with a loud thunk.

"Can you close that up?" Dax asks.

Again, Jes complies, crushing the top part of the bin down so that it encloses its contents.

"Bury that," Dax orders his men.

One of the guards attempts to pick up the container, then gestures to his companion that he needs assistance. Though the body has been reduced to a smaller size, it still weighs as much as a human. The two carry it out together.

"You can go," Dax dismisses the receptionist. "Feel free to take the morning off," he says.

She gives an awkward bow and dashes away as fast as she can.

"You should get moving also. I need you to get me what I need before anyone realizes something has happened to Romo."

Jes sighs, resigned to the task before him. Without another word, he takes his leave. In the elevator, he pulls out his node and has a look at the building schematics during the descent to the lobby. Romo's office is located at the back of the building, on a corner of the third floor. He can float himself up there, using the walls of the building as leverage, of course. This seems pretty straightforward.

The doors slide open and Bo's there, waiting.

"Wha... What are you doing here?"

Bo shrugs. "I thought you'd need some support. It never

seems to be anything good when you meet with him." He holds out a paper bag bearing the logo of the Bezan restaurant. "Want a crêpe?"

Jes is touched by the gesture, but he flashes on the mound of flesh he made of Romo's body, the look on the dead man's face, the eyeball in his pocket. "I'm not really hungry."

Bo accepts this. "OK. Do you want to come over for some barat and reef?"

He wishes so much to say yes. "I've got something I need to do." He heads for the exit and Bo falls in step beside him.

"Can I help? What is it?"

Jes looks around to make sure nobody's in earshot, then confides, "I have to break into a Magistrate's office and find a file."

"Ah." Bo pauses. "Need a lookout?"

His first reaction is that he wants to keep Bo far away from this Dax business, but he honestly would like to not do this alone, and Bo's already helped once with a Dax task. Plus, he feels a gentle tug of intuition to go ahead and accept this offer of company. "OK."

The two hop in a roto waiting at the stand in front of the Luna Lux, and direct the navbox to the Magistrates Central Bureau.

"So, what's the plan?" Bo asks.

Jes pulls out his node, projects the schematic of the building and indicates the window he has to access. "I float myself up to that window," he says. "Then once I get in, I need to find this crystal," he swipes over to the crystal, "and find a file. A design of some kind."

"Huh," Bo says. "Don't you need leverage to raise yourself up once you make yourself weightless?"

Jes is touched and surprised that Bo remembers this detail of how his gravity works. "Yeah. I'll just push off the wall."

"The Magistrates' building is treated with this anti-friction coating," Bo explains. "It's a security measure. It's impossible to climb up or rappel down the building because you can't get footing on the walls. Nothing sticks."

Jes sits back in the seat, brings his hands up to his face. He does not need this. He feels a panic attack rising, brings his attention to his breath in an effort to keep it at bay. "How do you know this?"

"Beni needed some extra scratch one time and took an odd job on the crew that applied the coating. He told me about it."

"What the fuck am I supposed to do then?" He's on the verge of tears and his voice cracks.

"Hey," Bo says, taking his hand, "hey. Don't freak. We can figure out…" His face lights up and Jes susses the unmistakable surge of revelation. "I have an idea." He lets go of Jes's hand, pulls out his node and taps out a message. He looks up at Jes after sending it. "Don't worry. We got this."

Something about Bo's confidence calms Jes down. "What's happening?"

"You'll see. Show me the building again?"

Jes projects the schematics from his node once more. Bo nods, the glow of the projection lighting up his face. "Yeah this will work. Hey, did you see that there are security cameras?" he points out the locations of the cameras, indicated by red circles on the plans.

"I can take care of those," Jes says. They ride in anticipatory silence, and after a few minutes, arrive at the back of the drab, gray building.

The roto spirals open and in short order, Jes crushes the two security cams. "Somebody's going to notice those are out before too long," he says as he climbs out of the roto. "What's your plan?"

"Arriving now."

Just then, another roto rolls up beside theirs, and Beni and the triplets come pouring out.

"What… What are you guys doing here?" Jes asks, unable to contain his surprise.

"Bo tells us you need a ladder," Beni says.

"We do this in the show," Zazie adds.

"It's easy," Lula chirps.

"One humanoid ladder coming up," Jujubee adds. "Where are we doing this?"

"Don't you want to know what we're doing here?" Jes asks.

"It doesn't matter," Beni says. "You're our friend and you need our help."

Bo points to the third-floor corner window. "He needs to get up there."

Without another word, Beni takes his position beneath the window, then Bo hops up on his shoulders, then Beni gives the first of the triplets a lift with his hands and she flips up to Bo's shoulder, then the next triplet, then the next. In seconds the five acrobats form a ladder, reaching to just below the target window.

Jes looks at the tower his friends have made for him and can't help but tear up with the swell of affection he feels for these people. He says to Beni, "OK. I'm about to do something you might find... unusual."

"Your gravity trick," Beni replies nonchalantly. Registering Jes's surprise, he adds, "I live with these people. I pay attention. Now do your thing."

A deep breath as he flexes his fingers. His blue field winks on, surrounding him, and he loosens the flow of gravitons, easing the coherence of their waves until they release their hold and he begins floating.

"So cool," Beni says, watching with awe.

Jes smiles at this, then, placing his hands on the shoulders of his friend, he pushes himself up. "Thank you," he says to Bo when he's face to face with him.

"I got you," Bo replies. "We all do."

Jes continues his climb, up, up, up. At the top, he settles on Zazie's slender shoulders, keeping himself weightless so he's not weighing down on her and the rest of them. Besides, he's not sure he could stay upright this high with gravity pulling at him. The window is locked with a standard magnetic latch. A neutralization pip would do nicely, so he searches the lock kit and plucks one out. He attaches it to the window frame. Three taps on the top surface of the pip, and the window clicks open. The gang back in Nooafar Prefecture would have loved to have a kit like this. He smiles at the memory of the janky, haphazard collection of tools they used and misses them for a second. Weird feeling. Back to the task at hand.

He's in through the window and drops to the floor after releasing his field. He sticks his head out, looks down at his friends. Zazie turns her face up towards him. "Thank you!" he says. "Now get out of here. Leave a roto behind."

"Good luck," Zazie says before she begins her dismount.

He doesn't watch them, but he's seen the way their bodies unfold down each other as they disassemble the ladder so many times in rehearsal that he can imagine it down to every last gesture. He makes his way to the desk.

He doesn't see any crystals though the scrying device is right there. Sliding his fingers over the surface, he feels for seams. A panel. But how to open it?

His intuition pings him with a hunch, and he pulls out the pip he used on the window. He activates it again and slides it around the perimeter of the panel. A click, then the panel slides open and a small shelf rises. It contains a set of crystals: an amber cylinder, a green pyramid, a blue diamond, a red sphere. He grabs the sphere, but the cage enclosing the scanning bed is locked. Right. The retinal lock.

He pulls the glass tube from his pocket and dread and disgust fill him as he looks at the eye. He feels implicated by its unwavering gaze, as if he himself were the one who plucked it from its rightful place. Queasiness threatens to overwhelm him, so he turns his attention back to the task at hand. He tries to position it so that the retina can be scanned through the tube. The machine's error beep is the only result he gets from this approach, and he reluctantly accepts he has to touch the thing. Bracing himself, he opens the tube and slides the severed eye into his palm – the optical nerve and tissue is wet and slimy, but the eye itself is surprisingly dry. He holds it up to the scanner which recognizes the retinal pattern, and the device wakes up, its screen flaring brightly. He puts the eye away, shoves the tube back in his pocket, then places the red sphere on the unlocked and illuminated scanning bed.

A file tree appears on the screen and Jes scrolls through the branches looking for "syntax". Syntax, syntax – no syntax. He scrolls through every path and option and there's no syntax. The interface labels are in Mudra-nul, but he recognizes the symbol for the find function, a diamond shape with a wavy line across its center.

Jes enters the commonscript file name. Nothing.

A tingle of intuition itches his fingers. Not "syntax" but "sin tax". A file pops up. Opening the tree, he scans the file names, spots one called *Collateral*. He taps it and there it is: *medallion*. A circular design appears on the screen: a winged serpent swallowing its own tail. He takes a snap with his node and pings it to Dax.

After placing the sphere back in its place on the shelf, he presses the panel back down into the desk. He shuts down the scrying device when he hears guards outside the door.

Fuck!

No time to make a run for it, he ducks down, scrunches himself as small as possible. His heartrate spikes as he holds his breath. The office door slides open and the guards chat as they enter.

"I heard Romo keeps a well-stocked bar in here. His own private stash, even."

"Well I heard he's a twitch-fiend. That's how he works so much."

"The head of narcotics – a twitch-head." Scoffing. "I bet he's on Niko Dax's payroll."

"Wouldn't surprise me. Where do you think he keeps it? His desk maybe?" Footsteps sound towards the desk.

No no no! Jes panics about what he can do here. Maybe he can use his ability to hold them while he floats himself back down? He's never split his focus like that – could he do it? The footsteps draw closer, just a few more steps and he'll be discovered. He reaches out with his gravity sense and creates a field around one of the approaching guards' feet. He increases the gravity by just a bit, causing the guard to stumble and knock something off the desk as he catches himself.

"Quit messing around," the other guard says. "Don't break anything. We have more checks. Plus, you think the chief won't notice somebody dipping into his stash?"

"You think the chief narcotics officer is going to issue a memo about somebody stealing his illegal drugs out of his office?" Jes susses the man is barely containing his laughter at the thought, and also mocking feelings toward his partner.

"Let's get back to it, stop being a dick."

"Fine."

The door slides shut and Jes releases his breath. He makes his way back to the window and contemplates how he's going to do this. He decides to face toward the building and gets himself floating before pushing himself out the window. The office door slides open again–

"I forgot to check... Hey!" The guard shines a light in Jes's face and Jes panics, losing focus on his field, and plummets to the ground three stories below.

"HEY!" he hears above as the ground rushes at him. He tenses every muscle in his body so tight that he almost spasms from it. He gets his field back just in time and is suspended mere inches from the street, his heart pounding loud and fast. There's a pulse of weapons fire and instinctively, he projects a field of heavy gravity, which diverts the bolt to the street in front of him.

Jes drops himself the rest of the way before the guard can

get off another shot. He makes the weapon so heavy that the guard's arm is pulled down and smacks against the wall beneath the window. The guard finally drops it, and it falls, cratering the street below with the force of extra gravity.

Jes dashes toward the waiting roto, beside which Bo is waving frantically. Jes has never been so happy to not be listened to.

"Behind you!" Bo points wildly towards the space above Jes' head. Jes spins around, sees the security drones zooming down from wherever they'd been stalking, alarm lights spinning bright white beams around the alley. Jes creates fields around them and they smash to the pavement with a sharp tug of gravity. He overdoes it somewhat and they don't merely crash to the street, but flatten thin as paper with the pressure he exerts, releasing sparks and smoke.

He throws himself into the roto where Bo already sits, and catches him in a tight embrace. The roto heads off down the alley, and his heart pounding in his ears is even louder than the whir of the engine. His sweat-damp shirt sticks to him. He pushes himself up from Bo, who catches his fingertips for a quick hold. Their eyes lock. "You sure know how to make your own fun," Bo says with a chuckle.

The node in Jes' pocket pings. "Sorry. I have to–"

Bo nods with understanding.

Well done

Jes messages back: *What do I do with the eye?*

Dispose of it

Bo waits for the node to be put away before he asks, "How many more jobs are you going to have to do for him?"

"Until the Institute calls off their bounty? Until he stops threatening to pull the plug on the circus or do my friends bodily harm?"

"There's got to be a way to get him off your back. To get them all off your back."

"Let me know when you figure it out," Jes says with more bitterness than he intends. "I got nothing."

"Hey – hey–" Bo grabs both his hands, kisses their backs one at a time. "You're not going through any of this alone, okay? Did the ladder show you nothing?"

Jes squeezes Bo's hands as his vision blurs with tears. "Thank you. I don't really know how to–"

"–have friends and accept support?"

Jes wipes his eyes, laughing. "Yeah. It's a new experience."

"Get used to it."

They hold hands and sit in silence the rest of the ride.

"Big day tomorrow," Jes says as they pull up in front of Essa's place.

Bo takes a deep inhale and exhale before saying, "I'm trying not to think about it. I gotta be in the present moment or I'll freak out." He leans in and gives Jes a lingering kiss on the cheek before saying goodnight.

After watching the roto roll away and disappear around the bend down the street, Jes sets aside the warm feelings Bo brought out in him, and turns his mind back to the business at hand. He pulls out the tube containing the eye, and generates a gravity field to crush it down into a sphere the size of a small bead. He drops it in a storm drain in the street. And so goes the last bit of Chief Magistrate Romo. The ease with which he performs this task takes him aback. What is he becoming?

When he walks into the apartment, he sees that the Voulos are over. He immediately susses tension, frustration, a sense of woundedness. Enovo and Quint sit on opposite ends of the couch, watching the women who stand around in states of aggravation. It's not quite an emotional minefield, but it's pretty close.

"Hi everybody," he offers, his tone somewhere between jovial and cautious. Should he go and hide in his room or stay and witness? He slides onto the couch closer to Quint. "What's happening?" he hoarse whispers.

"What's happening, dear boy, is that my family abandons

me at every turn." Eronda clutches her hands. It's clear she's the source of the hurt feelings.

"Please, Eronda," Enovo says wearily. This is clearly well-trodden ground. "There's no abandonment. I must appear at the Council meeting via holo-link for the conference. You've known about this since before we left home to come here."

"And Essa and I have to prepare for the show," Esmée adds. "It's opening night."

"Well, if *your* precious show and *your* precious conference are more important..."

Oh. She's being like that.

"You're perfectly capable of attending the function yourself," Esmée says, her exasperation radiating from her like pulses of headache pain.

"I am Eronda Solarey Voulo of the House of Emerald Flame. It would be most untoward–"

"–for you to attend a cultural event unaccompanied by escort," Esmée finishes her mother's tired refrain. "How many times must we say it? Nobody on this moon cares about homeworld protocols."

Jes susses it – the bright, gleaming truth of it that shines from Eronda like a beacon – she's afraid. He's surprised the others haven't picked up on it, but Asuna empathy is different, of course, and Essa's sussing isn't that fine-tuned.

"She's afraid," Jes says. "I can suss it clear as day." He faces Eronda, who's staring at him with an expression of shocked surprise. "What are you afraid of?"

"Is this true?" Enovo says, rising to his feet. "You're afraid of something?"

"Mother?" Esmée's face shifts from frustration to concern.

Eronda sighs. "I've never had to go somewhere without accompaniment before. And Port Ruby can be a seedy place..."

Essa laughs.

"It isn't funny," Eronda says in an attempt to reprimand, which doesn't work at all.

"All this drama over protocol not being observed," Essa says, her words punctuated by giggles, "when this whole time you're just afraid to go someplace in Port Ruby alone?"

"Well I never go anywhere alone!" Eronda exclaims. "I'm always accompanied by Enovo, or Esmée or an attendant. To expect me to suddenly go somewhere unaccompanied, much less in a rough and unknown city... it's a push too far! I'm not as resilient in the face of new experience as you lot seem to be."

"So that's the issue?" Jes asks by way of clarification. "You don't want to go somewhere alone?"

"Yes, that's the issue!" Eronda barks, annoyed her secret fear has been revealed to the room.

"It's just an opening and a reception," Esmée says.

"The museum is in a really nice part of town," Quint offers helpfully. Essa casts him a loving glance and a smile.

"I'm sure a roto can take you right there," Enovo says.

"I am Asuna of noble class. What if someone wants to kidnap me for ransom? Asuna are highly desired as sexual playthings – what if I'm sex-trafficked?"

"Oh, Eronda," her husband says.

Jes resists the urge at first, but intuition pushes him to it: "I'll go with you."

Everyone turns to look at him and he susses them all in overlapping pings: Enovo is relieved, Quint proud, Esmée and Essa surprised, Eronda confused.

"What?" she asks.

"I'll accompany you to this thing at the museum. I like art, I used to hang out with artists. Of a sort. I've never been to that part of town. It'll be a nice outing. What do you say?"

After a moment Eronda nods. "That would be acceptable."

"So, is this ordeal finally over?" Enovo rubs his eyes as he speaks. "Can we go back to our suite now? I need my rest."

The family says their goodbyes, gathers their cloaks and head out. "Thank you," Eronda offers to Jes on their way out the door. "I'll send a transport for you in the morning."

When they're gone, Essa turns to him. "That's so kind of you. You know you don't have to do that?"

"I really don't mind," Jes replies. "It'll give us a chance to talk."

"You say that like it's a good thing," Quint quips. Essa gives him a playful slap on the arm.

"Where've you been tonight?" she asks Jes. "What've you been up to?"

"It's probably better if you don't know." It's all Jes can muster by way of explanation. He excuses himself and makes his way to his room, where he immediately plops down on his bed and stares at the ceiling. He stares for a good long while, before he finally falls asleep.

CHAPTER SIXTEEN

The roto arrives mid-morning, alerts the apartment's caller display. "See you at opening night!" Quint calls. He and Essa have their morning tea in their bathrobes on the sofa, scrolling through newsfeeds.

"Have fun with Auntie," Essa offers, but when he susses her it's clear what she means: *better you than me.* Maybe he's projecting.

Esmée greets him with a peck on each cheek when he arrives at the curb where the transport awaits.

"What are you doing here?"

"Eronda didn't want to come here by herself," she explains. "I'm having breakfast with Essa and Quint and we'll head to the show together. Have fun." Is she smiling or smirking?

What, exactly, has he gotten himself into?

"Good morning, Jes," Eronda says as he clambers into the vehicle.

He flashes a smile as he settles in and soon they're rolling away. The silence is awkward.

"So, what's this event we're going to?"

"Are you familiar with the term 'asunasol'?" Eronda asks. He susses that she expects his ignorance.

"It refers to Asuna who have rejected the caste system, and live apart from Asuna society, outside the Crystal Imperium."

A wave of satisfaction when he susses her surprise. "Essa explained it to me."

"Of course. She would know. Well, there is an exhibition and reception for a well-regarded asunasol artist named Padroma Soren. I've quietly sponsored their work for some time, and it's a rare opportunity to meet the artist and see the work in person."

He can't help but be surprised at this. "You sponsor an asunasol artist?"

"I know what you're thinking. Why am I so opposed to Esmée pursuing this singing path away from Opale, away from the Imperium, when I sponsor someone else? All I can say is, it's different when it's kin." She looks at him and her expression is placid and cool though he susses pity. "I don't suppose you would know about that, being estranged from your family."

"My family never had much use for me," he says. *Except for the fee they were paid,* he wants to add, but he doesn't care to share that much about his story with her. He knows Esmée would have kept his confidence about the Institute and all that.

"As I understand it, asunasol aren't permitted contact with the homeworld. How is it that you can sponsor this person?"

"There's a network. Unsanctioned, unpromoted, but those in the know, know. We recognize that there are Asuna with gifts that cannot find full-flower within the caste system, and those of extraordinary talent we help."

"So you'd have to be talented to get any help."

"We can't help everyone. And besides, it's generally those with a passion and talent for something outside their caste that become asunasol in the first place."

"Or those who find love with another species." He's thinking of Eminy, her sister and Essa's mother, and she knows it. She keeps silent.

Jes bristles at the elitism and restrictions of Asuna society but says nothing. He knows that there's much about them he doesn't understand. And who is he, a mongrel from a world far from hers, to complain about that? As if his complaint would change anything.

"So this artist who's worthy of support, what caste are they? What are they supposed to be?"

"Padroma is Amethyst, who are engineers, architects, industrial designers. They make things. They build bridges, spires, domes. This park is lovely."

Jes takes the hint and doesn't ask more, and looks out to see where they are. The avenue they roll down is lined with flowering trees, their boughs bright with golden flowers. The hue of the blossoms is so intense they seem to be illuminated from within. Past the trees, paved paths wind through a manicured garden, and curved white buildings rise in soft mounds, laden with lush terraces topped with all kinds of plants. A fountain burbles in the distance.

"Such a different style of building here," Eronda says quietly.

"This looks like Indran architecture," Jes comments. "The curved white buildings. The vertical gardens."

She looks at him with surprise on her face. She really doesn't think he knows much at all. Jes isn't insulted though, he's used to being underestimated.

They arrive at the museum and step out of the roto. "The air even smells different out here," he says.

"I'll take your word for it." Though her tone is dismissive, Jes spies her taking a surreptitious sniff.

They stand in front of a metallic structure, grand in form and gesture, an explosion of curves. There's an arc at the top, the only feature that's pale yellow gold. The skin of the building is deep violet-blue in color, and metallic with a matte finish. Veins of light run across the surface, cycling through a rainbow of hues. The entrance is flanked by large banners bearing the artist's name and the title of the exhibition: *Loharzamira*.

"I know that 'zaiharza' means soulstone and 'zaimira' refers to the vaults where the stones are stored. 'House of Souls', right?" Jes looks to Eronda for confirmation and she offers a slight nod. Once again, he susses her surprise at his knowledge of Asuna culture. "Do 'harza' and 'mira' have the same meanings in this context? What does the 'lo' indicate?"

"Lost," Eronda replies. "The title translates as 'House of Lost Souls'. Come."

They enter an atrium to see groups of people standing and staring up at the structure that dominates it: a dome made of what appears to be thousands of bits of colored glass suspended from the ceiling. There's a border of cobalt blue containing a circle of pale yellows, orange and pink, and star-shapes made of gray and colorless glass jut out from the surface, like embossing. They stand under it, staring up at the way the light from the top of the atrium filters through.

Jes likes the colors, and appreciates the craftsmanship, and the wow factor of such a large and vibrant structure being made from bits of glass hanging on the ends of strings. He susses Eronda, and her experience is clearly different – there is wonder, and recognition, and grief.

"It's beautiful," he offers. "Is it a zaimira? Or a rendition of one?"

"Yes." Her voice is soft, the usual haughtiness shed from it. "The dome here is comprised of the colors of the Keepers of the Flame, the Asuna Consciousness Holders. The stars are zaiharza, the hearts of the dead. These are colorless, which I take to represent the asunasol, the banished, the lost ones."

They stand and contemplate the piece some more, then a wordless agreement passes between them, and they head into the main gallery. The exhibition consists mostly of shadow sculptures made from piles of detritus: broken glass, bits of wood, crumpled pieces of paper, mechanical parts, disassembled nodes, and other technological devices. A pinlight is focused on each pile, and on the wall behind them, the shadows they cast are silhouettes of recognizably Asuna figures. Some are just a profile, some are full figures in traditional robes. The spirit of the people lives, even in bits of cast-off trash. Because these silhouettes are made of shadow, there is no coloration, which means that the colors of the crystal halos that determine caste are erased. Rendered the same.

Eronda takes her time contemplating each one, and Jes keeps pace with her, staying at her side like a good companion. He wants to explore more quickly, check out other exhibits and rooms in the museum, but he's here for Eronda now and he can always come back. Maybe this would be a nice thing to do with Bo.

After making their way around the whole gallery, they enter a smaller room which features just one piece at its center: a hologram of an Asuna figure dressed in a traditional robe, but the robe cycles through the fabrics and patterns of cultures from throughout the 9-Star Congress. While the figure remains Asuna, its skin morphs color from the deep tan common to humans, to the violet tones of the Bezan, and the pale blue of Rijala. When the figure takes on the russet copper tones of Hydraxians it also sprouts two additional arms. At one point its skin becomes a dazzling rainbow prism, and the figure's eyes grow bulbous, and two antennae sprout from the top of its head, the robe taking on the surface texture of soft shell.

Off of this gallery is a space cordoned with gold velvet ropes. Jes chuckles at this – the markers of VIP status are the same, whatever the venue, whatever the species. Eronda produces a pass she slips out from the folds of her robes, flashes it to the Rijala attendant, who waves them through, casting a curious glance at Jes. He susses her curiosity and doesn't need full telepathy to know what she's wondering: why is this hybrid trash accompanying a high-born Asuna?

The artist holds court, chatting with a group of humans. The artist is dressed in the style of Indran humans, loose flowing slacks, a silk tunic and vibrantly colored shawl. Their halo is a shade of purple so deep it looks as if it may contain another dimension within it. Their eyes lock on Eronda, who heads straight for them.

"Padroma," the artist says, bowing deeply. "You honor me with your presence, Eronda of House Emerald. It is a pleasure to meet you in person after all this time. I hope the work you have helped create pleases you."

"I may have helped support it, but the creation is all you. The zaimira is profound."

They continue conversing in Mudra-nul. The rhythms and elongated vowels roll like wind and water over Jes's ears, and he's carried along by the enigmatic and ear-catching buzzes of their language. He understands not a word, but he susses the emotional interplay between Eronda and Padroma, how they infuse their words with feeling. It's different to the human way of sussing, which is to let feelings be while being attuned to them, without guiding and focusing them the way Asuna do. It's not manipulation, but another layer to the conversation. But what does he really know, anyway? What he thinks of as the human way may just be his grandparents' way.

Padroma laughs, returns to Ninespeak. "That may be. It was for the cross-market appeal." They cast a glance at Jes. "And who is this?"

"Jes," he says with a bow.

"Jes is…" Eronda pauses, surprised by her uncertainty over what to call him. "A friend of the family."

Padroma raises an eyebrow at this and Jes susses the gears turning in their mind as they try to grasp why an Asuna highborn would call a non-Asuna hybrid a family friend. "You must be special indeed, to merit that distinction."

"I have my moments."

A smile. "I'm sure you do." Their silver shimmer glints under the cerulean shawl, against where the purple crystals sprout at their crown.

"How long have you been asunasol? Is that the right way to say it?"

"My *solzajira* began at my edermapor. Do you know what that is?"

"The age of entering into contracts."

Clear, unmitigated surprise, which Jes can't help but revel in a little bit. They continue, "Well that was five Opale years ago. What's that, three and a half in 9-Star common?"

"I don't imagine you get used to it," Eronda says. "Is it lonely?"

"I thought it would be at first. But I'm surrounded by people who I share values with, and who value all of me. More importantly, we share a mindset that features of our biology shouldn't decide what we do with our lives. Shared mindset and values offers a far greater sense of belonging than merely being the same race." A look of concern Eronda's way.

"And what about family?" she asks, her voice soft but a defensive undercurrent burbles in Jes's sussing.

"I would have preferred to follow my heart's calling and maintain contact with old friends and kin. But I have new friends and family by choice now. I'm not lonely. I do miss the falls at Allele."

"Where are you settled?" Eronda asks.

"I'm on Indra, a little island in the Jasper Archipelago called Qo. A short ferry ride to the main island and the capital. Lovely neighbors, a fantastic studio, marvelous light. Right on the Amethyst Sea, which is fitting considering my station." The purple stone of their halo is burnished smooth, not faceted the way the Voulos' are, and at certain angles the light of the room is contained within it. They turn to Eronda. "The sponsorship of the network helped make it possible."

"I'm just happy to see your talent in full bloom." She locks eyes with Jes and he susses worry, fear, an anxious kind of sadness coloring a proud insistence on being right. Could he dance with those feelings the way Padroma does? The way Esmée did with the hostess at the Apogee Club?

"The network has helped so many of us," Padroma says. "There are a couple more on Indra and I'm in touch with some who reside in the Bezan Embrace. There's an intersystem network of asunasol, but I'm not as active as I feel I should be. That sense of obligation never really leaves us, I suppose."

"Well, I'm happy to meet you in person, and to see your work. I wish you a good journey."

Padroma bows, gives a nod to Jes, then turns to greet those stepping up to meet them.

Jes susses the familiar greedy hunger before he sees the one who exudes it, and as they head for the exit, Niko Dax steps in their path. "Jes, dear lad! I didn't know you were a follower of ex-patriate Asuna art. And who is this distinguished madame who allows you in her company?"

Jes sighs. "Eronda Solarey Voulo of the House of Emerald Flame, meet Niko Dax – Port Ruby–" he catches Dax's sharp look "–businessperson."

"Eronda," she says, bowing. He doesn't deserve her bow.

"Niko," Dax says, returning the gesture. "Wonderful exhibit, isn't it?"

"Yes. Quite profound. Moving."

"I especially liked the shadow pieces. Within castoffs lies the soul of a people."

"That's overstating it a bit, but I appreciate the sentiment." Eronda is impatient to move along but doesn't wish to be rude to the local businessman who enjoys Asuna art, as unconventional as it is.

"I so appreciate this chance encounter." Jes susses that Dax is mostly sincere, but the edge of his agenda is sharp as ever. "I had heard that an Asuna cultural minister was on the moon and hoped to make your acquaintance. I'd hoped we might discuss possible collaborative projects in the future? Projects of mutual benefit to our peoples?"

Jes hasn't a clue what the man could possibly be on about, but he is completely sincere in his appeal, which Jes finds somehow more worrisome. He lets his apprehension of Dax rise to the fore of his awareness; he knows the Asuna way of sussing is different, but hopes that what he's doing is enough for Eronda to pick up on.

"I'm here on a personal matter," she replies smoothly. "And besides, it's my husband that's the cultural minister. I'm afraid we won't be able to accommodate you. But I'd be happy to maintain correspondence, or perhaps we could holo-conference in the future?"

"Oh, that's disappointing. I was especially hoping we could talk since you're the mother of one of my resident circus's shining new stars."

What is he doing?

This catches her attention. "Your resident–" she looks from Dax to Jes, puzzled.

"I am the proud owner and proprietor of the Luna Lux Resort Casino, where the newly coined Circus Infinite is set to debut. This evening, in fact. Considering we are already connected, by dint of Esmée having such a prominent role in the production I'm a benefactor of, I'd hoped you'd be more open to conversation."

Jes is dismayed to suss Eronda wants to know more. Dax smiles, senses he has a hook in. That satisfaction makes Jes queasy.

"We really need to get going." He charges in gracelessly, but effectively. "It's a big night and I have to get to the circus."

"I'm about ready to depart this place," Eronda says. She turns to Dax. "I'll consider your invitation."

"I look forward to it." Dax smiles as they walk away and Jes feels his steps grow leaden as if he were in one of his own gravity fields.

He lets her lead the way out through the galleries. There's a line of rotos waiting for passengers at a stand nearby and Eronda is about to head towards it when she hesitates. "How much time do you have?"

"I don't have to be at the circus for a few hours."

"So having to depart right now was a ruse to get away from that man."

Jes nods.

"Fine with me, I'm not sure I liked him."

Relief.

"Would you mind a walk in the gardens before we head back into town?"

They begin walking away from the museum; Jes follows Eronda's lead not knowing if the direction they're walking is intentional or not. They're heading for beds of flowers on the other side of the trees with golden blossoms. They walk in silence while Jes turns over in his mind the fact that Eronda sponsors an artist in exile, that she said *I'm just happy to see your talent in full bloom.* He susses a restless worry from her.

"You seem to have something on your mind," he offers, trying to project a supportive feeling. "Do you want to talk about it?"

"I'm thinking about the situation with Esmée," she answers. This doesn't surprise him.

"You don't agree with the choice she's made."

"The life of an asunasol can be lonely." The moon turns from full day, and the curve of the planet begins to peek over the horizon.

"You heard what Padroma said about sharing values and mindset. Esmée's found her people here. She has Essa." He susses wavering in her resistance, that like her insistence that she be accompanied to this event, this disapproval of Esmée's choice is rooted in fear, that the cultural basis for her argument is just a front. He leans into this and continues, "And besides she wouldn't truly be asunasol, would she? She's not defying caste, since Emeralds can be artists and performers even if that's not as common as Rubies," he draws on that tidbit of information Esmée once shared, and by the shift in Eronda's feeling, he can tell it was the right thing to say.

She turns to face him, and a mild, pleasant surprise emanates from her. "You certainly do know more about Asuna culture than most jorai."

"One of my best friends is Asuna. I pay attention when she tells me things."

A smile.

He presses on, "I think you're afraid of letting go."

She sighs. "She'll be light years away."

"She could be light years away even if she went to another planet within the Imperium."

"Within the Imperium she'd be among her own kind. Out here she'll be lost."

"It seems to me she's found herself, found a way of being that suits her. Back on your world she might conform to expectations, she might be under your watchful eye, but she'd be more lost. Lost to herself. To me, that would be the worst fate of all."

They've stopped at a flowerbed overflowing with a heady fragrance, sweet and uplifting. The flowers that are the source of the scent are shocking pink, with delicate petals like crêpe paper. Tiny red-throated birds hover around the redolent blooms, feeding on nectar.

"Is that why you left your homeworld? To not be lost to yourself?" She doesn't look at him when she asks this, just keeps watching the birds.

"My homeworld never felt like home. Just because you're born someplace doesn't mean you belong there, or that you have to stay there forever. We live in a big galaxy. We're citizens of an alliance of worlds. Shouldn't it all be home to us?"

"That is the promise of the 9-Stars, isn't it? Such openness has never been the Asuna way, though we are founding members of the Congress. The trade in technology and resources, access to the slipstream – these were the things that attracted my people. Cultural exchange was never part of it, you know this. But for Esmée's generation, and yours," she casts him a sideways glance, "it seems to be the future you want." She sighs. "Certainly it's what my daughter wants. Maybe I should get out of the way. It's what you think I should do, isn't it?"

The fear he'd sussed earlier has faded into a sort of resignation. "I think that Esmée has decided what she wants. You holding tightly to her or resenting her choice will lose her to you more surely than if you let her follow her heart."

"I can see you're a good friend to her," Eronda says with a feeling approaching appreciation. "Now, don't you have a show to get to?"

CHAPTER SEVENTEEN

Jes, in his all-black running crew outfit, sits in the dressing room with Bo and some other cast members as they get into costume and makeup. Everyone is trying to ignore the pandemonium outside on the lawn and in front of the Luna Lux – hordes of fans and paparazzi have descended, and the chaos throws the cast and crew, not to mention the hotel and casino staff, for a loop. It turns out Jasmine Jonah, without a word to anyone, announced on her tour vlog that she was "so excited" to see Circus Infinite, the new show opening at the Luna Lux by the former Cirque Kozmiqa. "Aleia Siqui, the producer and director, is a brilliant showmaker," Jasmine says on her broadcast. "I can't wait to be there opening night."

It's all Jes's idea: he'd asked Bo to ask Tasso to ask Jasmine to plug the show, and she graciously did. Jes figured that raising the profile of both the circus as a must-see attraction in town, and Aleia as its mastermind, could only benefit them and give Dax more reason to keep Aleia around. Being the person to fire the strategist who revamped a show in such a way to earn Jasmine Jonah's endorsement would not suit the image Dax wishes to project. Jes is well aware the PR boost guarantees nothing, that it's no inoculation against Dax's whims, but anything that can boost the circus and Aleia's value in his eyes is worth the effort.

Bo's in his costume, applying eyeliner in a brightly lit mirror. He mumbles to himself the show sequence, his transitions, the esoteric names of the individual moves in his first tumbling pass. Jes sits behind him, watching the preparations. He probably shouldn't be here – he doesn't want to be a distraction – but he's compelled for some reason. It's his first time being in a show, and though he's just crew (and also secretly floating the triplets) he's not performing, not really. Not like Bo.

"You're amazing," he says. He hopes his tone conveys his sincerity since he speaks from the honest core of himself – anything else would come off as putting on airs and mark his comments as obvious attempts at reassurance, rather than actually reassure. "You'll be fantastic out there."

Bo lets out a nervous squawk; Jes senses he should leave him alone to mentally prepare however he needs to. "I'm going to check in with Quint and get into place. Break a leg." He reaches out a hand, pauses, touches Bo lightly on the shoulder. Bo's face lights up at this and he smiles in the mirror.

In the backstage studio-workshop that is inner space, Moxo Thron and some of the clowns practice their juggling. On the far side of the room, Essa, the triplets, Gregor and the Hydraxians go through the stretches that prepare their bodies for the feats they're about to perform. And somewhere in the warren of circus subcultures, Esmée trills through her vocal warm-ups. Jes can feel pre-show jitters flitting about the room, discrete packets of feeling in a prevailing air of calm. Everyone has their acts down, and feels pride in what they've made, and they all know they know their stuff. These are the circumstances that give rise to confidence.

"You ready to run the sets?" Quint asks, "And, you know, the other thing?" He raises his eyebrows up and down and looks so goofy, like a very stoned mountain equine pretending to be a horny human. Jes has to laugh.

Aleia taps him on the shoulder and indicates she wants to step onto the table where the clowns sit around and get baked after closing. Jes takes her hand, places his palm lightly on her back as she steps up. She calls for everyone's attention by tapping a tuning fork to a bowl, both of which had been absent-mindedly left on the table. A bright tone rings like a benediction. Everyone hushes and turns their attention to the statuesque woman in radiant purple Asuna satin. Her pale blue skin is electric against her evening gown, and her blue-white hair is in a loose tussle. She's effortlessly glamorous and shines.

"I want to thank you all for working so hard to make this show special. For those of you that have been here since the days of Cirque Kozmiqa, thank you for rolling with the punches and adapting as you needed to. And for sticking with me. For those of you new to what is now Circus Infinite, thank you for joining your story to ours. We are all the better for it. To the ones who got Jasmine Jonah to endorse us, thank you whoever you are…"

Jes knows she knows who they are.

"Your continued presence here means more than I can express," Aleia continues. "Thank you for being part of our circle. We're going to change what entertainment means on this moon. We'll show the galaxy a new way of telling a story." She raises her glass as the room cheers. "House opens in five."

Jes once again takes hold of her hand and helps steady her as she steps down from the table. "I hope Mr Dax is pleased," he says. "As pleased as he can be anyway. We've achieved turn-away crowds, the afterparty at the Singularity is an even hotter ticket than the main show, and we got the endorsement and presence of the galaxy's biggest popstar. We can't have done much more. I mean…" He pauses, meets her eyes. "You even kept up with the increased tithes. Even as the old show closed. Even as we went dark."

"I gave up my salary and most of my savings." She holds his gaze. "The funds for the Singularity had to come from somewhere."

In the shared glance, he understands their battles are joined.

"I'll be watching the show with our esteemed guests of honor, Mz Jonah and Mr Dax - and their entourages of course. I'll see you at the reception. Have a good show, Jes."

Jes watches the show – the parts of it that he's able to – from monitors backstage. He wishes he could be out in the audience to witness this creation, the biggest thing he's ever been part of in his whole life, but then wonders if he really could see the show the way an audience member who knows nothing about it does. By the time of the first run-through, even, he'd seen all the acts in development, he'd heard the band rehearse. He'd witnessed Aleia setting the order based on the narrative framework. The surprise, for him, is gone, wonder vanquished by a peek behind the curtain. But what's behind the curtain holds its own sense of wonder. And awe, and respect. Still, he envies the audience out in the dark outer space; their curiosity presses soft waves against his empathic sense.

The opening invocation by Kush O-Nhar sets the scene and the mood as the Mantodean assumes a tone of high oratory, prefacing the about-to-unfold tale with a reflection on identity and fate and the vagaries of spacetime. *Who is it that rises when your personal stars ignite?* he asks the audience. *Where leads the path of your gravity?* The sort of metaphysical what-the-fuck people expect from his species. Even from backstage Jes senses the audience's titillation at being let in on a secret and witnessing the novelty of a Mantodean performing in a show like this.

Then Bo makes his appearance, doing basic juggling tricks and some tumbling, a carefree vagabond in a sylvan glade. Then the wormhole opens, all projections and wind and fake fog and he goes tumbling through. The first person he meets on the other side is Gregor, spinning in his Single Wheel. From there it's on to Essa, who after her exquisite lyra act, hands him a talisman that reminds him of her mother's zaiharza.

The Hydraxians make their appearance with their crazy beautiful hand-to-hand-to-hand-to-hand acro-balancing dance, and they seem all friendly at first, then they turn on the vagabond, their two bodies moving as one. Then the chase through the poles set to intense percussion in a human style known as Klang. Then the clown-acrobats dive through increasingly tall stacks of rings, and so on through the acts. Jes switches equipment in and out, places set pieces for the duration until Moxo Thron's juggling set. That's his cue to get behind the control panel set piece. With a silver mask over his face and gauntlets over his crew blacks, he plays the panel's operator, fiddling with the controls while generating his field from the stage.

Moxo takes the orb in hand, glides through a single-ball routine full of butterflies and body rolls and balances and illusions. His motions are liquid, and he opens a gate through which Bo's vagabond walks. There, he meets the three sisters trapped in their diamond shaped cage. Esmée sings a tune in Bezti that sounds like ghosts whispering over cold plains. Jes has been feeling waves of excitement, anxiety, and awe from the audience but he has to shut all that out now. He's not a set-runner for the next seven minutes, he's the ineffable energy that bears the triplets aloft, and he has to focus.

They start on the ground, hanging and swinging from the bars of the octahedron-shaped apparatus. Then they set it spinning and it lifts up into the air by the cable it hangs from. The triplets each take a position to form a line across the shape: one each at opposite corners and one at the center top. They bend and pose, making graceful shapes as they rise. The apparatus stops its spin and the lighting effects hit the scrim that wraps it. The moment has arrived.

Jes projects his energies and generates a field within the apparatus. The triplets dive toward the center and move, gravity-free. When they shift from their grounded flips and poses to air ballet, the audience inhales as one. Even though his concentration is on the field, he feels the waves of shock and wonder that ripple through the crowd.

The triplets move through their routine, tumble in the air, their bodies bending and twisting in ways that seem impossible to people of normal flexibility. The formations they cycle through are glyphs transmitting a secret code to those watching. Despite himself, Jes susses the audience, and it's like each person's heart is opening to its own mystery.

The apparatus returns to the ground and the three sisters look at the vagabond hopefully. He raises up his sphere and beams of light shoot out of it. The octahedron cage opens, coming apart at one corner. The vagabond dances with the triplets, fastening harnesses to each of them as they complete a solo tumbling sequence one by one. Then they rise, pulled up into the air by wires, waving down at the vagabond as their former prison is subsumed by mist. They disappear into the fly-space, twirling, twirling, twirling, as the audience cheers.

Throughout it all, the band maintains the steady pulse of the show, adding just the right amount of dramatic flair to what's happening on stage without taking over. Esmée's vocals are crystal clear, warm, glorious. She performs two songs with nothing else happening on stage, between scene changes, and she holds the audience spellbound.

The rest of the performance goes by in a blur as he runs on autopilot. Suddenly it's over and the cast take their bows to a standing ovation. Jes hangs towards the back of the stage with the rest of the crew, happy to be one of the anonymous black-clad runners. He whoops loudly along with everyone when Bo takes his bow. Bo, Essa, the triplets, Esmée – all of them so radiant in the lights. The ambient vibration in the air can't be denied: the crowd is dazzled.

The mood is ebullient backstage as the cast and crew bask in their success. Spliffs are sparked and shots are poured. Jes changes from his crew-blacks into the suit Aleia made him wear to that first meeting with Niko Dax. Esmée talks him into glitter in his hair, some on his face.

"Enchanting," she quips with a smile.

"No, you are. You were great tonight. How does it feel?"

She squeezes herself and grins, "So amazing. OK I'm going to meet my parents for the party. See you out there?"

Jes nods as Bo comes bounding up. He's changed out of his costume and now wears a sparkling, diaphanous tunic and form-fitting shiny pants. "Ready to be my arm candy?"

"It'll be an honor to be beside the star of the show. You were amazing tonight, Bo."

"Thank you. It feels good." Bo isn't bashful – he knows he did well and is proud. He holds out an arm and Jes takes it, then the two walk out to join the inaugural VIP event.

Most of the cast is there in the new tent, but Jes and Quint are the only crew members present, being the escorts of cast members. Essa charms a group of human admirers as Quint stands by, part boyfriend and part bodyguard. Niko Dax chats up Esmée's parents, and Jes hopes they don't get talked into a meeting or whatever scheme he has cooking up. On the other side of the room, Aleia chats with Jasmine Jonah and Esmée and they wave Bo and Jes over.

"Congratulations, my dear boy!" Aleia raises her glass as they approach, and everyone congratulates Bo on a job well done. He soaks it in and Jes feels both his pride in Bo and Bo's pride in himself. It's a wonderful feeling.

"And to you too," Bo adds with a bow towards Esmée, who accepts the compliment with a curtsy and bow of her head.

"We have some news," Aleia says, then defers to Jasmine.

The popstar soaks up the light, casts it back on the assembled group so that they all feel touched by a tendril of fame. "I would love to include some acts from Circus Infinite as part of my next run of shows here," she says. "I'd love to include the triplets and the spinning-in-a-ring man and the acrobats, the human and Bezan group. And you to tie it all together, if you're willing."

Bo stammers. "Of course I'm willing! Thank you!"

"And she'll be paying the circus a handsome sum," Aleia adds, meeting Jes's eyes. He knows that she hopes some additional tithing might get Niko Dax to back off. It's not an unreasonable hope, but Jes does wonder how realistic it is.

"I'm so happy!" Jasmine gushes. "I never realized the circus could be so... artful. The story was just enough for it to hang together without getting super-complicated. And the set design, and costumes and choreography and the feats! It's just amazing what you all can do with your bodies and props... it's like you're dancing with gravity."

At this last remark Bo gives Jes a nudge and Esmée winks.

"The way those triplets looked like they were floating! That was amazing. You must tell me how you did that, or maybe I should ask them?"

"That's a trade secret, I'm afraid," Aleia says smoothly.

They all mingle after that, Jes sticking with Bo, basking a little in his light. He's never had any aspirations of being a performer of any kind, but he sees the appeal. Bo, Esmée – everyone – put themselves into their art. He's seen the training it takes for them to do what they do with their bodies, the collaboration and negotiation required for group performances. He's seen the ways that each of them, respectively dedicated to their own piece, contribute to the larger work. He even contributed too, in his own small, anonymous way. To have all that effort cheered and appreciated, and then to have the high-rollers of Port Ruby society offering congratulations, to want to be seen at the party – Jes gets how rewarding that is. He's never seen any of his circus friends be as happy, as satisfied, as they are now. In fact, he's not sure he's ever experienced *anyone* this happy.

And then there's Moxo Thron. He's smiling friendly smiles and chatting up fancy folks in the crowd, but whenever he's in proximity, Jes susses resentment and low-key irritation.

"Congratulations, Moxo," Jes says in an interstitial moment

while Moxo has walked away from a stylish Rijala couple and heads for the bar. He hopes he's making a peace offering. "Your act is really beautiful."

"Flattery will not make me like you more," Moxo says through a steely grimace. He gestures around the Singularity. "I envisioned this long before you ever showed your mutt face here but it's you who gets the credit."

"Maker of all," Jes replies with exasperation. "What credit? It's not like my name is on anything! It's not like I got a bonus. I had no idea Aleia shot you down for the same ideas I suggested, OK? I didn't even know that you'd suggested them. If you have a problem with how all this happened, maybe you should take it up with her."

"Everything OK here?" Bo asks as he sidles up, handing Jes a drink as he sips on his own.

"Fine," Jes says sharply. "We're all good here." He tugs on Bo's arm, leading him away from the juggler. "He is really starting to get under my skin," he says under his breath. Bo gives his arm a squeeze.

Zazie, Lula and Jujubee make their way through the crowd doing walk-overs – because why would they walk like regular people? Nobody here wants to see that. They approach Aleia from different directions and surround her as a spotlight focuses.

"I want to thank you all so much for celebrating the debut of Circus Infinite," Aleia says as she addresses the crowd. "I'd say we have a pretty good show on our hands, what do you think?" She beams beatifically as those gathered offer their applause.

"We call this space the Singularity, where we'll host our VIP packages going forward. Tonight, it's a big party, but in its regular mode, it will be a much more intimate experience, so I encourage you to come back another night. Bring friends, family, visitors from off-moon, all are welcome. And now I'd like to make a special announcement." She pauses for dramatic effect.

"We have a special guest with us this evening, the extraordinary pop performer and the young woman who represents the zenith of fame in the galaxy, Jasmine Jonah."

A spot opens on the diminutive singer and she shines in it, almost as if she's illuminated from within. She waves to the guests as they cheer. "I loved the show!" she calls out to more applause and laughter.

Jasmine continues, "As you all know, my intergalactic tour has four more performances in Port Ruby, picking up in a few days. Well, I was so blown away by the truly stunning beauty and magic of the circus, that I've invited a few of the acts to join me as my special guests for the final shows."

Murmurs of approval sweep the crowd. From across the room, Jes sees Niko Dax arch an eyebrow. He's too far away, and there's too many others between them for Jes to get a read on him, but his curiosity burns.

Aleia speaks again, "Please keep an eye out for announcements from Jasmine's tour and catch the Circus Infinite Edition if you can! Enjoy the rest of your evening!"

After everyone settles back into mingling, Jes and Bo find themselves chatting with Essa and Quint in one of the side booths. The crowd thins out, and some folks move outside to smoke. The faint scent of chordash and reef wafts in through the opening of the tent. They're in good spirits generally, though Essa carries an air of melancholy.

"Why do you seem down?" Jes asks.

Essa chuckles. "No hiding a bad mood from an empath, eh?"

"She's sad she didn't get picked for Jasmine Jonah's show," Quint says, and Essa immediately follows up with a jab to his side and an angry glare. "Well it's true," he mumbles.

"It's... I've been here before, the exciting opening night, you know?" Essa explains. "I was once the sparkling new thing and I know I still have my place here, but the kids are rising. It's as it should be and I'm so proud. I mean, I helped train the triplets! But it still makes me a little sad to be one of the old standbys, and not the bright new star. Oh maker of all, I sound so narcissistic."

"You're a legend, Essa," Bo offers.

"You're sweet. The boys are really going to be chasing after you now."

Jes bristles at this, though he's not really sure why. He and Bo have their bond, but sex is off the table for him, and the idea that there will be boys who'll want Bo to fuck them is not so outlandish. In fact, it's obvious now that he thinks about it. Bo's attractive, fit, and the star of the hot show in town. Is he holding Bo back from a relationship he'd find more fulfilling? More passionate? Before he can go farther down this path of thinking, Esmée walks over with her parents. They both radiate pride in their girl.

"Congratulations, lad, on a remarkable performance!" Enovo enthuses to Bo. "I couldn't have moved my body like that even when I was your age. Truly astounding. You should be proud."

"Thank you," Bo says, unusually bashful. "I've been training for this since I was a child. You may have been able to do more than you think if you'd started that young."

"It's never too late to learn something new," Esmée says to her father, laughing.

"What do you think, Eronda? Get some new tricks for this old dog, eh?" Enovo laughs at whatever private image he holds in his mind of himself spinning around a pole.

"If you learn how to do backflips, I will never complain about anything again," Eronda replies.

"If only I'd known that's all it would take. Good thing we'll be here a bit longer, maybe Bo can give me some lessons."

"You've extended your stay?" Jes asks.

"Yes. Eronda told me about the exhibition you visited earlier, and I'd like a chance to see it myself. And also continue to bear witness to my talented daughter's gifts."

Esmée blushes at her father's words and squirms

uncomfortably. Jes susses from her both pride and embarrassment. She knows she's talented but is humble enough to get flustered by compliments, and he loves that about his friend.

Enovo continues. "Seeing – hearing – what my daughter has been able to create in this environment has made me see the limitations of the Asuna strictures in a way that I hadn't seen before. I have some drafted reforms in mind to present to my colleagues back home. So yes, we've extended our stay. For research purposes.

"I haven't witnessed firsthand the blending of cultures as exhibited in your circus. The members of the 9-Star Congress have peaceably coexisted, but there was no true blending until the Emergence of Indra, and its people. That emergence, after the passage of time, can now be seen clearly as a catalyst. Look at how quickly humans took to the galaxy, how many human hybrids there are now. Each world maintains its own identity, each species its own culture, but out in the open territories, like here in the Vashtar system where there is no indigenous species, it's those with the urge to make a new culture that have settled.

"Consider Jasmine Jonah – what is her heritage? Human, Bezan, and Rijala? That's simply a new type of person. She's the biggest star in the galaxy. There's a reason for that. Not only is her biology mixed, her music is too. People look at her and listen to her and it's the future they witness. Our daughter and the younger generations of multiple worlds wish to be part of that future. I think our culture should catch up."

"And how do you feel about all this?" Jes asks, turning to Eronda.

"I am in full support of cultures evolving. As long as traditions are maintained and respected on the homeworld."

"I suppose now we'll have time to meet with that insistent Rijala…" Enovo turns to his wife. "What was his name again?"

"Niko Dax," she says. "I'd rather not. He seems rather suspect to me."

Bo circulates through the crowd, accepting the praise rightfully flowing his way. He keeps his hold on Jes's hand the whole time, and Jes realizes he's serving as Bo's anchor, his grounding. He's happy to be that for him. After a while though, he needs a little break, so he excuses himself and steps outside. He takes in the sight of Persephone-9's sister moons hovering in the sky overhead, and Persephone herself looming large with the halo of Vashtar, the planet's sun, glimmering around her mass – the half-night sky.

Small groups are scattered about the lawn, and a line of three Hydraxian guards stands across the entrance to the hotel, to keep away curious guests wanting a glimpse of the popstar everyone knows is here. A small fire flickers several yards away with flames of gold and green and blue. Silhouetted by the light is a familiar insectoid being. Jes walks over. "Hi Kush O-Nhar. Have you had a good night?"

Clicks, then words. "The circus had a successful opening. I've been 'telling fortunes'. I do loathe that term but it's the phrase most people understand. I've sat with and read the heartsick and the ambitious and the hopeful and the fearful all night. I've offered accurate assessments. Not everyone has enjoyed the experience. Does that sound like a good night?"

Kush O-Nhar blends into the dark because of his coloring. The fire catches glimmers of faint iridescence across his bulbous eyes, and the light carapace of his thorax and abdomen.

"I'm not sure how to answer that. Did *you* enjoy the experience?"

"I am where I need to be. Why did you come over here, Jes?" Clicks.

Jes doesn't know. He saw Kush O-Nhar and felt compelled. It's a moment of what his grandmother would have called an intuitive pivot, when one's intuition guides one's actions without one being consciously aware.

"I thought so," Kush O-Nhar says, understanding. The two stand in silence and listen to the rustle of the colored flames before them. "Have you had enough of the party?"

"I just needed a little break. My empathic sense is like a muscle, kind of. And it needs rest when there's been a lot of exertion. I don't feel anything from you though."

A series of clicks. "No, you wouldn't. Mantodeans don't have the same emotional resonances as humanoid species. So, being around me is relaxing for you, then?"

Jes laughs and looks into Kush O-Nhar's eyes of flame-tinged shadow. "In a way."

A series of clicks and waves through the antennae as he laughs.

A question that's been in Jes's mind ever since the day that he met Kush O-Nhar comes up again. "What's the deal with you and Niko Dax?"

"Why do you ask?"

"Well, you live in the restricted gardens of his property. He must have given you personal approval to do that. What do you do for him in exchange? He doesn't strike me as altruistic."

"I consult."

"On what?"

"Business matters. What steps will maximize profit, minimize loss, neutralize aggressive efforts by rivals. Matters of empire for him, but trivial for me and all other sentient life." Clicks.

"Why do you do it?" He's about to ask if Dax has anything on him, but holds his tongue. He suspects Kush O-Nhar would be insulted by such a question.

"That private garden is the most suitable place for me to nest in Port Ruby. The environment. The lack of noise and crowds. Mantodeans have extremely sensitive hearing, and we can feel sound vibrations through our antennae, our legs, our carapaces. A more populous area of the city would be highly uncomfortable, physically, for me to reside in. As you so noted previously, the Mytiri Forest would be much more suitable for one of my kind wishing to reside on this moon. But I need to be here. Lending Mr Dax minimal use of my talents in exchange for nesting in his rather expansive garden is a fair exchange. Not to mention, Mr Dax enjoys flaunting the fact that he has Mantodean counsel at his beck and call. Bragging rights are a valuable commodity to a certain personality type. I'm happy to provide them if I can."

So Kush O-Nhar was part of Dax's collection then. But he wouldn't enter the arrangement without an agenda of his own.

"You need to be here. For the circus? Is the circus something special, in the grand scope of things?"

"Oh now, Jes, you are getting close to the heart of the matter." He clicks, rubs his two front legs together.

"Why?"

"An event of significance is on the horizon. The circus is somehow part of it. The Weaveseers don't know specifically what the event is, but it could be cataclysmic, or it could be transformative."

"Jes!" Bo calls from across the lawn. He and Esmée wave from near the entrance of the Singularity.

Kush O-Nhar grabs his attention again with a series of harsh clicks. Then he says, "Heed this: *A time of glory comes, and with glory, treachery.*"

Jes doesn't like the sound of that. But before he can ask a follow-up question, he's dismissed.

"You should rejoin your friends. Good evening, Jes."

"Good night." Jes turns away from the fire and the being beside it and makes his way back to the Singularity where his friends stand waiting.

"Did Kush O-Nhar bestow words of wisdom?" Bo asks.

"Glory and treachery," Jes answers. "Clear as mud."

THE INSTITUTE

"They used to make us in test-tubes and raise us here," Rosa tells them one day. They're allowed supervised time outside, and they all relish the air and the sun. "We're the first generation born naturally and raised by parents."

There's a wall with art supplies they can paint on, but it reminds him too much of the old gang putting up unsanctioned murals and he avoids that area of the yard. They have children's playground equipment – monkey bars, and swings, and a spinning platform thing. Are there children here? Or does the staff here think of them as children?

"What made them do it that way?" Jes asks. "My parents hated raising me, as far as I could tell."

"The ones they raised in the lab ended up going a little crazy once their paratalents manifested. They couldn't control them. The subjects couldn't control their powers."

Jes cringes at the term "subjects". Could some of them have been brothers or sisters they never knew?

"My parents never seemed like they much liked each other," Minu says.

"Mine didn't hate each other exactly," Rosa adds. "But they never seemed like they were in love or anything. It was all very... professional. Like they were just doing some kind of job."

"Maybe we were the job," Jes says. "And now their job is done. That would explain a lot."

"Aren't you sick of it?" Minu paces beside the bench where Jes and Rosa sit, hugging himself. "Not having any say in our own lives? This whole situation is fucked up."

"You're expressing uncooperative ideas."

Jes and Minu look at Rosa after she speaks. After the session with the Counsellor, they put her through some kind of compliance treatment. She's mostly normal, until somebody says something critical about the Institute and their methods. She returns their looks with a blank stare.

"Look who's coming," Minu says under his breath.

Striding toward them across the lawn is the Counsellor herself, flanked by two orderlies. Jes tugs at his collar as one of the panels gets hot when he sits too long in direct sunlight.

"How are you three doing today?" She smiles but it doesn't seem genuine to Jes, even without his sussing.

"Enjoying the fresh air," Rosa says. "Thank you for this time."

Jes glares at her, hardly believing this is the same girl who threatened to fry the Counsellor's face. He notices the Counsellor staring at him, apparently waiting for a response.

"Fine," Jes says. "I'm fine."

She turns to Minu. "Please come with me. I understand we need to make an adjustment to your collar. We'd prefer you not use low-key telepathy."

"No!" Minu exclaims and backs away.

The Counsellor gives a signal and the orderlies move with speed, taking Minu by the arms.

"It's better if you don't fight this," the Counsellor says.

Minu looks around, his eyes dart back and forth between Jes and Rosa. He fixates on Rosa. "You! You told them."

"We need to cooperate," Rosa says. "We're all responsible for the project's success."

"Get off me!" Minu cries. "Leave me alone! Get the fuck off me!"

The Counsellor jabs a syringe into his neck, and he immediately goes limp. The orderlies take him away, his feet dragging across the grass as they do so.

"You didn't know about Minu's little telepathy trick, did you?" The Counsellor glares at Jes, and it feels like a dare.

"No. I don't know what you're talking about."

She just stares at him for a long second. "Well, it doesn't matter now." She walks after the orderlies.

Jes wants to be mad at Rosa for selling their friend out, but she's clearly been altered. Is she even really acting of her own accord? She stares after the Counsellor, the orderlies disappearing into the building with Minu's limp body between them. He wishes he could suss her. Is she proud of what she's done? Remorseful? Does it even matter?

"Why did you tell them he could access his telepathy?"

"He wasn't supposed to. It was a breach of protocol."

"Protocols are important to you now?"

"They only exist to keep us safe."

"The key words here are 'keep us'. Don't you want to ever get out of here and have your own life?"

She looks at him, eyes wide. "Why would you want to leave?"

He's flabbergasted. "You mean you don't?"

"They take care of us. And anyway, we have to go along. What else can we do?"

Could this be why they've allowed them time together? Because she has completely, utterly, acquiesced to their power and control? She's part of their mission now? And she'll influence him and Minu to do the same – is that what they hope?

To his dismay, she keeps talking. "I know his methods seem harsh, but Doctor Matheson just wants to protect me. Protect us. And the world! We don't know what we're fully capable of. What if we do something terrible, or hurt people? Our uncontrolled powers are dangerous."

The poor thing, she's completely bought into the Institute's story. What the hell even is this place?

"What if we have more control than you think?"

She ignores his question. "People like us are rare. We have a duty. And besides, I wouldn't want to lose control of my paratalent. Electrocution is terrible – I don't want to do that to anybody, least of all myself."

"I still think we should have a choice. And not be tortured."

"Some of the procedures are uncomfortable, but it's important that the parameters of our talents are measured."

He looks at her with disbelief, with pity. Has she so bought into the Institute's agenda that she no longer values her own personhood? Or maybe whatever they've done to her isn't as harsh as what they've been doing to him. Doubtful, but really, he has no idea. He wants to tell her she can learn to control her powers without succumbing to the Institute completely. He wants to tell her they all can. But the truth is, he's not so sure.

CHAPTER EIGHTEEN

The stadium, from the stage, is cavernous. Empty of people, it's intimidating thinking that so many will be watching them soon. Jes only needs to generate his field, like he's done countless times, but he still feels nervous. The triplets, Gregor, Bo and the tumbling crew are all completely unfazed, and as Jasmine Jonah's stage director and chief of crew explain where and how the circus acts will be incorporated, they each walk the stage calmly, making note of their marks and cues. The clowns go through a couple of their tumbling runs to demonstrate to the director how much space they'll need. It's just another show to them.

Esmée, on the other hand, is freaking out. Jes is right behind her as they all first set foot on the stage, and he watches as she looks out into the space, takes in the multitude of seats rising up around them, and susses a tidal wave of panic from her. He's worried she might start hyperventilating. She has three days to get it together, and he tries to think of ways he can help. He owes her, after all.

Jasmine takes her aside and the two work out their material; Esmée will be doing "The Witch's Chant" from the Circus Infinite show and duetting with Jasmine on her track "Zodiac". The focus on the material seems to calm her down a bit. Did Jasmine know that it would?

The triplets confer with the crew chief, discussing the placement of their rigging and accompanying set. They're pointing and gesticulating and the man demonstrates remarkable patience.

"Jes," Lula calls for his attention in her snippy mode. "We need you over here." As much as he wants to help Esmée, whatever she's facing is beyond his experience, and Lula's call reminds him of his place here.

"The rig will descend from up there," Zazie explains pointing up to the trusses above them, "and these pyramid things will surround it, along with the control panel. They'll rise up from below the stage. Maybe you can check out the space down there?"

"My people have it under control," the crew chief says. Jes can sense he feels imposed upon by his inclusion. "They've been doing it all tour."

"I'm onstage for this," Jes explains, "working the control panel."

The crew chief shrugs. "Fine. Silas!" he calls over one of his crew; it's the human who had joined the tour with Tasso. Jes hasn't seen him since the night of the house party.

"Hey man, Jes, right?" Silas says as he walks up. "Good to see you again."

"Show our guest here the trapspace, would you?" the chief asks wearily.

"Follow me," Silas says and leads Jes backstage. After they've walked some distance from the rest of the group, he adds, "You're looking better than the last time I saw you."

Jes flushes with embarrassment; the night he met Silas was not his finest moment. "I overdid it that night, I guess."

"It happens to all of us." Silas leads him down a short set of stairs, then they take a sharp turn and they're suddenly underneath the stage.

"There's trap doors all over the place on this thing," Silas explains as they head deeper into the structure. Trusses rise from the floor and crisscross overhead. "Jasmine loves stuff popping up and popping down." He winks knowingly.

The innuendo bothers Jes, but he says nothing about it.

"You take all this apart, travel with it and then put it together again?"

"Yeah, that's right. Biggest show in the universe. Here's where the set rises up." His tone is straightforward but Jes susses pride. They've reached just about centerstage. A set of hydraulic platforms arranged in a semi-circle surrounds them.

The control panel set piece is flanked by two pyramids. "I have to get to this and go up with it."

"That's no problem. Do you know your cue?"

"Right after Esmée's solo."

"Alright. We'll make that happen." He pulls a node out from his back pocket and taps notes into it, then turns and they head back out the way they came.

"Do you like this life better?" Jes asks. "Than the circus, I mean."

Silas is silent until they walk out from under the lip of the stage and Jes susses that Silas is closing himself off again. Was it something he said?

"I like the travel," he eventually says, his aura fully closed. Curious. "No time to do much sightseeing though. But it's cool. I won't do this forever." He stops and turns to face Jes. "So, your cue is when the Asuna girl sings her song. That's what leads into the triplets. That's when you need to be at your mark, down below where we just were. Got it?"

Jes nods and Silas says, "I'll tell the chief we worked it out," then he stalks off, back to whatever he was doing before. He was a lot friendlier at the party.

The crowd is thoroughly warmed up and ecstatic when it's time for the circus to go on. Jasmine thanks the crowd for being so welcoming, says some kind words about how great it's been in Port Ruby, makes a bawdy joke. "I've made some good friends since I've been here," she says, "and I'd like to bring some of them out onstage with me."

Standing together in the wings, Jes senses Esmée's nerves as she shakes her arms next to him. The audience roars its approval, but they don't know who's coming out. They're just excited to see who Jasmine considers friends, or maybe are hoping some other pop stars will join her. There are none of her magnitude in the galaxy, but some come close. Jes worries for a second that the circus crew will be a disappointment, but he dismisses that – this crowd will love what Jasmine loves.

"As some of you might know, there's this amazing show here in Port Ruby, based at the Luna Lux. You might have seen my vlogs about it…" Applause. After the opening night performance Jasmine had posted a glowing review video, so at least some here know what she's talking about. "They're called Circus Infinite and you should totally go see them. They're magic!" More applause. "Joining me now is the star chanteuse of the show, Mz Esmée Voulo!"

The opening notes to her album-track "Zodiac" – familiar to any true fan – begin and the die-hards in the crowd recognize it immediately.

"Here I go," Esmée says as she flashes a look of terror. Then she walks on, waves to the crowd as she crosses the stage to join Jasmine.

The song is deep into its intro measures and a wave of surprise floods Jes – he can see on the monitor that a giant holo-image of Esmée has joined the one of Jasmine and the whole stadium can now discern that an Asuna is onstage with their idol. None of them have ever witnessed an Asuna like this before and the surprise soon gives way to curiosity and anticipation.

The song is a departure in Jasmine's catalog of mostly upbeat, catchy songs meant for dancefloor exaltation, and steamy grinders meant for seduction, and weepy ballads of lost love.

This song is from her more recent experimental EP, brooding, melancholic, psychedelic. Many fans are excited for the new direction they sense coming from their queen, while some others hope she doesn't completely abandon the throbbing beats that made her name. In any case, the song is perfect for this moment as Esmée's crystalline voice weaves together with Jasmine's along the sinuous melody. The effect is hypnotic. Jes is so caught up in it that he almost forgets to wonder how Bo is doing on the other side of the stage. He's due to make his entrance towards the end of the song–

And there he goes, tumbling and dancing towards center stage where a silver holographic circle appears. His movements are crisp, assured. His image is projected on the huge screens hovering all around the stadium. Jes senses appreciation. It's strange, being able to suss the entire audience as if it were one consciousness. Is it because they're all fans?

Gregor rises from under the stage, sitting in lotus position as the ring's motion draws silver sine waves around him. He begins.

Though he wants to see the full routine, Jes leaves the wings as it's time for him to get backstage. He joins a couple of crew members watching on a monitor. "This is pretty cool," one of them says to his friend and Jes feels a swell of pride. Gregor finishes to enthusiastic applause and the opening strains of "The Witch's Chant" begins – Jes's cue.

He dashes under the platform of the stage and makes his way through the trapspace to the set. Silas is there and gives a nod of acknowledgment, "Ready?" he asks.

Jes nods and steps to his place. He adjusts his gauntlets, then moves to slip on his mask and realizes with a start that he doesn't have it. He turns to Silas, panicked. "My mask – I had a mask."

Silas looks confused. "I haven't seen a mask." He steps off the platform.

"I need my–" but he doesn't finish his sentence before the

platform begins its ascent. The set rises from the stage as the crowd is still cheering and Jes is blinded momentarily by the sudden lights. All he sees are lights, the huge crowd invisible in the darkness beyond the edge of the stage. Bo does more of his acrobatic dancing as the triplets descend in their apparatus from the shadowy heights above. The music starts and Jes taps at the fake controls, waiting for his lighting cue. Instead of the projections, it's just a spotlight on the rig, the triplets hanging inside it. The sheer fabric of the scrim shimmers prettily, but the camouflaging effects aren't there. Panic rises in him, and when the triplet facing his direction – he thinks it's Zazie – shoots him a look, he goes ahead and does his part, letting his gravity field unfold within the shape of the rig. The triplets do their thing.

Any worry Jes carries that the grace and beauty they exude would be lost in the enormity of this venue is dispelled – the audience is enthralled. He notices people in the front row recording on their nodes, and at least a few of them move to take in the stage, including Jes. He doesn't like that, but there's nothing he can do about it now. When the triplets take their final positions, the pyramids spin away while he pushes the control panel himself.

Bo and the crew of acrobats conclude the Circus portion of the show with high energy tumbling. The group splits and half make their exit on one side of the stage and half the other. Bo exits where he's standing and beams, happy with the performance and the reception.

Jasmine rises from under the stage, having changed into a glittering white costume for the energetic final stretch of the show, which features all her most popular dance songs. She stands atop a glittering pedestal.

"Can I kiss your cheek and hold your hand?" Bo asks.

Jes nods.

Bo's lips are soft and linger on his cheek longer than usual, while simultaneously his fingers snake between his own. Heat radiates off of Bo's body, and he smells of sweat. He has a mildly spicy odor to him that Jes wants to smell again after it fades from the nose.

"That was amazing." Bo's eyes are bright and wide.

"Awesome show," Theetee says to Bo as she places a set-piece in position. "Hi, boys." It's also the first time Jes has seen the Hydraxian since the party. Though they only had a brief exchange, Jes senses an easeful camaraderie from her that he appreciates. Jes and Bo step out of the way and Jes marvels that the same set-piece that Theetee sets by herself apparently requires three humans to move.

"You just here for moral support?" she asks as the piece she just placed – a glittery backdrop of stars and moons – slides out onstage to frame Jasmine and her dancers, pelvic thrusting to fast beats, ponytails twirling, the singer's breathy oooh ooohs somehow holding it all together.

Bo squeezes Jes's hand. "Something like that," Jes replies.

After the show, after the encores, Jes and Bo head towards the green room. They walk by Silas who is wrapping some cables. He shoots Jes a curious look as they walk past. Jes tries to suss him but doesn't get anything.

Esmée, the triplets and the others are already there when they arrive, drinking water and tea.

"That worked," Zazie says.

"Yeah," Jes affirms. "But I think Silas wonders what I'm doing onstage."

"You're our good luck charm," Jujubee says in her innocent pixie girl way. She laughs, shakes off the dippy persona. "Don't worry. We'll get him sorted. He always had a crush on Lula back when he was with the circus."

Lula rolls her eyes. "Like he'd have a chance."

"I always thought he's kind of cute," Zazie says.

"Oh no doubt he's physically attractive," Lula agrees. "But he's got a strange vibe. Don't you think so, Jes?"

"I can't read him at all," he replies. "He's totally closed off. And yes, that is weird."

Before they can go off more on Silas's weird vibe, Jasmine enters the room with her backup dancers and band, positively giddy.

"Oh, that was marvelous!" she exclaims, bee-lining for the circus group. She compliments each of the performers in turn. "Three more nights! And so you know, on closing night I'm having a party on my starcruiser, you all should come. Invite the whole cast."

They all hang out for a little bit longer, but before too long the performers start peeling off and heading home. The next show doesn't start till mid-evening, but they still need to get plenty of rest.

Jes, Bo, and Esmée share a roto to the Circus Mansion. They are all sated by the evening and ride together in contented silence. It's special friends that can enjoy a comfortable silence.

"Want to come in?" Bo asks. "I know it's late. You can crash if you want. There's plenty of room."

Jes nods. He's reminded that staying with Essa, and now Quint too, was supposed to be temporary but things have moved at such a clip that finding a place hasn't been the most pressing need, and his hosts don't seem to care. He'd had the passing thought that moving into the Circus Mansion might be an option, but since he and Bo are being romantic, he doesn't think that's the wisest move.

"Well I'm turning in straight away," Esmée says as she ascends the stairs to Quint's former room, now hers. "Good night, darlings."

"You were amazing tonight," Bo says.

She pauses halfway up the stairs, turns dramatically and blows them kisses.

"Don't forget about us when *you're* the biggest star in the universe."

She giggles at that and disappears upstairs. They follow and Bo leads the way to his room. The chatter of the triplets arriving home bubbles up from downstairs, but it quiets once they're in the room with the door closed.

"Night light," Bo says to the house controls and soft indigo and purple lights set the walls softly aglow.

The room is dominated by a large net, woven out of thick ropes of brightly colored fibers that glow slightly in the blue and violet light, like Bo's hair. A set of wooden struts supports the net, and its multiple levels are connected by woven tubes that look just wide enough for a person to fit through.

"What is this?" Jes eyes the set up curiously. This is the first time he has been in Bo's bedroom, but neither of them comments on that fact.

"It's a tubeweave hammock," Bo explains as he lights some fragrant incense. "It's a Bezan traditional furnishing. We hang out on them and sleep on them. This one accommodates eight, unless they're Hydraxians. My family's home on Bez has one that's big enough for twenty-four. Climb up." With that he scales the netting up to the top level, then scuttles over to the corner where mounds of pillows lie in wait.

Jes puts his foot in a loop of netting, grabs onto a couple above him and pulls himself up. He climbs it like a ladder, only it's more awkward because there's no rigidity to the structure and the whole thing sways under him. He makes it to the top, utterly lacking Bo's grace, and joins him in the corner.

"Welcome to my sanctum," Bo says, tossing Jes some pillows. They settle in next to each other, feet touching.

"Wow, it's almost like you're floating." The area where they've settled is comprised of a much tighter weave than other parts that are more open. Patches of the tight weave are scattered throughout this, as well as the lower levels.

"The netting is no gravity field, but it's cool, yeah? The tubes that connect the levels are representative of the wormholes Zo provides, that connect the star systems of the 9-Star Congress."

"I wonder what Zo looks like," Jes comments. "I wonder if the slipstream tubes look anything like this from the outside."

"We're taught the patterns were seen in the visions of the Ones Who See the Tree, back in the early days of the formation of the Congress."

Knowing what little he does of the Bezan mystical tradition, that the practices of the Ones Who See the Tree yielded a vision of the slipstream isn't surprising. Still, Jes wonders how true the story is.

He lays back, the scent of the incense soothing him, and he looks at the stars painted on the ceiling, and a carving of the Bezan tree motif, backlit in warm yellow and amber light on the far wall. "I recognize the tree," Jes says. "The Bezan Tree of the World, right?"

Bo nods. "It's the tree that calls the Ones Who See. They're our world's Consciousness Holders. They're the only ones that have laid eyes upon the actual tree. The rest of us just have this image based on visions and stories."

"There's an actual tree? Is it in a hidden forest or something?"

"I'm not sure it exists in the physical realm. Something the Consciousness Holders of all the worlds have in common is this... other place they can go. In their minds, right? It's all very mysterious. There's this temple they go to. Some people speculate it's in there. Only the initiated know for sure."

Jes nods. "My grandmother used to tell me about the 'astral plane'. She always said that maybe I'd see it someday. My grandparents were psions on Indra, but they'd retired from Consciousness Holder duties around the time I was born."

"I had a grandfather who was one of the Ones Who See the Tree. Once a Bezan takes on the role, they're not really seen or heard from again. I never met him, only heard about him. It's rare that someone gets called after starting a family. But once he was called, there was no question he'd go even if it meant leaving the family. It's the most sacred role in Bezan society. I went the circus route, despite what my family wanted. Street circus though, not high circus. Gregor and Moxo, those two trained at the Branch of the Tree Academy. How Moxo juggles like he's doing ballet? Gregor's ring thing? Those are high circus. Well, there's no precedence for what Gregor does really, but the apparatus he's riffing on, the double-ring-wheel, that's a high circus thing."

Jes considers the way Bo moves – virtuosic to be sure, but there's a rough and tumble edge to it that's different from the highly refined grace that Gregor and Moxo possess.

"Most off-worlders who come to Bez to train go to the Academy," Bo adds. "Most of the apparatus-based stuff is considered high circus. I trained acrobatics and poles at the other circus school, Bez School of the Circle. It's mostly just Bezan that go there."

Though he's been talking about circus and Bezan society, Bo has exuded an undertone of want which stirs in Jes a memory of rain. He remembers a day his grandparents brought him to the Grove of the Seed in the Divina region of Indra. The petrichor combined with the scent of a flowering vine called honeysuckle produced such a lovely ache, and that's what Bo's wanting feels like now. He wants to share about his culture, where he comes from, and he wants something else too – a deeper connection. Something more intimate within Jes's boundaries. Jes feels all of this from him and mirrors it. They rub their feet together and look each other in the eye. Jes makes his way across the net, bouncing them both as he goes, and settles in next to Bo.

"Getting to know you has been the highlight of being here," he says. "I wasn't expecting to…"

Bo grins. "To what?"

"To get close to someone."

"You're tight with Esmée. With Essa and Quint."

"Not like that. You know what I mean." Heat floods his cheeks. "I know you know what I mean. Empath, remember?"

"I really wanted to kiss you that night at Lake Tourmaline."

"I thought maybe you did."

"Can I kiss you now?"

In response Jes puts his hand on the side of Bo's face, takes in those amber eyes. Heart pounding, he leans in and touches their lips softly together. Infinity in a moment.

"Wow," Bo says. "I know that's a big deal for you."

"You're a big deal for me," Jes responds. "OK. Cuddle."

Bo rolls over onto his side and Jes curls up against him, puts an arm around him. Comfort from physical affection requires feeling close to someone. Bo meets that standard, and Jes wants to dive into this, have this experience with his circus boy, have this experience of being in love. He holds Bo, the position he's more comfortable with, and takes in his warmth, the spicy smell he exudes. The two savor their closeness, emotional and physical, as they finally succumb to sleep.

THE INSTITUTE

Minu is in the lab when they bring Jes in. He's stripped down and wired up the way Jes normally is. What's he doing here?

"We're taking a big step in our research today," Matheson explains. "We'll be testing the interaction of two different paratalents. How does Jes's gravity interact with Minu's strong nuclear force? This is a very exciting day for us."

A technician removes Jes's collar, and he relishes the relief of the weight, his skin being able to breathe, and the rush of his sussing sense flowing back to him. He stands on a platform opposite Minu, and the two make eye contact as the technicians wire Jes up. Minu nods, still collared, and to Jes's surprise, flashes a goofy grin as if the two are about to play a fun game.

Matheson's mood verges on jolly – Jes can't remember ever sussing him quite so happy before. The technicians are focused, a sense of anticipation buzzes among them all. Minu is hard to suss though – could the collar he still wears be working as a sort of barrier? He supposes it's possible.

Once the technicians have Jes all hooked up, he and Minu are instructed to stand together on the dais between them. There's a pedestal there, upon which sits a sphere made of a blue-tinged metal. Jes recognizes it as the alloy Indra is known for.

"This is how it will go," Matheson explains. "Minu, you will use your talent to deconstruct the orb. Jes, you will use yours to maintain its shape. We'll run this several times, as well as test Minu's ability in a zero gravity environment. This first time is just to establish the baseline readings." He's adopted his collegial way of speaking to his subjects again; Jes likes it better when he's cold and detached. It's more honest.

"Now remember, Minu, no telepathy." Matheson instructs casually as a technician releases Minu's collar. "Unfortunately we can't suppress one of your abilities without suppressing all of them, so it is on your honor to refrain from using it. Tell me you understand."

"Yeah, I got it." *Fuck your stupid rules though.* He maintains eye contact with Jes but his face remains blank, though Jes susses he's amused with himself. A laugh tickles in Jes's throat and he struggles to keep from smiling, but he manages to keep it in check.

Once Matheson steps off the dais, there's a flash and crinkles of light around them as a tube-shaped containment field activates. The pad that the sphere rests on begins to glow. In the control booth, familiar glyphs float, lighting the researcher's faces with their ghostly light: the telemetry that the sensors transmit.

A beep sounds and Minu cups the sphere's smooth curve with his palm. To look at the scene by itself, nothing much is happening. The researchers, however, murmur excitedly as the glyphs spike and diminish in time. Minu furrows his brow as he focuses his attention on the sphere, but there's no energy field glowing, or anything particularly dramatic going on that would correspond to the readings in the booth.

The orb starts to slip out of focus, just the edges at first, then the fuzziness spreads to its center. It's almost like a projection going out of whack, but it's a real, solid orb there. Slowly, Minu withdraws his hand, no longer maintaining physical contact, but continuing to focus on it.

"OK, Jes," Matheson's voice instructs through the intercom. "Try using your gravity to keep it from falling apart."

Oh sure, that. He's supposed to just hop to and do this thing he's never done before.

Do what you did to that cube. The one you crushed from the inside.

Minu's voice in his head is reassuring. Matheson would freak if he knew, even though Minu's only helping this process along.

Jes understands immediately what to do and generates a field vaguely in the center of the orb. It's a strange sensation as there's nothing solid there anymore, not really, it's more like a cloud, a blur. He generates waves of gravitons from this central point, increasing it as the orb loses cohesion and begins to dissolve. He strengthens the field, and winces with discomfort as the tug of gravity seems to pull on his insides. Wait. *He's* not feeling that – he's sussing what Minu feels.

I'm OK. Keep going.

There's more chattering from the booth, and waves of excitement and intrigue, in addition to Minu's discomfort verging on pain. He doesn't normally suss other people's physical sensations – is this happening because their abilities are interacting? Minu's face shows the strain of his effort and Jes feels sweat beading all over his own body. The orb maintains more of its cohesion, but Jes feels the atoms yearning to fly apart – is this what Minu does?

"Don't let the orb dissolve," Matheson instructs. "Keep doing what you're doing."

There's a lurch deep in his guts – his or Minu's? It's hard to tell. With one strong pulse, the orb's form coheres and shrinks. In a few seconds, it's half the size it started as. Minu collapses and Jes's legs buckle, but he catches himself on the edge of the pedestal. The researchers are abuzz, something about density increasing…

The containment field releases and a pair of orderlies attend to Minu – one of them prepares an injection. His friend seems stunned but otherwise OK. *That was intense. I felt what you did inside the orb...*

"We'll let you rest up and then go again," Matheson informs them.

"He could feel my gravity inside him," Jes protests. "I don't want to hurt him."

"How do you know what he felt?"

"I... I could suss it." The truth, but not all of it.

Matheson seems to buy his explanation and doesn't suspect Minu of using his telepathy in defiance of orders. Matheson is very pleased with himself. "I understand your reservations. But peering into the secrets of creation is bound to hurt a little."

CHAPTER NINETEEN

The roto pulls up alongside Jes and Bo as they arrive at the back-gate, on their way to rehearsal. Jes knows who it is even before the mirrored outer shell swirls open to reveal Niko Dax settled inside, a predatory insect feeding on dread.

"Would you join me, please?" Dax grins, beckoning Jes into the vehicle.

"We have rehearsal," Bo says defensively.

Jes susses the force field Bo projects with his words, and the affection this sparks in him floods him with warmth. He savors it for a second before turning to Dax. "We're expected at the circus."

"I'm sure your crew boss will understand." Dax's eyes flit over to Bo. "You can run along. I assure you no harm will come to your boyfriend. If he does as he's told."

Jes flinches at the word "boyfriend" – he and Bo haven't even called each other that word yet. To hear it from Dax first feels like a violation.

"I'll come with you." Bo is speaking to Jes but maintains eye contact with Dax. What is he doing?

Dax smiles and shrugs. He is maintaining an air of indifference, but Jes susses his curiosity is piqued. "If you insist."

"I really do."

"It's OK." Jes presses a hand against Bo's chest. "You don't have to come. I'll be fine."

"I'm not letting you do this stuff alone anymore."

"Decide quickly if you're coming or going," Dax says, just a hint of impatience in his voice. "I've got a full day."

Jes sighs, climbs in, and slides closer to Dax to make room for Bo.

"Well isn't this cozy?" Dax comments with a chuckle. The inside of this roto, Dax's private ride, is shaded and cool, blue lights ring the ceiling. Subtle music chimes softly. The whole scene is almost soothing. "Oh, and congratulations on going viral." He smirks.

"What are you talking about?"

Dax pulls out his node, taps and slides, and a vid clip is projected into the space of the vehicle. Jes recognizes the footage immediately – the triplets in Jasmine's show. The shot pans from the triplets floating to the rest of the stage, but never captures him maskless behind the control panel. A bit of relief which Dax is quick to snatch away.

"I'm not sure this will help your efforts to lay low." There's a restrained laugh under his words and Jes resents him for finding humor in the situation. "I know from seeing the performance at the Luna Lux that you normally wear a mask, and there are lighting effects to make the whole thing look like an illusion. Could Mz Jonah's crew not accommodate you?" He doesn't really care about what happened at Jasmine's show, he just knows it will make Jes uneasy and maybe even a little paranoid.

Jes ignores the question. "I thought we were done." He hopes he's being assertive with this statement, and not too impertinent.

"As long as you do what I ask, I will keep your location hidden from the Institute. You did what I asked, and I told you your secret was safe. And now I'm asking you to do a new thing."

Bo gives his hand a squeeze. He squeezes back.

"You did quite a bit of damage to the Institute's facility on your way out," Dax says.

The sound of crumbling concrete walls and beams splitting apart fills his ears once again. The looks of surprise on the orderlies' faces flood before his eyes as the building tumbles down on top of them.

"I guess."

"Oh, don't be modest, Mr Tiqualo. I've seen the pictures of the rubble you left behind. Quite impressive. Well, now I want to show you an eyesore right here in Port Ruby that I'd like you to take down, like you did the Institute. You'd be doing this town a favor. But first, I'll need you to help me clear some garbage."

"Fine. Whatever you say." The quickest way to end this encounter is compliance.

"Oh, come now. I'm giving you an opportunity to exercise your gifts! Surely that's more rewarding than hauling lumber for that Hydraxian brute or getting no credit for providing the magic that elevates the triplets' rather trite performance."

"Quint's not a brute. He's one of the kindest people I've ever met. And the triplets are amazing–"

Dax waves dismissively. "Yes, yes. I'm sure what you say is true. My point is that you could rise to a much loftier position, with a talent like yours." That greedy feeling wafts off of him and fills the space of the roto, taking over Jes's awareness for a moment.

"I'm happy where I am, thanks."

"We'll see how long that lasts. You're young and carefree now. Relatively. Ambition to use one's talents comes to everyone with talent eventually. The desire for recognition. For some modicum of power."

"Maker of all, project much?" Bo interjects. "Why are you so interested in Jes? Why won't you leave him alone?"

Jes winces at Bo's interference, grateful as he is for the backup.

Dax meets Bo's eyes, speaks directly to him, a strange sight for Jes to witness. "Jes is a treasure that's fallen into my lap – Bo, is it? I'd be remiss not to leverage such a gift to my advantage as best I can. Jes has his gravity talent, and you your acrobatics. Making the most of opportunities – that's my talent. Ah, here we are."

The roto glides to a stop and swirls open. They're at the back entrance of the Apogee Pleasure Club.

"You two know this place, from your little outing here not long ago, yes?"

Jes and Bo clamber out, then stand waiting for Dax like they're his valets.

"This place has outlasted its usefulness," Dax continues. "I'll need you to take it down. But first I need your help with something inside."

"I don't know if I can bring down this whole building–"

"I saw what you did at the Institute."

"I was under duress–"

"As you are now. You understand my terms. Do as I ask or the Institute gets a surprise ping from this little out-of-the-way moon."

They walk through a storeroom and enter the club from behind the bar. The place is quiet, much quieter than it was the last time he was here. As if reading his thoughts, Dax says, "The club is closed at the moment, so we have the place all to ourselves. I hope you appreciate the exclusive access." He chuckles at this.

In the lounge area, one of Dax's gray-uniformed guards stands watch over three men bound together, their hands behind their backs.

"Please, no more," one of them says weakly. It's Hollan Zola. His face is bruised and puffy and blood drips down the side of his jaw, from the gash where his ear used to be.

Jes blanches at the sight of Zola and the others, bleeding from their mouths. He susses Bo's shock and rising dread –

this scene is more than he bargained for, despite his vivid imaginings.

"This is the garbage I needed your help with," Dax says with a sweep of his arm towards the bleeding men. "Crush them like decrepit rotos at the junkyard. Crush them like you did Mr Zola's hand."

Nausea ripples through him as Jes wraps his arms around his belly, like that will actually defend against anything. Bo's freaking out – anxiety and fear stab through Jes's sussing, intensely bright and sharp. His earlier boldness fades quickly as he faces the reality of the situation. Good. Jes would be worried about him if he wasn't scared.

"I've never... I..."

Dax smiles. "You've never taken a life before? Don't think of it like that. You're helping these pitiful examples of men into their next phase of existence. Souls that live on? Consciousnesses reborn? Matter and energy reabsorbed by the engine of creation? Don't you want to be the kick in the ass that sends them spinning off into all that?"

Bo's close to him now, a hand on his back, another on his shoulder. "It's OK," he soothes. "You don't have to do this."

"But I do..."

"Don't let him make you a monster like him." Bo's voice is quiet, and urgent. "Once you do this, there's no turning back."

"But the Institute–"

"We won't let them take you. You've got me and Esmée. Quint and Essa. Folks at the circus. We all have your back. Don't do this. I'm here with you. Let me be your rock."

Jes squeezes Bo's hand, sighs heavily. Their eyes meet and Bo gives a little nod. What would he have done if Bo hadn't been here? He hopes to never find out.

"No." Jes faces Dax, who's still maintaining that frozen, creepy smile. "I can't do this. I'm not a killer."

Dax's face falls. "I see. Well, that's disappointing. Very well." He snaps his fingers and the guard fires three quick rounds from his pulse weapon. Orange spheres strike each man in the chest and they seize and flop, lifeless against their bonds.

Jes stares at the dead men, surprised that he's hardly feeling anything at all.

"Come on." Dax doesn't wait for a response before he's charging out the way they entered. They follow him back out to the roto they arrived in. When they get to it, Dax turns to Jes once more. "Bring it down."

OK. He couldn't do the other thing, but this he can manage. He takes in the building's black exterior walls, the discreet signage at the gate to the smoking patio. The place gave him the creeps, but he's aware it's the livelihood for many people who don't deserve to be suddenly out of work, and he feels bad for what he's about to do. But at least it's not taking a life.

He closes his eyes, reaches out with his gravitational sense. He locates what feels like the center point and finds a place where two support beams intersect and opens a field there. Positioning his hands as if holding a sphere, he condenses gravity at that join, increasing it until the walls of the building begin to shake and buckle. It's the same process that he used in the storage room lock the last time he was here, and what he did to Zola's hand, only scaled up.

Right at the point the building starts to cave in on itself, he holds steady, stops increasing the field lest he break the street or the whole block. With a rumbling crash, the outer shell of the building – the walls, the roof – all fall in towards the gravity well he created. He releases the field and dust billows out from the wreckage; Dax waves a cloud of it away from his face.

The patrons at the café next door have all leapt to their feet, crowded away from the fallen building. People on the sidewalk stop and gawk and the street is full of chatter as people snap pics on their nodes.

"Most impressive," Dax says softly as he stares at the fallen building. For the first time, he susses as somewhat awestruck. Turning to Jes he adds, "But as impressed with and grateful for this demolition as I am, you did fail to fulfill a request. Reprimand is called for."

Jes sets his shoulders back, lifts his head. "I'm not sorry I didn't kill those men."

"They're dead anyway."

"But I'm not a murderer."

Dax smirks. "Well, I hope the peace of mind you get from that is worth the price."

Price? What's he–

The flash of a familiar blade answers the still unformed question. Dax pivots like he's dancing, and the curved edge sinks into Bo's shoulder, up to the hilt. Bo screams as Dax twists and thrusts the knife before pulling it out. There's not as much blood as Jes expected but Bo's arm dangles limp, dead weight.

Jes reels from the shock of Bo's scream and the terror he susses from him.

"No!" Bo cries. "What... What..." He moans, clutching his shoulder, wavering on his feet. "Oh fuck..."

Jes glares at Dax. "What did you do?"

"Severed some tendons," Dax says cheerily. "He'll live, though his acrobatic abilities might be hampered somewhat."

Jes feels resentment and hatred so intensely it would have melted Dax's face off if his eyes were lasers. How does he feel about taking a life now? He could so easily do to Dax's head what he just did to the Apogee.

As if sensing his thoughts, Dax says, "You should know that I've prepared a little data packet that will transmit word of your presence here, in the event of my untimely demise. I share this with you just to head off any ill-conceived notions you may harbor of escaping my influence."

"You–You're –" he stutters, distracted by the distress he susses from Bo, the sound of his whimpers and moans. "I–I'm aware of the consequences."

"I've already summoned medics," Dax says as he taps his node. "Don't say I never did anything for you."

The side of the roto swirls open, and he pauses before climbing in. "I have another engagement. And speaking of engagements, I would still like a sit-down with the esteemed Asuna couple in your orbit. The Voulos. I've tried setting up a meeting with them, but I get the distinct impression they're avoiding me. I'm sure a nudge from a trusted friend, such as yourself, could sway them. That's not such a huge favor to ask, is it?"

Is he really asking this now, with Bo wounded and in pain? "How exactly do you think I can sway them? You overestimate my influence."

"You can think of something, you're clever. I would be most disappointed if they leave this moon without a friendly conversation about what we might accomplish together. Especially since their daughter is one of the bright stars of my show. Tenant agreements can be so fragile, you know. Along with pretty singers' throats."

Jes clenches and unclenches his jaw as he struggles against the urge to scream obscenities at Dax. "I can't make people do what they don't want to do."

"The power of persuasion is a worthy skill to master, Jes." Dax settles into his seat. "Consider this an opportunity to practice. Now, I really must be off. I trust you can take care of your friend and yourself from here, yes? That's a good boy." The roto's side swirls shut and it rolls away just as a silver medic station glides up.

"What happened here?" one of the medics asks, addressing Jes though his attention is on Bo. His partner takes a scan as he preps the stretcher.

"An accident," Jes says. "It was an accident."

After accompanying Bo to the medical center and receiving assurances from the doctor that Bo was no longer in pain, Jes leaves him, sedated and sleeping, and makes his way to the circus. While Bo's shoulder can be repaired, they can't predict how much functionality will return, so he must let Aleia know that the star of the show is out of commission.

When he arrives at her office, Danae is there, looking a mess. Streaks of makeup run down her face, and she looks at Jes fearfully with red and puffy eyes. He susses waves of distress, grief, and a hint of rage that is almost drowned out by the other feelings.

"I know he knows and I know you helped him know it," she says, glaring at him.

"I'm sorry," Jes offers lamely.

His sentiment is rebuffed immediately with a humorless laugh. "I'm sure you are."

"Don't blame him," Aleia scolds her sister. "You're the one who wanted in on the local swirl market. You're the one who went against Niko. I told you not to try it, in case you've forgotten."

"How could I forget your cowardice?" Danae spits out. "We could have done it together and you left me to do it alone. Now my club is gone, and my men killed, and you still have your precious circus."

"It's called consequences, sister." Aleia's anger bristles the air. "What the fuck did you think would happen? You know what he's done to others that have crossed him."

"He destroyed my club! He killed people! Maybe if it was one of your performers you'd have a little more sympathy."

"Bo's hurt," Jes tosses out awkwardly. "He's at the medical center. Dax did it." He glances at Danae who perks up at this tidbit.

Aleia's face pales, and Jes susses that she's more shaken by this information than what her sister shared with her. "Hurt how?"

He tells her about Bo's shoulder.

"Why would he do that to him?"

Jes hesitates, looks down at his feet, feels the shame sending a rush of blood to his face. "I refused to... do something he wanted me to do."

He casts a glance at Danae as he says this, and she stops the nervous worrying of her hands, goes still and stares. "What is it that he wanted you to do, exactly?"

"He wanted me to hurt – to kill – Hollan Zola and the other two at the club."

Now it's Danae's turn to pale – the color drains from her face, her blue skin going ashen. "You were at the club." It's not a question, just a statement of fact. "Why did he bring you there?"

"Jes." Aleia catches his eyes, and he susses protectiveness and caution.

His mind goes blank as he struggles to make up a story about what happened, and all that comes out is the truth. "I have abilities. Like Emerged abilities, but different."

Danae takes this in; no surprise at all emanates from her.

"You used those abilities to bring down the club." Her emotional state goes flat and still, but it feels like a false calm.

"Yes. He wanted me to use them on your men. But I couldn't do that." He turns to Aleia. "That's why he hurt Bo. If I'd just–"

"You're not a killer," Aleia says hotly. "And what happened to Bo is not your fault. It happened because Niko Dax is a monster."

Danae brings her hands up to her head, tugs on her hair and lets out a wail of frustration, anger, loss. But no more fear.

"He has something on you, doesn't he?" She doesn't wait for him to answer, knowing what the answer is. "Oh, you're in it good now, kiddo."

Jes had been bracing himself to reveal the nature of his abilities to her, but Danae doesn't seem to care.

"We need a regime change in this town, sister. Do you see that? Everyone is sick of the tithing, and Romo's replacement is sick of the Magistrates being neutered lapdogs. This can't go on."

"People have been saying that about Niko for years," Aleia

counters. "And if you haven't noticed, he's more powerful than ever."

"We need a mager to do that mind-warp thing they do."

"Their powers don't work off-world–" Jes begins to say.

"I'm well aware how Emerged abilities work!" Danae snaps. "I'm just saying he would never pull this shit off against a mager or psion or whatever. He creates his little empire here where they have no power. Just like a coward." She stands abruptly. "You won't help me then?" This question is directed to her sister.

"I'll support you how I can, but I'm not moving against him."

"Give me my stash."

Aleia walks behind her desk, slides open the cabinet behind it and pulls out what Jes recognizes as a case of swirl. She hands it to her sister.

"Thanks for nothing, sis," Danae says. "This is how you are, even after I supported you when our parents opposed your transition."

Waves of exasperation emanate from Aleia. "Of course I appreciate your support. But my gender identity and your stupid actions are nowhere near similar circumstances."

Danae huffs at her sister before turning to Jes. "Stay away from me and mine. I don't care what he's got on you. You move against me again and I will hurt you." With that she takes off, leaving the door open as she goes.

When she's gone, Aleia turns to him sadly. Although he susses something other than sadness from her – fear. She's afraid of him, she always has been, and there's a new dimension to it now. It's a fear that borders on existential dread, and this realization brings a heaviness to his heart, like she's wrapped her own gravity field around it and is bringing it down. "I didn't realize you were powerful enough to bring down a building? I thought making things float and… crushing hands, was the extent of it."

"I could do it to him. What he asked me to do to those men."

"Oh, Jes. Have you ever done that? Killed anyone?"

He hesitates before answering. "I could do it, then take off again. Find somewhere else to go. He said he has a message ready to send to the people looking for me if something happens to him."

Aleia shakes her head as if shaking off a dream, a delusion. "No. We're not going down this road. I'm not going to ask you to… to corrupt yourself like that. My sister got herself into this mess she's in. It's hers to deal with."

"I won't hurt her," Jes says. "If he asks me to. I'll refuse."

She comes out from behind her desk, walks over to him and reaches out a hand. "May I?" After his nod, she places her hand on his shoulder. "I appreciate your loyalty. I'm not sure my sister deserves it."

THE INSTITUTE

Minu grows increasingly weak as the days and tests go on. He can no longer walk on his own, so an orderly must glide him into the lab on a hoverchair. It's clear that the interaction of their powers causes him physical distress, but Matheson is determined to plow ahead, not allowing time for Minu to recover and rest. While the interaction of their abilities is also uncomfortable for Jes, Minu bears the brunt of it. What Jes hates most is being the cause of his friend's pain.

Minu's face is wan and grim as they set up across from each other for the day's big show. Rosa is a part of this one. She's hooked up on a third platform just like they are, only she's in a bodysuit, tethered to a monitor by the cables that sprout from its back. An array of sensors forms a burst pattern on her chest and she looks for a second like a uniformed member of some fantastical fighting force.

Then she's their fellow test subject again, trying to look bored and above it all. She susses anxious, though. It buzzes against Jes's sense like a persistent fly. But at least there's energy there, which offers some promise of agency, as opposed to Minu who's a hollowed out version of himself and doesn't even make sarcastic telepathic comments anymore. His eyes are sunken moons, and all Jes susses is a heavy listlessness, like something drowned. He's defeated and unwell and Jes wishes there were something he could do for him.

Jes is on standby for the first phase of the process and keeps his attention on the booth while he waits for them to begin. A team of physicists has joined the usual group, and they're as interested in the physical phenomena being generated as Matheson and his team are by the question of how these bodies can do these things. The physicists don't seem concerned about their bodies at all. They're not people to them.

The chatter and the emotional flux up in the booth quiets down as they get ready to start and the containment field winks on. With a sigh, Minu touches the sphere before them. It starts to lose coherence as usual, then Matheson gives Rosa the signal for her to begin. She extends her index finger and electrical current flows from her fingertip to the sphere. Jes hasn't seen her ability before – it's beautiful. Are they trying to magnetize the particles or molecules or whatever little bits Minu dissolves the sphere into? Jes puts the question out of his head – sharing the same curiosity as the researchers fills him with loathing and resentment and a sense of betraying his fellow subjects. Betraying himself.

Minu gasps and winces and moans, but he doesn't drop his field. Why does he try so hard to please these assholes?

"Increase your charge," Matheson instructs.

Rosa extends another finger and the golden-yellow bolts that fly from her hand increase in size, brightness, intensity. Minu howls – a sudden, sharp declaration of pain and a wave of force ripples the air between him and Rosa. Whatever he's done, he didn't mean to, it was a reflex. She stumbles backwards, her bolts ceasing as her arm and the upper part of the torso where it connects lose coherence. She falls to the floor, thuds down face first, her arm and the upper quadrant of her torso dissolving into a bloody goo.

"Rosa!" Jes takes a step towards her but stops in his tracks when he susses a wave of despair and guilt from Minu. Vaguely he hears the alarmed shouts of the researchers. He's aware of the containment field's deactivation and the rush of orderlies.

"I'm sorry," Minu says through tears to Rosa's lifeless, partially dissolved form. "I'm sorry," he says, meeting Jes's eyes.

"No!" Jes calls and lunges forward, but he's too late, too slow. Minu has touched his hand to himself. He opens his mouth in silent anguish as the molecules of his own body fly apart; the semblance of form that it still contained falls to the floor in a shower of black dust.

There's only emptiness in the places of Jes's sussing, where Rosa and Minu once lived and shone.

"Get the subject out of here!" Matheson calls.

A collar clamps back down around his neck, and his sussing is muted once more. For once, he's glad of it.

It's not quite chaos in the lab, but it's frantic as researchers pore over the telemetry recorded of what just happened, as they scan Rosa's body and what's left of Minu. An orderly takes him by the arm, guides him out of the lab. As soon as the door shuts, it's all quiet in the corridor.

Once sealed back up in his room, Jes sits on his cot. He knocks on the wall, knowing there won't be a knock back this time. He wants to cry but he's too empty to cry. He stares at the wall, tries to make himself blank.

CHAPTER TWENTY

"Entering synchronous orbit," the smooth A.I. voice says as the ship's acceleration pauses. *"Welcome aboard the Epiphany."* They enter the lounge where the party is already abuzz, greeted by the stylish guests whose backdrop is a large porthole framing the moon and its planet. Jes walks beside Bo as they board Jasmine Jonah's personal starcruiser, placing a hand at Bo's back, like Bo had done for him before. This situation is totally different, and Jes doesn't know how best to offer support.

"It's my arm and shoulder that's fucked up," Bo says. "I can walk just fine."

Jes susses the annoyance and defensiveness and backs off. He looks at Bo's arm in its sling – festive and spangled, courtesy of the costume shop. A luminous white disc pulses on the front of his shoulder as it powers and guides the nanites tasked with repairing the severed tendons within. It's still unclear if his arm will return to the same strength and range of motion as before. Bo isn't truly as nonplussed as he seems – he's actively avoiding thinking about how his future performance ability will be affected by the injury. Jes can't help but wish he'd simply done as Dax asked, and crushed those men to bloody pulp.

"I know I can't suss, but I can tell you're fretting," Bo says. "Let's just have a good time tonight, OK? How often do we go to parties on popstar's personal ships? Let's not spoil it by dwelling on what that psycho did to me."

Doubt and worry lurk beneath Bo's brave front, like a bruise that hasn't appeared yet. Jes doesn't mention it. If Bo can put on a strong face, he can too.

The lounge is a large, oval-shaped room that contains no corners; it's like the inside of an egg lit soft pink and gold with twinkling lights in the arc of the ceiling. Another porthole looks out into deep space, and it holds a view of the gate that contains the slipstream's shining vortex when it opens, as it does now. Tendrils of purple and green and white light form a tunnel into space, and a ship, tiny in comparison, emerges from the swirling vortex. Once the ship is clear, the vortex swirls shut again, and the ring of the gate holds empty space once more.

A server walks by with a tray of drinks, something pink and bubbly.

"Here's to the time of our lives," Bo says as they clink glasses. He smiles, and Jes follows his lead, but it's Dax's face that smiles back, with that look of utter glee as he drives the knife into Bo's shoulder. That pleasure he'd sussed smears across time to this very moment. But look – they're here, on this ship, above this world, together after a creative triumph even if the future is uncertain. That's worth a real smile.

The lounge door slides open, and the gathered partygoers raise their glasses and cheer. Jasmine has arrived, flanked by her entourage. She blows kisses around the room, beaming as she steps into the center, taking possession of the space and those gathered with her upheld hands; it's like she's beaming silence from her palms. She commands attention so easily – did that quality contribute to her being a star, or does being a star confer this quality?

"It's been a spectacular run here on Persephone-9! I want to especially thank Aleia Siqui and the cast of Circus Infinite – you all have taught me a different kind of showbusiness, and enlightened me on what circus can do, and what it can be. Thank you to Esmée, and Zazie, Lula and Jujubee, and Gregor, and Bo and the other clowns – thank you for adding such richness to my show. You better watch out Aleia – I might poach your talent one day."

"I'll fight you!" Everyone chuckles at Aleia's retort.

"At the very least I'll scope the talent of the Bezan circus schools before my next tour."

Bo and the other Bezans present let out a whoop of approval at this.

"We have a couple of stops left on this tour, and after that I'm taking a break, and working on new material. I've learned so much here. I might even want a Mudraessa singer on the next project – anybody know where I can find one of them?"

Recognition ripples through the crowd and everyone turns to face and applaud Esmée, who's by the bar getting a drink. She waves. She shines.

"You and I are gonna talk," Jasmine says, pointing at Esmée. "Thank you so much for the warm reception," she continues. "Enjoy the party, and my roving home. Feel free to wander about the ship."

Music comes on, the Indran genre called Thrum, marked by droning sounds overlaid with percussive beats. Some people begin dancing.

"Hi, friends," Tasso says as he strolls up. "So sorry to hear about your accident." He offers a sympathetic look to Bo, places a hand gently on the uninjured shoulder.

"I'll be better than ever when I'm all healed up."

Jes susses the glimmer of doubt and worry, but keeps smiling.

"That's the spirit. Gotta get your hotness back on stage where it belongs," Tasso says with a wink.

Bo laughs, blushes. There's a surge in him at these words, towards Tasso, that Jes has sussed before, at other parties. And between Quint and Essa. At the sex club.

"You two enjoying the ship?" Tasso continues. "I've been

aboard a few times, but it never stops being cool. Maybe it's because I know who owns it."

"The ship's impressive," Jes says. "It's a Rijalen design."

"You an expert on starcruisers?"

"My parents brought me to parties on a couple of them when I was a kid. Ambassadors and stuff."

"So, you're fancy!"

"What?" Jes susses curiosity and secretiveness from Tasso and looks at him with an expression of what he hopes is only mild interest.

"Oh, me and Silas were wondering if you came from a privileged background. If you were going to ambassadors' parties as a kid, I guess that answers that."

Jes tries to laugh casually. "Well, I didn't enjoy it. You and Silas talked about me? And what makes you think I'm privileged?"

"Just an air about you."

Bo turns to face the view out the porthole with what Jes susses as relief, and seems only half-listening to the conversation.

Tasso seems mildly embarrassed. "Not as gossipy as that sounds! Mostly Silas was wondering about the floaty trick with the triplets. He was wondering if you had something to do with it since you're onstage with them, but only pretend to operate the fake controls."

A mild prick of panic rises on the back of Jes's neck, the hairs on his forearms. "I've got nothing to do with that circus magic," he says, repeating a phrase he heard from Aleia. "It's a trade secret though."

"Well you guys will have plenty of time to talk about it since he's going back to the circus."

An intuitive flash at this news, urging caution. "Silas is coming back to Port Ruby?"

"Yeah. He says life on the road is wearing him down. I get it, I guess. I might too if I was hauling shit like him. I mean, he and the rest of the crew are missing out on the party because they've got to pack everything up and get it loaded on our cargo transport before we leave. Luckily, we can sleep while we fly. Anyway, it's party time! You boys care to dance?" He turns to Bo. "Been a while since I've seen you shake those hips."

"Not in the dancing mood at the moment," Bo answers, indicating his shoulder.

"You don't need your arm to thrust," Tasso says, winking again – and there it is once more, the feeling Jes sussed earlier, the unmistakable swell of lust.

"Maybe later," Bo offers.

"Alright," Tasso says without another glance at Jes. He bops away, making his way to the dancefloor.

Bo smiles as he watches Tasso, and Jes picks up a wash of affection, nostalgia.

An unwelcome thought arises in Jes's mind. He tries to push it away, to not acknowledge it, but the image of Bo and Tasso together, naked and entwined, is too vivid in his mind. "Did you and he used to be a thing?"

The question intrudes on the space between them – or maybe he's just imagining it. His feelings are a jumble.

"Not exactly. I mean..." Bo flushes hotly, and Jes susses trepidation. "We played around some, a while ago. It was nothing serious. Just sex. Not like you and me."

Jes pulls his hand away when Bo reaches for it.

"Jes–"

"No, you're right, I guess that's not like us at all." It's irrational, but he feels the ice and distance crystallizing around his voice, around his heart. He's not good enough, he never has been and never will be. He's flawed and broken and what the fuck was he thinking getting into a romantic relationship with someone sexual? "I need a minute."

He can't even look Bo in the face before he dashes across the room and out the lounge door. Once he's out in the corridor, the door glides shut behind him and the din of the party is muffled and far away.

He worried about this from the beginning; people of different orientations in a relationship, an ace and a sexual person. It's true that Bo hasn't made a pass or suggested sex or pressed for it at all in the time they've been... doing whatever they're doing. What he sussed between him and Tasso was mild, though undeniable. Without his sussing ability, would he have picked up on anything at all? Bo has been nothing but respectful of his boundaries but now he wonders if they're fair to Bo. Maybe the two of them just shouldn't be romantic at all. It makes logical sense to call it off, yet the thought of it hurts his heart. It isn't just learning about Bo and Tasso that bothers him though.

He walks over to the nearest wayfinding panel and speaks his destination into it. "Restroom." The lights in the wall flash the path he needs to take, and he follows their illumination absentmindedly.

In an attempt to get his mind off the situation with Bo, Jes contemplates the other revelation Tasso offered – Silas is returning to the circus. In the limited times they've interacted, Silas was more closed off in his auric field than is usual for humans. Jes supposes that it's because he's a Loran human, who are not open in the psychic way that Indran humans are. His grandparents always said Lorans were more like how humans were before the Great Emergence of Indra; that they were like those that destroyed their own homeworld, the place called Earth, nearly a millennia ago. But what does that mean, really?

Over the last couple of nights, Silas had been perfunctory with Jes – they both had their jobs to do. Jes didn't really think anything of it. Still, there was a guardedness, a wariness he sussed from Silas that at first he thought he imagined, but now he's not so sure. Tonight, in fact, as Jes got into position, it seemed like Silas was inspecting him. He felt he was being checked out, but not in a sexual way. Could Silas have been looking for equipment or gear that could have created the antigravity effect so integral to the triplets' act? Did he think they had some heretofore unknown antigrav tech?

The wayfinding system beeps at him and he enters the washroom, making his way to the sink to splash cold water on his face. With damp hands he sweeps back the shag of hair his father always said was like a wild animal. He must confess, the old man may have had a point. He hasn't had another haircut since that day with Moxo. It doesn't seem lately that Dax cares how he's dressed, or how he presents himself. Dax is interested in other aspects now. Deeper aspects. Jes shakes off the disquieting feeling that Dax knows him better than he knows himself.

"Let yourself have fun, you stick in the mud," he says to his reflection. "Stop fretting."

As he approaches the lounge, he hears the crowd and sees that the doors are open and some of the party has spilled out into the corridor.

"There he is!" Esmée exclaims as he approaches. "This ship is fantastic! There's a games room and a holo theater, and a garden! I want to see the garden. Will you come with?"

Jes can't resist his friend's enthusiasm. He could use some company and he's not ready to head back into the main party yet. "OK."

Esmée takes his arm and leads them away from the lounge, down a different corridor than the one Jes just walked. She's in a stellar mood, and why shouldn't she be? She's the Circus Infinite's new star, tapped by Jasmine Jonah for a special project, a budding media darling for the Asuna people's emergence into galactic cultural participation. Who, in such a position, wouldn't be happy, excited, thrilled at what the future holds? He can suss her feeling and wishes he could feel it organically, within himself – an echo isn't the same.

They reach the garden, where green doors slide open to

reveal a park. The place is lit with artificial moonlight and has a gentle slope - upon its crest stands a ring of trees laden with white and pink flowers. There's a bench to one side, and flowers and other plants occupy small beds around the edge. Two Bezans occupy the bench and pass a reef pipe back and forth; they wave as Jes and Esmée enter. One large, viewing port opens into deep space; stars twinkle out in the abyss.

"Oh this is lovely!" she exclaims. "Let's sit on the hill."

The two friends walk up the slope and sit themselves down in the middle of the trees, taking in the heady scent of the blooms.

"So, I hope you don't forget us little people when you're a big star." Jes glances briefly at his friend, then looks out the viewport at outer space.

She giggles at this and flushes, which intensifies the pink highlights in her shimmer momentarily. "I certainly did not think I would end up here, that day we met on the shuttle from Rijal."

"It's been pretty great for you," he says.

She crinkles her brow in concern. "I know dealing with Dax and his demands has been tough," she says. "And there's always the threat of the Institute discovering you. But you have friends, and a community, and a place here. And you have Bo."

"Do I?" Jes realizes he's taken on a self-pitying tone but he doesn't care. He meets Esmée's curious look and relays what he learned about Tasso and Bo, what he sussed between them. "It felt like I was pushed aside," he goes on. "That's not what happened. I know that in my head, but that's what it feels like. And now I wonder if maybe being in a relationship isn't the smartest choice for either of us. He deserves someone who can return sexual feelings and I don't want to have to enforce boundaries all the time. Maker of all, I feel like such a freak."

Esmée pouts with sympathy at Jes's words, and her eyes are wide and shining. "You know my people understand desire in all its permutations."

"I'm aware."

She continues, "And there are asexuals among us too. They're well respected in our society. In Mudra-nul it's *alano*. Among my species, all forms of desire that don't infringe on the sovereign rights of another are respected. Asexuals – or aces, I think is your word for them? – are treasured as friends. Our empathic sense is finely tuned in to sexual desire, and spending time with those that don't experience it is something we savor."

"So we're just a break for you?" There's more bitterness in his voice than he intends, but again, he doesn't care. He's so attuned to other people's feelings *all the time* he hardly pays attention to his own, and it's time to shift that dynamic. Maybe this is something he could have gotten more adept at if he'd spent more time with his grandparents? His parents definitely never taught him to connect with his feelings.

"I suppose you could put it like that. Or you could consider that you're treasured for your specialness. Mixed orientation relationships aren't common among us, but they do happen. What matters is that the people involved value their heart connection above all. Bo has clearly chosen you. I sense it and I know you can too. Speaking as your friend – and speaking empath to empath – sometimes we have to choose which feelings to focus on. Focus on the love and let that guide you. The rest will sort itself."

Jes blinks tears from his eyes, wipes them with the back of his hand. He hopped on that shuttle to this moon seeking refuge; he hadn't expected to find friendship and belonging and love. "Thank you," he says.

"Any time."

The party is in full swing when Jes and Esmée make their way back to the lounge. Just inside the door, Beni makes out passionately with a human guy from Jasmine's crew. The pair's lust is haptic feedback against his sussing, pushing him away. The music thumps, shaking the floor and Jes's bones – it's a remix of a duet Jasmine did with Petra Kli, a Bezan rising star. Jes remembers the original version from before the Institute, how the people he hung out with made fun of it, but he'd always liked it and was embarrassed to say so. *Shine your light!* the chorus goes, *see how they all take flight with you...*

Tasso has stripped down to a sparkling thong and spins himself about a pole that wasn't there the last time Jes was in the room. Esmée whistles and cheers at this provocative display and Tasso beckons admirers of all genders to him. Jasmine Jonah herself is right up front cheering him on. He's also rouged his nipples so that they're livid pink against his lavender skin and they catch the light in bright flashes. Even Jes must admit, it's all quite a sight.

He looks around for the one person he wants to see right now. His eyes pass over Aleia, Essa, Quint, Moxo. Zazie, Lula, and Jujubee are right at the base of the pole beside Jasmine offering up encouragement. Finally, he sees Bo, watching the spectacle with a bemused look on his face. He's standing by the window where Jes left him. Did he leave and come back? Did he stand there the whole time? It doesn't matter. Jes heads straight for him. He does something he's never done except with his human grandparents – he steps up to Bo and wraps his arms around him in a tight embrace, being careful of the injured shoulder.

"I love you," he says. He pulls back and sees the look of astonishment pass across Bo's face, his eyes welling up.

OK, Jes thinks. *OK. This is home.*

PARENTS

It happens by accident – he's practicing his balance walking along the high wall of the garden at his parents' house. His friends are at the park, but he doesn't feel up for their usual shenanigans and besides, he has a bet with Ramis he's determined to win. There's a high window at the squat where Ramis and the others stay, and he thinks it's possible to climb into it from the outside, but nobody else does. When he explained how he'd do it, Ramis challenged him. So, he practices. To do what he says he can do will require traversing a narrow ledge – and the top of this wall is just about the right width.

He's getting the hang of it when he slips. *This is gonna hurt* runs through his head and then suddenly he stops falling. He's enveloped by a bubble of blue light and floats, inches off the ground. What the hell? The blue light winks off and he drops the remaining short distance. When the light goes away, he feels something inside him click – could it be… could *he* have been the source of the light, the floating?

He runs inside, sees if he can do it again. He soon discovers that when he points his hand at something, he can make the blue light appear around it and levitate it. Excitedly, he floats different items around the house: dishes, a vase, a chair, a table. He floats himself again. This is new. This is cool. Is he

Emerged? But this seems like a psion ability, not mager, and he's not on Indra. He doesn't ponder that mystery though, he's too thrilled at being able to make things float.

He can't wait to show his parents when they get home. He rarely shares anything with them at all, but this is something big. Something momentous and important. Might they be proud of him at last? Stop thinking of him as a waste of space? They might even come to love him? Maybe he'll get to go to Indra to train, to live.

Mother opens her mouth in surprise when her favorite vase lifts off the surface of the end table. Father's face remains stoic, but he susses awe and a bit of relief. Why relief? Does his father see some value in him now?

"Is this telekinesis?" Jes asks. "Can I train with the psions on Indra?"

"We'll see," Father says. There's some tentativeness there, but he doesn't think much about it. "We'll talk about it more in the morning."

"This is all very exciting," Mother says. "Let me fix you a cup of tea."

Mother hasn't made him tea in a very long time. He doesn't really want tea at the moment but agrees just because his mother is offering. He susses a sudden lightness from both his parents, replacing the sodden disappointment that's usually there. His heart swells. He's turned a corner with his parents – this ability he doesn't understand has elevated their esteem for him. It sucks that it took having a special ability to get there, but it's something he's wanted for years and years and he's glad for it now.

Halfway through his cup of tea he's woozy, sleepy, and the room darkens around him as he slips out of his chair to the floor.

When he wakes, he's on a gurney, restrained. "What is this –

what's happening?" His head is fuzzy, and he gets a bit dizzy when he tries to sit up. Was his tea drugged?

His parents are speaking with a human man, one with pale skin and sandy colored hair. He must be Loran – Indran humans aren't that light-skinned.

Something's off, something's missing. He looks around the room – there's two Rijala men in white uniforms at the foot of the gurney he's on, his parents and the other man. He feels the restraints tight against his wrists and ankles, the rough texture of the fabric on the gurney, the smell of the flowers in the vase he floated earlier, the sound of low voices. But no feelings.

He's not sussing anything. Then he notices another sensation – something is around his neck.

"What's going on?" he asks again, alarm growing within him.

"You're coming with us," one of the men in white says.

"We'll take good care of you," his companion adds.

Mother walks over. "These men will take you somewhere to learn more about the power you showed us." There's a new lightness in her eyes, a relief that registers even without his sussing.

"Why am I tied down? Why can't I go to Indra? I don't want to go."

Father is signing something for the human man he's talking to, hands over a datapad. "I believe that fulfills the contract."

"What? What contract? What's happening?" He struggles against the restraints.

The human turns to face him and walks over. "You'll be with me and my team at the Paragenetic Institute of the 9-Stars. We have much to learn from you. You'll be staying with us for a while."

"Who are you? I don't want to stay with you!" He pulls harder and the restraints seem to get tighter as he does so.

"We'll sedate you again if you keep that up," the human says.

"Why are you letting them take me?" he cries. His tears sting; he's ashamed and embarrassed that he cares, but he does care. "Why did you even have me then? Just to throw me away? Please! No! No! Where are you taking me?" There's a Rijala in white at each end of the gurney, and they're bringing him to the door.

"I'm your son! Why don't you love me? Please don't! I'll behave! I won't get in any more trouble, I promise. I promise!"

Mother leaves the room, walks into the kitchen and doesn't look back.

Father stands by the door. "He's all yours," he says to the human.

"Why? Why are you doing this?" Jes asks again.

"We are fulfilling our duty," Father says. He doesn't even say goodbye.

Duty? What duty? What the fuck does that mean?

Jes is wheeled into the back of the medical transport waiting outside the house. He stares up at the sterile interior that surrounds him. The human leans over him, smiles a creepy smile. "I'm Doctor Matheson," he says. "We're going to be great friends."

CHAPTER TWENTY-ONE

The buzz of Jasmine Jonah's presence in their orbit sticks with the cast for a couple of weeks after she leaves, then things fall into a new normal. The flow of the new show clicks into place, and the line-up for the VIP afterparties in the Singularity settles into a regular rotation. Aleia surprises Jes by tapping him to be the host and greeter at these post-show events.

"It's your idea, so it's kind of your party," Aleia says, offering the role. "And besides, you look good all dressed up. You can use your empathic sense to... guide the guests to their most optimal experience. Plus, we need someone to introduce the acts."

Although he's a bit nervous at first, Jes sees the wisdom in this approach, and he appreciates having a larger role in the circus and the bump in pay that comes with it.

"You're moving up in the world," Quint comments. "It's a good thing Silas is back. I'll put him right back where he was, in your old spot, which was his old spot. It's perfect."

Yes, perfect.

"They're serious about you being their good luck charm, huh?" Silas says as he and Jes go through the now-familiar routine of Jes stepping down off the set-piece as Silas secures it backstage. The act once again elicits sustained applause which doesn't fully die down, even as the next act is ready to begin.

Silas locks the wheel as Jes takes the steps down from the platform. "You sure there's nothing more to it than that?"

"What more to it could there be?" Jes replies. Instinctively he tightens up his auric field, brings it into himself as if Silas were a telepath who could probe his thoughts. He realizes this can't be and relaxes a bit, trying instead to suss out Silas's intention behind the question. He senses nothing from him. Like usual.

"It's just a to-do to get you onstage with them when – well – you don't do much out there."

Damn. He'd always thought it was a flimsy rationale, but the triplets had been able to sell it, especially Jujubee. But maybe it's time to figure out another ruse, no matter how obvious and desperate. "The triplets insist. You know how divas are," he says, feeling rather lame.

"I don't remember them being that way before."

Jes shrugs. "People change."

Silas seems about to say something else when Jes cuts him off. "I have to get ready for the afterparty." This is true.

Jes goes into the dressing room to change out of his crew-blacks into the suit he wears to host at the Singularity, something the costume shop tailored to him. This one is a deep purple velvet, subtly studded with sequined stripes of the same color. The pants are form-fitting, as is the black shirt. The jacket he leaves hanging as he sits down to do his make-up.

Essa is back there too, touching up her look for her next act, the one with the silks. "You seem troubled," she says.

Jes takes the station next to hers and fixes his hair, then applies some make-up and glitter to his face like Esmée taught him. He hadn't really wanted to get all made up, but Aleia explained that as far as she was concerned, he was another character in the Circus Infinite experience, even if he's not onstage performing physical feats. He applies some white around his eyes, some violet and silver and white glitter that looks a bit garish in the bright lights of the makeup station but work quite well in the dimmer, atmospheric lighting of the Singularity.

"Silas is asking a lot of questions about my being onstage for the triplets. It might be time to figure out another way."

Essa sighs as she pins on a sparkling red headpiece that accents her halo brilliantly. "You're a character in the act. It's not up to crew to question artistic decisions." She gives him a wink.

Jes pauses his preparations, and with eyes closed he basks in the comfort and acceptance he susses from his friend. When he opens his eyes again, he decides that's enough glitter and powder.

"How's life in the circus house? Quint and I miss having you around."

"Longing for my return already, huh?" Jes misses them too even though it's only been a week since he moved out.

"You're a very calming presence, Jes." She turns her face to one side, then the other, giving a final look at her make up. "Plus I liked it when you did the dishes. How's Bo?"

Bo's role has gone to Beni, who capably performs the feats, but lacks Bo's panache and appearance of ease. He pulls it off, and Bo has stopped coming to the shows.

"He doesn't have to wear the sling anymore, and he says he's not in pain but I know that's not totally true. He can't even get into a handstand, or hang, so he's far from being able to take back his old part. It bothers him more than he lets on."

"Well, there's a lot of love around him. I can't imagine going through that. To not be able to do what I do…" She trails off as she stands, turns and examines herself in the full-length mirror behind them. The moment of vulnerability passes as her show face slips on. "I'm doing canes tonight at the afterparty. See you there." She gives him a wink before dashing through the curtains to get to her mark.

Essa's act is two acts from the finale, which means it's time for Jes to get to the check-in before tonight's service. Satisfied with his look, he leaves the backstage area and heads out one of the side exits of the main tent and crosses the lawn to the Singularity. A familiar buzz sounds that is at first quiet and distant, but quickly grows louder and closer behind him. He senses the presence landing lightly on the grass beside him and susses nothing. Still, a deep presence draws his attention.

"Hi, Kush O-Nhar."

A series of clicks before the response in words. "Good evening, Jes. All ready to play host?"

"As ever."

The Singularity's interior space includes a private room, which some nights is used by Kush O-Nhar to offer one-on-one consultations, and other nights is used for small private groups. Tonight is clearly one of the former. Jes lets the Mantodean enter first, then follows. As he steps through the curtain, he wonders what the night will bring. The entire experience is still new enough that Jes can't quite say that it's settled into routine, but now, on the ninth night, he has a good idea of what to expect.

Each night has a set number of reservations, so there is no walk-up business. As he takes his station, he's put disconcertingly in mind of the hostess at the Apogee Pleasure Club.

Every party that arrives – sometimes a couple, sometimes a platonic group, the occasional polyamorous triad – Jes greets with a smile and the appropriate air of mystery. Sometimes the female-identified are overtly flirtatious, sometimes the male, occasionally someone on the spectrum who is no discernible gender, and Jes rolls with it. It's not the range of genders that took getting used to, but the flirting. Flirting is just another form of flattery, he's realized, and those that do it aren't necessarily operating from a place of sexual desire, but sometimes a place of assumed desire on his part. He doesn't have to return it, and nobody really expects him to in his role, but he is slowly figuring out how to respond in kind so that no one is insulted, so that egos are stroked when required. He knows how to compliment the fit of a dress or suit, express surprise at someone's true age, pay deference to a guest's authoritative manner...

Flirting has been the most revealing dynamic, however. It's couched in a nebulous haze of desire but expressed – usually – with the aim of manipulation to get something they want: a better table, a discount on drinks or reef, some form of special treatment. On a few, rare occasions, it seems the flirting is just for fun and this he finds most difficult to understand; engaging in such behavior for a transactional reason makes sense, but to do it just for the sake of it? He doesn't get that.

"Welcome to the Singularity," he says to each arrival, his standard greeting to everyone who passes through the curtain. He tries to make each guest feel special, that their presence is an honor. As an introvert, this isn't a role he'd ever seen himself performing, but he finds he likes having a part to play. When he knows he's been less than warm or the guest feels slighted for whatever reason, he makes up for it by offering gratis a bowl of reef, or a round of drinks if the party aren't into that. Everyone who comes to the Singularity likes to get a buzz on something.

Once everyone is seated, it's time for Jes to perform his other duty. "Oh, most esteemed and adventurous guests," he says with a newly adopted formal enunciation he deploys only in this context. "Thank you for joining us at the Singularity. We remind you that recording of any kind is prohibited and will result in your immediate exit. Emergency routes are marked by the red circles at each quadrant." As he speaks, he walks from the center of the performance floor to a seat at a booth near the entrance. "If anyone is interested in a sitting with our resident Weaveseer, Kush O-Nhar, please see me at the hospitality station. Other than that, our attendants can see to your imbibing needs." He takes his seat. "Please enjoy the Circus Infinite's Singularity Salon."

The spotlight winks off and darkness quickly fills the tent before a warm amber glow takes its place and Essa is there with her canes, standing beside them, one hand on a wooden handle. Then, placing each hand on a cane, she slowly presses herself up, then raises both legs as she articulates them with a motion like walking right up invisible stairs that are also upside down, and then she's in a handstand, and then she bends her torso gracefully to one side. She lifts a hand, and holds the position on one hand. The crowd is with her by this point. She flicks her head up so that she's looking straight out at the darkness of the lounge and the golden glint of her halo flashes and her shimmer gleams so quick it's almost a trick of light.

Jes hears a late arrival come through the curtain and susses a wave of nervousness. He gets up to greet the new guest – it's Aleia. "Has he arrived yet?" she asks.

He doesn't need to ask who she means. "No. Do you want to just head back to his booth?" There's a four-top that's reserved exclusively for Niko Dax and guests.

"Oh no. He hates it when someone's at his table before he arrives."

"You know me so well, Aleia."

His voice startles both of them, who turn to see him stepping through the curtain. He smirks with the satisfaction of someone who knows he was just spoken of in fearful tones.

"That's why we work so well together," he continues. "You're so unlike your traitorous sister."

Jes susses Aleia tensing with apprehension though she does a remarkable job of not letting it show.

"I have to announce the next act…" Jes begins to explain apologetically.

Dax waves him off. "I know where my table is. I appreciate your consideration of protocol, Mr Tiqualo."

Jes cringes at being called that. Especially by him.

"Oh, and by the way, Mr Tiqualo–" It's as if Dax knows just how much that bugs him, "–I'm still waiting to meet the Voulos."

"They're very busy," Jes says lamely, as the crowd, thankfully, applauds Essa's act. Dax and Aleia head for his booth while Jes takes center stage.

"Another round of appreciation for Essa, our most versatile performer!" he exclaims cheerily and smiles at the shadows around the room. With the stage light on him, he can't see the audience at all, but he can suss their emotional discharges. There is respect, and a dash of envy and a fair bit of lust for the performer. Essa must feel that too, especially in such close quarters. How does it not distract her from her performance?

"Our next performer is an example of the beauty that's possible when a world that values brute strength allows grace to rise in its midst. Please welcome our master manipulator of objects – Moxo Thron!"

A murmur from the crowd as Moxo makes his appearance. He begins with butterflying a single ball in each hand, his four arms waving gracefully back and forth in a syncopated rhythm.

Jes makes his way back to his station. As he crosses the floor, he casts a glance over to where Dax and Aleia sit at the Reserved booth. He's not sure he wants to know what they're talking about.

The rest of the show goes by in a blur. The triplets do a grounded set. A human girl does a dance with hoops – she's a new hire for the Singularity line-up but isn't in the mainstage show. There's a static trapeze act by one of the Bezans that joins Bo – now Beni – in the chase-through-the-forest part of the show. Jes introduces all of them and barely remembers doing it when he's done. This gig does seem to be becoming second nature. During all of this he also books a few sessions for Kush O-Nhar, and processes the payments for that service.

After the short stage show, the place switches into lounge mode, and the performers come out and speak with members of the audience casually. An exhaust fan comes on as the air becomes redolent with reef and chordash and Jes hears it, ever so slightly, in the background just under the music, the pragmatism that undergirds the fanciful and makes it work. They'd gone back and forth – he and Aleia – about the proper volume, and finally arrived at the conclusion that softer music and hearing a whisper of the fan was better than turning the music up loud enough to cover the fan noise, which also would have made having conversations more difficult. He focuses on these details to keep his mind off of what Aleia and Dax could possibly be talking about all this time.

He watches Dax get up from the booth and give a slight bow to Aleia, as if he were the one in her service. He gives Jes a nod and flashes his oddly disquieting smile as he walks by on his way out. Jes looks over at Aleia, still sitting at the booth, staring at her drink. She stirs, as if feeling his attention on her, then waves him over.

"Can you come to my office after closing?" she asks.

He nods. "Sure. What did he want?"

"Not here."

After the Singularity closes, Jes says good-night to Essa and Kush O-Nhar who are chatting just outside its door. Moxo intercepts him on the lawn as he heads for Aleia's office.

"What *are* you?" he asks, his voice full of venom. He'd been calm and professional during the show and after-party, so this sudden harshness takes Jes aback even though he's well aware of Moxo's dislike of him.

"What do you mean?"

"I *saw* you," Moxo hisses. "I saw you with Niko Dax after the Apogee Club went down. I was at the café next door, in my usual spot, when the building fell. When I joined the crowd looking at the wreckage I saw you, and Bo. I saw Bo's supposed 'accident'. You did it, didn't you? You have powers. You make the triplets float. And Dax has something on you, doesn't he? It all makes sense now. What *are* you?"

"I think you need to calm down," Jes says, making the

appropriate gesture with his hands. He hates it so much when people do it to him, he can't believe he's doing it to someone else. He susses Moxo's increasing hostility. His heart quickens, his palms erupt with sweat and his head throbs in time with the flashes of white in his eyes.

"Don't try to gaslight me! Answer my question!"

"Is everything alright?" Essa calls over to them.

"Fine!" Moxo barks at her. He turns back on Jes. "Tell me what you are!" He lunges, reaching all four hands out to grasp Jes by the lapel.

Jes reacts.

Only not with his gravity powers. The headache building since the start of this conversation releases in a burst from his head. A white beam shines from the center of his forehead, connecting with Moxo's head. The beam is threaded through with crystalline patterns, like tiny, complex circuitry. Moxo's eyes open wide with shock and the top of his head begins glowing with the same white light. Vaguely, in the background, Jes hears Essa calling his name. There's a moment of connection – Jes feels his mind and Moxo's intertwine. Then a jolt from Jes, like an electric current across a wire, and Moxo seizes, then falls to the ground as the beam of light dissipates.

Essa and Kush O-Nhar rush over.

"Moxo!" Essa cries, and kneels beside the fallen juggler. She looks up at Jes, her face registering shock, and curiosity.

"It looks like your mager blood has asserted itself," Kush O-Nhar says. "You manifested a mental disruption pattern."

Jes stammers. "I–I've never done that before. I d-don't know what..."

"I thought those kinds of abilities don't work off the world of origin?" Essa says.

"Not usually," Kush O-Nhar replies. "But we already know that Jes is most unusual."

"I'm sorry!" Jes looks despondently at Kush O-Nhar and at Essa. "Oh, maker of all, Moxo! I didn't mean to hurt him –

I…" The soft pressure of an insect forearm on his shoulder. He turns to see the Mantodean face he's come to know, antennae quivering in a way he's never seen before. Is it concern?

"I can help him," Kush O-Nhar says. "He will be alright. I believe you have somewhere to be."

"What?" Jes is confused. "I don't know—"

"Aleia is waiting."

Oh shit. That's right. He'd been on his way somewhere when Moxo interrupted him. He doesn't think he'll ever get used to the way Kush O-Nhar just knows things. Sees things.

"Go," Kush O-Nhar says. "We'll take care of this."

Jes does as he's told, and heads for the main tent, shaking.

When he arrives at Aleia's office he is surprised – yet also not – to find Danae there as well. She looks haggard, her hair covered by a scarf, dark rings around her eyes.

"He's going to eliminate me," she says. "I haven't been home since Hollan and the others… since my club…"

Jes susses Danae's terror, frustration, resentment and self-righteous anger. "That's a hard circumstance. I'm sorry you're going through that."

She scoffs. "I'm sure you are."

"We need to take definitive action or we'll never get him off any of our backs," Aleia says.

"What did he want with you tonight?" Jes asks.

"He wants me to take over his swirl operation, run it out of the Singularity. I told him that was a ridiculous idea, but he won't hear it. He just had these delivered." She gestures to a tapestry covered bundle against the wall. Pulling the cloth aside, she reveals a stack of familiar black cases. On each one is an emblem he's seen before – the winged serpent eating its tail. The symbol he found on Chief Magistrate Romo's crystal reader.

"I know that symbol," he offers, and explains where he's seen it.

"It's a decoy syndicate," Danae explains. "It must be – I've never seen that emblem before, and I know them all. This is a tactic that I've heard the Magistrates are using. They create a fake syndicate with a fake emblem, which that must be–" she points at the serpent symbol "– since you found it in Romo's files. They use them to track the contraband circulating as bait. Sometimes it's narcotics, sometimes it's weapons. There's a bust coming, sister, and Niko wants you to take the fall."

Danae leaps up from her seat and paces. "If Niko had Jes discover the emblem, that means he knows it's a fakeout and he knows that the Magistrates are about to crack down on the swirl trade." She inhales dramatically, casts a fraught glance to her sister. "You're the chosen sacrifice now that I'm already destroyed."

"I thought he has friends among the Magistrates?" Jes says.

"He does, but the Magistrate Regents know this and some are working to root out the corruption in their midst."

Aleia turns on her sister. "This is all your fault, you understand. He's coming after me now that he can't hurt you anymore." She wants to say something else but holds back.

Danae can sense it and probes her, "Say what you have to say." It's a challenge, a dare.

"You just had to get greedy. On top of breaking whatever kind of heart he has, though I suspect he's just mad someone said no to him."

Danae holds up her hands. "If blaming me will help you, have at it! But please let's not forget – he wants to kill me! Maker of all, I've got to get the fuck off this rock."

Jes feels what she feels, all paranoia and panic, and he can't quite keep the pity out of his eyes, which he can tell aggravates her more. He wouldn't wish her plight on anyone, but he does see that she's facing the result of her own actions. The dispassion, even coldness, with which he thinks this takes him aback. Could he be learning the wrong sorts of lessons from Niko Dax?

He susses a snap of revelation. "We need his codex!" Danae

exclaims. "There are Magistrates who've been after Dax for years, who oppose the corruption in their midst. They've tried to get me to testify against him in the past. We turn the codex over to them, and they'll have all they need to bring down his network and lock him up on a penal station forever. Or for a long time anyway."

"What's this codex?" Jes asks.

"It's a data crystal," Danae explains. "All his contacts, the names and contact information for everyone in his organization, his ledgers, a diary of his deals, contracts, leverage. The Triple Moon Syndicate – even information on the Magistrates loyal to him – all of it on a crystal in his desk."

"Does anybody else know about it?"

She shakes her head. "Possible, but I doubt it. He only told me because we used to be… close."

"Why did you want to see me?" He directs this question to Aleia, and his tone is more curt than he means.

"To see if you knew anything about this," Aleia replies. "Since you've been… assisting him. Good thing too, or we wouldn't have known about the emblem." She gestures to the cases full of swirl.

"OK. We need to get the codex. How?"

A slow smile creeps over Aleia's face, which to Jes is strange and out of place, considering. "We need to break into his office. And I know someone who has experience with that sort of thing." She meets his eyes, and he knows he's got another task ahead of him.

"You're home late," Bo says when Jes walks into the practice room at the house. He and Beni are on the floor, both of them topless and barefoot, with Bo on his back, balancing Beni on his feet. Bo's shoulder is encased in the sheath that replaced the more obtrusive sling, now that the healing is farther along. The faint glow of the nanite disc pulses through the sheer black fabric. Esmée watches from the sofa, amused.

Beni hops off and Bo brings his legs down for a rest. He sits up slowly and rubs his recovering shoulder.

"You should be careful with that." For a moment Jes fears he sounds like an overly anxious, worried parent, but decides he's not going to hide his concern.

"My legs work fine. Circus business keep you?" Jes susses a twinge of annoyance and doesn't know how to answer.

"I don't get how the Hydraxians flip around the way they do," Beni says. "We can barely change positions without falling over."

"It's called a Risley act," a voice says behind him. "At least that's what they used to call it on Earth."

Jes turns and to his dismay sees Silas walking in, carrying two bottles in one hand. He crosses the room and sits on the sofa, hands a bottle to Esmée. They clink bottles and she beams at him as she rests her feet in his lap.

Are they...?

Silas continues, "It's named after the guy who developed it, hundreds of years before the Great Migration. So, like, a really long time ago. It was also sometimes called Icarian Games, but I don't really get that one. I think the Hydraxians call it 'foot tumbling'. Something like that. I think it's cool how similar acts have been developed by different species and different traditions on multiple worlds throughout time."

"How do you know all that?" Beni asks.

"I researched the human circus tradition when Quint first hired me," he says. "I figured I should know something about what I was getting into."

"Did you ever think about training an act?" Esmée asks.

He shakes his head. "No way. I don't like being upside down and I'm scared of heights. And for most of that stuff, don't you have to start when you're a little kid?"

"Depends on the act," Beni says. "But mostly that's true, yeah. The best way to get over being scared is to just climb way high, and hang or jump off something. Onto a mat or into water though. A hard surface would defeat the purpose."

"You don't say."

"We can get you set up at the space—"

"I'm good, thanks." Silas holds his hands up in protest. "I'd have done it before now if I wanted to. It's not like I haven't had the opportunity."

Jes is surprised that Silas would reveal a fear like that, he's always seemed so cagey. Somehow, knowing that Silas has this fear of heights makes Jes less wary. Is that what he wants though? To be less wary? To know that Silas is afraid of something? Maker of all, why does he distrust Silas so much? Moxo's outright hostility is easier to deal with.

Bo clears his throat, casts a curious look, and Jes realizes that he never answered Bo's question and has just been staring at Esmée and Silas on the sofa. In his mind he sees Moxo's shocked face as the beam he projected connected their minds. He sees Danae's anguished face, the fear he sussed from her echoes in him. This night has been too much already, and he doesn't think he can take anything else upsetting. Like one of his closest friends getting intimate with someone he's wary of.

"Aleia wanted to see me after the Singularity," he explains, struggling to keep his voice neutral.

"You're like her right hand, then?" Silas asks. "Host of the afterparty, getting called to midnight meetings. Plus coming up with the concept for the show."

"I know what the people want, I guess."

"Got your finger on the pulse, huh? What do I want?"

Jes feels the burn of everyone's attention on him and he really doesn't like it. "I don't know what you want, Silas," he snaps. "I mean, except for fucking Esmée I guess."

"Jes!" Esmée exclaims, eyes wide.

An awkward silence descends. Jes mutters a "sorry" and heads for the kitchen. He opens the refrigerator and stares at the contents. He thinks maybe he wants a beer but then decides he doesn't really.

"You OK?" Bo says, coming in behind him. He moves his injured arm gingerly, rubs the shoulder with his other hand and winces.

Jes nods.

They hear the front door opening and closing and then Esmée joins them. "That was rude."

"I'm sorry," Jes says. "Really."

"I might like him," she divulges. "I don't usually go for males. Or humans, not that I had much exposure before coming here. What do you have against him?"

Jes sighs. "He's good at closing off to my empathic sense and that makes me… trust him less? He's a diaspora human and they make me nervous? He's too curious about why I'm onstage for the triplets and that puts me on edge? I don't know. But date him if you want, Esmée. It's none of my business."

"Well you're right about that, it isn't any of your business. But it's a little soon to say 'date'. It's just been flirting so far."

"Has he asked about me?" Jes realizes the question makes him seem indefensibly self-centered but the intuitive ping to ask it is just too strong to set aside.

Esmée seems confused by the question. "What? None of this has anything to do with you–"

"Has he?"

Esmée sighs heavily and her annoyance burns between them. "Yes, actually. He's curious about your place in the triplets' act. Like you said. But I mean we weren't talking *about* you. We were just talking about the circus in general. I told him you're their good luck charm."

"I don't get what that proves though…" Bo says, turning to Jes.

"It doesn't prove anything except he has a reasonable question about an unusual situation," Esmée says, her annoyance clear in her voice, her face. Who needs sussing?

"You're right," Jes says. "His questions and not being able to suss him just puts me on edge, that's all. I'm sorry I was rude.

It's been a rough night. I'll apologize to him the first chance I get. OK?"

Esmée crosses her arms and nods.

"There's something else going on with you, isn't there?" Bo prods. "Something happened tonight."

Jes sighs, and tells his friends about what happened with Moxo, the manifestation of the mager ability.

"What does that mean that you manifested that ability off Rijal?" Esmée asks. "I mean, can other Emerged Ones do that too? Is it..." Her eyes open wide at the thought she tumbles in her mind. "Is it because you're a hybrid?"

"I don't know," Jes says.

"Maybe it's linked to you having the gravity power?" Bo offers.

"Could be," Jes says, his frustration mounting. "I don't know! You know as much as I do about all this."

"Are you going to try to do it on purpose?" Esmée is eager, cautious and curious all at once.

"I don't know about that. I don't know how I did it. I don't know what I did to Moxo, even. I could potentially fuck up somebody's mind – I might have done that already. I don't think I should mess around with it."

"You've got to figure out how to get it under control somehow," Esmée chides. "I understand not wanting to fuck somebody up, but that's all the more reason to practice or train it somehow, isn't it?"

"I think Kush O-Nhar is your best bet," Bo says. "If anybody on this moon can help you, it would be him."

"You're right," Jes agrees. "I'll talk to him as soon as I can. He'll probably come to me at some point. He seemed... *intrigued* by it all."

"So, what did Aleia want with you?" Bo asks, changing the subject.

Jes doesn't mind talking about something else and is about to answer when Beni walks into the kitchen. "I'm hungry. Anybody else hungry?" He makes his way for the fridge.

"She just wanted to… review the line-up for the Singularity."

Bo and Esmée both know there's something more, but say nothing since Beni's there. They know they'll hear about it soon enough.

CHAPTER TWENTY-TWO

"You want us to meet with that unctuous man?"

From her tone of voice and expression, Eronda is clearly incredulous at the request.

"It would help the circus a great deal," Esmée says, relaying the story she and Jes worked out ahead of this conversation. "He's keen to discuss a business proposition, and we also suspect he wants to get rid of the circus. You could hear out his ideas without committing to anything, and maybe ask him what his plans are for the circus? Maybe plug it, tell him how much you loved it? He holds you in high esteem, he'd value your opinion."

They agreed to not tell them about Dax's extortion and questionable dealings, nor about the fact that they needed a diversion to get Dax out of his office at a predictable time. Enovo wouldn't be good at keeping up the pretense, according to Esmée. Jes believes her.

"I can consider this policy research," Enovo says. "See how this Port Ruby business figure thinks we can collaborate. What possibilities might there be?" He's so earnest in this Jes feels bad for not sharing the whole truth. A little.

"I suppose a meeting isn't that heinous a request." Eronda stares her husband down over this point. A look passes between them, and acquiescing with a tilt of her head, she finally says, "Fine. We'll meet Mr Dax for tea."

And now the meeting with the Asuna couple that Dax has longed for is happening, right on schedule. When Jes gets word on his borrowed node – he doesn't want to use the one Dax gave him, which is sure to be monitored – first from Esmée that her parents have left for the meeting, and then from Bo who's been keeping an eye out for Dax's departure in the Luna Lux lobby, he knows it's time to move.

Aleia and Danae should be with Danae's contacts within the Magistrates by now. One of the many aspects of Dax's operation that can be gleaned from the codex is the identity of his lieutenants, which not even Danae knows with any certainty, though she counts as one of them. Counted. But they don't want any of them to have the opportunity to warn the others, or Dax, and so squads stand at the ready – right now – to be deployed to arrest all of them simultaneously upon receipt of the information on the codex. The information they're all waiting for him to grab. No pressure.

He stands on the roof of the Luna Lux, looking over the ledge at the gardens that sprawl below. From this height, the circus tents look like models in a diorama, and the people milling about are the size of bugs. In this moment, he's grateful he doesn't have Silas' fear of heights.

Jes generates a field around himself, and as he lifts off the rooftop, he turns so that he's facing towards the building, then steps off the edge. Slowly increasing the gravity, he lets himself sink gently, gently. He's lined himself up so that as he drifts down, he'll end up directly in front of the side panel window of Dax's office. Because the office is so high up, coming down to it from the roof is a far shorter distance to float than coming up to it from the ground. Also, there are fewer potential witnesses this high up.

He pulls out the lockpick tools Dax gave him, relishing the irony of using them to break into his office. He makes quick work of getting the window unlocked. After prying it ajar, he pulls it all the way open. The narrow opening is tight, but he manages to squeeze himself through with some effort, and he doesn't release the gravity field until he's more than half-way in. It's easier to maneuver himself through the window without also maintaining the field, but he waits until he is further in because of what happens next: a wave of vertiginous panic fills him as he feels gravity's pull again, and realizes how high up he is, which somehow didn't seem so bad when he was weightless. He focuses on the floor in front of him.

With an awkward tumble he gets himself down, lays on his back for a second to catch his breath, then sits up and goes straight for the desk. He remembers from his last time being here that Dax had put the data crystal in a panel in the top right drawer. It's locked, of course, but with the awl in his kit, he picks the lock easily. He remembers his father telling him once that he was wasting his life devoting time to learning such questionable skills, and chuckles. He pulls the drawer open. "Shit."

The panel that contains the crystal is also locked, and it's a bio-scan. It probably requires Dax's thumbprint or something – they should have foreseen this. The sensation of handling a severed eyeball comes back to him, and he grimaces at the memory. This isn't a lock he can pick. He considers trying to pry it open with the file he has but there's no opening, no visible seal. OK, there's no other option. He realizes he has to use his crushing technique, which is risky because he might damage the crystal, but he sees no other way. He takes several breaths using the technique Esmée taught him, then closes his eyes as he generates a field, a tiny one, inside the panel.

He focuses on his breath, and with each exhale he extends the field, feeling for the shapes within. He knows that the scanner, upon registering the proper data – fingerprint or DNA or whatever – releases a circuit, and with that release the field that keeps the panel shut deactivates and the thing opens.

He generates a field in what he estimates is the center of the box and expands it slowly, feeling for the edges of the inside of the case, feeling for circuitry, controls. He stops when the field envelops a familiar shape – the pins that hold the circuit, pretty much directly under the scanner. That makes sense – he should've started there.

The circuit buzzes through his field – a new sensation for him. Since he's expanded the field in order to search for the right part to break, it's now too big to break the circuit without doing any damage to the contents, so he releases it, takes several breaths and tries again.

This is the smallest field he's ever generated, and he finds the strain surprisingly difficult – bringing down the Apogee was easier, floating the triplets is easier. He focuses in on the area below the scanner and searches for the circuit again – there. A tiny pin, no wider than a hair, a filament of current. That's got to be it. He brings his focus to that point, a tiny spot on a tiny chip. He focuses on where the pin connects, creates a micro-point of increased gravity and the pin snaps away. As soon as he feels the pin snap, he releases. He doesn't want to collapse the case any more than he has to. The panel slides open and the crystal is revealed, softly glowing, held close by black foam padding. Jes exhales. His head hurts.

He grabs the crystal and remembers Dax showing him his Institute file while sitting at that table in the VIP lounge. Plus, there's the data packet he kept threatening to send – those items are probably on this thing. He wakes the interface and sets the crystal into the scanning bed on the surface of the desk.

Password

Of course it's password locked.

Closing his eyes, he brings his attention to his breath. Intuition has been tugging at him, and he decides to heed it. If only he could access the crystal. It was something magers were purported to be able to do – inscribe and edit information on crystals. Information such as memories they take from people's heads, or data – anything really. Could that beam he used to wipe Moxo's mind be used to access this crystal? It seems a totally different process, but both finding a password lock and erasing memories require accessing a system, retrieving information. Could he do it on purpose? Would it even work? How did he even do it in the first place?

He picks the crystal up; it's warm from the scanning bed and tingles a bit in his palm. He stares at it intently, willing it to open to him, willing the beam to burst from his head once more. His brow starts to hurt from the intensity of his concentration and his eyes begin to water – letting him know this isn't the right approach. How does his gravity power work? He doesn't try to activate it so much as he lets it arise. When he creates a field, he doesn't will it into existence – it's more like remembering what it feels like to generate it. What did that beam feel like when it manifested with Moxo? That night it was a reflex. Moxo had been coming at him, and he just wanted it to stop. But the sensation... can he call up the sensation?

He holds the crystal up between two fingers, its multifaceted tip glistening in the low light. He remembers how the pressure in his head felt, how he could feel his pulse inside his skull, the way he was hyperaware of the hair on that part of his head, like they were tendrils, livewires plugged into some reality beyond the physical world. There was mild pressure behind his eyes, but he knew it was the result of not knowing what was happening in the moment. The other main sensation was the warmth radiating from the center of his forehead and making his whole head warm, kind of like it's doing now. Then the buzz of the beam of white light – the warmth of it emerging from his head, the force of it projecting towards its target. He calls up the sensation of it.

The feeling of it arrives first, a prickling sensation in the center of his forehead, his third eye. Then a feeling like a magnetic pull between the tip of the crystal and that spot, then the buzz of connection and the beam ignites, illuminating the dark office. He's vaguely aware of the fractal, lacelike pattern of the beam when his mind is filled by the crystal's internal lattice, the files it contains like blooms at the juncture points. There's a net of light enveloping the data tree, and a knot of light holding it together. He brings his attention to the knot, and it unfolds like a flower, and at the center of the flower a single, glowing word: *3M00nNik0.*

He jolts himself out of the reverie, like waking from a daydream. After setting the crystal back in the scanning bed, he enters the password. He's in. He scans the file names and the first he finds easily: his surname, "Tiqualo". Upon opening the file, he sees that it is indeed his Institute file, and in the same folder, the notice of the bounty on him. Delete, delete. Next, he has to find the data packet. Where the hell would that be? He first checks a folder marked "Send", but it's not in there. A folder labelled "Opportunities" catches his eye, and his intuition pings. Right at the top of the file list is one labelled "Matheson". He opens it, just to confirm it's the right one, and sees that attached to the message is the bounty notice. The message itself is only two words: Port Ruby. Delete.

Relief overwhelms him as the file disappears from the menu. He shuts off the interface and closes the drawer, pocketing the crystal. He looks around the office and is tempted to snoop, but he's been here long enough. And how does Dax know Matheson's name since no specific individual is listed on the bounty? Pushing the thought aside, he climbs up onto the windowsill and looks around once more. It really is a nice office. The man has good taste, whatever else he is. A pale blue field surrounds him, then he steps out of the window and hovers there. Then he looks up at a field of stars and a sister moon traversing the night. He pushes himself off against the side of the building, and he floats up and away.

THE INSTITUTE

She had been his friend and now she's a specimen, splayed on a table, organs being weighed and catalogued. The top of her head cut open as they prepare to remove her brain, her face astonished, empty, eyes gazing into space, seeing nothing. He hopes they see nothing.

Matheson closes the privacy screen on the lab window, pretending to be quick, pretending to not want Jes to see, but Jes knows the view he got was intentional, even without sussing. Matheson's sadism is clear, as much as he wants to pretend everything he does is in the name of science.

Poor Rosa. Poor Minu.

"What happened to them?"

It's always a tossup, whether or not Matheson answers his questions, but given the severity of what transpired in the other lab, he's not surprised to actually get a reply.

"It was a sort of feedback loop. As we learned from your pairing with Minu, another paratalent interacting with his seems to affect his body as well. We suspected the same could happen with Rosa but didn't know for sure until we tried it. Her electromagnetic discharges were, apparently, more painful than your gravity fields. So when her lightning made contact with the sphere that was fully immersed in his dissolution wave, Minu reflexively released another wave – we think as a defense mechanism. Pity we can't figure that out now. Anyway, the wave he released followed the path of Rosa's discharge back to the source. He'd never projected a wave like that before. The wave, as you saw, partially disintegrated her before he reduced himself to carbon dust. It's a shame he cut the research short."

Cut the research short. Not his life, but the research. The work. And now he's a pile of dust in a jar somewhere in this place, and Rosa's dead too, cut open, a slab of meat. Whatever gland or muscle or strange new organ produced her electricity would be studied, along with the rest of her tissue. He wonders what they'll do with her when they're done.

"Why can't you study us without the cruelty?"

"I'm sorry you experience our rational objectivity as cruelty. But that's merely a limitation of your own thinking, don't you see? We're studying fundamental forces here. Fundamental forces don't have feelings."

Rosa and Minu forecast his fate. That's the fate that looms at whatever point in time Matheson decides he's gleaned as much as he can from him, when he decides his gravity fields have nothing more to show him. It's a point that's getting closer, and clearer all the time. Jes knows he has to get out of this place before that point arrives.

And he knows it's coming soon.

CHAPTER TWENTY-THREE

"I can't believe you used us as a diversion!" Eronda exclaims as they watch the newsfeeds on Dax's arrest. "We might have died!"

It's the day of their return to Opale, and they've gathered at Essa's place for a going-away meal.

Enovo guffaws at his wife's dramatic interpretation. "He wanted something from us, dear, we were in no danger. Had we known what was happening, we might have given the game away. It was wise to keep us in the dark."

"That was Esmée's idea," Jes says, shirking responsibility for the subterfuge.

"She knows her parents well." Enovo beams love and pride at his daughter. Jes is moved, and a little envious.

"What was the business proposition he had for you, anyway?" Esmée asks.

"Nightclubs," Eronda informs them disdainfully. "He wanted to open four on Opale first, starting with Ranara, and then license locations throughout the Crystal Imperium."

"It wasn't a bad idea, really," her husband says. "Except for his complete lack of understanding of Asuna culture, of course. But we can now return to Opale with a tale to tell. We played a part, however small, in bringing down a crime boss!"

Jes finds Enovo's enthusiasm for the experience cute. It may be the most exciting thing he's been a part of, well, ever. Even if he didn't know it at the time.

"Luncheon is served!" Quint bellows from the dining area.

"Your aqora is someone special, niece," Eronda offers Essa as the group takes their seats around the table. "I'd keep him around."

"Oh, I plan to, Auntie."

"This looks like a wonderful send-off meal, Quint," Enovo says to all assembled. "I think that you are the most accomplished chef in the family. It's good for both of us that Eronda and I can afford professionals."

Laughter all around. "It's been an instructive stay here in Port Ruby," he continues. "You've each expanded my view of the world and I see that the cultures of the 9-Stars have more to learn from each other than just technology and science, more to gain than access to rare resources. For that, I thank you." He turns to Essa, "I will do my part to open up Asuna culture. Perhaps one day, you can experience your family's zaimira yourself."

Essa wells up. "Thank you, Uncle. I would love that." She turns to Jes, "I can't believe you were dealing with all of that shit from Dax while working on the show too."

"I wasn't a featured player or anything. I could afford to be distracted by crime-world hijinks."

"Well, one thing I can say…" Quint begins as he passes around a basket of rolls. When he sees he's got everyone's attention, he adds, "you've earned a vacation."

Essa beams. "So during Dark Week, Quint and I are renting a cabin in the Mytiri Forest. There's a sauna, and hot tub, and falls, and a swimming hole a short hike away. We'd love for you to join us."

Dark Week is Aleia's new policy of having no shows one week per quarter, in order to give everyone, but the performers especially, a break. Eight shows plus four Singularity events a week is a lot – for the acrobats and aerialists especially – and Aleia has instituted the new plan in recognition of the physical toll on the performers. The performers had long lobbied for a break in the schedule every so often, but Aleia could never make it work given Niko Dax's tithe demands.

"That would be amazing!" Bo exclaims. He turns excitedly to Jes, "We stopped at Cosmia Falls the night of the Orbital, but there's so much more of the forest. It's so beautiful. You'll love it." This is the first time Bo's shown real enthusiasm about anything since the injury, and Jes's heart lifts at the sussing of it.

"It is indeed wonderful," Eronda adds. "We very much enjoyed ourselves. Would that we could join you."

"It's just as well that we're heading home," Enovo says. "I'm sure the young folks wouldn't appreciate us parental figures tagging along."

"I'd love to invite Silas, if that's OK," Esmée says, casting a nervous glance at Jes.

He notices Essa looking from him to her cousin and back again.

"Who is this Silas?" Eronda asks.

"Just someone from the circus," Esmée replies blithely.

"He's human," Jes tosses out, earning a stern look.

"You're seeing a human male?" Eronda asks, as waves of disapproval ping Jes's sussing. "You've not been with a male before. Is it serious?"

"Not in the least, Mother."

Eronda knows her daughter well enough to understand the truth of this and doesn't press further. Jes susses that there's more she wants to say, but she holds her tongue.

"There's plenty of room," Essa replies. "I don't see why not."

"That's great," Jes blurts. "I think it'd be great if he tags along. The greater the number, the greater the fun."

Bo squeezes his hand and whispers, "Stop saying 'great'."

"Well, as long as you approve," Esmée says, feigning sweetness. Jes meets her eyes across the table, receives daggers, and quickly looks away.

* * *

Later, Jes throws himself into doing the dishes while the others have tea in the next room.

Quint comes in while he's scrubbing the stewpot. He leans against the counter and crosses his arms. "So, you don't like Silas much."

Jes doesn't respond, and instead increases the intensity of his scrubbing. Eventually he says, "He's fine."

"Do you have feelings for Esmée?"

"What?" Jes is so astonished by the question that he drops the pot and the scrubber. "No, I don't have feelings for her. She's a dear friend but–"

"Then what is it? You clearly have a problem with him, and with them being together."

Jes rests his hands, covered in suds, on the edge of the sink. He looks up, meets Quint's concerned gaze. "There's a couple of factors. One is that he's been particularly nosy about my relationship to the triplets and their act. He was the stagehand that worked with me for Jasmine's show, and he's the one that works with me now at the circus. It's not unreasonable that he asks me why, but he keeps asking and he clearly doesn't buy the 'good luck charm' story. The other factor is, I can't suss him. He's learned how to block against empathic senses, so that makes me wonder why. Add to that what my grandparents taught me about diaspora humans–"

Quint fills in the rest, "–and how they're so much like the humans that destroyed their own planet out of greed and apathy."

"Exactly! They have a reputation." He leaves the stewpot alone and turns his attention to a cup, which he begins washing vigorously.

"I have to say, Jes, I'm surprised to see this from you."

"See what?"

"Prejudice."

Jes drops the cup into the sink with a thud and a spray of soapy water. "I'm not–"

"Is there another species you can't read with your empathic sense?"

"Sure. Mantodeans."

"So are you suspicious of Kush O-Nhar?" Quint asks the question with softness and patience. Jes can suss that Quint's not trying to be right, that he's coming from a place of caring about his friends and wanting to help Jes see. Which is even more frustrating.

"No," he can't reply any other way if he's going to be truthful. "But with Mantodeans it's a matter of their alienness from other humanoids. With Silas and diaspora humans, it's because they've learned how to close off and they do it on purpose."

"Maybe Silas closes off because he doesn't want somebody he knows dislikes him to suss his innermost feelings?"

This explanation doesn't sit right with Jes, but he must admit he has no logical counter. He reminds himself that Quint, Essa, and Bo all knew Silas from the circus long before he ever showed up.

"Look, Jes. The rest of us are inclined to have Silas along. It means a lot to Esmée. I hope you can relax into that and not make things awkward for everyone."

Jes considers this and understands that Silas hasn't actually done or said anything that off-base, really, and the decision has already been made. "OK," he says finally. "I promise. I won't be a dick."

Quint puts a hand on his shoulder and gives a squeeze. "Thanks, buddy."

Essa pops her head in. "Kush O-Nhar messaged me. He's asking that you stop by. I have a feeling it may be about Moxo. And it's really past time we got you a node of your own."

Since he turned the node Dax had given him over to the Magistrates as evidence, Jes has once again been without one of the devices. He sighs and turns his attention back to the dishes. He just wants to snuggle with Bo and not think about anybody else.

"I know it was an accident, what happened with Moxo," Essa says gently. "But you're going to have to deal with it some time."

Kush O-Nhar perches on his roof, rubbing his front legs together, antennae quivering in the dappled sun spilling through the leaves of his tree home. He raises an arm in greeting and Jes waves back. When he steps inside the abode, he sees Moxo across the room, beside the strange pod. His host approaches, saying, "We have some reparative work to do. Follow me." He leads Jes off the platform onto the floor of the cocoon structure. "You can walk like normal, this material is quite sturdy."

"It looks so fragile," Jes comments as he steps lightly onto the paper-like substance that comprises the floor, walls and ceiling of the structure. It's spongy underfoot, and gives each step a slight bounce. They approach the pod hanging over its platform. Light of a rich pink hue pulses in the interior of what, up close like this, looks to be a shell, but its surface textures give it the appearance of being woven. Tendrils curl towards the floor.

"So how do you know Kush O-Nhar?" Moxo sits beside the pod, isolating a clear crystal orb in each hand. The friendly openness Jes susses from the juggler takes him aback, considering the latter's more recent attitude towards him. How much damage did he do with that mind-blast?

"From the circus," Jes answers warily. "Kush O-Nhar, what's going on?"

"The mager ability you manifested in your last interaction erased Moxo's memories of you. His other memories remain intact, as well as his skills, but it's as if the two of you never met and he doesn't know who you are. It's a tricky maneuver you pulled off, to edit memories so precisely." He gives Jes a moment to take in this information before continuing.

"However, because your strike was unpracticed, the effects are beginning to impact his other memories. The longer his mind is in this state, the more of himself he'll lose. You need to restore what you deleted."

"Sounds like you did a number on me," Moxo says with incongruous cheerfulness.

Jes is bowled over for a moment by the magnitude of what he's done. That it was an accident is irrelevant – he understands this is his mistake to fix. "What do I need to do?"

"Take a seat and lower your psychic defenses. I will connect with your mind – you must not resist. Either of you."

Moxo puts away the orbs he's manipulating. "Understood."

Jes nods. "I understand." He takes his seat on the other side of the pod.

Kush O-Nhar takes one of the loose tendrils and touches it to the center of Moxo's forehead. Smaller filaments sprout out of it, take hold in a circular pattern. He then repeats the procedure with Jes. The connecting filaments tickle.

"Close your eyes."

Jes complies, and his timeline with Moxo unwinds in his inner vision, from last encounter to first meeting, from sitting in this chair to showing up for a haircut. He breathes and a rush of images flares brightly then fades away. Every interaction, no matter how minor, the two have had over the past weeks plays out in mere moments. Jes doesn't just see the events, but he can feel Moxo's emotional responses to them as well, from curiosity and skepticism at their first meeting to the anger and resentment of more recent times. Eventually, the visions and feelings fade, until there is only the rosy glow behind his eyelids. Before he even opens his eyes, he susses Moxo's disdain and resentment, returned in full force.

"I have a tea that will help you integrate," Kush O-Nhar says to Moxo before Jes can say anything.

Jes looks into the Mantodean's face and in a burst of intuition understands Moxo needs Kush O-Nhar's attention much more than he does.

"I'll see myself out," he says, rising to his feet. "Let me know if you need anything else." He wants to apologize to Moxo but knows any such expression would be inadequate. Once again, he traverses the spongy floor of the dwelling, and relief washes over him when he reaches the outer deck. Vashtar, the sun, sets while Persephone rises. He takes comfort in the fact that greater powers exist than his ability to erase memories.

ROSA

He appreciates her laugh when he hears it, on the days they're allowed to play games. Their favorite is an Indran game called "Portal" which involves laying smooth pieces of colored glass around a board that consists of concentric circles. His grandparents had tried to teach him the game when he was younger, but he could hardly grasp it then.

"It's about multidimensional thinking," Rosa explains one day.

Is he resisting or not resisting the Institute's tests at this point in time? He doesn't know. It doesn't really matter – some moments stick because of what happens and some stick because of the timing. Timing here doesn't matter.

"What do you mean?" he asks. He remembers Grandmother trying to convey a lesson about the multidimensional nature of time and reality once, but he didn't understand.

He can understand now, he's sure of it.

"See how the blue and green stones line up on the board?" Rosa asks, gesturing at the game before them.

He nods.

"See the patterns indicated by the cards of Fickle Fate?" She points at a line-up of cards arrayed along one edge of the board: blue green blue blue green and so on. "The pieces are our choices, and the pattern is chance, and when our choices line up with chance–"

"The portal opens," he says, sliding his piece down a level, one layer closer to winning, passing through a transitional space, liberation.

"You're starting to get this game," Rosa says, beaming.

CHAPTER TWENTY-FOUR

"Why do they think I'm your nephew?" Jes asks Niko Dax from one side of a glass divider. Disconcertingly, he thinks of the lie that he told Esmée when they first met, that he was coming to Persephone-9 to work for his uncle. He doesn't like how their lies fit together.

"Only family members are allowed to visit the accused," Dax says from the other side of the glass. "Thank you for coming to see me, Mr Tiqualo." He's in the drab gray coveralls of the Port Ruby jail, with a bright red patch indicating he's a high security inmate. "I hope the Magistrate coming to fetch you wasn't too disconcerting. You still have no node, so there was no other way to contact you really."

It's true that the human Magistrate who showed up at the house earlier had given him – given all of them, really – a bit of a scare, but he's not about to let Dax know that.

"What do you want?"

"Do you remember what you told me when I asked you what you want?"

Jes remembers. Those things haven't changed. "I said I wanted to find a place for myself. Find friends and community. Find a way to contribute."

"You certainly have done that, haven't you?" Dax just stares at him through the glass for a moment. Always with the assessment. "People seem to just like you, don't they? I certainly do. I thought I could make you mine."

Jes isn't sure he appreciates being liked by somebody like Niko Dax, but he supposes it's better than being disliked by him. He thinks about Hollan Zola. Actually, with people like Dax, it's probably better not being on their radar at all.

"That was never going to happen. Why did you ask me here? Are you thinking I'll break you out?"

Laughter. Genuine amusement. "I know that's just about the last thing you'd want to do. And besides, I wouldn't be so foolish to attempt it. It's not like I have henchmen waiting to ferry me off to a hiding spot. The arrests of my key people were remarkably well coordinated. I'm impressed. Aleia always did have a good mind for planning and logistics. The dim-witted Magistrates couldn't have managed their takedown operation on their own."

Jes bites his tongue. He'd been forewarned to say nothing about the witnesses against Dax, to neither confirm nor deny any suggestions as to their identity. Of course, Dax would have an idea – he's not stupid – but still, Jes says nothing and keeps his face impassive.

"No, my jig is up," Dax continues. "I know this. No sense in gnashing my teeth and wailing about how I've been betrayed. The authorities have me at last. All it took was somebody brave enough to make a move." He stares intently. Jes meets his gaze, unblinking. "Such fragile things, empires."

"Did you ask me here just to wax poetic about the impermanence of it all? Not really interested in being your audience for that."

Jes always got the feeling that beyond toying with him, Dax was trying to guide him in some twisted, indecipherable way. Teach him things. Mold him into one of his heavies. In a way he's not so different from Matheson at the Institute, but where Matheson made no effort to disguise the fact that Jes was anything other than a subject expected to do as instructed,

Dax indulged in the pretense that choice was involved in his demands. Technically that was true, perhaps, but is a choice between two terrible options really a choice at all?

Dax sighs. "I guess you can't buy loyalty. Compliance isn't the same thing."

"Why am I here?" A tinge of impatience.

"Why *are* you here? You probably don't like me very much. And now my leverage on you is evaporated. So why did you come when I asked?"

"Curiosity." That's the honest truth of it. "Closure maybe."

"Closure is overrated. But your curiosity I'll satisfy. I know something, Mr Tiqualo. About the Institute. And their breeding program."

"A friend of mine in the Institute told me about that..."

That sly smirk on Dax's face again. "So, you know that individuals descended from Consciousness Holders of different species are deliberately... mated? With the express goal of creating individuals with psionic-type abilities, or 'paratalents' I believe is the term the Institute uses. I can see from your flinching at that term I'm correct. Their aim is to create individuals with these abilities that don't rely on contact with the world of origin. Your mother and maternal grandparents were psions, were they not? And I believe your Rijala grandfather–"

"Was a mager. So, what are you saying..." A thought begins to form in Jes's mind. He'd always felt a distance from his parents, but he doesn't want to believe... The last time he saw them, Father said they'd had him out of duty–

"Your parents didn't *sell* you to the Institute," Dax explains, relishing the words. "They were paid to breed you, you were a commission, really. Then when you showed no signs of abilities, they thought they were stuck with a child to care for that they never wanted. You see, keeping the family unit intact was part of the deal. Just in case. All was finally worth it when you did manifest powers, and they got the remainder of the payment that was due them. I wouldn't be surprised if they split their fee down the middle and went their separate ways as soon as they were rid of you."

Jes clenches his fists, tries to will his stomach to stop churning. He wants to believe Dax is lying, but what he's saying makes too much sense. He susses him and it's clear that whether or not what he's saying is true, Dax believes it is. "Did your contact tell you all that? I'm surprised they were that detailed."

That smile again. Jes had hoped that maybe his public fall from grace would have humbled that smile out of Dax, but no such luck. "Not just my contact. My former colleague, Dr Matheson. You see, before I set about being my own boss here in Port Ruby, I used to procure subjects for the Institute, and it was I that contracted your parents and recommended they be paired. In a way, I feel like I'm your creator."

So that's where the feeling of possession he always sussed from Dax comes from. Jes feels his mind spinning away from him at this news and it's as if the floor has dropped from under him, his insides lurch. Dax is the reason his parents had a child they never wanted. Dax is the reason for his whole miserable childhood. Dax is the reason he exists at all. And if he was created by a monster does that make him...?

No. He's escaped that existence. And while Dax pairing his parents might be how he came to be born, they were the ones who chose to be assholes to him. Matheson was responsible for his own methods, not Dax. Still, the man behind the glass is why he's had the life he's had, and he can't help but wish none of it ever happened, that he'd never been born. But then he thinks about Bo and his circus friends. He's his own person now, and from this point forward, whatever life he makes is up to him.

"Did you know who I was when I showed up here?"

"No. You are hardly the first human-Rijala hybrid I've encountered over the years, and when you accompanied Aleia to that meeting, I hadn't seen the bounty notice yet. But when I did see it, I was delighted at how fate brought us together."

"Why are you telling me this?"

"Where you come from determines who you are, whether you embrace it or reject it. And I had a hand in your creation. Your turning up here was an unexpected opportunity to develop you further. The tasks I'd set forth for you were an effort to mold you into my indispensable tool. Something unique and powerful. Certainly a better fate than whatever Matheson had planned."

Jes laughs humorlessly. "Where you come from doesn't determine who you are, your choices do. I always hated people telling me what to be. I just couldn't get out of it for a while there. All you did was show me what I *don't* want to be, what I *don't* want to do with my abilities. We're done here." Jes stands up, the chair legs screech across the floor as he pushes it back. "My parents may have never wanted me, and the Institute might want me for terrible reasons, but I've made a place for myself here—"

"Yes, your precious 'community'. I had community too, and look what happened to them."

"People you intimidate and threaten and pay to do your bidding are not a community." Jes senses something else from Niko Dax now, something beneath the greed and the urge to manipulate – nothingness. An inner landscape of utter barrenness.

"The fact that you can't understand that is sad. Enjoy the rest of your life in whatever shithole they toss you in."

Dax looks surprised at this response – clearly not what he'd hoped to prompt with his revelation. He'd underestimated the distance his parents cultivated with years of their coldness, he'd underestimated the strength that can come from belonging. Without another word he turns from Dax, who is uncharacteristically silent. He indicates to the guard on the other side of the door that he's done. And he knows it too, as he exits the room and the door closes behind him. He's done.

On his way out of the Magistrates Hall, he passes Danae, who is on her way in. They are mutually surprised to see each other.

"I'm here to finish giving my deposition. What are you doing here?" she asks. Waves of suspicion emanate from her.

"One last conversation with our mutual friend. Closure."

"I see." She acts mollified but Jes can tell she's not. "I didn't realize you and he were... well, close isn't the right word but—"

He just wants to get away. "We're not. We're nothing. He wanted to shatter my world. He failed. And, to be honest with you, I guess I wanted the chance to tell him off. I have to go, though. Got a shuttle to catch – a bunch of us are going to Mytiri. Good luck with your deposition. It's almost over."

"So long, Jes." Her voice is calm, but her paranoia is palpable to his empathic sense. She knows he has powers, and she knows he destroyed her club under Dax's orders. But does she know why he obeyed Dax? Does she know about the Institute, or the facts around his conception? What does she think she knows?

No – he's not going to let himself fall into her paranoia. "Take care, Danae."

He walks down the steps but feels her attention stay on him. When he gets to the pavement, he looks back up at the entrance and she's gone.

CHAPTER TWENTY-FIVE

Dappled sun drifts through the purple leaves, one bright beam through a clearing warming the rock on which Jes lays. He's pleasantly stoned and sees dancers in the spaces between the leaves, acrobats performing a dazzling show against the backdrop of sky. A pale green cloud, all soft and puffy, looks close enough that it might graze the treetops. They're halfway through their week in the Mytiri Forest, and he never wants to leave. Maybe Aleia would want to start a show for the resort here. Maybe he could work at it. Manage it even.

The rush of the waterfall is a soothing music broken by Bo's whoop as he leaps off a high rock. Jes looks over in time to see him flip and twist in the air before splashing into the pool the falls pour into. The waters are a brilliant cerulean blue, the bluest he's ever seen. Bo emerges from beneath the surface of the water, laughing and splashing. It's good to see him have fun. The only one in the party who never takes a dive is Silas, which isn't surprising considering his fear of heights.

The sun dips below the treeline, and the air immediately cools though the rock he sits on retains its heat. Bo exits the water, dries himself off – he still favors his recovering shoulder. He doesn't have full range of motion back, and he still can't hold a handstand or hang, but it's getting better overall. Quint clambers up, water pouring off his shorts-clad form. "It's time we start heading back," he calls out to the others. "There's a different path I think we should try."

Once in a while a beam of light makes its way through the tall red-barked trees and the ground, covered with fallen purple leaves, turns a brilliant violet punctuated with emerald green shrubs, and yellow and blue flowers, and white mushrooms here and there. They come to a stretch of enormous vines that curl in and out of the ground like giant cables, and they walk through the arches they form, dwarfed by the dark green plants. They walk past another set of falls, after which the path narrows and they have to walk single file.

Loud pink birds caw and rattle in the tree branches above. Eventually, they get to a rope bridge that crosses a gorge. Jes senses a wave of panic from Silas – which is strange because Silas usually keeps himself so well closed off. The fear is so strong he's prompted to ask, "Everything OK, Silas?"

"I don't like heights." His face betrays his fear. Esmée holds his hand tightly, her brow knitted with concern. They stop and stand around him, a few feet from the start of the bridge.

"Quint," Essa calls. "Hold on."

Quint is onto the bridge already, turns and sees that the group has stopped. "What's going on?" he asks.

"Silas is scared of heights," Esmée explains.

Jes looks over at the bridge. It's narrow enough to require that they cross it single file, and consists of slats spaced an inch apart, and two "railings" of rope. The whole thing sways slightly in the breeze. It isn't that far across, but it does traverse a very deep gorge, with a stream rushing far below, perhaps a hundred feet.

"I don't know if I can do this," Silas says. "I might have to go back the other way."

"You won't make it back before dark going that way," Quint cautions. "Do you think you can do it if I back you up? I've got four arms, I can grab you if I need to. But I know you can do this buddy."

"I... I'll try," Silas says, struggling to keep his panic at bay. The look on his face betrays his feelings. For the first time since meeting him, Jes doesn't feel wary of Silas. He feels sympathy.

After everyone else has crossed, Silas and Quint are the only ones left. Quint steps onto the bridge first and keeps two hands on the ropes, one on each side, and holds two other hands out to Silas as he steps back. His weight sags the bridge, causing it to sway slightly. This seems to make Silas even more nervous, but Quint says something – they're too far away to hear exactly what – and Silas nods and steps forward.

They're almost all the way across when a board splits under Quint's foot. One of the guide ropes on one side snaps and the bridge twists, causing both Quint and Silas to tip over towards the gorge. Silas screams as he falls head first towards the rocks and water below. Then his scream fades away as he notices he's not actually falling at all. A blue bubble envelops him, and Quint too, and they hover in the air, neither of them making contact with the broken bridge any longer. The pieces of the broken board and rope drift as if under water.

"Thanks, Jes," Quint calls. He grabs the rope on the unbroken side and pulls himself towards the bridge, grabbing Silas by the ankle and pulling him upright. He pulls himself along the rope, one hand over the other, and indicates that Silas should do the same. Once they're both safely on the ground, Jes releases the field and the broken pieces clack together.

"There should be a warning sign," Quint comments.

Esmée rushes over to comfort Silas, who rests one hand on her shoulder, as he bends over and pants, releasing the remnants of his fear with each exhalation. He looks up at Jes.

"You have powers," he says. "I thought so." His guard is up again and Jes can't suss him.

Jes and Silas look at each other while the others stand around watching them.

There's no denying it now. "Yes," Jes answers with a shrug, trying to be nonchalant about it. He's not sure he succeeds.

"Are you a psion?" Silas asks. "Or a mager?" He acknowledges with his question both elements of Jes's heritage.

"I'm the product of a daughter of psions mated with a mager's grandson. I was bred for powers that will work no matter what planet I'm on. That's the mission of the Institute. Now it's your turn to answer something."

"What?" His tone is a peculiar mix of nervous and defiant. This sets off a flash of annoyance in Jes – as if Silas is the only one who gets to ask any questions here.

The focused attention of the others on this conversation magnifies every breath, every pause that's indicative of considering a response carefully.

"What are you hiding? What's your deal?"

Silas takes a deep breath. "First I want to make clear I've told nobody about you or my suspicions–"

"Suspicions?" Esmée asks, wariness entering her eyes as it rises within her.

"I come from a family of bounty hunters," he says. "I heard about a human-Rijala hybrid with unusual powers–"

Bo says, "You didn't…"

"No!" Silas exclaims. "I've told nobody about you Jes, please believe me. But yeah, my family are bounty hunters, and they told me about a bounty for someone that fits your description. Then we met at that party, and I didn't really think anything of it. I mean, human-Rijala hybrids aren't common exactly, but you're hardly the only one. You're not even the only one I've met before. But then you were onstage with the triplets for no apparent reason, and I saw the way they float during their show, and I got to wondering if it was you. But I haven't told anybody, and I won't. I promise I won't. I did ask you questions but it was just curiosity. Just wondering if you were the one the bounty was out for. I have no intention of claiming it." He looks from Jes, to Esmée, to Essa – everyone present that has some level of empathic sense. "You know I'm telling the truth, don't you?"

With a shared look, they all agree he means what he says.

"OK," Jes says. "We believe you."

Silas is so relieved he secms on the verge of tears. He's always been so closed and cool and above it all that this opening up, this vulnerability, makes him feel like a different person entirely. He turns to Esmée, "I wanted to get close to you because I'm... drawn to you. And all of you..." He makes eye contact with each of them. "You all seem like such a family, and I just wanted to be part of it. I'm sorry for raising so much suspicion."

"OK," Quint says resolutely. "New rule. No secrets. And now we get back to the cabin and have a decent meal, and maybe some hot-tubbing. Agreed?"

There are no arguments.

BREAKOUT

The alarms blare and whir down every corridor, and the cries
and moans and wails of the agitated subjects held in this
place echo through the sleek halls. The walls and the floors
reflect the yellow and white flashes of the sirens. A group of
orderlies gives chase, their luminous white uniforms cutting
illuminated silhouettes through the chaos of the alarms. He
increases gravity's pull on the ceiling, brings it down in front
of them, blocking the hall.

He runs.

"This is foolish, Jes," Matheson's voice echoes from all around.
*"Stop this now and we won't have to harm you. Listen to the distress
you're causing."*

"That's on you!" Jes bellows, but he doesn't know if
Matheson hears him or not. It doesn't matter.

He heads for an exit he knows opens toward the gates. Two
orderlies attempt to head him off, approach with stunsticks
in hand, spitting off their angry blue sparks. With a flick of
his wrist, the stunsticks become extraordinarily heavy, and
pull the orderlies' hands to the floor, where they're weighted
down by the weapons they held aloft so easily moments ago.
He generates fields around their bodies, and the gravity grows
so thick they can't stand back up. He walks between their
upturned faces and he susses their astonishment and fear.

He enjoys it for a second, then feels bad for being the cause, then he remembers who these men work for. He imagines Matheson's pasty face, his stupid glasses. He wishes it were him he was making afraid right now He makes it through the door.

He sees a group of orderlies, along with general security in their gray uniforms, running after him. Jes opens his arms wide, generates a field so large it encompasses the wing of the building, the wing the personnel who want to catch him all run down in this moment. He turns the gravity up several notches and the building starts to shake, buckle, then the whole thing comes down on top of the men. He hears yells of confusion, surprise, but these quickly blend into the ongoing whine of the alarms.

He runs for the gates, raises his hands in anticipation of the guards there who are preparing to try to stop him. They are not going to stop him.

CHAPTER TWENTY-SIX

Jes snaps awake shortly before dawn. His intuitive sense screams inside him, a yowl of warning from the root of his subconscious stabbing danger, urging caution, spurring him to full alertness in a second. He can suss them before he hears or sees them: the focused attention of orderlies as they hunt, their single-minded zeal like paths of polished stone. The desire to own him snakes through the cabin stalking its quarry, the desire to punish him for managing to escape, all stemming from a too familiar psyche he remembers from too much time in that lab. Matheson.

"Wake up," he whispers urgently to Bo. "They're here for me."

"Hey!" Quint's voice calls from down the hall. A weapon fires, a loud crash, then frantic yelling.

"Tranqs don't work on the Hydraxian–" a staticky voice through a comm device says before it's cut off with another loud crash.

"Out the window!" Bo calls and the two of them dive out together while Jes floats them down to the ground. "Head for the woods!" Bo tells Jes. "I'll stay back and help the others."

"I don't want to leave you all–"

A trio of orderlies in their stealth gear exit the house and step onto the deck. Two of them carry stunsticks sparking in their hands, but it's the one with the tranquilizer gun who strikes first, taking a direct shot at Jes. Bo shoves Jes out of the way and gets hit by the dart in his neck.

"Run…" he says to Jes before collapsing, unconscious.

The two with the stunsticks approach warily while the one with the tranq gun readies another shot. Jes envelops all three of them in a field and they bobble inches off the ground. They look at each other in confusion. Adrenaline and fear and, yes, hatred power this field in a way Jes hasn't felt before, and with the extra charge of these emotions, he doesn't just float them inches off the ground – they continue floating up, up, up. The one with the tranqs fires a dart, which rather than pierce the field, bends a curve into it. The dart moves in a quick half-circle before flying back at the one who fired it. The orderly takes it in the chest and immediately goes limp.

A voice broadcast from a drone flies into view: *"We'd like to not hurt your friends, Jes. Give yourself up."*

Jes reaches up, aims a field inside the drone and crushes it. The drone might as well be a crumpled up piece of paper. When Jes releases his field, the crushed husk falls to the ground.

Esmée and Silas run out onto the deck, and the two of them dash down the stairs that lead to the yard, at the far end of which the woods begin. They begin heading for the trees but Jes heads back to Bo. He gets him up off the deck, slings a limp arm around his shoulders, and drags him along. Silas runs up to Jes and grabs Bo's limp body from him, throwing him over his shoulder. They dash back down the stairs, joining Esmée.

"Where's Quint and Essa?" Jes asks.

"Essa's knocked out and Quint–"

A crash as two orderlies fly out of the second floor window.

"I guess he's doing that." Esmée is surprisingly calm.

"How did they know we were here?" Jes screams the question at Silas.

"It wasn't me!" Silas protests. "I swear I didn't!"

Then from the porch, a familiar voice, "Jes! You're looking well. Circus life agrees with you, I take it?"

Matheson.

Panic rises at the sound of his voice, but then, incongruously, Niko Dax in prison coveralls comes to mind. He helped bring down Niko Dax. If he could do that, he can put an end to the Institute's pursuit of him. He has to take a stand. Now.

"Please take care of Bo," Jes says to his friends. Then he turns and faces the human director of the Institute. Of course he'd come and oversee his capture himself. Good.

"What are you doing?" Esmée asks from behind him.

"Stay back," Jes says to his friends. "This is my fight."

"You floated a few of my men," Matheson says, pointing up at the orderlies floating high over the roof of the cabin. "I'd like for you to bring them down."

"If you say so," Jes replies, raising a hand and swiping it across the air in front of him as if he were working a holographic interface.

Confused and panicked cries fill the air as the orderlies feel gravity's pull again and begin their fall. They crash onto the deck, all of them thudding loudly and bouncing before settling into stillness. One of them moans but the other two remain silent, their bodies twisted on the wooden planks. Matheson looks down at the still bodies, aghast. Jes susses that he's surprised by this violence. Good.

"How did you find me?"

"I don't answer to you, Jes." If Matheson is shaken, he doesn't let his voice reveal that. "But, if you must know, I'll tell you. Had you contained your performance to the grounds of that casino, you could have evaded us, most likely. But the stage of a popstar who is a cross-cultural phenomenon is not so discrete. Your little act with the Bezan girls on Jasmine Jonah's stage was beamed over media everywhere, and it caught our attention. We weren't certain it was you making them float, but the effect was too uncanny and familiar. It was enough to bring us to Port Ruby on a hunch. Once there, your friend Danae Siqui was happy to tell us about this little trip to the forest with your friends, which you apparently mentioned to her. When we arrived on this side of the moon, we deployed a search for your brainwave pattern, which we, of course, have on hand. And here we are."

Two orderlies lead Quint out onto the deck, covered in a net of some kind. They prod him with stunsticks which make him grimace, but he doesn't yell out. Another one carries Essa; he pauses at the sight of his fallen comrades, but simply steps over the crumpled bodies, then lays her unconscious body on the picnic table.

"Do as I say or your friends–"

Two of Jes's fields appear around the orderlies holding Quint.

"What?" one of them says as their bodies sink down, curl, scrunch. The orderlies yell and moan as their bodies fall to the ground. The gravity within the fields that contain them increase to the point they can no longer hold themselves upright.

The orderly who carried Essa pulls out a stunstick and points it at Jes, who is out of range. Losing patience, Jes crushes the orderly's hand like he did to Hollan Zola's. The man screams, drops the stunstick and falls to his knees.

"I'd appreciate it if you left one of them alive. I can't fly the shuttle myself, and somebody will have to get us off this moon."

"I'm not coming with you."

"Oh, come now, Jes. Be reasonable. You've clearly been practicing with your abilities, but you and I have so much more to do together." He looks around, takes in the sight of his fallen and restrained men. "I didn't know you had such a violent streak, Jes. You've learned some interesting lessons during your time in Port Ruby. Don't you see how the Institute can help you? Don't you see the destructiveness of this path you've chosen since leaving us?"

"None of this is my choice!"

"Isn't it?"

Technically, Matheson is correct, and this infuriates him. Every action he took with Dax, what he's done here, has, indeed, been his choice. But the driving factor behind it all, was to avoid what's happening now. To escape Matheson and the Institute for good. He's not a violent, out of control renegade like Matheson is insinuating. He's not.

"Is it true my parents were part of a breeding program?" Jes asks. "That they were paid to conceive me?"

"You already know it's true," Matheson says. "You feel the truth of it don't you?"

Jes doesn't answer.

"Another truth you must grasp is that your place is with the Institute. What we can learn from you can reshape the very fabric of society within the 9-Star Congress. Imagine Emerged Ones not tied to their worlds of origin. Imagine the applications of that–"

"I imagine the Institute having its own superpowered security force."

"Cynicism is something else you've picked up on this moon, I see. It doesn't suit you, Jes. None of this suits you."

"Look what *you're* doing here!" Jes shakes, and balls his hands into fists.

"These deaths and injuries are on you," Matheson says with a smirk. "You could have come peacefully–"

"You mean allow myself to become your lab rat again? Give myself over to eventual vivisection? What did being 'peaceful' get Rosa? Or Minu?"

Matheson raises his hands in the manner of someone trying to calm down a person they know damn well has reason to be upset but will deny it. "I know it seems awfully unfair. I know you must be afraid. But what you can teach us is so much bigger than you or I or our individual lives. And besides, you are rightfully the property of the Paragenetic Institute of the 9-Stars, per the contract your parents signed. Come with me, Jes. Before anybody else gets hurt."

"Don't listen to him!" With the orderlies Jes took out no longer restraining him, Quint has managed to get himself out of the netting that held him. He stands at the table, seeing to Essa.

"We've only used tranquilizers here," Matheson says. "We can–"

"Shut up, Doctor Matheson. I never consented to being your experiment. The fact that you would take someone against their will makes you the worse kind of criminal, and I've met a few–"

"By that I assume you mean Niko Dax? I'm a bit annoyed he didn't turn you in before now. It's fascinating to me that he helped you at all. I know him from when he worked for the Institute, you know."

"I'm aware."

"Stop this foolish bid for freedom. Whatever life you think you have here isn't meant for you. You are the Institute's property."

"Well in that case, I declare myself emancipated." Jes encompasses Matheson's feet in a field and holds him where he stands. "I am an autonomous being who makes his own choices." Jes creates another field inside Matheson's head, something he once fantasized about doing to Niko Dax.

"Now Jes," Matheson says, holding his hands in that "calm down" gesture that Jes so despises. "Don't be rash. I understand how you feel–"

The corners of Jes's mouth curl into a smirk. "Fundamental forces don't have feelings. Remember? You taught me that."

Matheson's eyes widen in surprise, panic, terror as the pull of Jes's gravity squeezes and distorts his insides. He emits a scream that devolves into gurgling sounds as his head collapses in on itself.

"Jes!" Quint calls, but he sounds far away. "That's enough! *JES!*"

His friend's voice is a distant echo, and rational thought

seems to have evaporated – there is nothing but anger now. The rest of Matheson's body crumples up towards his head, limbs and torso twisting under the pull of Jes's furious gravity. Any sign of the human origins of the bloody blob of tissue Jes holds before him is obliterated.

He's vaguely aware of Quint calling him, but Jes can barely hear his friend through the wind of rage that howls in his ears. He increases the gravity again, and the bloody sphere of tissue and ligaments and crushed bone condenses even more, forming a perfect sphere that continues collapsing on itself. There's a weird sort of pressure, and the gravity he's focusing so tightly hits a limit, a barrier. It feels like something he can puncture… like fabric he can poke right into and shove the stain of the man Matheson through and disappear him from the cosmos. Erase him from existence.

The light changes suddenly: everything is purple, dark, like a sudden eclipse. He takes in the scene, and it feels like he's turning his head in slow motion. Quint is in mid-step, but appears perfectly still, as are the fallen orderlies. The blob that was Matheson begins to glow. He feels the pull of his own gravity, a tug pulling him right through spacetime. He's aware of the barrier again; a membrane limiting the concentration of gravity he's causing. His rage at the Institute fuels him, he can feel *how* he can break that membrane–

A familiar buzzing sounds beside him, a familiar presence. He turns and sees an insectoid face looking at him intently.

"Release your gravity field," Kush O-Nhar instructs.

Jes tries to do as he's asked, but the gravity is flowing inward, like it's pulling his consciousness into it. He's at first confused by his inability to release his field, then consternation gives way to fear.

"Gravity has taken over." Kush O-Nhar emits a series of clicking sounds. Jes gets the distinct impression that his insectoid friend is speaking to someone else, someone he can't see. "Don't be alarmed," he continues. The Mantodean stands in front of Jes, rests his two front legs on his shoulders, then leans forward, his open mouth descending around his head – then darkness, quiet.

Jes's gravity goes still, and the rushing wind sound in his head too quietens. He realizes his eyes are closed. When he opens them, he sees that he and Kush O-Nhar are enclosed in a sphere of violet and pink light, with strands of silver-rainbow-white running through it. He stands with Kush O-Nhar, and they're in the presence of a human, Bezan, Asuna, Hydraxian, Rijala and another Mantodean. Each of their bodies is made of light, or maybe they are the light, filtered through the consciousness and life of the Holder. Kush O-Nhar glows and Jes sees his own aura around him. It's aglow but his body isn't made of light like the others.

"Kush O-Nhar? What's happening?"

"We are in a psychic space," the Mantodean explains. "You are in the presence of the Council Most High of the 9-Star Congress. These beings before you are the chief representatives of each of the conscious worlds and their member species."

As is true of their species on the physical plane, the Mantodeans are the most alien here. Kush O-Nhar's body is of purple light, but the other Mantodean is multihued, with shades of green and pink and pale violet running throughout their body. They remind him of the Gateway from the Orbital. That night seems so far away. What looks like a gem, a sapphire, glows in the center of their forehead, between the two spots that sprout silver-white antennae. Their bulbous eyes are rainbow-hued and flecked with silver and look as if they contain stars. This other Mantodean's aura forms fractal patterns that pulse and swirl in the space around its body before disappearing in a pattern like breath. They exude a force like gravity on Jes's attention, an intensity of presence.

Between the Mantodean and Jes flashes the image of a dark star that blazes on the other side of visible light, its thoughts forming fractal geometry around it, geometry that will eventually emerge as matter. It's Zo, the mysterious sentient star from another dimension that brought together the members of the Congress, that created it with the gift of sub-light speed interstellar travel. He doesn't know how or how he knows, but he can tell that the space they're in is a manifestation of this star. And the Mantodeans contain its consciousness within them – they are the vessels by which it experiences the realm of matter and light.

"Why are you here?" Jes asks his friend.

"Aleia came to me as soon as she learned Danae revealed your location to Matheson. In addition, I perceived the possibility of a singularity, a tiny one that... branches out. In one version of events."

"A singularity?"

"What you were making of that human before I arrived."

That weird pressure... the barrier he could almost puncture... Was he on the verge of breaking through spacetime itself?

"A power such as you possess must be tempered," the other Mantodean says.

Jes hears the words, but it's like hearing a voice in his head. He knows – he just *knows* – that the Mantodean is speaking for Zo. A star, a fucking star.

"Not to mention your spontaneous manifestation of a mager ability while separate from Rijal," Kush O-Nhar adds.

"You are the first of your kind," the Rijala says. "Able to manifest an Emerged ability off-world. Among your other talents."

"You are the first that has retained your sanity and manifested an ability other than one of the classical psi-abilities," says the Bezan.

"You are something new in the universe," says the Mantodean. "For that reason we wish you to learn and master all the inner and outer boundaries of your ability."

The human: "My name is Pyrx. I offer you a place at the Mother Temple at Indra City where you can safely train, and study, and meditate among the psions of Indra, at the Academy of the Open Eye."

"Are you inviting me to be a Consciousness Holder?"

"No. That may be a path you choose to pursue in time, but for now, we wish to learn from you – in a gentler way than the Institute did. More importantly, you need to gain better understanding of your gravity ability, as what happened – or nearly happened – moments ago demonstrates."

"I could feel you making a hole in spacetime." The Mantodean stares at Jes – stars stream in their eyes and fractal geometry flares around their whole body as they communicate. A vision flashes from the Mantodean's mind to Jes's: a singularity, barely the size of a grain of sand, eventually compressing this moon, its sister moons, the gas giant around which they all orbit, down to infinite nothingness. The orbit of Lora and the other planets of this system thrown off kilter, the damage reverberating through multiple dimensions. All of this passes through Jes's inner sight in a second.

"What if I decline this invitation?"

"The creation of a singularity is not something that can be allowed to happen accidentally, Jes," Kush O-Nhar says. "I hope you can understand this."

"What if I decline?" He repeats his question, more emphatically this time.

"You can reside where you wish. I assume that would be Port Ruby and you'd keep your place with the circus. I would be assigned to watch over you and your power usage. I could provide some limited training. It would likely not be sufficient."

Jes must have made a face without realizing it because Kush O-Nhar quickly adds, "You can't be that surprised, Jes. You can manipulate a fundamental force of the universe. That's a matter of some significance. How the Institute went about studying your power was wrong, but study must be made. It would be dangerous and irresponsible to ignore that."

Jes can't argue with that.

"We'll be dismantling the Paragenetic Institute," the Rijala says. "It has done far more harm than good and has exceeded the bounds of the work for which it was created, which was simply to understand how psi abilities work on a physical level. But the possibility that others can manipulate such primal forces as you—"

"That path would lead to a darker reality than any of us would choose for ourselves." Flowers of crystalline shapes appear around the rainbow Mantodean and rise from the light of its body, then swirl into dagger-like shards that fade away into the space around them. "It would not serve the highest good of all."

"We will arrange transport for you should you accept," the one named Pyrx explains. "If you need to think about it, tell Kush O-Nhar when you decide."

Jes weighs the choice. With Niko Dax imprisoned and the Institute taken down, he can settle into a fluffy bohemian existence in Port Ruby with the Circus Infinite and his friends. And do what though? Host the Singularity afterparties and smoke reef all day? Float the triplets for years and years? He does wield a primal force of the universe, maybe he bears some responsibility in understanding what that means, to do something beyond circus tricks. Returning to Rijal is out of the question, Institute or no. He hates it there and besides the magers won't accept him the way the psions have offered to. The way the circus has.

He looks at the glowing forms around him.

"We can see that you have friends of many species," the Bezan says. "That's the sort of mindset that must be cultivated for further evolution."

"How can you see that?"

"Your life shines clear to us in this space," the Hydraxian says. He conjures two glowing orbs like tiny suns. "Who you are," he says as he holds up one, then the other, "and who you have been." He spins the two of them together in the palm of one hand, setting them off on a chase of each other. He's seen Moxo do the same move.

"The song of our lives rings out in this space if you know how to hear," the Asuna says. "We are vibrating bells." The crystals of her halo quiver and brighten, then emit a glow of colored light around her head.

"You don't have to decide your course right at this very moment," Kush O-Nhar says.

Jes meets his friend's gaze. He understands one of his choices will be more comfortable, and lead to contentment, at least for a while. The other is the way toward mastery.

Kush O-Nhar's eyes shine with a rainbow iridescence, but don't stream stars like the other one's do. He realizes he can suss Kush O-Nhar in this space. He's not at all curious, uncertain, or wondering about what Jes will do. He exudes a calm certainty, which means the universe isn't about to go off the rails. That means that Jes's choice, whatever he decides, is truly about him, and what he wants for his life. There's a certain comfort, just in knowing that.

CHAPTER TWENTY-SEVEN

"So, we are agreed this matter is closed, and the Magistrates in all jurisdictions of Persephone-9 will pursue no sanction against the witnesses?" Kush O-Nhar asks one more time of the lead Magistrate who was dispatched to the cabin – to put it crudely – to clean up the mess.

"This event is a high-security matter of the 9-Star Congress," the Magistrate repeats. "The Magisterial Record will contain notice of a domestic disturbance at this location that was resolved prior to the arrival of Magistrates."

"Very good." Kush O-Nhar speaks in his role as Weaveseer and liaison to the Council Most High of the 9-Star Congress, and has smoothed out what could have been a dicey situation for the group, what with the trashed cabin and multiple bodies.

Jes sits curled up in one of the deck chairs, wrapped in a blanket. He watches with a mixture of horror and relief as the bodies of the orderlies who fell to their deaths are carried solemnly away. The other survivors are tended to by medical staff, and Matheson's remains are placed inside a small, dense cube that requires two humans to carry it, each one holding a side. Jes answered a few perfunctory questions after Kush O-Nhar spoke to the squad leader and Chief Magistrate of Mytiri via holochat. He managed to remain impassive throughout the process, but that's a manifestation of the numbness that's overtaken him, not calm.

Now that he's truly free from the Institute, Jes should feel happy. More than happy – he should be elated. But he doesn't feel those things at all. Heavy weighs the memory of crushing Matheson's body down to almost nothing, of what he did to the orderlies. He wonders if he'd have found it within himself to do those things if Niko Dax hadn't groomed him with his requests. But also, what else could he have done against the orderlies and Matheson? Let himself get taken by them? Run off to another world and do it all over again? Let harm come to his friends? No. What happened needed to happen – the man he crushed had plans to dissect him. So no, he doesn't regret the actions.

He does regret becoming the person who could perform those actions. He's gone from being a neglected son, to lab rat, to fugitive, to bohemian circus ragamuffin, to unwitting henchman to... killer? This is not the course he ever imagined for his life. Although, to be honest, he never really imagined much beyond getting off of Rijal and finding his way somehow. Being part of the circus, being with Bo, opened his mind to the possibility of having people and finding love. But it's all shaded now with this darkness, with this moment of... vengeance.

Esmée and Silas are suddenly timid around him, and he susses they're a little scared of him, and of Kush O-Nhar too. He can't blame them really. He's a little scared of himself.

Quint steps onto the porch. "We're all set for the hotel," he says. "As soon as we get the all-clear here, we can be on our way." It's clear after the raid that nobody wants to stay at the cabin anymore. Quint's made arrangements for the group for the night as there's no more shuttles to Port Ruby until morning.

"OK, so you're freaked." Quint squats down so he's not looming over Jes as he speaks, but even so, they're not eye-to-eye. Close enough. "You can't believe that you could do what you did to that guy–"

"Matheson."

"Matheson. The scientist with plans to dissect you. Who attacked all of us."

Jes looks at his friend's face, so kind and concerned. His eyes well up.

"You fought bravely," Quint says. "You have nothing to be ashamed of. You did what you had to do. To save yourself and protect all of us. I'm grateful to you."

Jes knows he's right, and yet. He'd been afraid of the fact that he lost control with Matheson but he's even more afraid of the truth he senses – that he was very much in control the whole time. He remembers how his rage seemed to fuel his power. He remembers liking it.

"I don't think they need you out here anymore," Quint says. "No use sitting around staring at the damage. Why don't you check in on Bo and pack up your things?"

Jes nods silently and starts heading for the cabin, but then he turns and throws himself into an embrace with Quint, smashing his face against Quint's torso and hurling his arms around him, though they don't fit all the way round. Four strong arms wrap him gingerly and he lets himself go and sobs. All the abandonment and betrayal and torture and fear and resentment and alienation and every moment of cold, ruthless loneliness that he's held in his heart for his whole life before the circus, bursts and flows down his face, racking him with heaving cries and gasps for air.

Quint holds him gently. Even as Jes's pent-up emotions gush out of him, he susses his friend who, in this moment, is all softness and love. He leans into that softness, lets himself be held by it. The emotional body makes a stronger impression than the physical one, and Jes basks in Quint's fierce loyalty and care. After several moments, he pulls away and wipes his face. "Thank you."

Quint smiles down at him, and Jes sees his friend has tears in his eyes too. "Anytime, buddy."

He heads back into the house and finds Silas and Esmée cuddled on the sofa and Bo splayed out on a big pouf.

"I packed your bag," Bo says. "I think we're gonna head out soon."

Jes nods. "Thanks. How do you feel?"

"OK for being shot in the neck with a dart. It's a little sore but I'll be OK."

"How are you doing?" Esmée asks. She seems to want to say more but holds back.

"It must be a relief knowing the Institute is done for," Silas says. "You're finally free."

"It's weird." Jes sits himself down in the lounge chair beside where Bo rests. "I mean, yes it's a big relief knowing the Institute's work is over. And as much as I was afraid of the orderlies and hated Matheson…" He lets his sentence trail off. He doesn't really want to talk about it anymore, and even though he doesn't say the words, his friends understand.

"So, what are you going to do about the invitation?" Silas asks. Esmée jabs him with her elbow and throws him a glare.

"You have to go," Bo says before he has a chance to answer. "Your gift is too important, and what they're offering you is a big deal. I know you love the circus, and we love you…" He chokes up and stops talking. Jes understands that if he goes, Bo won't come with him. They haven't talked about it yet, but he knows in his heart that's what would, and should, happen. Bo's life, his work, is here, and besides, Jes won't have time for a relationship while he's studying at the temple. The understanding passed wordlessly between them when he first told them all about the invitation. But hearing Bo encourage him now, out loud, saddens him even as he knows it's the right path.

"We would be terrible friends if we held you back," Esmée continues. "Or let you hold yourself back."

Clearly, they talked about this while he was busy with the Magistrates, while he was sulking by himself. "I have decided," he says finally. "I'm going to Indra."

Bo sits up, reaches over and takes his hand. Esmée gets up from the sofa, squats down in front of him and takes his other hand. "Indra's just a few hours' slip from here," she says.

"I've always wanted to see that planet." Bo squeezes his hand. "I hear Indra City's amazing."

"It is a beautiful place," Jes concedes. "It'll be good to see my grandparents' house again. I wonder who lives there now."

"OK, let's not get too maudlin," Esmée says. "We were assaulted, vanquished the enemy, and we still have a night of vacation left. Let's just enjoy each other. Deal?"

CHAPTER TWENTY-EIGHT

"You made our act," Zazie says to Jes. "It pains me to say that."

"I'm surprised you did say it," Jes answers with a smile.

She sticks out her tongue.

The circus is throwing him a going-away party and the inner space is full of chatter, reef smoke, and cries of "Donkey Balls!"

"Real mature," Lula chides her sister. Then turning to Jes, "It was an honor to float in your gravity field."

"We learned a lot about movement," Jujubee adds. "Thank you."

He wanders the party, susses the whole room and basks in the feeling, everyone's affection like a warm sun. He approaches Aleia, standing by the drinks table arranged around one of the support trusses. "Thank you for letting me work here."

"A fortuitous decision, it turns out." She holds a spliff between two fingers and offers it to him. He declines.

"I'm sorry I told my sister about what Niko had on you. She came to me in such a state after running into you at the Magistrates Hall. I thought if she knew the seriousness of it, that she'd understand why you did what you did. But she turned out to be such a snake in the end. Which shouldn't be a surprise." She takes a puff and sends a cloud of smoke billowing around her face.

"I can't say I blame her really," Jes says. "Or you either."

"You are much more understanding than I would be." She puffs again, then exhales a plume into the air above their heads where it dissipates quickly. In his head, he hears Quint bragging about quality air filtration. "In any case, she's taking her immunity from prosecution and going to Lora. She's opening a spa."

"I hope she finds some peace."

"Oh, Jes. You're a bigger person than me."

"I had fun hosting the Singularity."

"You were great at it. I'm sure the new girl will do just as well, though." The former hostess at the Apogee Pleasure Club is his replacement. "I'll miss your good ideas. If you ever get tired of Consciousness Holder duties, you have a future in circus management."

"Good to know. And I'm just undergoing training. I might not take up the mantle."

Aleia chuckles. "You know, your ambition will get you farther in life if you own it."

Jes smiles at the remark. Maybe she's right.

Kush O-Nhar walks up, antennae quivering. He and Aleia exchange nods.

"You basically engineered it all," Jes says to his insectoid friend.

Clicks. "I merely nudged two parties into orbit of each other. It wasn't about you; it was in service of the Weave." More clicks.

Jes watches the movement of his mandibles and imagines how wide that mouth must have opened to fit his whole head inside it.

"I'm glad our paths crossed."

"They were bound to."

Jes laughs. "Are you ever not cryptic?"

Kush O-Nhar stares, keeping his antennae perfectly still. They stare at each other a moment until Jes finally laughs again.

"What are you doing?"

"Being cryptic." The Mantodean emits a series of rolling clicks and his antennae twitch. "I look forward to seeing how you grow in your abilities and understandings. You are a rarity in the galaxy. I have no doubt you will find your place in the fabric, and weave a wonderful path."

"Thank you for the vote of confidence."

A group of clowns, led by Beni, unicycles by, juggling among themselves as they weave through the crowd. For a moment, Jes sees a mandala pattern in the spaces between the clubs, then they're past him and the perspective changes and it's gone.

"Also – thank you for dealing with the Magistrates in Mytiri."

"What happened was a matter of some importance to the Council Most High. It was my duty."

"Kush O-Nhar," Jes pauses for effect, bows his head. "Highest respect to you, but you really could learn to accept gratitude more graciously."

Clicks and hisses and antennae wriggling with wild consternation as Kush O-Nhar's head rotates left and right. "Understood."

"Thank you for everything."

"Our paths will cross again, so this is no goodbye."

"Well, until next time, then," Jes says with another slight bow.

"Good journey to you," Kush O-Nhar says, returning the bow, his antennae at attention and curled at the top in mimicry of his gesture. He scuttles away.

Jes feels like he's been holding up the table he's been standing by and looks around the room for Essa and Quint. He spies them settled together on the sofa in the lounge area and begins heading over when he's stopped by Moxo Thron.

"Let me just be clear," the juggler says. "I don't like you and I don't trust you."

"A wonderful goodbye. So why are you even here?"

"I need to at least look like a team player. Don't mistake my presence for forgiveness."

Jes sighs. He hates leaving things this way, but he can tell there's nothing more he can really say to Moxo to change his attitude. "I never meant you any harm, Moxo. I know you don't believe me, but it's the truth."

"Your lips are moving but all I hear is blah blah blah."

"Goodbye, Moxo."

"Good riddance, Jes." With that Moxo turns and walks away, stopping to chat cheerily with some of the clowns.

Finally Jes makes it over to the couch where Essa and Quint sit chatting with members of the band. The band members, understanding the situation, turn from the couple and chat among themselves when he walks up.

"I don't know where I'd be if you two hadn't taken me in." Jes struggles not to get choked up.

"We had a good feeling about you," Essa says, getting up to hug him.

"The crew will miss you doing all the heavy lifting," Quint says.

Jes mimics Quint's impression of him using his power, wiggling his eyebrows, and they have a laugh. He turns to Essa, "I hope you get to go to Opale and see your family's zaimira one day."

Essa's eyes soften. "I'm sure it will happen in our lifetimes. I hope so anyway." She sighs, reaches out a hand, places it on his arm when she senses his consent. "You're a good soul."

Esmée and Bo walk up.

"It's time."

He leans in for a hug with Essa and Quint wraps four arms around both of them. He'll miss four-armed hugs. He grabs his bag and slings it over his shoulder. He's packed light, just a few articles of clothing. The suits he left behind in the Free Box, along with the cape he wore the night he arrived – one of the clowns wears it now.

As he walks to the door, the rest of the cast and crew line up, forming an aisle between two groups. They applaud as he walks between them, some of them wave good-bye. There are calls of "so long" and "good luck" and he susses an overwhelming fondness that really puffs him up. Silas steps forward, says, "It's been good knowing you. Good luck." He offers his hand, and Jes takes it, giving it a good shake.

Bo holds the door on their way out, and Jes turns, waves once more and gets a final look at the inner space before stepping through it. The door closes and it's quiet in the corridor where he stands quietly with his friends who are seeing him off.

"I've called a roto," Esmée says. "At the back."

They leave the tent, head for the gate in the hedges that Essa held for him his first night here. The roto rolls up just as they get to the pavement and they all slip inside. They're quiet for a minute, all of them looking out the window. Bo and Jes hold hands.

Jes susses strong melancholy among them. "Both of you, thank you for everything," Jes says finally. "You've been the best friends."

"And we will remain best friends," Esmée responds. "We'll be just a slip from each other. I've never been to Indra and would love an excuse to visit. I know–" She holds up a hand, cutting off Jes's reminder that he won't be able to receive visitors for a while. "Eventually."

"Share your news," Bo prompts, nudging her with his foot.

Jes looks at her inquisitively; her excitement is effervescent against his empathic sense.

"Jasmine's wrapped her tour and after taking some time off, she wants me to meet with her about recording together. Not just a collaboration. She wants to produce music for me. As a solo artist."

"Amazing!" Jes exclaims enthusiastically. "I can't wait to hear what you do. Look at you – on your way to fame and fortune!"

"That's not why I'm looking forward to it," Esmée explains. "It's going to be fun, and creatively satisfying, I hope. But also – I want to blow the culture open. Keep expanding the universe Jasmine created, you know?"

Jes nods. He admires his friend's ambition, and can't wait to see who she grows into. He meets Bo's eyes and immediately wells up. He looks away, puts his attention on the flash of the glaze on the roto's outer sphere, shimmering blue-violet.

"I'm always going to love you, you know." Bo looks intently at Jes, who can feel the look penetrating him. He brings himself to meet his gaze.

Jes susses Bo's feelings for him in all their ferocity and softness. "I'll never stop loving you either. Even when I'm in the psychic space or whatever."

They've arrived at the station and the roto pulls over to the passenger drop-off. They all get out and hug their good-byes.

"Have a safe trip," Esmée says. "Until next time."

Bo's hug is tight and strong. There are no more words really.

Jes turns from his friends, and crosses the bustling plaza of the spaceport. There's a new holoboard for the circus, featuring an image of Esmée and the triplets. He makes his way into the atrium and heads for the dock where the shuttle to Indra waits. Everything that's happened from the first night he arrived here up to this moment runs through his mind. Here he is, about to take off for another new world. But he's not running away this time. He's going to a place where he intends to grow into who he's supposed to be, a place that will nurture his growth, his abilities, and let him develop on his own terms. The only place, besides the circus, where he's ever felt comfortable.

Finally, finally, he's going home.

GLOSSARY

People and Places

Asuna – species who call their planet Opale; territory known as the Crystal Imperium.

Bezan – species who call their planet Bez; territory known as the Bezan Embrace

Human – species who call their planets Indra and Lora; territory known as the Human Diaspora

Hydraxian – species who call their planet Seraph; territory known as the Hydraxian Range

Mantodean – species who call their planet Ixizia; territory known as the Mantodean Protectorate

Rijala – species who call their planet Rijal; territory known as the Rijalen Expanse.

Zo – sentient dark matter star that provides the slipstream network that allows faster travel between star systems

Political bodies, collective designations, social roles

9-Star Congress of Conscious Worlds – a collaborative body of star-systems and the species that reside within

Consciousness Holders – subset of Emerged Ones, tasked with maintaining the consciousness matrix for their respective worlds and communicating with the planetary and stellar intelligences

Emerged Ones – sometimes referred to as Emerged; individuals of any species who activate expanded psychic awareness and species- and planet- bound abilities

Gateway – a class of Mantodeans who possess hona-producing glands and serve ceremonial purposes.

magers – Rijala Emerged Ones

Paragenetic Institute of the 9-Stars – Research body and facility investigating paratalents distinct from the standard Emerged talents

psions – Human Emerged Ones, typically from Indra but not always

weaveseers – Mantodean Emerged Ones

Places

Bez – homeworld of Bezans; it orbits the star Hejira

Indra – considered the cultural homeworld of humans though it shares equal political standing with Lora in representing human interests within the 9-Star Congress; it orbits the star Ai

Ixizia – homeworld of Mantodeans; it orbits the binary stars Ixia and Ixiz

Lake Tourmaline – a freshwater lake on Persephone-9

Lora – a world under human control that shares power with Indra representing human interests within the 9-Star Congress; it orbits the star Vashtar

Mytiri Forest – a large forest that occupies nearly half the surface of Persephone-9

Nooafar Prefecture – a municipal zone on Rijal

Ontari Canyon – a canyon on Persephone-9, the largest canyon in the Vashtar system

Opale – homeworld of Asuna; it orbits the star Injari

Opale Lunar Station – space station on one of the planet's three moons. The only port designated for interstellar travel and the farthest point of entry for most non-Asuna into the Crystal Imperium.

Persephone-9 – a terrestrial moon of the gas giant Persephone; it is in the Vashtar system

Port Ruby – main city/port on Persephone-9

Ranara – Principal city on Opale

Rijal – homeworld of Rijala; it orbits the star Oaloro

Seraph – homeworld of Hydraxians; it orbits the star Korana

Cultural Terms

---

aqora – Mudra-nul: loved one/spouse/life partner

asunasol – Mudra-nul: person who abandons tradition. Designation of Asuna in exile due to nonconformity with their assigned caste/role

barat – Bezti: a liquor made from the leaves and berries of the barato shrub, native to Bez

Bezti – language spoken by the Bezan

chordash – Bezti: the purple leaf of a fragrant plant native to Bez that is popularly rolled and smoked by multiple species

edermapor – Mudra-nul: the age of being able to enter into contracts

Emerged talents – abilities possessed by Emerged Ones, including multiple forms of telepathy, telekinesis, psychometry, clairvoyance, remote viewing, and others

halo – Ninespeak translation of Mudra-nul word: the crystal formations that grow from the skulls of Asuna

hona – Ninespeak term for a Mantodean concept: a viscous substance with psychotropic effects exuded by a gland possessed by Gateway Mantodeans

Indric – dialect of human language spoken on Indra

jorai – Mudra-nul: alien, non-Asuna person

Klang – Genre of music originating on Lora, consisting of aggressive rhythms and discordant sounds

Mudra-nul – language spoken by the Asuna. Regional dialects exist.

Mudraessa – Mudra-nul: Asuna opera, considered by those who have heard it to be the most harmonically perfect music in the galaxy. Access by non-Asuna offworlders is strictly limited.

Ninespeak – Common language used by all species within the 9-Star Congress

node – handheld communications device capable of many functions including messaging, starlink connect, transactions, registration, feeds and holoprojection

orrrkut – Mudra-nul term meaning "nice to meet you" or "nice to see you again"

reef – Ninespeak: the variant of a cannabinoid containing plant native to Indra, popular among all species except Mantodean

Rijalic – language spoken by Rijala

roto – mode of transport comprised of individual rolling spheres. Of Rijalen origin, ubiquitous throughout the 9-Star Congress, except the Bezan Embrace

shimmer – Ninespeak term for the iridescent effect on the skin of mature Asuna

slipstream – network of interdimensional tubes that connect different locations in the galaxy, allowing for travel between the systems at a fraction of the time sublight speed in simple space would require

solzajira – Mudra-nul: solitary journey, exile

suss – the empathic perception of another's emotions

swirl – a party drug with euphoric and psychedelic effects

Thrum – genre of music originating on Indra, heavily beat-driven and incorporating droning sounds

twitch – an amphetamine-type drug with euphoric effects

zaiharza – Mudra-nul: soulstone. The crystalline form that remains after deceased Asuna are cremated

zaijira – Mudra-nul: soulpath/journey/record. The period of mourning for the dead

zaimira – Mudra-nul: soulhome/garden. The vaults maintained by families in which the zaiharza of its members are stored

ACKNOWLEDGMENTS

Many folks contributed their loving attention to the creation of this book and the tending of its author.

Much gratitude to the team at Angry Robot, for plucking this little circus book from the slush and helping it achieve its final form. Thanks especially to Gemma Creffield for her support and belief in this book, and for the guidance that made it better.

My agent Amy Collins has been the advocate, cheerleader and support I'd always hoped for in an agent.

Many thanks to this book's first readers: Jon Bush, Katie Desmond, Paula Jo Endicott, Kara Owens, and Natasha Young. Thank you for the support and feedback on the early drafts!

Adam Dipert, the Space Juggler, talked me through the finer points of movement in zero-gravity. Alas, most of what I learned is not in the text, but certainly informs the triplets' and Jes's technique.

Big love to my fellow travelers in the flow arts. If it isn't obvious – the jams, rehearsals, and shows I witnessed and was a part of, are a huge inspiration for this book. Burn bright, friends.

To the WMC Discord group – thanks for the emotional support, encouragement, and commiseration, especially in the querying and waiting-to-hear-back phase of this process. Can't wait to have a shelf of all our books and to celebrate all your beautiful stories into the future.

A late-night conversation during a trip to Berlin reignited my urge to write, and pick back up a dream set aside a long time ago. Thank you, Geoffrey Szuskiewicz and Anah Reichenbach for the talk, and the pact, and the love. Geoffrey has been my first reader and stalwart sounding board for a few books now, and his encouragement and feedback helped get me this far.

Most essentially: my loved one Marty, who endures my ramblings of both enthusiasm and despair on every book. He's offered love and support in everything I've turned my hand to, writing and otherwise. Everybody needs a Marty, and I am grateful for mine.

CHAPTER ONE
The Bitter Blossom

When the murderer Gary Cobalt trotted into the Bitter Blossom, he nearly gave himself away as half-unicorn within thirty seconds. His prison-issued pants were hiked up so high that his hooves stuck out the bottom, clopping across the tile, calling all sorts of attention. He'd hoped people would mistake him for a common faun, but the bartender let him know that he wasn't fooled.

"Why the long face, son?" asked the barkeep pointedly, holding a glass upside down to catch the liquid flowing out of a bottle of Gravitas. He shoved the cork in, set the glass rim-down, and slid it to a uniformed Reason officer at the end of the bar. The officer caught the drink and tipped it slightly sideways with a practiced motion. A stream of Gravitas rose from the edge of the glass and into his mouth.

"Another," said the officer. Heads turned. Gravitas wasn't cheap. Even high-ranking Reason officers didn't carry around enough cash for more than one glass. The bartender obliged and turned his attention back to Gary.

"Just released from the Quag?" he asked.

Gary nodded and tugged his baseball cap low over his forehead. Ten years in prison for murder had taught him the value of lying low. That officer's freshly laundered Reason uniform did not bode well for him. Prison guards from the nearby Quagmire wore the same basic uniform, but their trousers were encrusted with mud and waste from a dozen races, both human and other. You smelled corrections officers before seeing them. This was no CO at the bar. A well-dressed Reason officer on a dead-end planet like Earth was either here for an official inspection or a resource collection. Gary hoped it was the former, because if it was the latter, the "resource" in question was likely him.

Everyone in the employ of the Reason government, whether filthy or clean, wore the same embroidered patch on their left shoulder. A trio of red spheres: one filled with a five-pointed star, one with a seven-pointed star, and the center one with a twenty-four-spoke wheel, not unlike a space station. Each sphere represented one of the three nations – the United States, Australia, and India – who came together to form the Reason. Everyone called that flag the "spheres and tears," but you'd never say that to an officer's face. Not unless you wanted to end up in the Quag on charges of sedition. Reasoners didn't have much of a sense of humor about their flag.

Nor did they care for even the gentlest ribbing about polluting their planet until it became a hot, uninhabitable marble in space. Humans were touchy about being forced to flee their home world en masse in hastily constructed generation ships. And the people left here on Earth – people deemed too sick or too poor for a chance at a new life – were the angriest of all. Gary didn't blame them one bit. Mostly, he kept his head down and tried not to attract any notice, but today he needed to navigate the labyrinth of human rage.

"I need to see Ricky about my stoneship." Gary kept his voice low and slow. He'd been a free man for less than an hour, but it wouldn't be difficult for a CO on break in the Blossom to find a reason to throw him back into the Quag. Or worse, they'd declare him a natural resource and he'd find himself on the business end of a bone saw. "I was told he bought it at auction–"

The bartender slammed a silver bowl onto the counter to cut him off. Liquid sloshed over the edge and sizzled onto the bar's high-gloss varnish. His eyes went right down to Gary's hooves.

"If you mean *Miss* Tang, then *she's* hosting the game table," said the bartender, lighting the bowl on fire with an ember perched on a golden fork. The flaming drink smelled like crushed limes and wax crayons gone soft in the sun.

"I'm sorry. I have apparently misspoken," said Gary. "The last time I was here, Ricky was a–"

"A charming host who you will find at the game table," finished the bartender firmly. "*Miss* Tang will be pleased to see you again."

The sharply dressed Reason officer studied their conversation over his second empty glass of Gravitas. Gary dropped his face toward the floor, but there was no hiding the line of his powerful jaw; strong enough to crush bones into powder. His stomach rumbled. It had been a long time since he'd crunched through a bone bigger than a rat's femur. Unicorns in the wild primarily ate trisicles – palm-sized chitinous beetles that thrived in the cold vacuum of space – but he could eat any type of bone or exoskeleton in a pinch.

The officer opened his mouth to speak and Gary turned quickly toward the game table. He had to make this fast. Whatever that man came to do, it wouldn't be good for Gary to be here when he did it. If they found out he was part unicorn, his magical body parts would be portioned off throughout the Reason. Best-case scenario, they'd take him at his word that he was a faun and he'd end up playing the flute in some wealthy family's summer home.

Gary had learned never to underestimate a human being's capacity for cruelty. He'd been a toddler when the Reason Coalition formed, but his mother had been on the first generation ship to meet alien life on their way to a new planet. It didn't matter that the alien Bala had familiar shapes known to humans through centuries of myth and legend; unicorns, fairies, and elves. Or that they offered to use their magic to help the colonists survive in their new home. The humans fired the opening shots in what would become a hundred years of war between the humans and the Bala. Growing up, Gary watched a ragtag collection of starving humans become a highly efficient colonizing machine. War galvanized them and gave them the will to live. Humans were never more persistent than when they were in the wrong.

Gary scanned the game room. In addition to the main table where Ricky Tang presided, there were a few dozen low-stakes games going on. Most of the players were off-shift correctional officers, but there was a single table of Reason officers playing poker among the COs.

Gary saw the simmering heat of disgust between the officers and the COs. Every so often, a CO would walk a little too close to the officers' table and the whole party would look up, daring the glorified Bala babysitter to talk to them. The CO would eventually turn away, but always made sure to hesitate a moment to show the spot on their uniform that bore the largest tear or burn – a souvenir from some violent skirmish in the Quag. Most of the officers hadn't seen a day of combat since the Siege of Copernica Citadel ended fifteen years ago. They might wear the same uniform as the COs, but there was a galaxy of difference between them.

Gary tried his best to walk like a full human. His equine bottom half – two-legged like a faun's – was suited to soft dirt and not slippery tile floors. He skidded across the slick surface, trying to look more like a drunk human than an awkward part-Bala. The hem of his pants collected tumbleweeds of sparkling elf hair and more ogre toenail clippings than could possibly be sanitary in a food-serving establishment.

As he neared the game table, his right hoof slipped in a puddle of dusky brown dwarf blood. He caught himself before he fell, but a few COs snickered. A headless blemmye, pale and doughy, looked over at them with the face embedded in its chest. Gary sniffed the air, trying not to flare his nostrils. Something about it was familiar – a flowery scent that wasn't the usual damp ichor smell of a blemmye. It made the fur on his legs stand on end.

Gary stood behind a pair of neofelis cats at the main table. The cats pushed their furry heads together and played one hand as a team. One studied their cards as the other swatted at a dancing light on the leather tabletop. A group of COs near the window cackled each time the cat reached for the reflection coming off their buddy's watch.

In the chair next to the cats, a fairy sat forlorn, his transparent wing hanging broken and twitching. To be out here in public, wings exposed, meant this Bala was desperate. Indeed, most of Ricky Tang's clients were.

The blemmye bent over its cards, considering for a long minute before placing a vial of angel tears into the pot. As it moved, the floral scent wafted in Gary's direction again. Memories flooded back so powerfully that he had to grab the back of a cat's chair to keep from swaying on his feet. That was Jenny Perata, the woman who had held him captive for nearly two years. That lavender soap she used would forever be associated with the feeling of a knife digging around in his skull, searching for slivers of horn to power her ship. *His* ship, that the Reason had confiscated and awarded to her for defeating him in battle.

The blemmye was a particularly competent disguise. Really, he'd expect no less from Jenny Perata. The thick, coarse robes even covered her wheelchair. She was one of the fiercest adversaries he had ever faced. His gut clenched when he realized he was now vying against both her and Ricky for control of his ship, because there could be no other reason why Jenny was here, in the Bitter Blossom, from which she had been banned for life.

Ricky Tang shook the vial of angel tears, researching its value on her ocular display. The blemmye held its breath while she came up with an answer and Gary knew for sure that its appearance was a subterfuge. Blemmye didn't have lungs.

A wooden girl, kneeling on her chair to reach the game table, looked up at Gary with a wrinkled nose.

"Half-breed," she muttered. She took a drag from her cigarette and blew the smoke in his direction.

In the dealer's chair, Ricky's head snapped up at the slur. Her face moved from ire to joy before the smoke had cleared.

"Gary!" she cried, tossing her hand into the air. The other players threw down their cards in disgust as her voided hand landed face up on the table – three, seven, jack, ten, and king.

"I hoped you'd show up today," said Ricky, tossing a strand of dark hair over her shoulder. "It's been ten years and you haven't changed a speck."

"You have changed quite a bit," said Gary. Everyone at the table froze, but Ricky waved off his words with a calm smile.

"Oh you know, the outside caught up with the inside," she said. "I expect you're here to join the game?"

"I'm here to collect what's mine," replied Gary, raising his voice louder than he intended. His tones were deep and powerful from the generations of royalty in his ancestry. A few heads rose to look in his direction. He quieted both his volume and his mind with a slow breath. "My stoneship does not belong to you," he said calmly.

The damaged fairy looked up at Gary through bleary eyes.

"Leave while you still can," the fairy lisped. His tongue slid past the spaces in his jaw where teeth used to be. Razor-sharp fairy teeth were harder than diamonds and invaluable in the Reason drill bits that cored Bala planets for their minerals. From the oozing, it looked like this fairy had been betting his teeth all morning.

"Don't be a downer, Cinnabottom," said Ricky. "You got a fair chance. Gary can play if he wants to."

"I'm not here to play. I'm here to collect my ship," said Gary. The table of Reason officers had stopped playing and were now openly staring at him, but the officer at the bar was still seated, gulping down another gravity-defying drink. This transaction with Ricky had to go down fast, or he'd be taken back into custody. Gary didn't prefer to fight, but he would if he had to. And he almost always had to.

"Have you even seen it yet... since you were released, I mean?" asked Ricky with delight.

She flicked her eyes up and left to raise the shades on the back windows of the bar. In the distance, on the city's highest landing platform, sat a Halcyon-class stoneship with the terrible aerodynamics of unicorn deep space design. The *Jaggery* looked like a chunk of rounded stone as large as a planet-killing asteroid. It cast a shadow over half the city. A crew of workers was painting an enormous pink blossom onto the stoneship's hull.

The Reason was supposed to return his property to him upon release from the Quag, but they'd shoved him out of the gates with barely a word. The ship had gone to auction this morning and the only person with enough liquid cash in Broome City to buy even a heavily discounted stoneship was Ricky Tang.

Gary took a step toward the window and swiped a hand across the stubble on his chin. Seeing the *Jaggery* again, it felt, for an instant, like he might cry. He slackened his face into an unreadable mask that was the result of years of practice. Ricky already knew how much he needed his ship; he didn't need to broadcast it to everyone in the bar.

"The ship was supposed to be returned to me upon my release," said Gary. Ricky shrugged. One strap of her dress slipped down her shoulder and she let it hang there.

"The laws have changed since you went in." She fixed him with a gaze that was also a warning. Of course he'd noticed that the laws had changed. He'd seen more Bala come into the Quag for minor offenses like incorrect immigration documents in the last few years. Those who came in stayed longer or ended up in a harvesting center for parts.

"I'm just the buyer, Gary. You want to file a grievance about the logistics of the property sale, talk to one of those people."

She gestured toward the table full of Reason officers. Their game had ground to a halt. Gary shoved his hands into his pockets and hunched back down. Officers wouldn't be fooled as easily as a drunk CO.

"How much?" he asked quietly.

"Oh Gary. I have waited years to negotiate with you. I'm honored." She pretended to wipe a tear from her eye. "But my ship is so pretty, I don't think you can afford it. In fact," she flicked a fingernail at each of the beings seated around the game table, "none of these quags can afford it either."

One of the neofelis cats stood up and hissed at the insult. Her empty chair made a whirring sound, not unlike a timer. The other cat gasped and pawed at her to sit back down. After a loud click, a dozen silver needles sprayed out of the chair, piercing the cat's thick fur and burrowing into her flesh. She screeched in anguish and clawed at her back. Her partner pawed ineffectually at the piercings.

"The game is not over until I say it's over," Ricky said to the yawling cat. "Get out. You're bleeding all over my upholstery. But your kittyfriend has to stay."

The neofelis slunk out of the bar growling under her breath, "Ricky Tang, you suck." The remaining cat licked her wounds without taking her eyes off Ricky.

"Damn right I suck," said Ricky with a saucy smile. She turned back to Gary. "If you'd like to play for your ship, a seat has just become available at my game table."

"No game. A straight offer to buy."

"Oh Gary. What do you think this is, Myer? We don't *sell* merchandise here." Her head tilted toward the tidy Reason officer sitting at the bar. "That would constitute illegal black market dealing in Bala goods. And no one's doing anything illegal in here." She waved at the bartender to pour a fourth round of Gravitas for the officer. That explained how he was able to afford such pricey drinks. Ricky was trying to appease him.

"What do I have to do to get my ship back?" snapped Gary. He bit the inside of his lip and willed himself to be calm, because no one won a fight in the Bitter Blossom except Ricky Tang.

"Well, what do you have, kid? The Quag lets you out with two hundred and a shuttle ticket. Two hundred wouldn't curl my hair and I certainly don't need a shuttle ticket now that I own that beauty out on the platform."

"A private ante," said Gary, lowering his voice until it was nearly a growl. He hadn't been alive for thousands of years like his father, but he was still old enough to be Ricky Tang's grandfather.

Ricky dropped into her chair and let it spin in a lazy circle. Gary wondered if this was her tell. She seemed thrilled beyond speech.

"Gary, Gary, Gary..." she whispered. "That is a bold move, my friend."

"I am not your friend," said Gary.

"You used to be," she said, and Gary heard a hint of sadness in her voice that evaporated like alcohol a moment later. "Anyway, I doubt you have anything worth a ship that fine."

Gary snorted, a sound so close to equine that his hand involuntarily twitched upward as if to stifle it. Ricky's cheeks plumped and pinked with the spread of her smile. She wasn't even trying to bluff any more.

"My ship has been in storage for ten years. It may not even run," said Gary. He was losing the upper hand in this negotiation. The others in this room might be clueless, but both he and Ricky knew that you could bury a stoneship in the core of a planet for a millennium and it would still run like new. Especially if the dwarves stayed on board to maintain the ecosystem.

Ricky shook her head.

"I did a walkthrough this morning. Boges kept everything in working order. Well, as much as she could."

And this is where he had her.

"Everything but the FTL," said Gary pointedly. Ricky paused to wipe her palms down the front of her dress. She nodded, searching his face for any clue to the location of his horn. He didn't know where his horn was – he hadn't for quite a long time. The only horn he had was the tiny shaving of growth under his hat that he'd been working on for years eating vermin bones in the Quag.

He had eaten thousands of rats and rabbits in order to grow

enough horn to power the *Jaggery*'s faster-than-light engine. The tiny shaving wouldn't get him far, but a few AU in any direction was better than sitting on Earth. He'd had a full horn when he was younger, like any other unicorn. It had been sawn off so he could hide better among humans. It was a big enough piece of horn that he might go anywhere in the universe, but his mother had hidden it to keep him safe. He didn't feel particularly safe without it.

Ricky opened her mouth to speak. She stopped when a furry paw reached across the gaming table toward the ante. She flicked her eyes across her ocular display and the second neofelis cat howled and clutched her backside.

"I don't think so," said Ricky. She pointed to a sign mounted above the table.

ALL BETS ARE FINAL AND NONREFUNDABLE

The neofelis hissed and yowled.

"Fine then, go. I'm not into pussies anyway." The cat limped off after her partner and Ricky settled back into her chair.

"Is this private ante in the form of a liquid or a solid?" Ricky asked.

"Liquid," said Gary.

Ricky looked dissatisfied and drummed her fingers on the leather tabletop. The wooden girl lit another cigarette and picked splinters out of her teeth.

"Nothing solid at all? A shaving?" Ricky asked. Gary knew better than to admit it.

"Not a lot of bones in the Quag."

"I hear you ate well before you went in, though," said Ricky, staring intently at the front of his blue baseball cap. Gary balled his fists, resisting the urge to come back with a hasty reply. Ricky's words were always calculated. She was trying to goad him toward making a mistake by bringing up Cheryl Ann's murder. He heard a soft sigh from the table. The blemmye looked distressed. The elfin magic that had been used to craft the disguise was starting to drip down its face in the warm room.

"Fine. Five liters," said Ricky cryptically. Gary knew what she meant. Even the notorious Ricky Tang didn't dare say the phrase "unicorn blood" out loud. If the clientele figured out that he wasn't a faun trying to trade wishes for food, they'd be clawing over each other to tear him to pieces.

"That would kill me. Two liters," said Gary.

Unicorn blood healed most wounds and was one of the most precious substances in the universe. The last place he wanted to be was in a bar full of desperate people who knew who he really was. There was also a healthy contingent of planetbound xenophobes who had never made peace with the fact that the first aliens humans had encountered were an envoy of talking unicorns who offered to teach them farming. Within a few generations, most of the Bala races had succumbed to the human doctrine of manifest destiny. If there was one regret Gary had in his lengthy life, it was that he'd had to watch so many of his friends die in a pointless fight for galactic supremacy, when cooperation had been offered from the start. Then again, he'd never had just one regret.

"I don't care if you're dead. My ship's not worth less than five liters," said Ricky.

"Three," said Gary.

Ricky looked out the window, considering for long enough that the blemmye risked wiping away the slimy wetness collecting on its chin. The wooden girl narrowed her eyes.

"I don't know why you let a blemmye sit at your table, Ricky," said the wooden girl. "Everyone knows they suck the luck right out of the room."

Jenny might not have been an actual blemmye, but the puppet didn't know how right she was. If Jenny Perata had risked Ricky's wrath by coming back into the Blossom, things were about to get contentious.

The blemmye lifted a doughy middle finger and grunted. The wooden girl spat a wad of dry sawdust back. It settled on the table.

"Everyone is welcome at my games," Ricky said to the wooden girl. She turned back to Gary. "Four liters. Take it or leave it." She flicked her head toward the Reason officers. "This is your only chance to get out of here. The laws have changed. On any Reason-controlled planet you'll be picked up within minutes. Your very existence is illegal. It's only professional courtesy that they've left you alone in here for this long."

A pair of COs recognized Gary from the Quag and spat slurred curses in his direction with all of the intensity they could muster after complimentary glasses of larval eggwine. The dark purple secretion seared the throat on the way down and shredded the esophagus on the way back up, but during the twenty minutes in between, the drinker stood in the presence of their god. The COs looked disappointed to be back in reality, but were very much enjoying heckling what they thought was an ex-convict faun. He'd gone by his mother's surname, Ramanathan, while in the Quag. The name Cobalt was synonymous with unicorns and he hoped neither Ricky nor Jenny would be foolish enough to use it in here.

"You have no other options, Gary. Four liters is a gift. A welcome back present from me to you," said Ricky, blowing him a kiss. Her brown eyes crinkled at the corners. For a moment, it truly did seem like a fair deal. Then his blood kicked in and removed the toxin that she had just puffed into his face and the deal seemed just as raw as ever. But it wasn't as if he had many other options.

"Fine," said Gary.

"I'm so excited," Ricky stage-whispered to everyone seated around the table.

"What about the blemmye?" whined the wooden girl. The blemmye shrank back in its seat, pulling up its hood to hide its face.

"Your luck problem isn't the blemmye," said Ricky, training her laser focus on the wooden girl, who shrank back in her chair. "The problem is the ancient card counter installed in your brain."

The doll's eyes went wide.

"Don't think I didn't notice the freshly cut access panel behind your ear. Or the gears creaking inside your head. They're louder than a fairy's orgasm."

The wooden girl's eyes were suddenly sticky with sappy tears.

"I would never cheat. I just need to win enough to bail my fairy godmother out of the Quag." She batted lashes that looked like toothpicks.

"You are a cheater and a liar and I know all about the money you owe the Sisters. You're never going to win, but if you want to keep playing, I'm happy to keep taking your money," said Ricky.

The wooden girl's eyes went from wide, innocent hollows to narrow slits dripping with anger instead of sap.

"I guess that means I don't need to pretend you're a girl any more." The doll dropped her cigarette onto the table where it smoldered on the sawdust she'd spit at the blemmye. Ricky picked up the stub and blew the ashes off the leather. She took a long drag and the ember glowed hot. She let it out with her eyes closed as if this was her first cigarette in years. The noise in the room died down to a murmur as everyone waited to see what Ricky would do. She'd killed people for less.

"When you come into a person's place of business and deliberately call them something they are not…" she paused to exhale a perfect ring of smoke and her eyes flicked up and to the left, "…you give the impression that you have no respect for that person."

The air in the room disappeared as the regulars sucked in their breath. A chair scraped across the floor. Ricky took the doll's hand into her own, tenderly, like a woman consoling a friend. She stubbed the cigarette into the tiny wooden palm.

The doll screamed and tried to pull away. Ricky's slender fingers clenched around her like a vise. Gary watched as Jenny pushed her hidden wheelchair away from the table, the blemmye disguise running down her face in little rivulets of moist magic. Straight brown hair showed through the blemmye's shoulder and the outline of a human face replaced the blemmye's blank expression. The eyes crinkled at the edges, like someone who laughed often. Gary had looked into those steely eyes many times. They looked tired now, ten years since he'd seen her last.

Anger tightened across his chest like a hand squeezing. All the nights he'd imagined what to say if they ever met again, and now here she was and he found himself at a loss for words. He looked away, pretending not to recognize her, but kept the wheelchair in his peripheral vision. Jenny was a formidable opponent who had bested him in the past. And unlike Ricky, who would use her wits to outsmart him, Jenny would have no qualms about besting him in a physical fight.

The chair under the doll clicked and popped. A strange creature skittered across her lap. At first it looked like a moving blanket snaking its way up her torso, but some of the blanket broke away into lines that led down her arms. Tens of thousands of insects swarming out of the upholstery and marching in unison up the girl.

"What are th... No!" The doll writhed and screamed, bugs skittering into her open mouth. The tendons in Ricky's forearm tensed as she held the girl in place on the chair.

"You think you can come into my bar," said Ricky over the agitated humming of insects, "try to cheat me and lie to me, not to mention speak to me in that manner? You have no heart, you dry-rotted, hardwood bitch."

The doll choked up clots of insects. A few clumps carried timing gears between them. Bugs wandered out of her eyes and ears, slow from eating their fill of macerated wood. Ricky let go of her hand. The doll tried to wipe away the invaders, but they swarmed too quickly.

"One time, a missionary came into my bar and asked if a creature like me had a soul, or if it had burned away when I turned against God," said Ricky. "Would you like to know what happened to that man?" She ran her free hand across the leather surface of the gaming table. "You've been playing on him."

The broken fairy lifted his head up off the leather and crinkled his button nose. The wooden girl slumped in her chair, her eyes two empty caverns. An undulating group of insects climbed out of her slack-jawed mouth, holding a small bit of dark wood. They marched across the tabletop and dropped it in front of Ricky. She picked it up and twirled it between her fingers. It was intricately carved into the anatomical shape of a heart.

"This will make a lovely necklace for a lovely lady," she said, sliding the wooden heart into the pocket of her dress. She swept the rest of the ante into a slot in the table and waved the rest of the players away.

"Game over. We have a private ante that takes precedence," said Ricky.

No one dared to move.

"Ah, right," she said, eyeing her ocular display. There were audible clicks from all of the seats at the table. With a flick of her eyes, Ricky's voice was amplified throughout the bar. Gary was about to find himself in the spotlight – anyone who hadn't noticed him yet was about to.

"Beings of Bala and humans of Reason," said Ricky, addressing everyone. "I apologize for the violence done here today. I take full responsibility for the incident. You see, it was my choice to *cedar* at the game table."

She flashed a saucy grin and everyone in the room began to breathe again. Ricky took Gary's hand into hers, squeezing his fingers reassuringly.

"You ready for this?" she whispered, looking up at him and pulling down his cap playfully. She ran a finger down his nose and he pulled away. "I forgot how big you are in person. Another time, another place, you and me could have…" Gary backed away. Ricky's face froze. "Oh. Are the legends really true? Unicorns are asexual? My apologies."

Gary stared at her for a long moment. He appreciated her beauty – and the way she carried herself with the surety of someone with a dozen traps hidden on their person – but unicorns did not often experience sexual urges. Most immortals didn't, or the universe would be overrun with the offspring of eternal beings. Of course, sexuality and love formed a complex spectrum and individual unicorns experienced it differently, which is how Gary was conceived by a unicorn father and a human mother. Though he did not experience sexual attraction, there were many beings in the universe that Gary admired, and even a few that he loved fiercely.

Ricky turned back to the crowd.

"Gentle beings and jewels of every gender, today I bring you a spectacle like none you have ever seen in any corner of the Reason. This man has offered to compete in a game of skill in an attempt to win my new stoneship." She gestured outside to the *Jaggery*, which now sported a pink flower the size of a building. "The ante he has put up is private, known only to him and me. It will be revealed at the conclusion of the game. Aren't you curious what this ex-convict owns that could be worth as much as my pretty new ship? Probably something Bala..." she teased.

The crowd pressed in close. The servers moved through them, ready to take orders.

"If Gary survives all three of my challenges, he will win my ship. If he fails at even one, I receive his private ante. Creatures both Reason and Bala, you're going to want to see this ante. Buy your drinks now so you don't miss a moment."

Hands went up and servers flicked their fingers across tablet screens with practiced speed. Bottles clinked as the bartender moved double time.

"Gary, do you agree to the terms of the game?" asked Ricky, waiting to record his verbal agreement on her ocular display.

"By the lengthy strides of Unamip and the hardy gallop of Fanaposh, the reverberating snort of Finadae, and the piercing whinny of Hulof, I invoke the strength of Arabis and the–"

Ricky slapped her hand over his mouth and rolled her eyes to the crowd.

"Pantheists, am I right?" she asked, who chuckled as they waited for their drinks to arrive.

Gary knew he'd have to negotiate for the *Jaggery*, but he had naively assumed it would be a private deal, not a public game of skill. Unless he was incredibly careful, he was going to out himself as a unicorn and end up back in the Quag before the game finished. He pried Ricky's hand off his face and adjusted his cap again.

A server dropped a plate of broiled cow meat at one of the tables. Gary smelled the roasted bone nestled inside the seared flesh. His knees nearly gave way from the wave of hunger that gnawed at him. Ricky grabbed his elbow.

"Steady there, big guy," she whispered off mic. "No fainting until I get my blood."

He looked for Jenny. She'd wheeled herself into a back corner where no one would notice as the disguise continued to slide down her face. She was clearly a human and not a blemmye, but everyone was so transfixed by Ricky's announcement of a game that no one saw as she wiped off the last of the elf excretions with her sleeve. It gave Gary the tiniest bit of pleasure to know that magic like that only came from elf semen, which she'd had to smear all over herself. The indignity of it was a small consolation, but he had comforted himself with those for a long time now.

Ricky reached under the table and pulled out a faded canvas bag printed with an elaborate script. It read, "The Atlantic & Pacific Grocery Company," an artifact from her sideline trade in Earth antiquities.

"For the first challenge, we use the baby bag," said Ricky. "Gary, choose your fate."

Gary reached in and dug into the bottom of the bag. Ricky often rigged the more difficult tasks to jump into players' hands. He pulled out one from deep in the corner, covered in crumbs.

Ricky took the tile from Gary and read it. She blew a low whistle that reverberated throughout the bar.

"Oh, this one is going to be fun. Who here wants to experience the moment of their death?" A few inebriated hands went up. Mostly Bala for whom magic was as familiar as breathing.

"Well you just got your chance." She held the tile above her head so everyone in the room could see the bird carved into its surface. A man in the back gasped. A corrections officer shuffled out the front door muttering that there was no way she was going to watch this shit. The rest of the crowd was riveted on Ricky.

"The Sixian parrot!"

Being half-unicorn gave Gary a better chance of survival than most people, but the Sixian parrot was by no means an easy challenge. There were entire institutions filled with humans who thought they could face the bird safely. He braced himself. He hadn't come all this way to end up trapped in the vision of his own death.